THE ORLOV LEGACY

Robert Marcum

Deseret Book Company
Salt Lake City, Utah

Library of Congress Cataloging-in-Publication Data

Marcum, Robert.
  The Orlov legacy / Robert Marcum.
    p.   cm.
  ISBN 1-57345-146-0 (pbk.)
  1. Inheritance and succession—United States—Fiction. 2. Fathers and sons—United States—Fiction. 3. Lawyers—United States—Fiction. I. Title.
  PS3563.A6368075   1996
  813'.54—dc20   96-873
                                                               CIP

Printed in the United States of America

10 9   8   7   6   5   4   3   2   1

To our family—

Erica, Bryan, Jordan, and Alyssa
Bryant, Bonnie, and Breanna
Aaron
Cameron
Jared
Matthew
Brandon
Christopher

Family is our most important earthly possession.
You have made our lives complete.
Your love, your example, your dedication to the Lord
have inspired us to live better and love more.
We thank God for letting us be a part of your lives.

1

ALEX FINISHED ADJUSTING THE TIMING SCREW by turning it a little to the left, the purr of the Ford engine a soft rumble in the confines of his garage. Perfect. He wiped the screwdriver with a rag, then put it into the roll-away toolbox and closed the drawer. Wiping his hand on the rag, he opened the car door and slid behind the wheel. The 1965 Mustang rumbled deeply as he pushed on the gas, its now rebuilt engine an Alex Barrett work of art.

He closed the door and shifted the stick into reverse. Backing from the garage, he entered the firm's parking lot. From there it was a hundred yards to a deserted stretch of road. As he swung onto the pavement, he shoved the gas feed to the floor. The dual carbs fed the hungry engine and spun the wheels against the asphalt, the gray-white smoke of burning rubber trailing the car as it catapulted forward. Alex adjusted the steering wheel as the rear of the car danced right to left, then shifted the standard from first to second and on to third. The new gearbox worked smoothly, the motor driving the mustang to sixty miles per hour before it hit the quarter-mile mark. He applied the brakes, slid to the right of the old roadway, and swung the car into a U-turn. Moments later the Mustang was rolling back into one of the bays in his shop.

Alex shut down the motor, lovingly dusted the dash, then removed himself from the car. The next day it was due at the upholstery shop, where it would receive a new interior of black leather—rolled and tucked—before heading to the paint shop for its final christening in twenty coats of jet-black paint. After that, new tires and rims. Then the job was done. In Vegas he could sell it for twenty thousand, a ten-thousand-dollar profit.

He checked his watch—time to get ready for work. Walking to the garage door, he pushed the down button. The high steel door descended while he did a once-over of the work area, making sure all his tools were put away.

There were seven cars in the garage, all classics—all but the '68 Corvette Stingray, the car Alex drove—in various stages of restoration. His hobby. The garage itself was fully equipped with the latest instruments and tools for body and engine work and took up the front half of a large warehouse in Centennial Industrial Park. The rest of the building housed Alex Barrett's living quarters and the thriving law offices of the firm where he was working to become a full partner.

He walked to the door of the shop that led into his apartment, switched off the lights, and passed into the room he called his mud room. Large and spacious, the mud room contained a row of cabinets and closets along one wall where he kept his coveralls, socks, shoes, and extra garments. A vanity with two sinks was along the opposite wall, and a large shower took up the rest. A two-foot door led into a separate toilet.

Efficiently he stripped himself of his greasy coveralls and threw them into a hamper. After turning on the shower, he finished undressing, pushed a button that turned on the morning news broadcast of KSL radio, then entered the shower. It was nearly 8:00 A.M. He had been up four hours.

Alex Barrett had been an early riser all his life. He didn't know why, but at four o'clock something went off in his head that made his eyes flap open as if they were attached to springs. They refused to close until around ten o'clock at night at the earliest. His body just didn't seem to need much sleep. Having the garage only a step away gave him something to do with those early morning hours. His weird internal clock had its advantages. For example, the six o'clock wakeup time during his mission to Finland and Russia had been a piece of cake for him while many struggled just to clear the edge of the bed for another fifteen minutes.

The apartment actually belonged to the firm of Ivanov and Associates. So did the garage. The apartment had been used to house clients from out of town, but it was so far removed from the city proper, its tourist attractions and nightlife, that it had proven unworkable. That was when Alex had convinced Victor Ivanov, the controlling partner, to give him a lease that included the apartment and the unused warehouse space behind it. Although costing him nearly two thousand a month, one restoration every quarter more than paid the rent.

After drying himself with a thick beach towel imprinted with a picture of Shamu the whale, Alex slipped into garments, then went through the hateful ritual of shaving the coarse, heavy beard from his face. How a man could have such heavy facial hair and still be sensitive to a razor was beyond Alex, but shaving always left him with a rash and a wish—the rash went away by noon; the wish remained—a wish that someday beards would make a comeback in the business world.

After dressing, Alex went to the kitchen and fixed himself a simple breakfast of toast and a bowl of raspberries in milk. Raspberries were in season, had been for several weeks, and he had eaten them every single morning. He never seemed to tire of raspberries.

While he ate, he scanned the pages of the latest *Salt Lake Tribune,* the *Deseret News,* and the *Wall Street Journal.* A new president, same old political games. Alex wondered if the country would ever get past partisan politics again, ever resolve the deep problems greed created for everyone. Over the past few years all everyone in Washington seemed to want to do was sling mud at one another, place blame, and spend money they didn't have while the country fell apart. If things didn't change, people would vote the Washington bureaucrats out of office, run them out of their townhouses, and take away their million-dollar retirement programs. In Alex's mind, that was long overdue. He hoped the next election would take care of it.

According to the weather section, the valley was heading for another blistering day of sunshine and pollution. On the front page, lower left-hand corner, the *Tribune* ranted about another scholar being excommunicated from the Church—the indignant voice calling foul again. The *Tribune* never ceased to amaze Alex.

It wasn't that he didn't think they should report the news; it would just be nice if they did it with less bias. But then, that was how a lot of newspapers worked the system. Titillation sold papers. And the name of the game was and would be, for some time to come, profits. How could they stay in business if they said exactly the same thing as that "other" newspaper in town?

He turned to the international pages and looked for anything on Russia and other former Soviet satellites his firm was dealing with. His responsibility was the Ukraine, a country in a whirlpool of inflation and turmoil run by an archaic political system still controlled by old Communists trying to keep their power intact. It was Alex Barrett's job to work over, around, through, under, and within those bribe-infested waters for Western clients wanting to buy and sell in the Ukraine. It wasn't easy, but Alex had been successful—so successful he was sure he'd be a full partner by the end of the coming year.

Opening the *Wall Street Journal,* he checked for news of the same kind, then did a quick rundown of the stock market. IBM was having another blue Monday, but Disney was still headed up. Investing in Mickey had been a gold mine, along with Reebok and a couple of other companies, but some of the stocks in his portfolio were floundering or barely holding their own. He considered calling his broker, then resisted the urge. He bought the stocks with the intent to hold them. With one exception he had held to that decision, and now wasn't the time to change.

He turned back to the *Tribune* and *Deseret News* and did a quick run-through of the society pages, a part of his morning he didn't relish but found good for business. His clients came from the upper crust and had egos the size of grand champion watermelons—egos that had to be stroked. He gleaned a couple of items, cut out the articles and pictures for his secretary (she sent notes of congratulations, his signature attached), then closed the papers. He folded, then deposited them on the considerable stack in a cupboard closet. Another week and they would be discarded in the recycling bin a few blocks away.

He emptied the dishwasher of cleaned silver, pots, pans, and plates, making room for another day's washing. Wiping the inside of the door with a dishcloth until it was spotless, he placed the dirty dishes on the racks and closed the door, sealing it with the latch.

While slipping into his suit coat, he glanced about the kitchen, making sure he hadn't missed anything. The room was large, all white, and glistened in the early morning sun that poured through the six feet of window over the dining table at the south side of the room. Pleased, he picked up the clippings and headed down the hall for his office door.

He looked back down the hall with a smile. He loved this apartment. It was a steal at the price, and better conditions for him would be hard to come by. He intended to hang onto it as long as Victor Ivanov would allow him the privilege. That meant no foul-ups, just good solid deals for the firm—something he had full confidence he could handle.

He entered the firm's suite of offices, turned left into his, hung his suit coat on a hanger, and placed himself in the leather chair behind a large cherrywood desk. After pushing a button on the intercom and letting his secretary know he was in, he began withdrawing manila folders filled with papers from his desk drawer. They were all neatly in order, just as he had left them before leaving the office on Friday. He opened the first and began poring over it.

Ivanov and Associates had been formed in 1994. Victor Ivanov, a Russian American, had started the firm a short time after retiring as head of the biggest corporate law firm in Washington, D.C. He hadn't intended to do so, but six months after he had retired, his wife had suddenly died, and he had found himself alone and with nothing to do. They had been vacationing in Utah at the time, and Ivanov, at fifty-nine years of age, had liked the place, settled in, and started over.

The "associates" included Alex and a half dozen other attorneys along with a dozen foreign troubleshooters, all natives of the four biggest countries in which the firm did business and all of whom lived in those countries' major cities.

Ivanov and Associates acted as agents for Western firms wanting to do business in the former Soviet Union. When a company like InterAmerican Steel wanted to sell building beams in Russia, Ivanov and Associates worked out the details, brought the necessary parties together, drew up the legal papers, and made sure payments were made and supplies received as promised. In Western countries companies usually did their own wheeling and dealing for business, but in the former Soviet Union, with its chaotic, archaic, and bureaucratic legal and political system, companies found the expertise offered by Ivanov and Associates indispensable. You needed contacts to do business in most East European countries, and knowing the legal ins and outs was essential.

Having served in the U.S. military as a Soviet expert during World War II and for some time thereafter, then having acted as counsel to presidents on Soviet politics and law after starting his own firm in Washington, Victor Ivanov had the necessary political and business contacts and was the undisputed master in that arena. It was easy to understand why Alex, at twenty-nine years of age, considered himself lucky to get his start under Victor's tutelage.

Alex picked up the phone and hit the proper numbers for Victor's secretary. "Good morning, Liz. Is he in?"

"Good morning, Alex. No, I'm sorry. He's still in Petersburg and isn't sure when he'll return."

"I thought he was coming back for the meeting this morning. We have—"

"He was, but the InterAmerican deal needs a gentle touch. It all but fell through Friday."

Alex wanted to ask what had happened but fought back the desire. Russia proper fell under another associate's responsibility, and it wouldn't have been good office politics to pry.

"He asked that you conduct this morning's meeting," Liz said.

"Fine. How's Mason doing on his mission?" Liz had a son in Brazil who had been out about a year and was having a bout with some sort of intestinal parasite.

"Much better. The Church gave him some medicine. They said he'll be fine."

"Good." Alex meant it genuinely. Having been sick for nearly three months because he had drunk contaminated water while traveling in Russia his last year of law school, Alex knew how miserable it could be. "Give him my regards."

"I will." They hung up.

Alex turned to his work. As he read the papers prepared by one of his assistant attorneys, he stood and began pacing in front of the room-length bookcases on his right. He was five feet ten inches tall, wide through the shoulders, with skinny legs. A thatch of dark, wiry hair graced his head, and his eyes were dark brown. His jaw was square and had a tendency to harden when he was angry. His teeth were not as straight as they could have been because he had refused to wear braces when he was thirteen years old, the one thing in which he felt he could rebel against his parents and win as a budding teenager. Later he had regretted it, even considering having braces attached after college, but he had put it off, unsure of how people would view him as a potential attorney if his smile were all silver.

Alex had been athletic, an all-state receiver in football at Park City High School and state runner-up in the hurdles in track. He had gone to BYU on a football scholarship, achieving all-conference honors his sophomore year, but had gone down with a career-ending knee injury in the middle of his junior year. That spring he had put in his papers and been called to the Helsinki Finland Mission, in 1984.

After Alex arrived in Finland, the mission president discovered that he had taken Russian classes at the Y and was "talented" in the language. The president asked him to teach other missionaries the basics of Russian, then be responsible for teaching the Russians proselyted in the Finland mission. He had always taken to the language as if it were in his blood, and he became even more proficient during his mission. He and several others were very successful in teaching Russian people who would return to their country and strengthen the Church there. It had been one of the great experiences of his life. He had learned to love the people of Russia, their language and culture; that had been the impetus behind his decision to major in Soviet studies on his return.

After returning to BYU for his senior year, Alex had poured himself into his studies, throwing in an occasional date just to keep his college-ward bishop off his case. He had continued his language studies and expanded from near-perfect Russian into German and French. From there he had gone to law school, studying international law with an emphasis on the Soviet Union.

Alex pushed the button on the intercom and spoke to his secretary. "Lillian, is Ms. Walden in yet?"

"Yes. She was here when I arrived at 7:45." A short hesitation. "The Ukrainian delegates left last night. She did a very nice job—"

"Thank you, Lillian. Have her come to my office. Now, if you would."

"Yes sir."

Alex placed the papers on his desk, then stood and propped himself against it, staring out the window. The view wasn't great, but Victor hadn't bought the building for the view. Alex focused his mind on Cynthia Walden.

A new staff attorney assigned to him, Cynthia was young, intelligent, a hard worker who seemed dedicated to getting the job done. Up to now he had been impressed with her abilities although he didn't know her well personally. Assigning her the CompuWest deal hadn't been his idea, but Victor had insisted. Now, Alex was thankful it had been the boss's idea, because Cynthia might have blown one of the biggest deals of the year.

Dick Samson was president of CompuWest, a firm that had placed the low bid on the delivery of nearly ten thousand computers that came under the government's new list of acceptable products for sale to former east bloc countries. After some intense negotiations the Ukrainian government's representative committee, chaired by Leonid Antonov, the minister of internal affairs for the Ukraine, had accepted CompuWest's bid and sent a contingent to Salt Lake City to sign it. At Victor's direction, Cynthia Walden had been given responsibility for their entertainment and getting their signatures on the dotted line, then transferring the first of a series of bank deposits into CompuWest's account. She hadn't accomplished it, and Dick Samson had been as mad as a nest of bees with a bear's paw in it—mad enough to call Alex at home on a Sunday afternoon. Mad enough to threaten a lawsuit. It had taken Alex ten minutes to calm him down. The bottom line was that Dick Samson had wanted to know what was going on and why, and he seemed to have every right to his anger. After they had hung up, Alex had tried to think of a single reason for such a failure by Cynthia Walden and had found none. It had been a done deal. He had drawn up the papers himself. There had been no loopholes, no one who wanted to back out or play games. The appropriate "fees" of nearly twenty thousand dollars had been paid by Ivanov and Associates. Everything had been in order.

But they had no contracts.

And if they didn't get them, the firm was out the twenty grand, its sizable commissions and its reputation severely damaged. And Alex would get the blame, even if Victor had assigned Cynthia as the attorney responsible. That was just the way it was, and Alex accepted it as part of the territory he had elected to live in.

He stared at the city center in the distance. But he wasn't just unhappy with Cynthia because her mistakes could damage his career. He had personally worked hard to make Leonid Antonov happy. The man's assistant, Sergei Davidov, had contacted him personally, told him what they wanted, and set the deal in motion. Then Davidov and his contingent had come to Utah, met with bidders, and been introduced to important people in business and political circles. They had even met with Alex's father, chairman of the board and owner of Barrett Bank. Alex hadn't liked that part. He and Charles Barrett hadn't spoken for several years, and Ivanov and Associates used Zion's Bank for their business services. But Davidov had insisted on Barrett Bank, and Alex had found himself forcing aside his personal prejudices to keep the deal healthy. And although Charles Barrett may have been a lousy father for the past few years, he had also built one of the best small international banks in the world. There would be no problems because of slipshod service by Barrett Bank.

The door opened as Alex seated himself behind the desk. He smiled at Cynthia Walden.

Cynthia was of medium height, had shoulder-length dark brown hair, and had green eyes set in a thin but pleasant face. Alex always noticed her eyes first because they were almost oriental in shape. Her complexion was on the light side, turning scarlet when soaking up sun. He knew she was of Ukrainian descent. It was one of the reasons she had been given the job at Ivanov.

"You wanted to see me?" Alex sensed only a tinge of nervousness. Surely she knew she had blown it.

Alex pointed to the chair in front of his desk.

"You sent our guests home?" Alex asked.

Cynthia smiled as she nodded and took a chair.

"Then why don't I have signed contracts on my desk?" He smiled back.

She relaxed in the chair, a perfect set of white teeth showing through soft lips. "We can give them a better deal," she said evenly.

"They were happy with the deal we proposed. CompuWest—"

She cut him off smoothly but without coming across as a challenge. "Their bid is too high, Alex."

Alex didn't say anything. He knew the deal favored CompuWest financially, but it also gave the Ukrainians more than any other company had even come close to putting on the table.

"I'm not sure what you're getting at, Cynthia. You've seen the other offers. CompuWest has beaten them all."

Cynthia leaned forward and put some papers on the desk.

Alex picked them up and looked through them. "A bid from . . . " He looked at the letterhead. "International Computer Works." He looked up after looking at the bottom-line price. "It's lower, but it's too late to add bids. We can't—"

"The date is on the letter of submission," she said.

"November 21, 1992. But if this bid—"

"Is real, they beat CompuWest by more than a million dollars and offer services through centers already set up in Germany, France, Russia, and most recently Kiev, Ukraine, itself. CompuWest has no such service centers and will be at least a year ramming through the paperwork to provide them, even if we do it for them. ICW can provide the computers, software, and service in a matter of weeks, two months at the outside."

"You're sure about this? The bid is real? Submitted properly, ahead of the deadline?"

"I'm sure, Alex. As near as I can tell, it was thrown out by someone. I think we should reconsider it."

Alex looked at her, then at the papers. He read through them more carefully while Cynthia waited, chewing on her thumbnail.

"Where did you get these? When?"

"From a friend at ICW. They have an office here, and he submitted the bid. He and I were out to dinner when he brought up the fact that he had never received a reply to their offer. After leaving the restaurant, I asked him for copies of the bid. He gave me what you have in your hands."

Alex leaned back. He didn't like what he was hearing because it meant someone under his responsibility might have squelched some bids. Ivanov and Associates had a reputation for honesty and fairness, and that suddenly seemed threatened. In a business where reputation meant a great deal, such a thing could cost the firm clients. He felt a little squeamish.

Cynthia kept talking. "I tried reaching you, but with no luck."

Alex smiled. "Out most of the evening." He had taken a drive north to Logan in one of the restorations he had just finished—a 1954 Chevy pickup with a souped-up 327 engine he had wanted to check out before turning it over to the new owner, a retired millionaire from San Antonio, Texas.

"I tried reaching Mr. Ivanov but couldn't," Cynthia went on. "He's still in Russia but was on the train from Moscow to Petersburg. With no one available, I did what I thought was right."

"You showed the ICW offer to the Ukrainians." Alex's brow wrinkled with concern.

She nodded. "I apologized to Davidov, the assistant minister and head of the Ukrainian contingent, for the mix-up and promised them new paperwork within a few days. Davidov was a bit disgruntled, even angry, until I showed the group what they'd save by doing business with ICW. He still seemed upset, but he really had no choice. The others weren't going to let him do anything but accept the ICW bid. He agreed to wait." She paused. "I asked permission to deliver the paperwork personally to Antonov in Kiev."

"Why?"

She shrugged. "I don't trust Davidov. He's a snake. I think he and Samson may have cooked something up."

"You mean Samson may have promised Davidov a kick-back."

She nodded again. "It wouldn't be the first time someone in Antonov's ministry has taken money under the table. Even Antonov makes a habit of it, although this time I think he got left out."

Alex was beginning to see there might be more to Dick Samson's anger than first met the eye.

"Who was responsible for filing the bids on this deal?"

"Alfred Franklin."

"Did you ask him about the ICW paperwork yet?"

"No. I thought you—"

"Good." He paused, thinking. "Victor would want to handle it. Have you talked with management at ICW?"

"Yes. Their bid is still good."

"Call them back, tell them it is accepted, and get me the president's name and number so I can personally apologize for goofing up on this. Then call Minister Antonov in Kiev and tell him you'll bring the proper paperwork as soon as it's completed. Give him and President Kuchma our personal apology." He gave her an appraising look. "You can do it in a few days, I assume."

She nodded.

"I'll talk to Franklin. Probably just an oversight. Misplaced paperwork or something."

She agreed but with about as much conviction as his own voice conveyed. He couldn't help thinking that Dick Samson and Alfred had worked something out so that Samson's CompuWest got the bid. If so, Franklin was about to lose his job, and Dick Samson wouldn't be welcome at Ivanov and Associates for a long time to come. Victor Ivanov was honest to a fault. He expected his employees and people wanting to do business with him and his firm to be the same.

Alex leaned back, placing his hands behind his head. "I called you in here to let you have it for losing the deal, do you know that?"

She gave him a knowing smile. "I figured Samson would call you when I didn't deliver the money into his account. I've been in the office since four this morning making sure I wasn't being fed a line and a late bid by a friend. I talked to ICW's main office, and they faxed me a detailed casework of the bid and a copy of the certified mail receipt signed by Alfred Franklin."

"Doesn't Victor's secretary usually sign those?"

"Alfred signed for this one."

"That's it, then. Make those calls and keep me informed, will you?"

She started for the door.

Alex leaned back in his chair. "One more thing, Cynthia." She turned to face him, one hand on the doorknob. "May I be honest with you about something?"

"Sure." Cynthia was a little shocked. Their relationship had always been very businesslike.

"I didn't want you as lead on this deal. I didn't think you had enough experience, and I thought from the first day you'd blow it."

"You really get into this honesty thing, don't you."

Alex smiled. "It's a fault the boss seems to like." He paused. "I was wrong and I apologize."

"Apology accepted." She closed the door behind her.

Alex picked up the ICW bid and read it in detail. Then he turned to his computer and typed out a memo of his conversation with Cynthia and sent a copy to Victor Ivanov by interoffice e-mail, along with his planned response. Franklin's possible collusion with Dick Samson and CompuWest finished the rather lengthy note along with a pat on the back for Cynthia. She had saved him considerable embarrassment and the company a severe blow to their reputation. She deserved the accolades.

He punched the key that sent the note through the system, then sat back, thinking.

He hadn't liked Sergei Davidov from the beginning of their relationship. The man had the eyes of a weasel and the moral backbone of a jellyfish. Around Davidov, Alex always felt as if he were being watched. Now he understood why. Davidov had been looking for someone to work with him, take some money under the table. The question was, what should be done about it at this point? A subject for discussion with Victor on his return. Alex glanced at his watch—fifteen minutes until the ten o'clock meeting. He shoved the matter from his mind and began preparations. With Cynthia on top of the Ukraine deal, Davidov could wait.

It was a decision he would regret.

2

CLAIRE BARRETT WATCHED HER FATHER from the kitchen. He was staring out the window, had been for nearly twenty minutes, never blinking, hardly moving, deep in thought.

Something was wrong.

He'd been this way for more than a week. Pacing the floor at night, thoughtful, distant all day. Even Melissa couldn't gather his attention for more than a few minutes. He had spent more time in his upstairs den in the past week than he had the entire time since she and Melissa had moved back in.

She walked down the steps to the sunken living room. Melissa, sitting on the couch reading a Sesame Street book for six-year-olds, looked up at her mother, smiled, then returned to her story. Claire walked to her father's side at the big windows looking across the east mountains. She loved the view, had always loved it.

"What's the matter, Papa? You seem worried."

Charles looked over at her with a forced smile. At seventy-three his hair was silver gray, his flesh a bit saggy, but he still held a handsome look and a clear eye. At six feet one inch, he had been a powerful man in his younger years, stately and highly respected in his later ones.

"It's nothing." He looked out the window again. "Just a little problem I'm working out." He paused. "Have you told Alex you're back with me?"

She shook her head. "No, not yet." She paused. "Soon. You usually talk to me, Papa. I don't understand why you're shutting me out this time."

No answer.

She sighed. She'd asked a dozen times, and it was always the same. Maybe it was time to take the hint. "I have a late doctor's appointment. It shouldn't take long. I'll take Melissa with me." He didn't answer.

"I can't ask for his help unless . . . until I work things out with him," Charles said.

"Who, Alex? What kind of help?" Claire asked, hopeful that her father would begin to open up about what was bothering him.

"Old business, Claire. Just old business." He didn't move his eyes from the distant hills. "You should talk with him—tell him about the baby."

She shrugged. "Plenty of time for that." She had put off talking to Alex because she had some decisions to make. Steve, from whom she was now divorced, had been cruel, had forced himself on her so many times it made her shudder to think about it. Then he had physically abused her. She wasn't sure she wanted to have his baby, and she knew Alex wouldn't want her considering abortion. Until she made up her mind about keeping Steve's child, talking to Alex would only confuse the issue.

"Do you think he's forgiven me, Claire?" Charles asked.

Claire was a bit startled by the question. He had never asked it before, and yet the concern in his voice seemed so deep and genuine she found herself wondering why not. The sad thing was, she didn't know. Alex was like their mother in that vein. Forgiveness didn't come easy; in fact, sometimes it didn't come at all. Because she was unsure of the answer, Claire chose to ignore her father's question.

"I'll see you later, Father." She took Melissa's hand. "Will you be all right?"

He nodded but didn't turn away from the window. Claire and Melissa both kissed him on the cheek, and he snapped out of it.

"I'll be fine." He smiled and walked them to the door, waving as they climbed in the car and left.

When they were gone, he went upstairs to his master suite and den, closing and locking the door behind him.

Pushing a false panel aside, he dialed the numbers on the safe and opened it. Taking out a small sack with some keys, then several notes clipped together, he laid them on the desk, staring at them with a look of deep concern mingled with fear.

He was beginning to understand what might really have happened four years earlier, how his life had been ruined, his marriage and family nearly destroyed, and it frightened him. It meant his worst nightmare might now be coming true, his entire family in danger from something, someone, from so far in the past Charles had nearly forgotten about it.

No, he could never forget. You didn't forget people like that, could never shove aside things that had happened because of them. You could only hide such things, shove aside such memories. And he had hidden them. He had pushed the memories aside as best as he could. He had hidden them from his wife, his children, everyone. But he had never been able to rid himself of the memories. Try as he might, it was impossible.

He thought back. The war. Before and after. They had accomplished so much, saved so many.

Then it had all fallen apart.

Could it be that someone from so long ago could have done this to him? And how had they found him after so many years?

He stood, rubbing his arms, trying to make the goosebumps and the anguish go away.

He had been found. He hadn't believed it at first, refused to believe it. But the notes kept coming, the phone calls, the tidbits of information about the past. He couldn't ignore them any longer, and he had no strength to run, to hide again. The time had come to face it.

Possibly he should have done so years before, should have been up front with Fontana before their marriage. But when he had met her, the past had been safely tucked away—the secrets a new identity and a new religion had cured, and there had been no reason to dredge it all up. Their life together had been good until the accusations of adultery, the doubt and mistrust, the anguish and denunciations.

The divorce and the pride.

Possibly he should have told her then, told his children, too.

But it hadn't occurred to him that the past might be connected to all that pain. It had been easier to blame the Church, the leaders.

He felt only anguish. There had been no reason to think his past was connected to his excommunication! He still wasn't sure it was. Was he? Could he be sure until he confronted all of it? No. He must confront it this time. For that he would need Alex.

And if they were connected . . .

It answered a lot of questions and gave reasons to the unreasonable.

And it could finally clear his name and show Alex, Claire, Fontana . . .

Fontana. Ironic. Now that he might be able to prove himself innocent, the one woman he wanted to see it was gone.

Tears sprang to his eyes and rolled down his wrinkled cheeks. He should have told her about his past.

There had been times he nearly had told her, nearly told all of them. Their visits to Israel had always been challenges. Such glorious times! So much to tell, so much he had wanted to share! But he had kept his secrets. He had known his enemy was still out there looking for him, all evidence to the contrary. One slip of the tongue, one photograph in the wrong place, and his family might have become targets for that enemy's hatred. He couldn't have taken that chance.

And they had the gospel, a new life. Why look back when they had so much? When the past held nothing but bad memories and danger? Those were the rationalizations he had used. They had seemed right then, but now . . .

Now it seemed all of his hiding had been for nothing.

He picked up the phone and dialed the number he had dialed a hundred times in the past few days—the number for Ivanov and Associates. It rang. He hung up, just as he had done every other time, afraid Alex wouldn't talk to him. And why should he? So much had gone wrong between them.

He looked at the clock on the wall. It was after six. Ivanov and Associates was closed anyway. It would be better if he went into the city, tomorrow, saw Alex personally. At his office. They would be able to talk there. He could show his son then, tell him everything. Things could begin again—differently this time.

After another twenty minutes of thinking, Charles removed a pencil from the container on the desk and wrote a three-digit number in the corner of one of the notes. Then he placed them back in the safe and locked it. He wasn't sure why he had done it—just a precaution, he supposed. Everything would be all right tomorrow.

He left the room feeling better. It would be good to tell Alex about the past. There were good parts, lots of good parts—things a son should know, things a father should tell.

He went downstairs to the small basement shop where he fiddled with a woodworking project late into the evening, content with his decision, thinking of what he would say, how he would say it. By the time he finished the small cradle for his granddaughter, he was looking forward to tomorrow.

A tomorrow that would never really come.

3

For Alex, the day that had begun by finishing his work on the Chevy with such great satisfaction ended up chin deep in averting a half dozen crises in legal projects the firm had near completion. For example, there had been the Moscow deal in which a construction firm wanted to build American-style housing but had run into half a dozen snags, each needing personal attention and substantial fees for resolution. Then there had been the Latvian shipping contract for American paper goods that had suddenly developed a near-fatal case of paralysis when the port authority refused to receive the goods unless a port tax was paid, a tax that had never existed until then. And the CompuWest fiasco had snowballed, with Dick Samson and his attorneys threatening a dozen different lawsuits by noon. Alex had taken all he thought he should before telling Samson and his threat squad he'd see them in court and had hung up. He knew he would hear from them. Greed would made sure of it.

So he had taken first steps he would rather have left to Victor. Calling Franklin into his office, Alex had confronted him with his role in the whole greedy affair. Franklin had declared his innocence, not very convincingly, and then threatened a few lawsuits of his own. Alex had fired him.

All in all? A terrible day.

And he needed therapy.

Now he was standing in the one place he always went for relief—his garage. He was standing at the side of bay three looking at his '55 Thunderbird's new right front fender, a puzzled look on his face. The old fender had rusted through in several spots, and he had ordered this new one, but it didn't seemed to fit as it should. Feeling underneath the wheel well with his fingers, he touched each screw, making sure they were tight. The third one down the well seemed wrong. He lay down and moved himself under the car so that he was looking up at the screw. It was fastened down tight, but he had missed the hole on the fender, and the screw was attached only to the frame, the fender lying against the screw creating a bit of a bulge at that point. He fumbled around with his hand until he found the screwdriver and began undoing the faulty work.

He heard the door leading directly from the office area to the garage open, but he kept working as the sound of high heels moved across the concrete floor in his direction. The stride was short, familiar. Seconds later he could see a pair of legs standing beside him and disappearing beneath a knit skirt. From his vantage, dimpled knees were as high as he could see. He shoved himself from under the car and squinted into the light coming from behind the woman standing over him.

"Hello, Claire." He sat up, looking at his sister in a state of mild shock. "It has been a while."

Claire wasn't particularly beautiful, but what she had she usually worked to keep fine tuned. At five feet seven, with a thin frame and a good figure, Claire decorated herself with expensive, appealing clothes that accentuated her attributes. Today, though, she looked twenty pounds heavier, pale, her dark hair showing signs of gray at the temples.

Alex stood, rubbing his hands with the grease rag because he didn't know what else to do. "Where's Melissa?"

"In the car. Have you got a few minutes?"

Alex tossed the rag into the barrel and put the tools away. He reached into a pocket and handed her a key to the front door of the apartment. "I assume you came through the office. Get Melissa, and I'll clean up a bit, meet you in the living room of my apartment. That will get you through the front door."

Claire started walking away, then turned back and looked at him. "You're looking good, little brother. It's nice to see you." She left by the side shop door.

Alex flipped off the lights and went into the mud room, beginning to clean up while wondering what the visit was about.

He and Claire hadn't seen much of each other since her second marriage. How long? A year and a half now. He scrubbed his hands. That meant it had been four years since their parents' divorce, two since their mother's death from bone cancer. As far as family went, it had been a miserable four years.

His mother had divorced his father at the ripe young age of fifty-three. His father had been sixty-nine. Irreconcilable differences. Alex had seen it coming from the moment his father had been excommunicated.

Charles Barrett had been a successful banker by the time he had married Fontana Payson Barrett. There were reasons, good ones, for his father's delay. Charles had joined the army when he was twenty-three and single, a year before the Japanese had bombed Pearl Harbor. He hadn't said much about the years of war, but Charles had ended up in Europe and had been in Berlin for the German surrender. He had stayed in the military for a few more years because, as he had put it, someone had had to do the paperwork. He had opted out when a fair-sized inheritance had come to him at his mother's death. His father had died before the war, a well-to-do industrialist in New York City.

When he was thirty-six years old, Charles had moved to Salt Lake City and started Barrett Bank. He had found two things that first year, the Church and success. The following year he had found Fontana Payson. He had been a member of the Church for a little over a year when they had met in a class on banking at the University of Utah. Charles, a young banker asked to share his ideas on the future of banking in America, had been the speaker, Fontana, a young college student working for a degree in business. Charles had been struck by her intelligent questions and dark good looks. With people rolling their eyes and whispering behind their backs, they had enjoyed a whirlwind romance and had been married in the Salt Lake Temple three months later.

From all that Alex knew, their marriage had been perfect except for the fact that Fontana had had a hard time having children. Claire, Alex's one and only sibling, hadn't been born until six years after the marriage, but even then complications had nearly cost Fontana Barrett her life. When it became clear that she would survive, the doctor had told her she could have no more children. But Fontana had a mind of her own and wanted a son for her husband. Three years later she had had Alex. Her sacrifice had been nearly total, her heart stopping during labor, but they had saved her. After that there *were* no more children.

As a child, Alex grew up in a happy home, but one in which his father was taken away more and more by business and Church responsibilities until they seldom saw him. Fontana Barrett kept the home fires burning but found herself pulled away by civic responsibilities related to her husband's position in the Salt Lake business community, and by Church callings. She felt obligated on both counts but was in constant turmoil over the amount of time her commitments took her away from her children. By the time Alex was twelve, maids and nannies, chauffeurs and tutors were pretty well running him and Claire from place to place, feeding them and putting them to bed at night. Claire was sixteen then, had a mind of her own and used it. From sixteen until her first marriage, Claire Barrett had rebelled against the Church, against parents, against convention. Alex had come to understand the prophet's counsel about mothers staying at home. It made a difference.

Alex might have gone the same route if he hadn't seen the fights, the misery, and the tearful nights his mother had paced the floor waiting for Claire to come home. He might have done something stupid if he hadn't seen his father enter a police station one night to get his daughter, hadn't felt the pain of the horrible silence that had hung between them for weeks until they had finally worked things out. But even then he might have gone as berserk as Claire if his mother hadn't quit all the junk that had kept her from being a mother and come home, if his father hadn't started coming to ball games and spending some time working at being a father instead of just a banker and a bishop.

Claire's Las Vegas marriage to a real loser at age eighteen had shocked them into realizing how far they had let things slide. They had been going through the motions of parenthood while putting everything else before being a parent, a mother and father who knew their children. They had changed that, and it had probably saved Alex, that and athletics. Sports had kept him off of drugs and booze. Not that those things hadn't been there; they had, and everyone had known it, but Alex had known he wasn't that talented, and if he wanted to be the best he'd have to pay a price. He had kept himself clean so that he wouldn't have to start over every week the way some of his teammates had, and it had worked for him.

But that wasn't all of it. Alex had always liked the Church and never doubted its teachings, even though he hadn't always done the right thing. The gospel, the core teachings about Christ and faith and commitment to God, had been important to him from early childhood.

There had been challenges, times he had wondered if it was all worth it, times he had felt alone because he excluded himself from the group, unwilling to go the direction they were headed. Having his parents start acting their proper roles again had made those times easier. He had had someone to talk to, a place to go that wasn't filled with strangers anymore. It made a difference when your parents were in the grandstands, but it was even better to know that they'd be waiting at home, ready to talk, excited about what you were doing. It was nice to know you had that kind of place waiting when you needed it, and it made things easier when it came time to say no to other places.

Even Claire had felt the change and made peace with their parents, especially Charles. Even though she had fallen into a lifestyle she had found hard to give up, Charles had learned to understand and accept her the way she was. It hadn't been that easy for Fontana. She had been raised a puritan when it came to morality and the Word of Wisdom, and she had struggled with her daughter's waywardness and Church inactivity. On top of that, Fontana couldn't stand Claire's husband, and it showed. Even though Claire came to accept her first marriage as a mistake later, she wasn't about to admit it then. It was a constant wedge between them, so Claire didn't come around the house much, and even when Claire had her first child she didn't involve her mother. It hurt Fontana deeply, and things got worse. All Charles could do was stay in the middle and play the referee. He did pretty well for five years.

Then Claire's husband left her and the baby, claiming he didn't like the responsibility of having a family. He went to Europe and continued doing what he did best—be a bum. Claire filed for divorce, and it was granted three days before she heard from her in-laws that her ex-husband had been killed, the victim of a robbery. Alex had almost laughed, wondering whose money it was the assailants had tried stealing. Jonathan Camber hadn't earned a dollar his entire life.

Claire moved home, and things seemed to get a little better, even though when Alex returned from BYU on weekends he sensed a lot of tension between his mother and sister. A year later, Claire moved out again and went back to school. During that time she and Alex talked a lot and started being friends.

Claire stayed in school while Alex was on his mission. She wrote often but seemed little affected by what he was doing. The Church didn't seem to matter to her, and Alex began wondering if it ever would. On his return, she was struggling to be a mother to a two-and-a-half-year-old, still angry with the Church, still staying clear of their mother. But she and Alex stayed close while she finished getting her degree and Alex went to law school.

Then their world fell apart.

It happened in 1989. Their father was excommunicated for adultery. The storybook marriage came apart at the seams, the love between his parents straining to the point of breaking. Alex had always thought of his mother as near perfect but had often witnessed her one glaring fault. He had first seen it in her treatment of Claire and Claire's first husband, John. His mother found it extremely hard to forgive.

Her husband's apparent infidelity ate at her like acid. When Charles refused to admit his guilt, even in the face of undeniable evidence, Fontana moved out. A year later, Charles still holding obstinately to his story of innocence, she filed for divorce and ended thirty years of marriage. It was a shock to both Alex and Claire, even though they knew their parents' marriage had its share of ups and downs. Alex, caught in the middle, watched his father tenaciously cling to his innocence and his mother grow angry, then bitter, even though it was destroying their happiness, their marriage, and their family.

Claire stuck with Charles, believed him, but Alex didn't. He and his father argued constantly, then stopped talking altogether. Alex quit calling the house in Deer Valley, moving all of his remaining possessions to his mother's place in Salt Lake City. Claire stayed with their father, commuting to school at the University of Utah to finish her senior year. Charles, still chairman of the board at Barrett Bank, threw himself into his work and sat on the back row at church.

The family was in a shambles.

Alex had witnessed his mother's anguish, watched it eat at her strength. She was still deeply in love with Charles but refused to forgive until he admitted his guilt. He wouldn't. Alex grew more frustrated with their behavior, angry at both of them for allowing stubbornness to destroy their marriage, their family. He was especially angry at his father. Alex had wanted to wring his neck because of his stubborn insistence that he had done nothing wrong. Alex saw it as nothing more than ridiculous, insipid pride and callous treatment of those his father professed to love. Because of those feelings, Alex stayed away from Charles and spent all his time with his mother, watching her waste away both physically and emotionally until her death on August 9, 1990, her last words being her husband's name. It had been a wrenching thing to hear, especially when Charles hadn't even come to the funeral.

Actually, Charles's absence had been the last straw for Alex. Even though Claire later told Alex their father had stayed away out of respect for their mother's wishes, Alex completely shut his father out of his life for it, and they hadn't spoken since. To punish his father further, Alex walked away from the Barrett banking empire and his father's wish to make it a family business. As far as Alex was concerned, Charles had made his mother suffer needless torment with his immorality and lies, and he wanted nothing to do with such a man or his empire.

Alex took a shower, put on fresh garments, then dressed in light slacks and a polo shirt.

The funeral had been a miserable experience all around. Alex had condemned Charles, railed against him for his nonappearance. Claire had fought back, trying to defend Charles and blame the Church for what had happened. She insisted the Church was out to get their father, for some reason she never could explain, that Charles hadn't done what they said, couldn't have been immoral! She talked of how it had nearly killed him, of how lonely he was without their mother! That even though Charles clung to his faith, the Church was responsible for all their misery because they stuck their nose in where it didn't belong, even if Charles was guilty.

It was then Alex had blown up.

In the first place, he told her, the Church didn't make mistakes like that, and they didn't "go after" someone. Second, the evidence spoke for itself, and she was crazy to continue believing their father was anything but guilty and completely at fault for what had happened to them. Third, if their father loved their mother so much, why didn't he swallow his pride and admit his guilt? And fourth, he told her that her attitude stank because it showed how her own lack of moral fiber had shaded her character and led her to support an insupportable position, and if she'd get her act together she'd be able to see the truth for a change.

She had slapped him.

Then they had cried.

It was hard enough burying their mother without hating one another.

They started having lunch when they could, spending part of Saturday together so that Claire's daughter, Melissa, would have a father figure in her life. They worked out their differences, became friends again, and left Charles out of their conversations.

Then Claire had married her second husband, and it had all ended. The guy was another jerk.

His feet bare, Alex combed his hair and rinsed his mouth with a little wash. When he left the mud room, it was far from the

usual spotless condition his fetish for such things demanded.
Claire and Melissa were waiting in his living room.

Claire smiled up at him from the couch. "Nice place. Better
than the one you had downtown. You have everything at your fingertips—the garage, the office. You've done well the past two
years."

Alex smiled his thanks while sitting in the chair across from
them. Melissa was six now, at least that's what he remembered.

"Hi," he said to her. Her black eyes stared at him, and a smile
creased her lips.

"Hi," she responded. Her eyes went to her feet that were
straight out in front of her. She seemed to be checking the polish
on her shoes.

"I was just about to fix a sandwich. Would you join me?"
Alex asked.

Claire looked down at Melissa, who smiled up at her and
nodded slightly. "Yes," Claire said. "That would be nice."

They got up and went to the kitchen.

Claire watched as her brother worked at putting everything
together on the center island counter. She didn't really have an
appetite—even the thought of food made her stomach queasy.
The first months of pregnancy were like that for her.

Alex noticed Melissa sliding onto a stool. She put her arms
on the table, her fingers entangling themselves in one another as
she watched him work.

"She's grown a lot since I saw her last. She's a real beauty,
Claire," Alex said.

Claire looked at her daughter. "At the moment, Alex, that
isn't a compliment for her, but it does help my self-esteem a little.
Thank you."

Alex put the sandwiches together, added some crinkly potato
chips and a pickle, then set the table, and they sat down to eat. He
gave a quick blessing, glad to see Melissa folding her arms and
bowing her head and Claire following suit. Alex poured them all
a glass of milk, and they started eating.

"You know how to take care of yourself." The comment was
genuine.

"Practice," Alex said.

"You should get a wife."

Alex didn't know how to reply so he concentrated on taking a bite of the sandwich and chewing it gracefully.

"How do you eat a sandwich like this and remain a lady?" she asked, smiling. "Mind if I get myself a knife and fork?"

"Top drawer, other side of the island."

She retrieved the weapons and cut into the sandwich waiting on her plate. Melissa pulled on her sleeve, and Claire did the same for her sandwich.

Alex was nearly a quarter of the way through his when Claire finished her first bite, wondering if it would stay down. Deciding it would, she cut a second piece and lifted it to her mouth.

"You didn't come all the way out here for lunch, Claire. Would you like to launch into your thoughts, or will it ruin my appetite?"

She wiped her lips with a napkin and sat back, eyeing her brother. "I left Steve. Melissa and I are staying with Dad again."

Alex put his sandwich down. "This one didn't work out either." It came out more coldly than he intended.

She looked at her hands.

"Sorry. That wasn't fair." He focused on the distant skyline through the window, his appetite gone.

Melissa pulled at Claire's sleeve and whispered something to her.

"Is it all right if she watches television. Her favorite show . . ."

Alex nodded, took Melissa's hand, and walked her to the living area. Sitting her on the couch, he handed her the remote. Seeing she knew how to handle things from there, he returned to the kitchen and sat down. He leaned toward Claire.

"I am sorry. The guy was a jerk. I'm glad you're out of it."

"It was worse than you think. He was abusive, Alex. I had to get out or be killed."

Alex felt the anger well up in his chest, but he wasn't sure who he was most angry with, the jerk for his abuse or Claire for marrying him. He had never liked Steve Navarro. The guy was cold with Claire and treated her like dirt. He worked for the county prosecutor's office, and Alex had asked around about him. Even though Steve was LDS, his lifestyle and moral ethics left something to be desired. Alex had told Claire so. She hadn't responded well. Alex wasn't surprised that there had been problems, but abuse hadn't occurred to him. He wondered why not.

"Did he hurt Melissa?"

"Twice. I left him the last time." Alex knew Claire would have stayed with the guy if he had abused only her. Her ridiculous stubborn streak. But with Melissa being involved, things were different.

"You stayed with him a long time. Why didn't you call? I could have . . ."

"He's a violent man, Alex. Bigger than you." She tried a smile.

"I would have had him thrown in jail, Claire."

The smile disappeared. "I couldn't have handled that—my pride and father's position in the community. People would have talked."

It was a lousy excuse, but Alex bit his tongue instead of saying so.

"What did Charles say when he found out?"

"He doesn't know the reason. Steve is running for prosecutor next year and agreed to a divorce on my terms if I'd drop the whole thing. He made me promise not to tell Charles. He knows father could ruin him."

Alex could see Steve Navarro needed a lesson in manners and decided he'd figure out a way to see that he got one. It would come as a surprise to the wife-beating son-of-a-mule, and it would come where it would hurt Steve Navarro most—in election results.

Claire slowly shoved her plate aside. "There's something else."

Alex waited.

"I'm expecting."

Alex smiled. "No wonder you look a little ragged around the edges. When?"

"According to the doctor I just met with, seven and half months."

He looked at her midsection. "You don't look pregnant."

"Give me another eight weeks and you'll think I overdosed on helium." She paused, losing the smile. "I . . . I don't know if I want to have it."

Alex had to bite his tongue again, sensing the confusion and fear in his big sister's words. He wanted to scream at her but stayed in control. She had come because she needed advice, not a tongue-lashing about the evils of abortion. He shoved his plate to one side, forcing himself to wait and keep silent.

"Steve . . ." The tears started to flow, but she quickly choked them back and rubbed away the residue with the back of her hand. "He raped me, Alex, or I wouldn't be having this child."

Alex had a fork in his hand and felt it bend in half as the anger rushed from his heart into his fingers. She explained what had happened, how often, and the beatings that followed. Alex listened, too angry to speak, finally understanding why she wasn't sure she wanted to give birth to someone who might have Steve Navarro's genes.

When she had finished, Alex leaned back in his chair, unsure of how he should reply. She was sniffing some, using a hanky, getting her tears and her emotions under control.

"I can't tell you what to do, Claire, but if you're worried about the baby turning out like its father, don't be." He forced a smile. "Steve was no good because of the way he was raised, not because of something in his genes."

She returned the smile as she drew in a deep breath. "What's wrong with me, Alex? Why do I always attract such losers?"

"No offense, Sis, but with few exceptions—in fact, I can't think of any—the company you keep isn't exactly fraught with wholesome males with high standards and strong fatherly inclinations."

"No, I guess not."

Alex leaned forward and took her hand. "Keep the baby, Claire. Melissa will make a great little mommy, and you'll raise a good kid. I'll help." He paused squeezing her fingers. "You'd regret an abortion. You may not be the all-American Mormon girl, but you have a conscience like everybody else, and you'd never forgive yourself."

She nodded lightly. The silence was a bit uncomfortable, and Alex knew something else was coming.

"Father wants . . . needs to talk to you," she said after the tears were gone and she was back in control of her emotions.

Alex felt himself going red in the face, his jaw setting. "Since when did the chairman need you to deliver his messages?" he asked.

Claire looked down at her hands again. He hated the way she did that. It always made him feel rotten, as if he'd used foul language or something.

"What's wrong?" he asked.

"I don't know. He won't say. He didn't send me, Alex. I came because I'm worried about him. Over the past week he's aged a dozen years. He's not going to the office; he seems preoccupied with something." She drew a breath. "He's been asking about you."

"What about me?"

She looked down at her hands again. "Nothing specific." Another pause. "I think he wants to turn things around, Alex."

"I'm not ready." He said it in a flat, matter-of-fact tone.

She gave him a cold stare.

"Sorry. I have a lot of anger inside. Most of it comes by way of Charles Barrett's pride and stubbornness, not to mention his blatant immorality."

"He made some mistakes. He knows that."

"No, he doesn't! He's still holding tenaciously to his old story." Alex shook his head. "I think he has actually convinced himself he never touched that woman!" He paused, leaning back. "But even if he did, sudden recognition doesn't burn away the past the way fire does chaff, Claire!"

He started to take another bite of sandwich, couldn't, and tossed it back onto the plate. "Look, he loves you and Melissa— that's great. It's nice to know he could still love someone besides a mistress, but that doesn't change what's happened between him and Mom. And me! I can't just forget it! I have too much anger inside. He killed my ability to feel love for him, and that love isn't going to suddenly spring into new life because he thinks he wants to turn things around."

Claire poked the sandwich she couldn't finish with her fork, hard, then shoved it away with enough determination that it nearly fell off the far side of the table.

"You make a mess, you clean it up," Alex said. It was a poor attempt at lightening the mood. She wasn't having anything to do with it. Fire danced in her eyes, and Alex could see that the only way it would be quenched was by burning him. He braced himself for what he knew was about to come.

"You can be so understanding one minute and so . . . so . . . annoying and self-centered the next!" Claire said angrily. She stood, walked to the island, and grabbed the mayonnaise bottle, screwing the lid on so tight Alex wondered if he would ever get it off again. Next came the mustard, the salad oil, and the vinegar. After that she started throwing vegetables into various bags and heaving them into inappropriate places in the fridge. Alex didn't dare move, afraid she might decide he was a good target and nail him with what was left of the tomato on the counter.

When the cabinet top was nearly clear, she took a deep breath and sat down again. "You were always so insufferable and self-righteous Alex! I hated it when we were growing up, and I hate it now! You're so good at looking down your nose at others while seeing yourself as Mr. Clean! You've been around people telling you you're so hot all your life that you can't see that your attitude is as wrong as father's!"

Alex's laugh was one of disbelief. "Oh no, big sister! You're not going to lay the fault for this at my feet!"

"Then forgive him, Alex. Start living your religion instead of just wearing it on your sleeve like eighty percent of this city!"

Alex took a deep breath. He was angry now, and he wasn't about to control it.

"Tell me, Claire, how long will it take before you forgive Steve for what he's done to you?"

She seemed to shrink, turn pale.

"How long? Can you forgive him today? Could you walk up to his doorstep and say, 'I know you didn't mean it, Steve, so I'll just let it go. It doesn't matter that you nearly killed me and beat my daughter until she was blue.'"

She slapped him across the face hard enough to make his head spin. She stood there, her face showing the anger, the confusion, wanting to hit him again. She started the motion, then redirected it, pummeling him in the chest, her other fist joining in. She cried, sobbed, pounding him until he grabbed her arms and pulled her to him, holding her close, trying to comfort her, wishing he hadn't said it.

But it wasn't so different. What she was feeling, the anger, the self-hatred because she thought everything that went wrong was her fault, the helplessness—all of it was what he felt for Charles. You couldn't just wave a magic wand and make it go away.

After long minutes she stopped shaking, and he was under control again. He kept his arms around her.

"Dad has changed, Alex. Even I have changed. I don't blame . . . I mean I feel different about things now."

"I know, Claire. You aren't the problem. Neither is Charles. It's me. I have to change, and I can't. I blame him for what he did to Mom, to all of us. It isn't something I can just click off and on. It's who I am. He taught me morality, Claire! You remember the business trips to Israel that he took us on, the vacations? The time we were in Shepherd's Field and he taught us what he hoped we'd become?"

"I remember," Claire answered. "I was starting to have problems then. He was talking to me."

"He was talking to both of us, and his lessons had a great impact on me. They were a big part of the reason I determined to keep myself clean. Then he broke those laws! Made a mockery of all of it. I feel what I feel because he's acting as if none of what he told me counted, as if we and the Church and God didn't even count! He continues to go to church every Sunday while continuing to declare his innocence! More mockery!"

His head went back, his eyes closing as he took a deep breath.

"He doesn't need me, Claire. He doesn't need anyone—never has. The bank is in good shape. I received an outside auditor's report on it because of a business deal we've got in the making with Ukraine. I wish all banks were so well off. He'll be fine." His tone was firm but filled with both frustration and bitterness.

"It isn't the bank, Alex. I don't know what it is, but it's aged him."

"Has he seen a doctor lately, gotten some bad news?"

She shook her head. "No. I asked him about his health, and when he didn't answer I called Doctor Wilson and asked him. His heart isn't what it used to be, but nothing the doctor is worried about at this point. It's emotionally that he's a wreck. I can hear him walking the floors at night. Mentally he's preoccupied, as if he's waiting for something."

"He has plenty of people he can turn to."

"Not really, unless it's business. I don't think this is. When he started acting funny, he also starting asking questions about you, and whether or not I thought you'd be open to talking. It's you he needs for some reason, Alex. Possibly your international law background or something." She shrugged. "I've tried to get him to open up. He won't."

There was a short silence. "I'll talk to him. That's what you came here about, isn't it?"

She smiled. "It didn't work out exactly the way I had it planned. I hate it when you yell at me."

He put a hand to his jaw. "Your slapping me isn't exactly the best part of my day. That's the second time. I hope it isn't becoming a habit."

She laughed, her smile returning.

"Will you keep the baby?"

"Yes, I think I'd better. I've messed up my life enough without adding something like that. I couldn't have done it, Alex, you know that."

"I know."

There was a long, comfortable silence between. It reminded Alex of when they were little and shared the same room because he was scared of the dark. Their mother would put up a blanket between their beds, but they'd lie awake and talk until they couldn't keep their eyes open any longer. There were comfortable silences then, too.

He thought about his father, the good times flashing through his mind. Could they get them back? Could it ever be the same?

Memories of his mother rushed in. The anguish of betrayal, the bitter loneliness caused by his father's immorality and pride. He'd keep his promise to Claire, but it was business. That's all it could ever be.

4

ALEX WAS INSTANTLY AWAKE THE FIRST TIME the phone rang, a feeling of foreboding coming over him.

"'Lo." His throat was dry, and he cleared it before repeating the word.

"Alex?"

The voice was barely audible, shaking, near weeping.

"Claire? What is it? What's wrong?"

"It . . . it's . . . father. He . . . he's in the hospital." The sobs filled the receiver, and he could tell she was fighting to get them under control. "Someone . . . broke into the house—after Melissa . . . Oh, Alex, please come! Please hurry!"

"Melissa? Claire, what are you talking about? What—?"

"Kidnap. They were trying to kidnap . . . " She began sobbing again.

Alex was holding the phone between his chin and shoulder, pulling his jeans on, fastening his belt. "All right, Claire. Where are you. I'm on my way. Take it easy! It'll be all right." He was forcing his voice to remain even, calm.

"LDS Hospital. Emergency room."

"Is anyone there with you?"

"A . . . a policeman, and Melissa."

"Okay." He fumbled with the buttons on his shirt. "I'll be there as quick as I can."

The phone clicked dead. Alex pushed the cellular's button to off and tossed it onto the bed, freeing both hands for dressing. Grabbing his slip-on oxfords, he put them on without socks, shoved his wallet and keys into pockets, picked up the phone, and burst through the door that led directly into the shop. He threw a tarp off the 1968 Corvette Stingray as the automatic garage door

lifted, revealing the faint glow of early morning light. As he
shoved the key into the slot and started the car, he glanced at his
watch. It was 5:35 in the morning. He jammed on the gas feed,
and the Corvette bolted through the opening and into the dark.

Five minutes later he was heading east on the freeway.

Alex found the room, along with a uniformed policeman at
the door who checked him for identification before allowing him
inside. As he closed the door behind him, his eyes adjusted to the
dim light. Claire stood by the bed, where a pale, unconscious
Charles Barrett lay.

Charles looked like a wax figure lying between sheets, which
were the same white color as his skin. His face was thin, making
his nose and ears look large, out of proportion, the flesh sagging
downward as if gravity had total control. Both arms lay on pillows, with IV tubes poking out of them like grotesque growths,
the blue veins a wide path down his arms and into his fingers.
Alex wanted to feel compassion for his father, but it wasn't there.
Bitterness, guilt. What was it he was feeling? Whatever it was, he
didn't like it.

They had moved Charles into a private room in the intensive
care section of the cardiovascular unit of the hospital. A nurse
stood next to Charles, checking an IV, then making notes on a
clipboard before changing a plastic bag full of clear liquid to
replace an empty one that hung on a stainless steel stand with several other bags. The green machine overhead showed different
lines and figures Alex didn't understand. The numbers were all
in the hundreds, and the lines were uneven, erratic. Alex didn't
have to be told his father was hanging onto life by the thinnest of
threads.

Claire heard him behind her and turned. Her lips were quiv-
ering, her eyes full of fear and deep concern. She took a step
toward him, and he wrapped her in his arms. Tears came then,
cascading off her cheeks onto his shirt. She put her arms around
his waist and hung on, sobbing. They stood that way for a long
time before Alex noticed Melissa sitting on a couch pushed

against the wall of the large room, her head lying on the thick padded arm, her lips wrapped around a thumb and sucking with quick successive pulls. Her eyes stared into his with apprehension. The look made his heart hurt.

Alex pulled away from Claire, putting one arm around her waist, giving support while moving toward Melissa. Easing Claire into a position next to her daughter, Alex stooped down, bent at the knees, and looked directly into the six-year-old's eyes.

"Hi." His tone reflected the deep concern he had for her condition. He had heard of children traumatized by things like this, going into a near comatose state. He didn't think it was happening to Melissa, but he wasn't sure.

She gave no answer, the thumb still in place, but the eyes were searching his. He was relieved there was at least some recognition.

"Do you mind if I hold you so I can sit next to your mom?"

Melissa nodded, slowly. Alex stood, lifted her from the chair into his arms, and sat down, Melissa in his lap. She put her head against his chest, and he smoothed her hair gently.

"She quit sucking her thumb two years ago." Claire's voice was filled with concern.

"Just a reaction. She'll be okay." Alex smoothed her hair, rubbed her arm. She seemed to relax a little. "What has the doctor told you about Charles?" he asked in a soft voice, his eyes still on Melissa.

Claire shook her head as if afraid, confused, even angry. "He . . . he said it was a massive coronary brought on by exertion." She took a deep breath, trying to control the sob that had lifted into her chest. "He went after them, Alex. They had Melissa, and Father went after them, fought them. Melissa was able to run to me, and we got away, to a neighbor's." She took another deep breath, a fist tapping her chest firmly several times as she tried to keep control of her voice. "They must have hit him. The doctor says his abdomen and chest are badly bruised. They had a . . . a pickup, four-wheel drive, parked on the ski hill below the house. I couldn't see what it was, only that it stood high off the ground, and I heard it . . . going down the hill in the dark."

There was a long pause. The nurse was at a computer and hit
several keys, checking the readings. Alex noticed numbers flashing in red in the upper left-hand corner of a machine pumping
oxygen through the tubes in his father's lungs. The nurse's brow
wrinkled with concern as she watched the various monitors and
made more notes.

"We . . . the neighbor and I, found Dad unconscious. The
ambulance took him to the Park City hospital first; then he was
flown here by helicopter." Claire leaned forward, placing her head
in one hand. She looked exhausted. She leaned back again, sliding
down in the seat slightly, her head against the back of the chair.
"It was a nightmare. Melissa's crying! Finding him lying there in
the grass! Then the police! Ambulances! Neighbors! A horrible
nightmare!"

Melissa was in a listless sleep, sucking gently on her thumb.
"Nurse," Alex said, "could you get my sister a pillow, and a blanket, please. And one for her daughter."

The nurse turned and nodded, then left the room. She
returned a moment later with the items in her arms.

Alex lifted himself carefully from the couch, holding Melissa
close, trying not to wake her. She stirred a little, fussed, then
sucked her thumb, but her eyes remained closed.

"Mrs. Navarro," the nurse said, "please, lie down. You look
exhausted."

Claire shook her head, standing. "Alex, lay Melissa down.
We'll use the blanket and pillow for her."

Alex started to argue but saw it was no use. Carefully he lay
Melissa on the couch, her head on the pillow the nurse had put at
one end. She didn't stir much. When the blanket was placed over
her, she unconsciously pulled it around her chin, her legs sliding
upward until she was in a tight ball, filling a tiny area of the
couch.

The door to the room swung open, and a doctor came in.
After asking the nurse several questions and inspecting the equipment and the patient, he removed his reading glasses and shoved
them into the pocket of his white jacket.

He tried smiling at Claire, then at Alex. "You are . . ."

"Alex Barrett."

The doctor pushed his hands into his pockets, his eyes going to Charles, his brow wrinkling. "The left side of his heart is badly damaged." He paused. Alex knew worse news was coming.

"In effect, Charles was dead, revived by the paramedics, but his brain was without oxygen. There is little activity. We're nearly sure the damage is permanent."

Claire stiffened. "What does that mean?"

"It means we can do little for him at this point. Surgery on his heart is out of the question right now; his heart is too weak and irregular. We might rectify that with medications, but the damage to the brain is a different story." A slight glance at Alex. "Frankly, your father's chances of coming back to you are less than twenty percent. Even if we replace his heart, the damage done to his mind can't be repaired."

Claire grabbed Alex by the arm for balance, her frightened eyes on the face of her father. She was biting her lip against another wave of tears. Alex put his other arm around her waist in an attempt to give her strength. It was the first time he had realized how dependent his sister was on their father, but with everything that had been happening in her life lately, he figured she had good reason.

The doctor went on. "I'm sorry, but it is important that you know his exact condition. If it worsens, you will have to make critical decisions about his care, and—"

"You mean whether to keep him alive, don't you." Claire said it stiffly.

"Yes, that is what I mean."

To Alex, Claire seemed to get taller, her soft flesh turning to cold stone against his arms. She turned herself away from him and walked around the bed to the doctor. The anger was evident in her eyes, and the doctor took half a step backward, an uncomfortable look on his face.

"You keep him alive, doctor. Do you understand? Regardless of cost, of what you think he might be if he remains alive, you do it!" Her words were commands, like those a sergeant would give to a wayward private in an attempt to remind him of his place.

But then, in Alex's view, the doctor needed reminding, his cold demeanor offending them both.

The doctor frowned, sighed, then moved toward the door. As he reached for the handle, he turned back. "For now I will do my best to fulfill your wishes. You had better get some sleep." He looked at Alex. "A policeman is waiting for you, Mr. Barrett—in the office just outside the IC unit. The door is one of those with a numbered lock. Just knock and he'll let you in." He left.

Claire moved to the couch and was sitting when the door clicked shut. She had put her head in her hands but wasn't crying.

Alex sat by her, careful not to disturb Melissa. He put his arm around Claire's shoulders. After a minute she stopped shaking, lifted her head, and took a deep breath.

"You're still using the name *Navarro?*" Alex questioned.

"No, it's been changed back to Barrett, but in the rush of things I signed the old way. They've been calling me that ever since. I'm too tired to explain."

He stood. "I'd better see what the police want. Will you be all right?"

Claire nodded without looking up at him, her eyes glued to their father.

Alex left and went into the hall, past the nurse's station, and out of the ICU, pushing on the metal door opener that swung the large doors to the sides.

"Mr. Barrett." Alex turned, facing the doctor behind him. The doctor began polishing his glasses with a handkerchief that materialized in his hand.

"I'll get right to the point," the doctor said.

"Yes, I've noticed you're good at that." The tone was equally methodical.

"As I am about to show you, I could have said much more. Your father's heart cannot be repaired. Survival will depend on our locating a compatible donor."

"A transplant."

The doctor nodded. "Something I do not recommend. Your father's system was without oxygen for eight minutes. In effect, he is brain dead and will remain so. In such a condition, a heart transplant would be foolish, especially when you consider that we must deprive another, more needful recipient of the chance for life."

The cold-hearted analysis gave Alex a chill.

The doctor folded his glasses and placed them in his pocket, then the handkerchief. "What this all means, Mr. Barrett, is that the chances of his ever getting out of bed again are nil; of speaking to you or your sister and the child, none. He'll need constant care. His bodily functions will all be completed with machines, from eating to disposing of waste. Is this what your father would want?"

There was a hard knot in the pit of Alex's stomach. "What do you want from me, doctor? I'm not the one who will make this kind of decision under any circumstances. My father and I haven't been on speaking terms for several years, and I don't think he will appreciate my making any decisions about his life or death."

"I'm afraid you will have to. Your sister is in no condition to do it. It's going to come to you, Mr. Barrett, whether you like it or not."

The doctor looked at his watch. "I have surgery. As cold-hearted as you think I am, you have to know the facts in order to do what is best for everyone." He turned and walked away.

"Wait."

The doctor stopped, facing Alex again. "I want something done," Alex said.

"Yes, Mr. Barrett, what is that?"

"No decisions without at least two opinions on his condition—yours and my father's personal physician."

"This is not just my decision, Mr. Barrett. We have a team concept here in which a number of doctors are consulted before giving advice to the patient's family. All of them agree with what I have told you."

"That's all well and good, doctor, but my father has a board of directors who are going to want another opinion. They know about our strained relationship and aren't about to accept my decision without the approval of Charles' personal physician. We'd just as well get him involved now."

"Very well. Whom do I call?"

"Benjamin Wilson."

The doctor's eyes lifted, casting wrinkles of concern across his forehead.

"It's apparent you know the man."

The doctor shrugged. "A GP without much experience in the field of cardiovascular medicine, but the evidence in this case is obvious, and it shouldn't be a problem. I'll see that he is contacted." The doctor walked away, headed for the nurse's station.

Alex knocked on the door with the numbered lock. A young man dressed in a light teal-green jacket, tan canvas shirt, and beat-up tennis shoes below a pair of faded jeans opened it. Alex didn't think he was more than twenty-five years old.

"Mr. Barrett." He showed his badge. "Dray Butterfield, detective with the Park City police."

Alex's smile was a bit forced. He felt exhausted. "What can I do for you, detective?" Alex asked, going to a chair to sit.

"The chief investigating officer asked me to come down here and fill you in on what we know—and to ask you some questions."

"Who is the chief investigator?"

"Brig Logan. He would have come himself, but he's at your father's house taking care of the investigation."

"How do you fit in?" Alex asked.

"I'm sort of his partner, at least on this one."

"I thought Logan was running your department—worked nine to five. What's he doing on a kidnapping?"

Butterfield looked away. "Orders. Your father—"

"Ah, of course. The chairman of Barrett Bank deserves better service. Well, fill me in but make it quick. I need to get back to the chairman's bedside."

"As near as we can tell, two men entered the house about one o'clock through the rear door."

"The one that leads directly to the ski hill."

"Yes. There is a hot tub on the porch," Butterfield said.

"And it's only twenty steps from Melissa's bedroom."

Butterfield nodded. "Apparently your father heard something

and went down to see what it was. He caught the kidnappers in the hall. As near as we can tell, one of them hit him, knocked him against a wall. Broke a picture in the process. It must have taken a few seconds, but he gathered himself together and went after them. He caught them loading the daughter into a four-wheel-drive outfit—we think a Toyota or Nissan. A man whose home sits below your father's heard a racket, went onto his porch, and saw such a vehicle leave the hill in a hurry about the time of the kidnapping."

"Did you get a decent description?"

"Dark color. Big tires. Roll bar with lights attached."

"Dozens of them in Park City. Thousands in the valley. No license number?" Alex asked.

"The only witness who got a look at it said it was smeared with mud."

"What happened to Charles?"

"When he caught up with them outside the house, he had a ski pole in his hand. We found the mate hanging on a row of coat hangers in the dressing area by the door. He used it pretty effectively until they hit him with some sort of heavy object—my guess is one of those big flashlights."

"What do you mean he used the pole effectively?"

"There's a good deal of blood."

Alex leaned forward. "How much blood?"

"The ground is soft, soaks things up. Forensics will give us a better idea this morning." Butterfield shrugged. "How much damage can you do with an aluminum ski pole?"

Alex smiled. "Charles Barrett? A good deal. Don't rule out hospitals, sergeant. Any descriptions from witnesses?"

"No. It was early morning, and only the one witness saw the pickup."

"Anything left behind? Prints, gloves, anything?"

"We're still looking." Butterfield removed a small notebook from his pocket. "I'm supposed to ask you the questions, Mr. Barrett."

"Why me?"

"Not you exactly. Anyone in the family I found here, except Mrs. Navarro."

"Her name is Barrett again. She's been through a divorce and had her name changed back."

"Logan said to leave her alone until tomorrow. She has enough on her mind."

"Good policy. What do you want to know?"

"Do you know anyone who might—"

"No. My father and I haven't been on speaking terms. I don't know much about his personal life over the past few years, but I can't say that everyone was his friend before that. Bankers are forced to foreclose on people and shut them down. Few of them like you after that. Tell Logan to contact Hal Frost, vice president of the bank. He and Charles ran in the same circle, and they have the same enemies. My sister can fill you in on the personal stuff later." Alex paused, leaning forward. "I can tell you this—if they were after money, Charles was a good target."

"Owner and chairman of the board of Barrett Bank. That's why Logan isn't home asleep, remember. What do you mean you aren't on very good speaking terms?"

"My father and mother divorced. When she left, so did I." Alex stood. "I have to get back to my sister. Anything else?"

Butterfield pushed his small notebook back into his shirt pocket. "Your past relationship—how deep were the problems?"

Alex got the drift and didn't smile. "Not deep enough I'd kidnap my sister's child, detective. If I wanted revenge on my father for some injustice, I'd ruin him through the bank." Alex turned toward the door. "Now if you will excuse me . . ."

"For now, Mr. Barrett, but don't leave the Salt Lake area without letting us know."

Alex hesitated at the door, biting down hard on the words that wanted to come off the end of his tongue. Instead he forced a smile. "Nice meeting you, Butterfield. Tell Logan I'll see him this afternoon. It would be nice if he'd have some answers." He closed the door behind him.

5

ALEX GRIPPED THE STEERING WHEEL in both hands, pushing against it with his arms, stretching, forcing the sleepy cobwebs from his head. The dial of his watch said it was nearly lunchtime. Another ten minutes and he'd be at his father's house.

He wasn't sure why he was going—mostly just an excuse to get away from the hospital. His father was still in a coma, still being kept alive by machines because his body was ruined. Claire had finally fallen asleep on the couch, and the nurses were taking good care of Melissa. There was nothing he could do there.

He shifted up a gear as the phone rang.

"Alex, this is Hal Frost. What's going on?" Frost was all business, but then, Alex expected him to be. As president and CEO of Barrett Bank, Hal was stiff enough that he didn't even need starch in his shirts.

"Hello, Frost. Yes, the chairman's fine. How are you?"

"I already checked on your father, Alex. What I want to know is why you're involved. Your father—"

"Claire called me. Haven't the police reached you yet?"

"No. I'm in Nevada. We're adding a family-owned concern here as a part of our expansion program." A long pause. "The family we're buying from is very touchy about publicity, so the merger has been kept extremely quiet. What are Charles' chances?"

Alex wondered if the question was born of concern for the life of the bank's chairman of the board or bred out of a need to make sure Charles' condition wasn't going to affect Hal's little merger.

Alex told him what Butterfield had said, then gave him a

quick rundown of the doctor's analysis of Charles Barrett's condition.

"That bad?"

"Yes, Hal, that bad. Kind of puts a cramp on business, doesn't it." Alex paused long enough to shift down again. That was the one thing he disliked about a stickshift in today's modern world. It didn't mix well with a cellular phone and a steering wheel. He caught only a part of Hal's comment.

"Say again, Hal. I had to shift."

"I'm not worried about the business, Alex, only about your father's health."

"I didn't doubt it for a minute."

"Do the police have any idea who did this?"

"Not according to the detective who came to the hospital. I'm nearly at the house now. Possibly Logan will have some answers, if he's still around the place. If not, I'll look him up on the way back to the valley and have him give you a call. What's a number where he can reach you?"

Hal gave him the number.

"Logan had better have answers." Alex hated the demanding sort of arrogance in Frost's voice.

"Leave him alone, Hal. This is one time we'd all be better served if you'd keep your ego in check."

Another long pause. Alex knew Hal was looking for an adequate response—one as biting. One that would put Charles Barrett's son in his place. Alex had enough time to turn the last corner, shift, speed the length of the block, and turn into the drive. There was a single police vehicle on the driveway, and the Corvette rumbled to a stop next to it.

"Why the sudden interest, Alex? You haven't exactly been Charles' biggest fan over the past . . . four years is it? Getting tired of being an attorney?"

Alex shut off the Corvette. "Don't get your pocketbook in an uproar, Hal. I have no interest in Barrett Bank."

"Then why are you—"

"Because Claire needed me and you were off gathering in another bank or two. She doesn't have anyone else she can turn to. Good-bye, Hal." Alex hung the phone up, cutting Hal off. He always liked cutting Hal off. Hal had his sights set on the chairmanship of Barrett Bank someday, wanted to run the whole show. He wasn't about to let the fact that Charles had heirs interrupt his goals. But then, neither was Alex. He wanted nothing to do with Barrett Bank. Maybe that's what made him so mad at Frost. Hal was constantly acting as though he needed to protect himself against Alex when Alex had absolutely no interest in taking his job.

He climbed from the Corvette, locked it, and descended the stairs to the front door. Removing Claire's key from his pocket, he let himself in. A man was standing in the step-down living area, staring out the window.

"You must be Logan," Alex said.

"Umm." Logan rubbed his bristled chin, his concentration on something outside, through the large wall of windows that looked east, across the ski run and over the valley below. He didn't even turn when Alex stepped to his side.

"Do you know who lives over there?" He pointed to the blue-gray house across the run, sitting in some trees. Alex squinted a little and could see someone sunbathing on the patio in a two-piece bathing suit.

"Haven't the slightest," Alex said.

Logan turned to him. "You're Alex Barrett, right?"

Alex nodded. "I've been to this house just once in the past four years. That house wasn't even there the last time I took a good look."

Logan turned back to the view. "Great view, isn't it?"

"Yes. Used to be even better." He pointed his hand at the dozens of houses below. "There was a time when none of those existed. You could look out over this mountain and have the serene feeling of being alone. Now it's nothing but back-to-back houses, and the thought of wilderness never occurs."

"Yeah, I remember." Logan paused. "I knew the guy who bought this property, subdivided it. He died a year or so ago—a multimillionaire. His three kids are fighting over the money in the courts. By the time they're finished, another couple of attorneys will be building houses up here, and the kids will be dirt poor."

Alex glanced at Logan, impressed with his straight talk. They were about the same height, but Logan was heavier, maybe a year or two older, with blond hair cut marine style. His face was somewhat flat and wide, with high cheekbones. His lips were thick but not heavy. Except for the blond hair, Alex thought he might be partly Native American. But whatever his genealogy, Alex didn't think anyone would dare call him handsome.

"Why, Chief Logan, you sound like a man disillusioned with our great capitalist system."

Logan laughed lightly. "Nah. It's crooks I'm disillusioned with." He removed a small pad from his shirt pocket. It looked like the twin of Butterfield's. "A clean, professional job. Except for your father's interference, we'd have nothing. When people are running for their lives they get sloppy, and we find them. We already found the vehicle in downtown Park City. A lot of blood on the floor and seat. Your father did a good deal of damage."

"The ski pole."

Logan smiled. "A very sharp ski pole."

Alex remembered his father's fetish for having the poles sharpened at the beginning of each ski season. It stemmed from an accident Alex had had on icy slopes at Park City. If he'd had sharp poles that day, his father said, it would have saved a couple of thousand dollars in doctor bills. The chairman had always been a master of cost-effective management.

"But no appearances at any of the hospitals?" Alex asked.

"Nope, not yet. But it shouldn't be long before the wounded man either checks in for help or we find a body with a nasty hole or two in its chest and abdomen."

"Fingerprints on the pickup?"

"Lots of 'em, but they all belong to the original owner. Kidnappers probably used gloves. They borrowed the vehicle for the evening from a parking garage. The owner was out of town until about an hour ago. Phoned in a stolen car report when he was forced to walk to work."

"Anything else?"

Logan let his eyes wander back to the view. "One thing. A ransom note was found in the girl's bedroom. Attached to the lamp shade with tape."

"How much did they ask?"

"They didn't ask for money."

Alex glanced quickly over at Logan, waiting.

"They were after cooperation." He pulled a piece of paper from his pocket and handed it to Alex. The message was several sentences long in the middle of a full sheet of standard typing paper. Alex read it aloud: "You should have listened. Provide us with the information we want or your granddaughter will pay the price."

"Nasty people," Alex remarked.

"Kidnappers are the most cruel kind of person. They hurt you where you never forget. Any ideas who might be behind this?"

"None." Alex handed back the paper. "Charles Barrett is a banker. He has access to money, and everyone knows it."

"Money. Could be the motive, I suppose." He shrugged. "They have contacted him before, that's evident."

Alex agreed.

"The kidnappers also knew the layout of this place," Logan said. "They knew where the girl's room was, the closest entrance."

"Someone who had been in the house before?"

"That's my guess," Logan said.

"Not many people have been inside Charles Barrett's inner sanctum, Logan. To my knowledge he never held a party here, even for close friends."

"Any relatives with an ax to grind? Somebody who needed something from your father but couldn't go through standard channels?"

Alex thought of Claire's ex-husband. He didn't think Steve Navarro had the brains or the guts to pull something like this. "No, but I'm not an authority. When you talk to my sister . . . I suppose you want a list. People who might be in financial trouble at the bank, might have known the layout of the house."

"As soon as you can get it."

"I'm out of it. Hal Frost and Claire can help you."

"Halford Benson Frost. Acting president, Barrett Bank. Member of the board of directors of Utah Power, former candidate for governor, and on enough political and public action committees to make your head spin." He smiled. "Hal Frost thinks he's the cock of the walk."

Alex laughed. "Sounds like you know him."

"City council. Trouble is, he does have some power."

"Powerful enough to get you out of bed in the middle of the night."

"Not Frost. I wouldn't get up before nine for Frost. The mayor, now that's a different story. A personal friend of your father's." He faced Alex. "Butterfield tells me you and your father don't get along."

"We get along fine as long as we don't get within sight of each other."

Logan smiled, turned, and headed for the front door. "Not much left to do here. Under normal conditions I'd tell you not to leave town, but I don't think you did this."

"Nice to be on your good side."

"Yeah, a lot of people say that. I'll keep in touch." Logan turned at the door, a grin moving his heavy lips into a wide smile. "Lock up. I wouldn't want to be sued for allowing this place to be cleaned out."

Alex could see Logan through the glass in the door as the cop ascended the steps leading to the drive. He decided he liked Logan.

Alex went up the stairs from the sunken living room and into the kitchen. He felt hungry and grabbed an apple to stave off the rumbling in his stomach. Then he wandered. Downstairs he did a once-over of Melissa's room. It was a little messed up but nothing to make him think the kidnappers had a problem getting her out of bed and out of the house. He walked down the hall, turned right, then left, entering the small ski room that led to the back porch, then went outside. He gnawed at the apple while standing on the porch and surveying the scene.

The hill sloped away from the house at a fairly steep rate. The ground was covered with wild grass and flowers in their natural state, but it looked matted. Alex thought Logan must have had a small army going over the grass to look for clues. A hundred feet away tall stakes were driven into the ground, and yellow plastic ribbon with black writing on it was tied to them. Must be the place where the pickup had been parked.

Alex finished the apple, thought about tossing it into the grass, but changed his mind. If the cops weren't finished and came back to look things over, they might think it was a clue of some kind, and that could only cause grief. Two more bites and the disposal of a few seeds, and it was gone.

Descending the steps from the porch to solid ground, he walked the short distance to the yellow plastic ribbon. As he approached, he could see where the tall grass had been ripped by heavy tire treads, leaving the landscape scarred two inches deep in wild grass and brown earth. His eyes followed the trail until it disappeared some hundred feet down the hill. Alex searched the area around the barrier. It was ludicrous to think he would see something a couple of dozen cops had been on their hands and knees looking for, but he searched anyway.

The dark rust red of dried blood was noticeable in one spot. It clung to thin blades of grass and marred the face of half a dozen wild flowers near the right edge of the barricaded area. Alex stooped down to get a closer look, touching the dried substance with his hand.

"What are you doing?"

The voice came from the trees to his left. Alex stood, squinting a little to see into the shadows. A child was standing there, near the trunk of a large spruce tree.

"Are you a policeman?" The child took a few steps into the sunlight. Alex could see then that it was a little girl with a doll in her arms. She had short blond hair in a pageboy cut and was decked out in shorts and a white T-shirt that said "U of U" on the front.

"No, not a policeman. My name is Alex—Alex Barrett. What's yours?"

"Linda." She pointed through the trees to the house next door.

"I live there. My dad is named William. My mom is Linda too, so they call me Lindy."

"How old are you, Lindy?"

"Six. Where is Lissa?"

"Melissa is at the hospital with her mother."

"Is she hurt?"

"No, she's fine. Charles, her grandfather, was hurt."

Lindy smiled. "Charles was nice. I hope he gets better." Lindy walked toward the yellow ribbons.

"You're not supposed to go past—"

"I know; the policemen told me. Do you know where the policemen are?"

"Probably back at the police station or doing other jobs, helping other people."

Lindy's face wrinkled with concern.

"What's the matter?" Alex asked.

Lindy pulled down on the zipper of the small pack around her waist and pulled out some sunglasses. "I found these." She handed them to Alex and pointed to the far side of the ski run. "Over there, in the grass."

Alex took the pair of glasses. They were wire-rimmed with bifocal lenses. Prescription. Along one earpiece was a word he couldn't make out and a series of numbers.

"Can you take them to the police? They told us if we found anything we should give it to them right away," Lindy said.

Alex felt his heart start to pound. "Can you show me exactly where you found them?"

Lindy nodded, then started walking down the slope and away from the house. They went across the ski run and into some trees on the far side before she stopped.

"Do you know anyone who wears glasses like these?" Alex asked.

She shook her head in the negative.

Alex looked at the houses through the trees, then back at his old home. It was a good hundred yards. "Do you know the people who live on this side?"

She nodded, pointing at the closest house in the trees. It was the blue-gray one with the sunbather. "Angela lives there. She plays with Melissa and me sometimes. We play here because Angela's mother won't let her leave their yard." She walked further up the hill and pointed at the ground. "There. I found them in the grass right there."

Alex bent down and carefully pushed the grass aside, searching for what he didn't really know, and he wasn't surprised when he didn't find it. "Angela's father, does he wear glasses?"

"Her father lives somewhere else. She only has a mother. She wears sunglasses sometimes but not like these." She glanced nervously toward her own house. "Will you take them to the police?" Lindy asked.

"Yes, if you want me to."

Lindy looked relieved. "I have to go now. My mom and I are going to lunch somewhere with my dad." She seemed pleased and started the walk back.

"Thank you, Lindy. I'll tell the police it was you who found these."

She smiled over her shoulder but kept hurrying across the ski run. Alex watched her until she climbed the back stairs to a patio, then did a more careful inspection of the grass. Possibly the glasses belonged to an unfortunate skier who had made contact with the tree, but he didn't think so. If Lindy played in this spot often, they would have found them before now. He looked through the trees at the blue-gray house, then started off in that direction.

Approaching a stairway that led to the patio, he began the ascent. At the top he found the woman in scanty swimwear asleep in a chaise lounge, a pair of sunglasses with oversized lenses hiding her eyes. He cleared his throat.

"Hello," he said as the woman sat up, a look of surprise on her face. She removed the glasses to get a better look and seemed pleased with what she saw.

"Well, hello." She gave him a seductive smile. "What can I do for you?"

Alex felt the wave of red climb into his face as she adjusted her suit but left the light robe lying on the floor beside the chair.

"I'm Alex Barrett. My father—"

"Across the run. The old gentleman caused quite a stir this morning. How is he?"

"In a coma."

She looked genuinely concerned. "And Claire?"

"Okay."

She stood, the sun glistening off her well-tanned and oiled skin. She could see his discomfort with her scant attire and with a half-smile picked up the robe and slipped into it. Her hair was brown, long, but was fastened up, away from her shoulders. She was about five feet six and thickly proportioned. Her face was round and seemed out of harmony with the rest of her, even though it would be pleasant enough to look at if she would just use less makeup.

"I'm Della—Della Ames. My daughter, Angela, plays with Melissa, and I know Claire quite well. She told me about you but never said you were so good looking."

Alex ignored the attempt at flirting and handed her the glasses. "Have you ever seen these? Lindy found them down on the boundary between your property and the ski run."

She looked the glasses over, shaking her head, then looked again, sudden recognition crossing her face. "The guy from the resort. I saw him down there a few days ago. He was digging, so I went down to make sure he wasn't doing it on my property. He asked me to keep the kids out of the area for a few days. He had glasses like these."

"Did he say what he was doing?"

"Some sort of preparation for placing snow-making machines along this run. Said they had to survey it, that sort of thing."

"Did he have any instruments with him? Surveying equipment—"

She nodded. "Yes, but he never really used them." She thought a moment, then walked toward the edge of the deck. "Another one came later. They marked several places on both sides of the run. Took nearly all of one day to do it."

"Did they seem . . . did they have an interest in Claire's place?"

Della turned around. "They spent some time over there near the house, digging and fooling with their equipment. But it didn't strike me as unusual once they told me what they were doing."

"Anything to verify they were who they said they were?"

"The name of the resort that owns the ski hill and lifts was on their hats and shirts." She shrugged. "That was good enough for me." She paused, giving him a curious look. "You don't think . . ."

"Maybe. I'll have the police check it out with the resort." He started toward the stairs.

"Would you like something cold to drink? I have some iced tea."

"No thanks. I'd better get going, but I appreciate the offer."

Alex gave her a parting smile as he reached the bottom step and looked up. "Nice to meet you, Della." He walked through the trees and across the hill. When he climbed to the house and entered by the back door, he glanced across the ski run. For the most part Della's house was obscured by the trees, but the deck was visible. Della was back in position in the chaise lounge, sunglasses in place, robe discarded. He wiped the sweat from his brow and locked the door before going back to the main level, then the front door.

He'd drop off the glasses on his way back to the valley.

6

LEAVING THE PARK CITY police department parking lot, Alex headed for the nearest freeway entrance. He had wanted to give the glasses to Logan personally, but the police chief wasn't in and wouldn't return for a couple of hours. He left the wire-framed lenses with the desk cop.

As Alex reached the freeway, entered, and made his last shift, he picked up the phone and dialed the hospital.

"Hello, this is Alex Barrett. Connect me with my sister staying with our father, Charles Barrett."

"Hello." Claire's voice seemed fresher.

"Hi, any change?"

"None."

"You sound better."

"I feel better, a little. I want to stay the night with Father. Can you take Melissa?"

"You need a good night's sleep, Claire. You and Melissa can stay at my place. I'll stay with Charles."

"No. I've made arrangements for a bed here. I must do this, Alex, please. You come and get Melissa, all right?"

She was right. She was the one who had stuck it out with Charles, and she was the one who would experience the sense of loss when he was gone. "If you think Melissa will be all right."

"She likes you Alex. Always has."

"It's been a few years. She seemed a little reluctant to strike up where we left off."

"She's shy with people at first, remember? She needs to get away from here."

Alex agreed. "Do you need anything else?"

"I'm fine. Father's resting, and I'll grab some sleep as soon as you pick her up." A pause. "Thanks, Alex. I know this is asking a lot, but I haven't many choices."

Alex thought about Steve for all of one second. The jerk was a lousy father, and Melissa would only be in danger there.

They broke the connection.

Driving to the office, he parked the Corvette in the garage and went to his office through the apartment. He tried working, but it was nearly impossible. He felt as if his life was coming unraveled and he couldn't do a thing about it. He didn't like the feeling. Didn't like it at all.

He forced himself back to his paperwork. It was going to be a long afternoon.

Alex heard the doorbell but didn't believe it until it rang a second time. He shook off the sleep, turned on the night-light, and found his robe. Thirty seconds later he was staring at the TV monitor that showed the outside entrance area to his apartment. He saw Logan standing on the step. He blinked several times, wondering if he was having a bad dream. He opened the door and checked. He wasn't dreaming.

Brigham Logan had a tired look on his face. "A guy could die from exposure before you get to the door." He stepped forward, and Alex moved aside to avoid a collision.

Alex followed Logan into the living room, stifling a yawn and working at getting his eyes completely open. "To what do I owe this honor?" Alex asked.

Logan faced him, a bit of a smirk on his face. "I was in the neighborhood and wanted to see how the guys in the fast lane live."

Alex glanced at the clock on the wall. "I take sarcasm better between the hours of nine and nine. It's nearly five in the morning, Logan, and, in case you hadn't noticed, Park City is a long way from this neighborhood."

Logan lowered himself onto the couch. "We found the guy your father used the ski pole on. He was dead."

Alex sat down, the pixy dust fleeing from his mind like a flock of startled birds. "Charles killed him with a ski pole?"

"Not exactly, but he was badly wounded. He was finished off with a .22-caliber hollow-point bullet put through his forehead. We figure his partner considered him a liability."

Alex sat back, his mouth dropping open. "Have you identified him yet?"

"Yeah." Logan looked away. "Steve Navarro, your sister's ex-husband."

Alex felt sick inside, weak in the knees. His chest tightened, and it was difficult to breathe. He sat forward and lowered his head a little, trying to keep the room from circling around him. It took a few minutes to get under control.

"I know it's hard to believe, but I recognized him the minute I saw him. I knew him, Alex. He was a prosecutor, and I dealt with him on a couple of cases." He took a deep breath, looking even more tired.

"I thought of Steve when we talked at the house this morning. I didn't think he . . . "

"Yeah, I understand. He's not the type you'd figure to kidnap his own kid." He paused. "We did some preliminary checking. He was in deep trouble financially—living way beyond his means."

"He got used to it when my sister was paying the bills," Alex said weakly.

"He made regular junkets to Las Vegas. Nearly a hundred thousand in debt to some boys down there, guys that charge high interest and don't take no for an answer."

"How'd you find out—"

"He keeps records. Gave us a couple of names in a little black book. I called Las Vegas and had a guy from the state's racketeering division lean on 'em a little. They verified he was into them." He leaned forward. "They received full payment yesterday—by courier and in cash."

"His partner paid him up front?"

"Probably more coming later—after they got a few million out of your father."

"Any ideas on the other guy?"

"None yet," Logan said. "Those glasses you brought by—did they belong to Navarro?"

Alex shook his head. "Steve didn't wear glasses."

"We're tracking them down. Foreign make so it won't be easy."

"Foreign?"

He nodded. "German, we think."

"But they sell them in this country."

"Not so's you'd notice."

Then the men were silent, each in his own thoughts. Logan finally spoke.

"I think I can tell you this and trust you'll keep it under your hat." It was almost a question. "We think whoever tried this was a professional. He needed access to the house, someone who knew the layout, and did his own little survey of the most likely candidates. He came up with Navarro. To do all that takes time. If the lady you talked to, this Della, is right, they've been watching the place for at least a week, putting together their plan, waiting."

"Waiting?"

"The note implies that pressure was being applied. When your father didn't respond, they had a second option—kidnapping Melissa."

Alex let it sink in.

"Your dad had a lot of connections abroad, through the bank, right?" Logan asked.

Alex nodded. "Hal Frost—"

"I talked to him." Logan smiled. "He doesn't like me asking him questions. Always considered me below him. I forced him. As near as I can tell, Charles wasn't dealing with anyone outside his usual circle. Frost gave me a list, and we're doing some checking." He leaned forward. "I didn't come this late just to tell you all this. I need your help, on two counts."

Alex felt exhausted, overwhelmed.

"Come with me to talk to your sister. This is going to the media in a few hours, and I think she needs to be prepared. At the same time, she has to give me some answers before her mind becomes so muddled she forgets something."

Alex cringed inside. This wouldn't help Claire's already weakened state. "What else?"

"We need to get hold of your father's personal papers. I think his enemy may have come out of his past."

Alex agreed. "I'll see what I can do." He remembered the house guest with whom he had spent a great evening. "I have Melissa here with me. I'll need to make arrangements for someone to come and stay with her."

"How is she doing?"

"Fine. There don't seem to be any lasting effects from her experience last night."

Logan sat back, his eyes searching Alex's face in concern. "I've dropped quite a load on you. You gonna be all right?"

Alex smiled while lifting himself from the chair. "I'll change and make a call. My secretary lives alone and can be here in thirty minutes."

Alex went into his bedroom, his brow wrinkled deeply with worry. He was back in his father's life now, whether he liked it or not.

7

ALEX STARED AT THE HEADLINES.

"Assistant Prosecutor Murdered in Bizarre Kidnapping Attempt." It covered half the front page of the *Tribune*. The story was sketchy but had Steve Navarro and Charles Barrett as prominent characters. Of course, that pulled Claire into it, and even the name of Alex Barrett was mentioned half a dozen times, but only as potential heir to the Barrett millions.

Until now Alex hadn't realized how much speculation went into a major story like this one. It was wild. And people said only the *Enquirer* pulled out all the stops! This was bound to become the valley's story of the year.

He lay his head against the back of the chair. Melissa was safe with Lillian and was probably getting enough attention that she wouldn't have time to miss her mother—at least not much. Claire was asleep after having been given a sedative. He had been proud of the way she had held up, answering Logan's questions and responding to a small contingent of reporters.

Then Charles worsened. Another attack. His body was carrying on few of its own functions now. The doctor had already suggested they consider letting him go. They had discussed it, but Alex could see now was not the time to force such a thing on Claire. And he wasn't up to it either. It had exhausted both of them, but Claire had needed something to knock her out, help her pull her emotions together.

Claire hadn't given Logan many more answers than he already had—at least not that Alex could see. She hadn't lived with Steve for months and, even though aware of his gambling problems, wasn't able to tell them much about them. She had known one thing—Steve was careful. He had never gone over his limit. It was clear to Alex that the hundred-thousand-dollar debt was a shock to her. He wondered if Steve had been set up.

Alex closed his eyes, trying to shut down his mind, let it rest, but it wouldn't.

Alex knew where their father kept his personal things—in a safe in his bedroom study. But he didn't have the combination, and neither did Claire. It was just as well. They were in no condition for a search right now. Alex was grateful that Logan had postponed it.

He heard soft leather soles come to a stop in front of him and opened his eyes to find Hal Frost standing there, all starched up prim and proper. But he did look pale.

"Sit down, Hal. You don't look so good."

Hal sat in the chair across the table, his eyes going to the story on the front page of the paper lying between them.

"With news like that, your phone is probably a bit busy," Alex said.

"Every big account, every client . . . " He tapered off as if about to cry. "I . . . they . . . we are very nervous. The board . . . our business . . . "

Alex could see that Hal Frost was beginning to realize his importance didn't amount to much when compared with that of the bank's founder and chairman.

"What brings you out so early on a Sunday morning?" Alex asked. "I thought you had Church meetings." Alex had only shaken his head when he found out that Hal had been called as a member of a stake presidency. But then, that was one of the signs of the true church. It survives in spite of some of the people who serve in it. Besides, Hal had some good qualities. He could get things done and was about as conservative a man as Alex had ever known. He lived modestly, recycled everything, and had a plaque on his wall that said "Waste not, want not." It was good for a bank to have that kind of second-in-command. It wasn't bad for the Church to have him working at it, either.

Alex noticed that Hal was glaring at him. "Your father is important to me, Alex, and contrary to what you think, not just because my job might hinge on whether he lives or dies. He has trusted me, let me do a lot of things other banks wouldn't even have considered. He's been a good friend. So lay off the snide remarks and insinuations, will you?"

Alex was pleasantly surprised. The man had a backbone. "Sorry, Hal," he said genuinely. "I grew up a cynic—my father's fault."

Hal breathed deeply, then reached into his pocket and pulled out an envelope, handing it to Alex. "A living will. Your father left this copy and copies of other pertinent papers with the bank's attorney. When the story hit the papers this morning and the world found out about your father's condition, he delivered these to my doorstep with instructions to deliver them to you. He'll join us later."

Alex could see Hal didn't like the responsibility the attorney had placed on his shoulders, and it made him apprehensive about the contents of the letter. He read it. It was the usual thing, a legal document removing any liability from his family if the time came that they needed to make a decision to let him die or leave him hooked up to machinery. But the last paragraph nearly took his breath away.

"Claire is not emotionally capable of fulfilling my request in this matter. Therefore I leave it to my son, Alexander. As an exceptional attorney in his own right who knows and understands the laws of this land and state, Alex is to have full decision-making responsibility in this matter. I leave the decision in his hands."

It was signed, witnessed, and notarized. Then a brief note followed.

"Alex. I know you think I betrayed you and don't deserve your consideration of my wishes, but I ask for it, nevertheless. I won't burden you further than this, but please, don't let me die without dignity. Dad."

Alex couldn't have felt any more tired. He stood, the document clinched in a tight fist, and walked down the hall, his shoulders sagging under an unwanted load.

Alex sat in the corner, his chair and head against the wall, his feet propped up on one of the four other chairs that surrounded the small table. It was nearly lunchtime, and the hospital cafeteria was busy. Alex hardly noticed.

Claire walked through the tables and took an empty chair next to him. He forced a smile.

"You're looking better," Alex said.

"I feel nauseous, drug out. I hate medication." She lay her purse on the table. "The doctor has been looking for you for the past two hours," she said.

He glanced at the will lying open on the table. Her eyes went there as well. "Hal told me." She placed her forearms on the table and played with the napkin holder. "Father is right. I can't do it, Alex. You have to." She was near tears.

"I can't either," he said. After a long moment in which she gained control he continued. "Do you know how many times I dreamed of this chance? Father in Heaven forgive me, but it is more than I can count on hands and toes!" He leaned forward, his shoulders slumped. "Now, I can't."

"He has asked, Alex," she said, her eyes glued to the will. "The doctors give him no chance." She brushed back the tears. "Giving him a new heart would be foolish. He's brain dead, nothing but a vegetable lying there . . . " She choked, unable to finish. She put her head in her hands, covering her face, trying to get control again. It was several minutes before she removed them, took a tissue from her purse, and dabbed at her eyes.

"I'm sorry. It's not fair. I couldn't do it either," she said. "He is our father, and taking his life . . . "

"You don't understand, Claire. I don't know *why* I would be doing it, don't you see? Would I be pulling the plug out of mercy or out of vengeance? I've wanted to kill him, especially the day we buried Mom and he was nowhere in sight. If I could have had his neck in my hands then, I would have wrung the life out of him! That would have been murder, Claire, and this is no different. It's what is in my heart that God will judge me on, and what is in my heart is hatred and vengeance. I'd love to go up there and pull that plug, but don't you see that's just the problem. I'd love it! That's why I can't!"

Claire was stunned. She knew their parent's divorce had affected Alex but hadn't realized how deeply bitter he had become.

"Do you really hate him that much?" Claire asked. "After all this time? How can you justify it, Alex? Even if he did what has been said of him, he was a good father to you for more than twenty-five years! The gospel . . . even I know it teaches compassion, mercy, forgiveness. Even for enemies. This is wrong, Alex! Wrong!"

Alex pushed the will across the table to her, his jaw set firmly. "I won't pull the plug, Claire. I don't care if he rots in that bed, but I won't. You give that to Hal and tell him to have the attorney find a way around it if you think it ought to be done, but I can't do it." He stood and started away.

"Alex!"

He turned back to face her, anger in his face.

"Yesterday you asked me if I could forgive Steve for what he's done. Today I find that he committed even worse by being involved in the attempted kidnapping of my daughter and putting Father in this hospital." She took a deep breath, her eyes boring into his. "But I can honestly say I don't hate him, Alex. I hate what he did to me, to my family, but I don't hate him. Not like you hate father. It's the hate that will get you in the Judgment, Alex, whether you unplug Dad's machinery or not. If you value your soul so much, you ought to consider forgiveness. Only then will the hate go away."

He turned and walked away.

Claire sat there in a pained stupor. It was a long time before she picked up the will and her purse and left the cafeteria. As she went up the elevator she read, then refolded her father's living will. It almost seemed that Charles was forcing Alex to face all this. Was it a cruel form of revenge on her father's part? An effort to make Alex look deeper at what had happened? If so, it wasn't working.

The door slid open. Hal, the two doctors, and the bank's attorney stood near the nurse's station. They were talking quietly together, but when they saw her they stopped. Hal took a step toward her.

"He said to give you this. He won't do it," Claire said, handing the will to the attorney.

"If he abdicates, refuses to accept the patient's will, it falls into the hands of the family. That's you, Claire." The attorney's demeanor was solemn, concerned.

"No, it belongs with Alex by Father's request. Alex will have to deal with it. At least for now. I'm going home and get some sleep." She realized she couldn't go back to the house in Deer Valley. It would be surrounded with press now, and it was the place where all this nightmare had begun. "No, not home. I'll be at my brother's apartment. That's where Melissa is anyway."

She turned and walked into the just-opening elevator. Hal thought of saying something, but the door closed. The four men stood there, just looking at each other. Hal finally spoke.

"See that he's kept alive, doctor," he said. "That is the apparent wish of the family."

8

ALEX FELT THE BED MOVE. He opened his eyes to see Melissa leaning against the side of it, fully dressed.

"You sleep a long time," she said.

He looked at the clock on the night table. It was 6:00 A.M. A Monday morning. He had slept in.

"Really? What time do you usually get up?" he asked.

"Five. Mommy and I clean the house. Grandpa, when he was feeling good, took us walking at seven. Then we had breakfast."

"Are you hungry?"

"No. Can we go for my walk?"

"Is your mother up?"

She shook her head. "No, she's really tired, Uncle Alex. Come on. Let's go."

He sat up in bed, the blankets falling away from his dark-blue pajamas. "Give me twenty minutes?" he asked.

"Yup. I'll make some orange juice if you have any."

He smiled. "You're quite handy for a six-year-old."

"I'm an only child." She said it as if it explained everything.

"Yes, I know. Does that bother you sometimes?"

She nodded. "I asked Mommy to get me a little brother."

Alex laughed. "What did she say about that?"

"She said she'd ask Grandpa."

"Umm. The orange juice is in the freezer compartment of the fridge. You'll have to—"

She was already running from the room. "I know. Thaw it out. I know how."

Alex lay back on the pillow, rubbing his fingers through his hair, thinking. Claire's parting words in the hospital lunchroom had hit him in the stomach like a fist. He had let his father's sin

make him hate everything about the man. It had become a beam
in his eye, and for the first time in four years Alex realized his
father wasn't the only one responsible for what Alex felt. Alex
couldn't, wouldn't, excuse his father's conduct. It wasn't his to
excuse. But he could do something about his own feelings. He
could stop hating. He had to, or it would eat him alive.

He had taken a long drive south to Fillmore and back in the
Corvette, attended a late afternoon sacrament meeting there, trying to get his heart right. It had helped, but he still had a ways to
go. Making a commitment to rid himself of such a thing at the
sacrament table was one thing, doing it quite another.

After making his commitment and partaking of the sacrament
to seal it, he left the chapel in Fillmore to come home. As soon as
he walked out the door, the hatred, the hard feelings returned. He
got behind the wheel of the Corvette, then prayed for strength.
Peace of a kind returned. Another twenty miles down the road he
had to fight the same battle again. Four times he had been forced
to pull over and plead with the Lord. Four times peace had come.
It wasn't total, but it was better. Now he knew that it could be
done. He just needed more time, a chance to get things right
inside. He couldn't make a decision about his father's life until he
knew his own heart was right.

He threw off the covers and headed to the bathroom to
shower and shave. When he was finished and dressed in running
shorts and a T-shirt, he took his shoes and socks and headed for
the kitchen. The juice was in a pitcher on the table. Melissa was
standing on the counter getting a couple of glasses from the cupboard.

"Don't fall. You'll break my floor."

She laughed. Even less evidence of the trauma today. A good
sign.

He took the glasses and placed them on the island, then
helped her down. While he put on his shoes and socks, she poured
the juice.

"What do you like for breakfast?" he asked.

"Muffins and cold cereal."

"Me too." She drank her juice, but he ignored his, pouring it back in the pitcher when she left the room to get a sweatshirt. He had another eight hours to fast.

They left the apartment. The walk took them down the street a mile, then back. She strutted right out, and Alex found himself taking good-sized steps to keep up. When they returned, he was ready for a rest.

"You take your walking seriously, young lady," he said. He pulled some blueberry muffins from a sack in the bread drawer, then retrieved some cold cereal and bowls from the cupboard.

"Mommy says it's important to keep in shape."

Claire appeared at the door between the hall and the kitchen.

"Hi, Mommy!" Melissa said, running to her mother. "We're having muffins. Would you like one?"

"That would be nice." She smiled at her daughter. Melissa went back to the counter and removed two more and placed them on the plate. Alex put them in the microwave to warm.

Claire was in her robe, but her hair was wet, as if she had just showered. She looked better than she had since walking into Alex's garage a few days earlier.

"You're looking pretty good this morning, Sis," Alex said.

"You came in late," she answered.

"I went for a ride. What you said in the cafeteria made me think." He looked her way. "You were right. Give me a little time and I'll work it out."

She nodded. "I know. Do you have any coffee?"

He shook his head. "Sorry. Some Postum?"

Her face wrinkled. "No caffeine? I'm addicted to caffeine."

"Stick around, we'll break you of it."

"Have you called the hospital this morning?"

He nodded. "No change."

There was a pause.

"Alex, do you remember when we were young? Dad gave us blessings. Maybe you should . . . "

"I thought about it on the way home last night. I'm not quite ready . . . worthy . . . for that either. God gives the blessing. I have to be in tune enough to hear his voice and then speak his words."

"He needs it now, Alex." She said it carefully, refusing to have another argument.

"Maybe someone else, Claire."

She shook her head. "No. It has to be you."

Alex gave her a side glance encasing a bewildered look.

"What?" she asked when she saw it.

"You have changed, haven't you. A year ago you would have laughed at the idea of a priesthood blessing."

She smiled. "You'd be surprised. On the outside I may have given that impression, but inside the idea of getting a blessing occurred to me more than once."

"When?"

"When Melissa would get sick, when Steve would hurt us. I was just too proud to ask, too independent and determined not to need God." She rubbed her finger around the top of her glass, her eyes on its edge. "He's brought me down a notch or two. Now independence doesn't seem as important as survival."

Alex took her hand. "I can give you a blessing."

"Yes, that would be nice."

"After breakfast, before I go into the office. I'll have my suit and tie on then."

She nodded.

Alex removed the muffins from the microwave and placed them on the table. "Have a seat, you two. I'll grab the milk, and we'll have all we need."

Melissa volunteered to say the prayer.

"You've raised quite a lady."

"She told me you washed her hair two nights ago. You'd make a good father."

Alex didn't answer. He excused himself and went to the front door for the paper. When he returned, he busied himself with reading and ignored the food.

"Why aren't you married, Alex? I'm sure you've had offers." Claire buttered a muffin for Melissa.

He blushed lightly. "Scared of girls." He turned the pages until he reached the financial section.

"You've changed since high school, then," she teased.

"Lots of things have changed since high school, Sis." He folded the paper and lay it on the table. "Seriously?"

She nodded.

"I've just never found someone I want to spend eternity with."

Claire laughed. "You've got to be kidding. Here, and at the Y? These places are crawling with eligible women."

"At the Y I found a lot of them—shallow, here-and-now types who liked the idea of a mansion on the hill more than they did mansions in heaven."

She grinned. "Surely out of sixteen thousand Cougarettes you could have found at least one who would fit your concept of the ideal!"

"Did. Dozens. They were usually taken." He shrugged. "It just didn't happen. Sure there were some I liked, even dated seriously, but the feelings—the deep ones—just didn't happen."

"Maybe you expected too much."

"Mom and Dad were going through the divorce. I was a bit disillusioned by that, and afraid. If their marriage could fall apart so easily, so could anyone's. It made me nervous, and I decided I was in no hurry."

The phone rang. Melissa was busy pouring herself a bowl of cold cereal, so Alex got it.

"You busy this morning?" It was Logan.

"Yeah, why?"

"We have a picture of the guy we think owns the glasses. I thought I'd show it to your sister's friend in the blue house across the ski run from your father's place—the one you said talked to the guy who lost them."

"What time?"

"I'll meet you there at nine."

"You asked about my father's personal papers. They're in a safe at the house."

"Good, after we've finished getting this Della woman to ID the picture, we can wander over to your father's place and take a look at them."

"The safe isn't accessible. Neither Claire nor I has the combination."

"I have a man who can help us with that. See you at nine."

Alex hung up. Two hours. He could at least clear his desk. He started to get up, telling Claire what was happening.

"I'm coming with you," she said.

Alex glanced at Melissa.

"She can play with her friends while we go through Dad's papers."

He agreed. "I'll dress and give you that blessing." He left the room. Claire finished her muffin, then began clearing the table, but suddenly she felt woozy. She had nearly forgotten about the new baby. Quickly she ran for the bathroom.

Melissa finished the dishes.

The drive was pleasant, the weather sunny and warm, and the Corvette with its wings removed allowed all the smells of late summer to fill their senses.

Alex turned into Della Ames's driveway. Logan was already there, sitting in his car on the opposite side of the street.

He got out as Alex stepped from the Corvette.

Della and her daughter, Angela, came to the entrance. Angela and Melissa met halfway, hugged, then disappeared inside.

"I hope you don't mind watching her for a while, Della," Claire said as the two women gave a cursory embrace. "We have to do some things at the house . . . "

Della smiled. She was clad more appropriately for company this time, in a white silk blouse and black pants of the same material. Alex noted that the usual heavy makeup was in place.

"Angela misses Lissa, Claire. They'll love it, and so will I. Lindy has gone on vacation with her parents, and Angela has made a basket case out of me with no one to play with."

Alex introduced Brig Logan, who flushed with the sudden abundance of attention he received.

He pulled an eight-by-ten photo out of a brown envelope and showed it to Della.

"Yes," she said, "that's the guy—the one who worked for the resort."

He removed a photo of Steve Navarro. Alex watched Claire look away. Della looked at the picture, then at her friend. "It was in the paper." She looked at Logan. "I recognized him then. Yes, it's the other guy."

"You never met Mrs. Navarro's husband before?" Logan asked, a little surprised.

Claire answered. "We didn't come up here much. Steve came even less. She never met him."

After an uncomfortable bit of small talk, Della excused herself to check on the kids, but not before inviting Logan back when he wasn't so busy.

They walked around the house and across the ski run to Charles's place. Alex still had Claire's key and used it to open the back door and let them in. Going upstairs to the main floor, they were careful to stay away from the windows. Members of the press were out front, and Alex and Claire had no desire to let the parasites know they had come in the back way.

The study and master suite were on the top floor. They went up the stairs and began looking around while Logan waited for his safe-cracker at the back door.

Alex looked around. The remnants of a man's life. Colognes, shaving cream, old-fashioned straight-edged razor. He remembered watching his father use it, a habit Charles had never changed.

In the closet were rows of suits, white shirts, a dozen pairs of shoes, and a small number of casual golf shirts and tan slacks. The suits were arranged by color. So were the slacks and the shoes. It was all very familiar; his closet was arranged exactly the same way.

Alex was surprised to find some of their mother's things still hanging on her side of the closet, her discarded shoes in a neat row underneath.

Claire stood near the large window that looked east across the ski run, her arms folded in front of her.

"I shouldn't have come," she said. "He'll never come back here, and I'm not ready to face that yet."

Alex didn't answer, but he was struck with the thought that
until yesterday the idea might have left him sadistically happy.

He walked through the double doors into the study. He knew
where the safe was and how to shift the false panel to one side to
reveal it. Its cold, gray steel and black and silver dial appeared as
he pushed the button. He checked his watch. The safe-cracker
should have arrived by now.

He looked around at the walls. They were covered with more
pictures than there used to be, but then, he hadn't been in this
room since the day he carried his mother's luggage out of it. In
the center of the far wall, opposite the large walnut desk, was an
enlarged photo of a snapshot. Alex remembered when it was
taken. It was their last trip to Israel and was shot in front of the
Wailing Wall. It was just before his last year of high school. Next
to it was the last family portrait. They were smiling even though it
had been a difficult time. Claire's first husband was standing
behind her and next to Alex. Alex had forgotten what his first
brother-in-law had looked like—a fact that made him uncomfortable.

He looked away. The wall to the right was filled with more
pictures. One section was reserved for Israel and had a small
Israeli flag at its center. They had spent a good deal of time in
Israel because Charles Barrett had had a lot of banking business
there. At one time they even owned a home, sort of a summer
place. Those were good years.

The rest of the wall was of family but closer to home. Pictures
in ski gear, hiking boots, and prom dresses and tuxedos. There
were a dozen of Alex, mostly newspaper clippings of his football
exploits. One was of his mission call. The rest were of Claire and
Melissa. Only two had Steve in them, and none had Claire's first
husband grinning from their flat surface. The main picture was a
large oil painting of Fontana Barrett. She hated that picture;
Charles loved it. She thought it was old fashioned; he said it
reminded him of pictures in Europe, of royalty. She deserved to
have a queen's portrait, he had said. But that was before—before
his adultery. What had happened?

"His rogues' gallery," Claire remarked.

"I didn't expect him to keep it intact after Mom and I left."

"He didn't stop loving either of you, Alex. In fact, just the opposite. I caught him many times in here just staring at the walls, a slight smile on his face, or tears running down his cheeks. It was one of the things that made me feel he was innocent."

Alex looked at her eyes. He could always tell when she was lying. She was telling the truth.

Logan and another man came into the room. He glanced at them, aware that he had came at an awkward moment. Then he covered it by introducing Sam Biggins.

"Sam is presently residing in our lockup," he said.

Biggins had a small plastic toolchest with him and a smile that made him look like Howdy Doody.

"Sam wants to show the courts that he can be cooperative, maybe get a little off the sentence he is about to get for trying to clean out the safe of one of our local establishments. Caught him myself."

Sam moved to the safe, replacing the smile with the look of a concentrated professional. Five minutes later, the door swung open and revealed the items inside.

"Nice," Biggins said. "Hard to break unless you have the experience." He smiled. "I'd replace it though. Get one of the new ones. They're expensive but a lot tougher to break into."

Logan escorted Biggins and his small box of tools back to the uniformed policeman waiting in the entry. Alex started removing the papers.

They had been at it for ten minutes. All of the family's papers were there—the deed to the house, another copy of the living will, half a dozen plastic pages with rare stamps in them, and a file of ledger papers and other documents, some written on foreign letterhead, that showed just how rich Charles Barrett was. Claire and Melissa would never go without, nor would their grandchildren and their grandchildren's grandchildren. It also listed the attorney's name who held the wills, as well as deeds to all bank and personal property. Alex thumbed through them, then laid them aside.

Claire's marriage licenses and divorce papers were in a large envelope along with Melissa's birth papers and a picture of her grandfather holding her shortly after she was born. It was taken in the birthing room. Claire looking happy but a little washed out where she lay on the table next to them. Alex had a sudden regret for missing that moment.

What surprised him was the lock of his sister's hair from when she was just two, a small pair of baby shoes belonging to him, and a file filled with memorabilia from each of their lives—something Charles had never showed them.

"What's in the bag?" Claire asked.

Alex shook them into his hand. "Keys to safety deposit boxes at the bank. Dad keeps the stocks, bonds, and other ready assets there. You remember the stamp and coin collections he bought us when we were kids? They're in one of the boxes. I saw them just before my mission along with some gold ingots, silver coins, and some diamonds." Alex returned them to the small bag, then put them on his lap.

A stack of personal papers came next, and Alex quickly thumbed through them. Assets were listed on computer printouts. They were sizable, in the millions. There were letters from a couple of banks, including one from Leumi in Israel and one in Geneva. He passed them on to Logan, who looked them over a bit more carefully, then laid them next to the other items, impressed by Charles Barrett's monetary worth.

At the very back of the safe, Alex found a rare first edition of the Book of Mormon and his father's Hebrew copy of the Torah, both collector's items. Charles knew Hebrew, had learned it quickly when deciding to work with Israel's Leumi Bank, but the Torah was older than that. Charles said he had picked it up during the war. The Book of Mormon had a note inside: "See that Alex gets these." Alex lay both aside.

"What's this?" Claire handed the stapled notes to Alex. Logan peered over his shoulder as Alex looked at each one.

He read. "Arkadi and Pavel send their best. I'll be in touch." He turned the note over. "That's it, no signature."

He looked at the next one, then read it aloud. "I have given consideration to your answers. They are unsatisfactory. The shipment still exists. We expect more information."

The third was longer. "You were the one who took the shipment out of the country. You know the location. You will reveal it or I will be forced to take further steps against your family." None was signed.

Blackmail notes all typed neatly on heavy, inexpensive paper, folded, as if they had once been inside envelopes. Alex handed them to Logan, who slipped them into a plastic bag. Alex looked one last time inside the safe.

"Anything else?" Logan asked.

"Nothing. I hope those help."

"Everything helps, Alex. Do either of you recognize the names? Arkadi? Pavel?"

They both shook their heads.

"They're Russian," Alex said.

"Possibly the war," Claire added. "Father never said much about those years, but he was in Berlin at the end, and there were a lot of Russians as well."

"Does your father do any business in Russia now?"

"Not that I know of," Claire said.

"Check with Hal; he'll have a better idea," Alex said.

"Hal might even know who they are," Claire added. "Especially if father did any real business with them."

"The use of the word *shipment* bothers me," Alex said. "Not exactly banking terminology."

"More like drugs," Logan commented. "Or a truckload of toilet paper."

"Father never dealt in either, detective." Claire said it with a bit of a smile at Logan's way of saying things.

"No, I know he didn't. Just giving examples. Sorry."

Alex smiled. Logan seemed flustered. Alex put everything back in the safe except the three keys to the deposit boxes.

Those he slipped into his shirt pocket without Logan and Claire noticing.

Claire looked at Alex. "Aren't you going to keep the books? A first edition of the Book of Mormon and—"

"It's still his, Claire." He stood. "I'm going back to the office." He shut the safe and turned the dial a couple of times, then picked up the paper on which Biggins had jotted the combination. He gave it to Claire.

Alex started from the room, and the others followed. They locked the doors behind them and crossed the ski run to Della's house.

Logan got into his car and left, anxious to get the notes to forensics, while Claire decided to stay awhile. Della promised she'd take her to the hospital when she needed a lift. Alex got into the Corvette after promising he would pick her up there.

He drove off the mountain quickly. He wanted to get to the bank. Logan probably didn't know Russian, and Alex didn't think he had figured out the significance of the numbers written in that language on the last note.

"Six-four-six." It was the number of one of the deposit boxes. He had the key in his pocket.

The question was, who wrote it? His father wasn't Russian.

9

WILLIAM THOMPSON WATCHED FROM THE ROAD above the Barrett house as the Corvette disappeared around the turn. He started the engine of the rented Taurus and began his pursuit. Thompson had done this dozens of times before, so it wouldn't be a problem. There had been enough of those already.

Thompson was worried. The first part of his instructions had been clear. Charles Barrett had something the people who hired him wanted. Thompson was to deliver the notes to the banker, apply necessary amounts of pressure to get a positive response, then kill him once the banker gave them what they wanted. But the old man had been a reluctant participant, dragging his feet, uncooperative. Thompson had turned the screws with threats, but the old man remained a tough nut. More pressure had been needed—definite pressure the banker couldn't resist. The kidnapping had seemed like the answer. It wasn't, and the old man's condition had put Thompson in a bad spot.

Charles Barrett would never give Thompson's employers the information they were after. Not now. His condition wasn't going to allow it. Under normal circumstances that wouldn't have bothered Thompson. Usually he worked on a no-lose contract with fifty percent of his hundred-thousand-dollar fee up front, but this time he would get his money only when his pressure paid off. One million dollars. It was a lot of money if you did things right—a waste of time and expense if you didn't.

His employers were expecting results and were more than a little miffed when they read in the papers about Charles Barrett's condition and the attempted kidnapping. After cursing Thompson's parentage, they told him the banker was their only source for what they were after, and with him out of the picture, prospects were dim.

Worse for Thompson, he wasn't getting paid.

So he'd lied to them—told them he was onto something, that the old man had passed information of some kind on to his son. All Thompson needed was a little more time in which to get the younger Barrett to cough it up. They had given Thompson an extension: three days.

It wasn't much, and Thompson had moved quickly. He had watched Alex, bugged his phones, bugged the old man's house in half a dozen spots, and kept constant surveillance, hoping for a miracle.

From the look of things, he might just get one.

He saw the Corvette a few cars ahead of him, just coming to a stop sign before turning right toward the freeway entrance. Nice of Barrett to drive such a recognizable car.

Steve Navarro had been a mistake. He had had the backbone of a jellyfish, deciding at the last minute he wasn't going to go through with kidnapping his own stepdaughter. Thompson had threatened him, and the sweating coward had picked the girl up and started from the house. Then the old man had showed up in the hallway.

Navarro had panicked and nearly removed his mask before Thompson hit the old man and pushed Navarro out of the house to the pickup. He had thought the blow to the old man's midsection would be enough to keep him down, but the banker had kept coming, attacking Navarro with the ski pole as he struggled to get the girl into the vehicle, ramming it a good inch into his former son-in-law's chest. Navarro had dropped the girl, and she had taken off, whimpering and screaming for her mother. Barrett had valiantly placed himself between them and his granddaughter, giving her a chance to get away and forcing Thompson into a battle with the ski pole, while Navarro had rolled on the ground, acting half dead and screaming for a doctor. Before their tussle was over, Thompson's mask was gone, and the old man was having a heart attack. Thompson slugged Navarro to shut up his screaming and threw him into the pickup. When he looked back, the girl was climbing the hill, her mother coming after her, and neighbors were making noise in the darkness. Retreat seemed the best decision. He didn't think anyone but the old man and the little girl had gotten a look at him, and he wasn't concerned about her. Six-year-olds weren't good with mug shots, and he didn't intend to let her see him again. For twelve hours he sweated the old man, then discovered his condition and considered the heart attack a mixed blessing.

Navarro had gone nuts—screaming, yelling threats if he weren't taken to a hospital, and generally making William believe he was nothing more than a big mouth who would get them both long prison terms. Thompson had killed him. He hadn't enjoyed it, not exactly. It was business. Security measures. Spending the rest of his life in a federal prison was not Thompson's idea of a good time, especially because a gutless wonder like Navarro couldn't control a tendency toward diarrhea of the mouth.

On the freeway now, Thompson kept pace with the Corvette while maintaining a safe distance and half a dozen cars between them.

Alex Barrett was onto something, Thompson could smell it. Bugging his phone, monitoring the call with the cop, then hearing the conversation in the old man's den. All of it was paying off.

They took Foothill Boulevard and went north. At 1300 South, they turned west and drove for several blocks before the Corvette pulled into the main offices of Barrett Bank. Thompson pulled into a parking place a dozen spaces away from Alex, then followed him into the bank at a safe distance. If he was lucky—if the banker's son could find something—he'd be back on track and get what he was looking for before the deadline his employer had set.

The entrance door closed behind him, and he found himself inside the conservative interior of the bank. On his right were half a dozen tellers, all with customers, and more customers waiting between felt ropes strung from portable silver posts. Barrett was approaching a woman at a desk nearly on the other side of the bank. From the hug, it was apparent they knew each other. They had a short discussion, then the woman removed a set of keys

from a locked desk drawer, and they started toward the stairs leading to the basement. There was a sign at the top. "SAFETY
DEPOSIT BOXES," it read, with an arrow pointing down.

Thompson moved to the desk at his immediate left and took a
seat. A moment later a young lady joined him.

"May I help you?"

He smiled. "Yes. I'd like information on opening an account."

He turned his chair slightly to his right so he could keep an
eye on the stairway. The woman started her spiel. He listened
without really hearing, wondering if Alex Barrett was actually
going to be kind enough to solve his more pressing problem. The
young man was sharp. Thompson figured the chances were very
good.

———————

Alex felt apprehensive. All the way from Deer Valley he had
wondered what might be in the box designated by his father, and
his heart was thumping now that he was about to open it and end
the wild speculations going through his mind.

He and Natalie inserted their keys and removed the box from
its assigned slot in the bank's stainless steel wall of boxes. He put
it on the table provided, thanked her, then watched as she left the
area through a door in a wall of steel bars on the other side of
which sat a guard at a desk, far enough away that he couldn't see
what customers were doing with their boxes but close enough that
he could be of assistance if needed.

Alex put the key into the hole and turned it, then lifted the
top. The box was a large one, one foot wide by two feet in length,
with a depth of six inches. Inside he found a Jewish prayer shawl,
folded, and a worn yarmulke. Although his father collected such
items, especially from Israel, Alex had never seen this set. From
its appearance, it was very old. He set it aside. The other item was
an envelope nine by twelve inches. He removed it and closed the
lid. Wiping his sweating hands on his pants, he undid the clip and
lifted the flap. Reaching inside, he pulled out the stacks of papers
and other objects, laying them on the table. As he was about to
shove the envelope aside, he realized there were still some things

inside and lifted it, letting them slide onto the polished surface of the table. Two war medals and a key with what looked like French writing on it: *Beau Rivage.*

He put it aside and picked up the first photo. It was yellow with age and had writing on the back identifying two Russian and two American soldiers at a monument outside Hitler's bunker. Alex recognized the first names of the two Russians as those in the blackmail note—Pavel and Arkadi. Pavel Grachev and Arkadi Lutria. So the connection *was* an old one related to the war years; Claire had been right about that.

He also recognized the name of one of the Americans— Arthur Hainey, retired general and intelligence officer, in on the beginnings of what became known as the Central Intelligence Agency. Hainey was an aging, powerful Washington insider. Alex remembered reading about his recent participation in a fund-raising event for the Republicans in which he had made a fool of himself by forgetting the name of the man he was to introduce as the keynote speaker. The paper had discussed the retired general's recent illness and speculated that Hainey was probably suffering from Alzheimer's disease or a similar illness.

With a closer look, Alex realized the other American looked something like his father—thinner, younger, but with the same long face and narrow, square jaw. The eyes were somewhat different, the nose and lips, but . . .

He looked at the names on the back of the picture. Michael Poltoron. His heart skipped a beat, but he put the picture aside and picked up another bunch encircled by a rubber band. He removed it and thumbed through the pictures. All of them contained Michael Poltoron in military uniform. One was with a young woman Alex didn't recognize but who looked happy to be standing in front of a barefooted Poltoron with his arms wrapped around her in a friendly embrace. He couldn't believe the similarities between Poltoron and his father. They looked the same, yet different. Possibly it was a cousin—maybe even an uncle or something.

A note was jotted on the back. Myself and Nadia, 1945, Berlin.

Picture two was a stately looking man along with Poltoron and Arthur Hainey. Alex turned the picture over. General William J. Donovan. Alex whistled. Important man—head of the OSS during the war and, some said, the man responsible for the development of the CIA.

The woman in the third picture was the same pretty blond Michael Poltoron had been embracing in one of the other photos.

The man next to her was Arkadi Lutria. One of the children standing in front of them had one finger in his mouth and wore dark shorts and a white shirt open at the collar. The other child, held by his mother, had lighter hair and seemed to be just getting over a cry. In the background were the familiar domes of the Church on the Blood in St. Petersburg. Alex turned it over. It read: *Nadia, Arkadi and their kids.*

The next picture was of Poltoron and the two Russians, their arms around each other's shoulders, big smiles across their faces. The backdrop was the Tsar's Cannon inside the Kremlin in Moscow. He turned it over. "Self in the center. Arkadi on the left, Pavel on the right."

How did they meet? Why were they so happy? And what was Poltoron, an American military man, doing in Moscow during the war?

The next one took his breath away. According to the back of the picture, whose corners were worn, it was of Michael Poltoron and his parents. Alex had seen those parents before, in two large pictures hanging on the wall of his father's study—eight-by-tens of Charles Barrett's parents!

Alex couldn't breathe. He stared at the picture, the similarities coming into precise focus. Michael Poltoron and Charles Barrett were the same man. Sure, there had been some alterations to the face, probably some kind of surgery, but for reasons Alex could only guess, Michael Poltoron had taken a new identity. He had become Charles Barrett!

Alex picked up the next piece of paper, which was folded. With slightly trembling hands he undid the folds and opened it. It was a map, about twenty-four by eighteen inches. It was German, old, with military symbols and what looked like red markings placed on it by a sturdy red pencil.

He turned it so that the print faced the right way and found it was a map of Germany after Hitler had conquered most of Europe. It took him a few minutes, but he found Frankfurt, then Munich, then Vienna, Austria. The map covered even further south, going as far as Greece and Italy. It looked like it might be a troop movement map with railroads and highways clearly marked in heavy black ink, along with circles around some cities and their surrounding areas. Alex had no idea what it meant or why Charles would have had it. He thought it must be some sort of souvenir of the war. The red pencil line followed a railroad that went near Breslau, Poland, south to Prague, Czechoslovakia, then southeast to Budapest, Hungary, and from there west to Vienna. Troop movements? An escape route? A tour Michael/Charles and others had taken after the war? As Alex looked at the markings and let his college history course refresh his mind, he knew it wasn't troop movements. The red line left the railway at the Swiss border and meandered west across Switzerland by road. The Germans never entered Switzerland. A trip then? It had to be! In the years following the war, American soldiers stationed in Europe took the opportunity to see the sights, often with a pretty young local like Nadia on their arms.

But the Russians didn't, and this map started in what was Russian territory in 1944.

Nadia. How did she end up clasped to one Charles Barrett, alias Michael Poltoron, if they really were the same person, then, apparently, married to Arkadi Lutria?

And what did any of this have to do with the notes in his father's safe? And why would Charles, or Michael, need a new identity? It was all crazy!

Alex rubbed his head. It was starting to hurt.

He focused on the map. The line stopped outside Geneva, Switzerland, a good tourist spot, unaffected by the war. Probably a hot spot for all kinds of Allied soldiers looking for a place to burn off steam and celebrate when getting leave from duties in occupied Germany or France. He looked more carefully. Actually, the line didn't reach Geneva but extended only to a little town nearby. Voltaire. He knew nothing about Voltaire, Switzerland.

He refolded the map and set it aside, picking up the picture of the three soldiers. His father! A second identity—with Russians at the end of World War II. Why? How? And what had they done together? How did it all fit in with a blackmailer fifty years later?

Maybe it didn't!

Then why would Charles refer to this box in the blackmail notes?

He turned back to the items in the envelope. The next document was on parchment, also folded and yellowed. Alex unfolded it carefully. A birth certificate. American. State of New York. For . . . Michael Poltoronov. Born December 5, 1918. Father Dimitri, mother Larissa. Russians. Michael Poltoron had been Michael Poltoronov, had changed his identity not once but twice.

The first time was prior to 1940, probably because of the fear of Russians in those days. Communists and the red scare. The second? Because he was a spy? He needed to hide and now, after fifty years, had been discovered again? What else had his father hidden from his family all those years? Had his mother known who he was? What he had done? No. His life had changed before they ever met. He was Michael Poltoron in 1945 but Charles Barrett ten years later. When did he change his name? It had to have something to do with the OSS during the war and just after. How else could he explain Poltoron's pictures with the likes of William Donovan and Arthur Hainey?

The next item was a passport. Dates 1948 through—he thumbed through the numerous pages—1953. Civilian picture. Stamped for Paris, Geneva, Berlin, London, Vienna, Helsinki, and Istanbul. There were a dozen trips to Israel. He was still Poltoron until at least 1953—four years before he met Alex's mother.

Alex thought back. He knew little of his father's past before the meeting of his parents, and whenever the subject had come up between him and his father, it had been quickly closed or skirted. Those moments of evasion were beginning to make sense now.

The next item on the table was also a passport. Russian, in the name of Mikhael Koniev. But it had Michael Poltoron's picture. Several papers of identification were stuffed inside, indicating that Koniev had the right to travel freely in the Soviet Union. There were also some military papers—Koniev had been a hero of the Great War.

Another identity.

This was crazy! His father wasn't Russian, didn't even have a hint of an accent. And yet all these papers said he had been born Russian, traveled in Russia, knew the language well! That also explained who had written six-four-six on the blackmail note.

He squinted at the pictures again until his eyes hurt. Michael Poltoron and Charles Barrett *were* the same man.

Frustrated, he tossed the passport onto the map and picked up the stack of four letters. Removing the string that tied them together, he turned the first over and read the address on the envelope, then searched for the postmark. There wasn't one. Hand delivered?

"To Michael Poltoron. 1243 Walnut Street, Washington, D.C."

He removed the letter, grateful he could read Russian.

He sifted through the three small, handwritten sheets to the last and read the signature: Arkadi. Alex went back to the first and began reading it to himself.

"Dear Michael,

"Your last gift was a joy to receive, and I and my family were most grateful. It is difficult here, and expensive. Your generosity allows us to get much-needed clothing for the children. My meager wages do not account for much. Thank you for sending it in rubles. I know it must have been difficult. I hope the enclosed material will be adequate return on your investment."

Enclosed material? Alex looked through the pages again. Nothing was there. He went back to reading.

"Our decision to be involved in this venture has given us a good deal of contentment, but we feel we can do so little. We pray that our last delivery was received without consequence.

"On a personal note, we are Russians in a foreign land among a foreign people who do not wish to be ruled by us. Since the beginning of my new job as military attaché at the embassy here, in what is now being called East Berlin, I have seen much that makes me sure about Comrade Stalin's real intent. Many people suffer at the hand of the military police, and we know that no matter what we may do, one day they will come for us as well. I suppose that is the purpose of it all—to keep us in constant fear so that we will obey. It takes much effort to keep such thoughts to ourselves, but we know that our survival and success depend on wisdom in such matters.

"I know of a friend who was recently arrested. He was a good man and did a good work. You would remember him as Stenka Pushkarev. We pray he will forget his friends. It is rumored that in Moscow much worse is taking place.

"Whole families are being sent to work camps, like Magadan and Karaganda, former heroes of the war becoming jailers for our own kind in the Siberian north, or worse, prisoners.

"In response to your question, I have not seen Pavel lately. He moves up the ladder of the NKVD and considers it a great honor to root out the enemies of the state and kill our people. He does it with, I think, a bit too much of a flourish. We are becoming worse than the Nazis. But it is such men that will rise in my country. To my knowledge, he has no suspicions of our relationship.

"I am grateful for your messages, as is Nadia. She misses you almost as much as I do. The boys grow and are the love of our lives.

"The method of delivery is still safe. I hope to hear from you soon.

"Friendship,

"Arkadi."

Pavel Grachev. Alex knew the NKVD was Lavrenti Beria's domain. Beria was Stalin's henchman. In the years after the war, Stalin returned to his former paranoia and started using Beria and the services of the NKVD to eliminate more of his perceived enemies. Men like Pavel were Stalin's best servants. From the sound of the letter, Michael knew some of the people caught and destroyed by its widely flung nets. And he knew some of those who had cast those nets as well.

Alex wondered what kind of secrets Lutria was delivering to Michael Poltoron.

He placed the letter back in the envelope. Nadia. Just a friend to Michael Poltoron? It seemed that way. Either that or good friend Arkadi was the winner in the battle for her allegiance and love.

The next letter was also addressed to Poltoron, but the address was in New York City on 17th Street.

Alex opened it. The date at the top of the page was August 1, 1950.

"Michael,

"Your letter was well received but dangerous in the coming. All communication with outsiders is forbidden now, and the secret police are working hard to ferret out all of us with any Western ideas and feelings. I have burned all our correspondence for fear that it will be used against my family. I am sorry and embarrassed. My country is under the rule of a madman. The postwar five-year plan is near completion and has driven us mad. We have people starving in the cities, yet Stalin builds canals that lead nowhere and plants that produce only appliances for death instead of ways to bring us new life.

"Following your suggestion, I resigned from the military, and we leave Berlin for Leningrad in two weeks. You are probably right—Berlin is a place from which escape takes place only to the east.

"In a way it was Pavel's action that finally made me realize we must go. I fear Pavel and his hunger for power. He will stop at nothing. He is only one step away from leading the NKVD in our half of this once-great city, and he is a man possessed with obtaining it. He considers it his passport to the higher echelons in Moscow. To get what he wants, he must produce. He comes to our home often, and Nadia caught him there just last week after coming home from shopping—in our locked house, alone. Even our home is not off limits to him and his prying suspicions. Thanks be to God, he did not find our depository and delivery system.

"But now I leave him behind. As good a friend as he once

was, he is a changed man now. It is a sad commentary on our times that a man who lusts for power as Pavel does may some day achieve it.

"Once again your generosity has brought us good things. I can leave this nasty business and go to the home of my father in Leningrad. He is worse than ever before. After surviving the siege of our great city, he now suffers from cancer of the liver. Your rubles will give him the medical treatment he needs, and he will at least die in comfort. He will soon go to meet his God, and we, heaven forgive me, will have one less thing binding us to holy Russia, although our love of her is still our greatest shackle.

"It is with heavy heart that I close this letter. I know you are aware of events here, possibly better even than I, but I have a deep sense of foreboding and desire to run from this place and to hide myself from the likes of Pavel Grachev. But such a thing is not a freedom I have at present.

"I live only for the hope that I can save my country for our children's sake and that you and I can be reunited within its holy borders.

"You are right about Pavel. He would have betrayed us if we had included him at the end of the war. We did the right thing. I pray all is safe until our country is free again.

"Friendship,

"Arkadi."

Alex folded the letter and placed it back in the envelope, anxious to read the next.

The third was addressed to Michael Poltoron, again in New York City. The date was December 1952.

"Dear Mike,

"We are attempting to set up the escape route you requested. You will meet your contact in Helsinki at the appointed place and time. Get them out using whatever means you can muster. Stalin is going through another one of his moods and lopping the heads off anyone in sight. If any taint of Western influence is connected to them, they are in extreme danger. Pavel Grachev is now in the central office of the NKVD because of our recent losses. His treatment of our mutual friends tells us just how far downhill he has gone. Reports indicate that he is much like Beria; he kills for pleasure. Even his old friends are not safe.

"As you know, I have established contacts in Moscow and Petersburg (I refuse to call it Leningrad. Somehow even to say the man's name is difficult. He started all this mess and has caused us all great pain, but especially his people. To name a city after him seems unholy. It would be like renaming Berlin Hitlerville.) The network is slowly being picked apart. We have more we must try to save. Please be at the appointed place to discuss method and timing and possible deterrents to further collapse. Your offer to use your father's place is tantalizing, but I must have further details.

"I hope all went well in Finland.

"Our business relationship stands on strong footing. Investing with you has been profitable. Your talent for making money is astounding but predictable.

"Yours,

"Arthur Hainey

"Interim Research Intelligence Service

"Berlin Office."

Alex didn't put the letter away. With a knot in his stomach, he quickly removed the next one from the last envelope. As he unfolded it, a newspaper clipping dropped free. He opened it. It was actually three articles taped together. The first was from the Russian newspaper *Pravda*. He read the headline: "American Spy Ring Uncovered."

"Comrade Pavel Grachev, newly appointed member of the NKVD central apparat, has uncovered a plot by elements of the American intelligence community and spies within our own country in which an attempt was made at removing secrets of value from the Soviet Union. Included in the plot and named specifically for their crimes are Arkadi Ilyenevich Lutria and his wife, Nadia, who had close ties with a former member of the American army intelligence organization in Moscow during the war. It appears that Lutria set up communications with the Americans through a contact known as the Fox, whom Comrade Grachev has identified as one Michael Poltoron, a Russian

American who has been an undercover operative for the intelligence organization of the United States government determined to overthrow the Soviet government of the people. We wish to congratulate Comrade Grachev on his achievement and know the judgment handed down to Arkadi and Nadia Lutria will be a lasting example of the consequences of betrayal of the free people of the Soviet Union.

"Congratulations, Lavrenti Beria, head of NKVD."

Alex felt empty, then sick as he read the second clipping. Arkadi Lutria had been executed for his crimes at Lortovo Prison, his wife and children sent to Siberia for "rehabilitation."

The third article startled him at first but made perfect sense in light of what he was discovering. It was an obituary for Michael Poltoron. He had died in an automobile accident on May 3, 1953, and had been buried in the family plot next to his parents in New York City. There were no surviving members of his family.

The letter in the envelope was from Arthur Hainey. It gave his condolences for the loss of their friend Arkadi, a few curses for Pavel Grachev, and then a postscript: "Pavel was in Beria's camp. Stalin will die, and Beria will go with him. Khrushchev will be the winner. Pavel will die. I hope you have healed and that you find your new life acceptable." It was written in a matter-of-fact style that made Alex shiver.

The next article was clipped from the *New York Times* and was dated several years later. It detailed the disappearance of Lavrenti Beria and seven other leaders in the organization then known as the NKVD. Among the names listed was that of Pavel Grachev. The name was circled in heavy red pencil.

Alex placed the letters back in their envelopes, his mind spinning. His father's attempt at saving his friends from Grachev had apparently failed.

He shook his head, running one hand through his hair. His father—an intelligence operative of Russian descent, one of the CIA's first field agents. A man who changed his name, taking a new identity, that of Charles Barrett, at the time he was connected to Arkadi Lutria, an intelligence operative working for the over-throw of the Communist regime in Russia.

He took a deep breath, his eyes going to the ceiling. It was like reading a work of fiction only to discover that the plot was true and that the main character was alive and living next door.

Why the trips? So many different places. All part of the work? And how many times had Michael Poltoron actually been in Russia as—who was it? Koniev?

And what was the operation he and Arkadi had worked on at the end of the war, and why had they left out Grachev? Why would his father have been involved with Grachev and Arkadi Lutria at all during the war? Was he an agent of some kind even then?

Whatever he had done—they had done—it was somehow connected to the attempt to blackmail his father. But who was doing it? And how did they find out that Michael Poltoron was still alive as a much-changed Charles Barrett?

Alex needed answers. With his father in his present condition he would never get them from him, and Grachev and Lutria were both dead. That left Arthur Hainey and a visit to his home in Washington.

Alex rubbed his eyes, then his temples. His head was split-ting!

After a moment he shoved the papers back into the package. Picking up the medal, he thumbed it for a moment. Michael Poltoron was a war hero. You didn't get a Purple Heart for sitting on your hands in an office.

He thought he knew his father. How could a man so com-pletely hide something like this? Obviously his mother and Claire knew nothing of the past, of Michael Poltoron. When Michael Poltoron died, Charles Barrett had been born, a new identity, a new face, a new future, and a new past. From that moment on, only these few papers said otherwise.

Alex pulled the picture out again, the one of the four men together. Looking at it carefully, he could see that the surgery had been very good. It would take someone very familiar with his father to recognize him as the man they had known as Michael

Poltoron. The nose was completely different now, and the mouth and lips were thinner, the teeth straighter. The hair was heavy, black in the picture, and wavy. Even in younger years he remembered his father as having dark but very short and thin hair, with a balding spot that became prominent at about fifty. Alex had recognized the eyes and the forehead. Couldn't others have done the same? How had Charles avoided recognition all these years?

Alex thought a moment, realizing that his father had always avoided the camera. Until just a year ago, Alex couldn't recall ever seeing his father's picture in the paper. He never attended a bank opening and gave interviews only to columnists he considered good friends willing to abide by his no-pictures rule. Charles had never been a public figure, had shunned the limelight, even when his charitable contributions had cried for attention. It seemed a quirk, an eccentricity. Now it took on greater dimensions—a man hiding from his past.

Alex put the medal back into the envelope, then picked up the key. It was of an older style, fairly large. The words *Beau Rivage* were engraved on the side. An old hotel key? Possibly. But why save it? Like everything else in this box, it had to be attached to the life and memory of Michael Poltoron, a part of the man Charles Barrett hadn't wanted to give up.

He put the key in with the other items, placed them back in the box, then locked and slid the box into its slot. Then he used the intercom to call for Natalie, who used her key to close the second lock on the box.

They left the vault and went upstairs.

"You're awfully quiet," Natalie said, setting her keys to one side.

"Long day," Alex answered, forcing a smile. "May I use your phone?"

Natalie smiled. "Your father's office is upstairs. Why don't you use his?"

Alex returned the smile. "Thanks, but no thanks."

"How is he?" Natalie asked, pointing at her phone.

"Bad." Alex frowned. "Do you have out-of-state phone books?"

She nodded. "Which one. We have all the bigger cities in the back."

"Washington, D.C., and surrounding area."

She walked away. Alex could see she was going to miss her boss as she rubbed a finger under an eye to catch a tear. Charles was good to his employees, personable and caring—always had been.

Alex had forgotten.

Punching the numbers, Alex waited.

After searching the phone books for Arthur Hainey's number without success, Alex had remembered that he and Victor Ivanov had been friends. With a degree of reluctance born of concern for a sick friend, Victor had finally given the number to Alex, but Alex had to promise to bring him up to date on what was going on when he returned to the office in the morning.

The phone rang for the sixth time. Alex's stomach was in knots, and his mouth was dry. If Hainey was in the hospital . . .

"Hello." The man's voice was tired, but Alex was grateful to hear it.

"Arthur Hainey?"

"Yes, and who is this?"

"Alex Barrett, Mr. Hainey." He paused. "I'm Charles Barrett's son."

A long lapse, but the breathing was heavy.

"I don't know—"

"Does the name Arkadi Lutria mean anything to you, Mr. Hainey?"

The breathing stopped and there was a long hesitation. "Is . . . is Charles all right?"

"No sir, he's not." Alex told him what had happened.

Alex could tell that Arthur Hainey was struggling with some kind of illness.

"Can you come to Washington?" Hainey asked.

"Yes sir. I'll be there later tonight."

"Call when you know your flight number and arrival time. I'll have someone meet you."

The phone went dead. Alex placed his on the receiver, an empty feeling in the pit of his stomach.

"Bad news?" Natalie had entered the board room, where he had retreated for privacy.

"What? Oh, no." He forced a smile.

"Want me to take these books out of your way?"

He nodded. "I need you to let me back into that safety deposit box first."

"Sure."

"And let me use a copy machine?"

"While I clean up this mess." She looked at the dozen large phone books on the conference table.

Half an hour later Alex had completed his task and was coming back upstairs just as Natalie was exiting the back storage area. He moved quickly to her desk and dropped her set of keys there. Precautions. Moments later he promised to call her if anything had happened to his father, said good-bye, and left the building.

He had to hurry. His plane was leaving for Washington in less than an hour.

10

THE PLANE ARRIVED AT DULLES INTERNATIONAL at eleven in the evening. Alex was tired even though the flight had been direct. He had never slept well on planes, and hours of boredom coupled with the events of the past few days had formed a train hard to pull.

Walking from the jetway, he spied his name floating on a piece of paper in the crowd and greeted the well-dressed and stockily built chauffeur behind it, grateful the young man calling himself David was willing to take charge of his carry-on. Alex kept his briefcase.

Once in the back seat, he opened the case and removed the papers, photocopies of the documents and pictures in case Hainey decided he wanted to plead no knowledge. The originals and the other items remained in a safe place at the bank. There was still an outside chance Arthur Hainey was the enemy.

While waiting for the plane at the Salt Lake airport, Alex had called Claire and told her he would be out of town until late tomorrow afternoon. He put off the questions born of his sister's natural curiosity, telling her he'd fill her in on his return. By then he hoped to sound like something less than a blubbering idiot.

He'd also called the hospital. No change. Charles Barrett was nothing more than a vegetable, kept alive by technology Alex was beginning to wish had never been invented.

He contemplated all that he had learned about his father over the past few hours. He felt driven to learn more. One side of him cherished his discoveries, while the other reminded him that Michael Poltoron was not Charles Barrett, at least not the Charles Barrett who had deserted Fontana Barrett and made their family a shambles. Michael Poltoron was more like the Charles Barrett

Alex remembered from his childhood, the man with unshakable principles and a dedication to honesty, the man who had never turned another away and would challenge anyone trying to trample on the beliefs of a human being. What had happened to that Charles Barrett?

Inside he knew this was the way to find out. And the way to find his father again.

He flipped on the limousine's overhead light and went through the papers again. Some things were apparent to him. Michael Poltoron had been with the intelligence services during and after World War II. Poltoron had made friends among the Soviets and continue¹ corresponding with at least one of them, Arkadi Lutria. When Lutria was executed by Stalin's government, Michael Poltoron disappeared into a new identity. One of the first questions Alex had for Arthur Hainey was *why*. What had happened that had so dramatically changed the rest of his father's life, and who was behind it?

Turning into a gate, the car headed up a short drive to the front of an old, vine-covered house. It was large but not a mansion. Two small columns of white marble supported a roof over the entry of the two-story stone building. The windows were dark, except for one on the right front where a man stood, a dark shadow with a dim light behind him. He watched Alex get out of the car but stepped away as Alex walked forward and faced him.

The chauffeur opened the front door, let Alex enter, then followed. After placing Alex's bag next to a table adorned with a large bouquet of flowers, the chauffeur walked to the door of what Alex thought to be the study and knocked, then entered. A moment later he came out, motioned that Alex should go in, then closed the door after him.

Arthur Hainey sat in a high-backed chair in front of a fireplace, the low light of the gas log bouncing off items in the room, giving them the eerie look of a Vincent Price movie.

"Mr. Barrett," Hainey said without looking in Alex's direction. "I hope your journey wasn't tiring."

"A bit, but I'll survive once I get a good night's sleep," Alex said.

"I asked David to put your bags in the corner bedroom, upstairs and at the end of the hall. Would you like to freshen up before we talk?"

"No, thank you, but I appreciate the hospitality."

"Have a seat, then." He pointed at the other chair opposite his own. To Alex it seemed hot in the room, but Hainey was wearing a sweater. Alex removed his jacket and laid it over the back of the chair. He moved his briefcase to the side of the chair as he sat down.

Alex could see Hainey better now and recognized that Victor was right. This was not a well man. His skin looked waxen and was drawn tightly over his bones, with liver spots dotting its gray surface. His hair was thin, almost fuzzy. His eyes, sunk into shadows, only showed pupils when light from the fire glinted in them. Alex decided he would make this as brief as possible.

"I'm sorry to intrude. Victor Ivanov said you were ill, but I didn't realize—"

"Victor?"

"I work for his law firm."

Hainey smiled. "The new one he started after Faye's death. The man never could keep still." He stared into the fire as if looking back, remembering. "Victor and I have known each other a very long time." He paused. "As for my health, Alex Barrett, you have come on one of my better days."

"I'll try to make this brief."

Hainey smiled. "I am stronger than I look, but I appreciate your concern." A cat came from a dark corner of the room and jumped onto the old man's lap, curling up there. Hainey stroked its long white hair absentmindedly, as if he had done it so many times he knew each strand by its length and size.

"Why did Michael Poltoron have to die?"

Hainey faced the fire, its light glinting for a moment into strangely tired eyes. "We buried Michael a long time ago. Are you sure you want to resurrect him now?"

"I'm sure. Poltoron is my father, isn't he?"

No answer, just a slight nod.

Alex told him about Claire's worries over their father, about the attempted kidnapping, then the discovery in the safe at the house and the deposit boxes at the bank.

"You feel your father intended you to find the pieces of his past in the vault."

"Why else would he write the safety-deposit-box number on one of the blackmail notes?"

"But why didn't he talk to you personally?"

"I think he wanted to, but our relationship . . . Since my parents' divorce, Charles and I haven't been on speaking terms." He paused, taking a deep breath. "I'm sure it has something to do with the attack on him and my niece. Father can't tell me the connection. I need your help if I'm to discover the truth."

"I cannot think of any possible connection." There was a long silence before Hainey went on. "He thought of telling you about his past many times." Hainey sighed. "But there always seemed to be reasons why he shouldn't." He stiffened in his chair as if mustering the determination to give Alex what he wanted. "All right then. Your father was the best operative we ever had. He was of Russian descent, and even though he was taught Russian from the time he was small, he could speak perfect English. His mastery of both languages, along with his hatred of Stalin and the Communist movement, made him the perfect selection to work in the Soviet Union."

"My father was Russian?"

Hainey smiled. "The fact that this is such a surprise to you tells me Michael was perfectly successful at his new identity, but then, he had a number of years to practice before he met your mother. Yes, he was born shortly after his parents fled their country. Like so many others, they were forced to leave their homeland when the Bolsheviks came to power under Lenin. Your grandfather lived under Tsar Nicholas II as a wealthy businessman. When he heard that Nicholas had abdicated, he made arrangements to get him and his family out of the country, along with a sizeable portion of their wealth. They settled in Toronto, Canada, where your grandfather was a prominent member of the banking community."

"Apparently Michael went into the family business," Alex said. "My father came by his banking skills naturally."

Hainey nodded. "He was gifted in financial matters. The Midas touch. When your grandfather died suddenly a few years before the war, your father took the reigns of his considerable empire. Michael was in his early twenties then, but he moved in as if he'd done it all his life.

"The year your grandfather died, Michael and your grandmother started moving the bank's main office to New York. They completed that task in 1939 and became U.S. citizens the following year. Michael then settled into the business of running the bank and working with the underground until 1942, when he joined the army."

"The underground?"

Hainey smiled. "Your grandparents were Jewish, as were some of their ancestors supposedly back to Moses. The anti-Jewish movement was another reason they left Russia.

"Michael was not an Orthodox Jew, but he was a Jew, and he worked very hard with the Jewish community in New York to bring Jews out of Russia from 1940 to 1942. Although most of what the Jewish League did was provide financial support for immigrants getting a start in the United States, Michael took a more personal interest. He made two trips into Russia in 1940 and 1941, secretly, to set up a better system for smuggling Jews out of the country."

Alex sat back. That explained his patriarchal blessing. He had never understood why his lineage had been that of Judah instead of Ephraim, like most members of the Church. It also explained the prayer shawl and yarmulke in the safety deposit box and his father's love and deep understanding of everything Jewish.

"As you see, he became involved in clandestine operations at an early age," Hainey went on.

"When did he go to work for military intelligence?"

"In 1942. He joined the army with that in mind. The director of OSS, William Donovan, heard of Michael's work in the Russian Jewish community and saw immediately how useful the

young man could be. Donovan went to him personally and convinced Michael to join our modest effort."

"Who took charge of his financial interests while Michael
was gone to war?"

"Your grandmother." He smiled. "She was very talented, very
aggressive. She moved the bank into wartime industry, bought
several armament plants, and put them into full production. After
the war, she and your father quickly adapted those factories to
postwar manufacturing, making refrigerators and other appliances. In the spring of 1948, they sold the companies for a handsome profit."

"That accounts for the considerable inheritance from his
mother he told us about—the money he started Barrett Bank
with."

"Yes, part of it, but Michael was an extremely wealthy man,
Alex, with much more to his financial empire than just the funds
from the sale of a few appliance factories. In fact, that wealth
caused us some concern. When he had to disappear, all of it had
to as well. Ingeniously, he set up a system for hiding it while still
giving him use of it without anyone being able to trace it to him.
He used accounts held by banks in Geneva and Israel. He told me
once that the accounts will go to you and Claire only after his
death. Then you will discover just how wealthy Michael was."

Alex remembered the papers in his father's safe, account
ledgers from foreign banks, millions of dollars in special
accounts, money that had nothing to do with Barrett Bank.
Hainey was right; it was considerable.

"When did grandmother die?" Alex asked, regretting that he
had never known her.

"In 1948. Pneumonia. Michael was on assignment in Russia
at the time, incognito, and I and your grandmother's rabbi took
care of the burial. There were no brothers and sisters, no aunts
and uncles. Even though all of us sorely missed her, it made
things easier when he was forced to disappear."

"He always talked of them with respect, had pictures of them
in the house, but he never gave us much detail, only that they
were great people and we could be proud of them," Alex said.

"There were times he thought of sharing this with Fontana, and with you and Claire, but for many years there was the need to keep Michael Poltoron hidden because his enemies might still seek him out. In fact, I'm not sure your father ever felt safe, even after the enemy he feared most was dead and buried." He sipped from his glass. "Then there came a time when he wondered if he shouldn't just let it go. He had a new life, a good life. Why confuse it, confuse all of you, with something that didn't matter anymore?"

"It mattered. He should have told us."

"I am sorry, Alex, but your father felt there was good reason."

"Where did he serve during the war?" Alex asked. There was a slight pause as Hainey thought back.

"In 1943 he was assigned to the American military mission in Moscow. It was shortly after that when General Donovan, head of the fledgling Office of Strategic Services, or OSS, tried to establish intelligence relations with the People's Commissariat of Internal Affairs, or NKVD."

"The Soviet department that controlled state security, ran the corrective labor camps, that sort of thing?" Alex asked.

"Yes, but more important at the time was their complete control of information and intelligence operations for the Soviet system. For OSS to serve the American military machine as it moved against Hitler, it needed to cooperate with all Allied secret service agencies, including that of the USSR. At that point, because of past ideological differences and fear of the Soviets' well-known goal of reducing capitalist countries to rubble, nothing had been done with the NKVD."

"What did Donovan propose to do in this relationship?"

"Joint operations behind enemy lines to gather information, other large-scale intelligence operations in which the Nazi power in a given area could be undermined and the local underground forces armed and trained to fight guerrilla warfare. And the trading of intelligence that would help unite us in the effort to destroy Hitler's Reich." Hainey rubbed his thin, bristly jaw. "There was a lot of support for the effort, but J. Edgar Hoover and several others threw their weight against it, using the argument that it was dangerous for the United States because of the Russians' stated intentions to overthrow our government."

"Wasn't it dangerous?"

"Some, but we weren't inviting them inside our borders, and the rewards were well worth the risk in the European military theater. We knew they might use the opportunity to solidify Communist political groups in occupied countries so that when the war was over, they would have greater strength for their ideologies there. But we could do the same for pro-Western politicals. All we had to lose they could lose as well. But both sides agreed we would, for now, stop spying on one another long enough to concentrate on our common enemy. As far as information was concerned, we traded only what would stand against our enemies and help the allied war effort. Hoover's gang read too much clandestine nonsense into it and used standard fear tactics to defeat it. But then, Hoover saw a Communist behind every tree, under every rock. He was a paranoid, small-minded man with too much power."

"They defeated your efforts."

"Yes, in a roundabout way. President Roosevelt said no, but because he knew the conservatives would use any cooperation with the Soviets against him in the next elections, not because of any inherent evil he could find in cooperating, even with Hoover's incessant stream of misinformation." He laughed lightly. "Sad, isn't it—votes instead of national security determining wartime policy. But when has it been different? The war could have been shortened and many lives saved except for this politically expedient decision."

Alex sensed the stiffness in Hainey's voice, the edge of bitterness. "And Michael Poltoron's role?"

"Roosevelt didn't outlaw everything, and General Donovan received permission to exchange information as long as it was cleared by the Joint Chiefs of Staff. The military mission in Moscow was used, and your father acted as chief liaison with the Soviets at NKVD headquarters. His group and their Russian counterparts developed a very good working relationship and did a lot to get valuable information traded between camps. They exchanged material on sabotage methods used by the Germans, arms and factory locations we needed to bomb at the times of troop movements and invasion, Far East matters that helped us fight the war with Japan, Balkan issues such as what was being done to undermine the German authority and military presence in Rumania and Bulgaria, plus hundreds of other bits of information that helped us fight the war on the economic front and shorten it. It was invaluable."

"Michael met Arkadi Lutria and Pavel Grachev during this time."

Hainey nodded. "Grachev was an NKVD operative. Arkadi Lutria was assigned through the military. Your father and Arkadi developed a relationship much like that of brothers, and even Grachev was civil in those early days. I worked with Michael then—with all of them. They were successful times." He sighed. "But your father wasn't happy as a paper pusher; none of us were. So when the opportunity to move into a more active role presented itself, we took it."

"What opportunity?"

"As early as May of 1944, the American Army Air Corps asked OSS to put together operations for saving the large number of its downed bomber crews being held by the Germans in Rumania and Bulgaria. A plan had been created but was put on hold because of other needs, but by the end of August of the same year it became imperative."

"Why?"

"We learned the Bulgarians and Rumanians were planning a revolt against the Germans, were going to leave Hitler's Axis forces. That would leave the prisoners of war totally at the mercy of the Germans, who would slaughter the airmen rather than leave them behind to return to active duty and drop bombs on Germany. When we received word from the Russians that the revolt was inevitable, we rushed in a rescue team to save those pilots. It was successful."

"And Michael was a part of it."

"Not directly. There was a small group of Russian airmen in the same predicament in a camp further north, near the German border. He, three other Americans with Russian backgrounds, and four Russian natives from the NKVD were sent in to get them." He smiled. "It was the only joint field operation between OSS and the NKVD during the war."

"How many were rescued?"

"Twenty-four. Your father and three other men stayed behind to organize resistance forces and perform intelligence functions. I was one of those men."

"Lutria and Grachev were the other two."

He nodded. "Neither side would agree to any operation until it was evenly split. All of us knew each other from our work in Moscow, so we were chosen. Things went very well, but Grachev was a disappointment. As the war neared its close, he became more caustic in an effort to please his superiors and put himself in a position for better things after Germany's final capitulation. His obsession began taking precedence over mutual agreements and even friendship. Michael got fed up with it, and when I left to take some important intelligence information back to our people, Michael, responsible for the operation, sent Grachev with me. Michael and Arkadi were left behind and carried on with operations with the underground in southern Germany. It took them another two weeks before they returned to Breslau, Poland, and by then Grachev and I had been reassigned. We all four renewed our acquaintance in Berlin after Germany surrendered."

Alex sat back. "But none of this explains why Michael had to disappear ten years later."

"Patience, Alex. I'm getting to that." He coughed, sipped from the glass on the table, then wiped his mouth with a handkerchief. "At the end of the war we found ourselves in Berlin with events hurtling past us. It was suddenly nation against nation, grabbing for every inch of German soil. Battle lines were drawn, and the ideological madness of Communism versus the free world, especially American-style democracy, caught up with our little group. Each of us had choices to make as we were confronted by the political camps our countries created. Grachev went willingly and became a part of the rather zealous NKVD anti-American intelligence organization that began thriving in

Berlin. Although Lutria was also put to work in his old department in the Russian military, he maintained ties with your father,
and when he married Nadia two months later, Michael acted as
best man. As you can imagine, it was a very private wedding,
away from the prying eyes of the NKVD and our own OSS. Both
looked down on any association between American and Russian
troops by then. At the wedding, Grachev had visibly changed. He
was upset with Arkadi for defying their authority and continuing
a relationship with the two of us. He used every moment, except
for the ceremony itself, to belittle Allied presence and what he
called capitalist imperialism in Europe. He paced, nervous, afraid
they would be caught and his life would be ruined. He finally left
after he and Arkadi had an argument. Actually, Michael threw
him out of the place." He smiled. "I doubt that Grachev ever forgave him for that."

"He went to the authorities."

"No, Michael had something on Grachev, even then—enough
that Michael could tell us not to worry about him. He did caution
Arkadi, though. He knew he had made an enemy, one who would
use the first opportunity to make everyone's life miserable and get
vengeance. Pavel was like that. He was not the kind of man you
wanted for an enemy. He could not forgive."

"A dyed-in-the-wool convert to radical Marxism?"

"Grachev wasn't necessarily a Marxist or a Communist, but
he was always the opportunist. He saw where the future lay in his
country and became a dedicated Communist because it looked
like the only way to succeed. Then he turned to recruiting others,
even us. When he could see we weren't about to join, that even
Arkadi despised him for his false front, it angered him. He threw
himself even more fanatically into his work for the NKVD and
warned Arkadi and Michael to stay clear of each other."

"And Michael and Arkadi? You?"

"Michael and I went to work for the OSS in Berlin. General
Donovan, and many of us, wanted to create a lasting intelligence
organization after the war. We had seen that the communists were
returning to their old determination to fill the world with their ide-
ology, and we saw what they were doing in shadow warfare to

bring their dream to reality. We knew we must have something as good or better to combat the clandestine operations. We worked hard, trying to show President Roosevelt and congressional leaders that in the coming era it was the Russians who would need watching and that there would always be a need for our services. We did some important things, such as keeping track of troop movements by the Russians and clearly showing that Stalin intended to make the entire German nation a Soviet satellite. Of course, our government took steps that prevented that from happening.

"But our efforts weren't enough. The war was over. The country wanted her boys home. We went from three and a half million soldiers in Europe to half a million in a matter of months. Budgets were cut as the country geared up for the postwar era that would turn into a boom. In September of 1945, Harry S. Truman, who had replaced Roosevelt at his death earlier that year, signed the order abolishing the OSS."

Hainey coughed again and took another swallow of water. His appearance made Alex wonder how much longer he could keep talking, yet he seemed to have no intention of stopping.

"After the OSS was officially disbanded, a small number of us continued under what was called the Interim Research Intelligence Service, or IRIS. It was intended that IRIS handle the paperwork to move the assets of the OSS back into several other departments, but we dragged our feet and worked for the resurrection of the organization."

"You must have been successful. The CIA comes out of IRIS, doesn't it?"

"In part, but General Donovan had been working all along to make the OSS a viable, postwar institution, and the crusade was continued by many parties after its initial dissolution. Our role was simply to keep some vestige of the OSS in operation so that when the work of many others bore fruit, we'd have a running start.

"More important to matters that concern you, Alex, your father saw another way of showing how important continued intelligence operations could be. He sat up a working intelligence network behind the Iron Curtain."

"And Arkadi was his first recruit."

"Your father visited him and Nadia in East Berlin, secretly, and laid everything on the table. He knew they were unhappy with the government, especially with Stalin and his extremely poor handling of the war. Millions died because of the dictator's stupidity, and Arkadi and Nadia knew it. They and others were convinced that Stalin's continued leadership would only lead to cataclysmic results for the postwar Soviet peoples. Michael asked for their help in doing something about it."

"And they agreed."

"Immediately. Once they were committed, they recruited others, and the usual methods for getting information in and out of the country were set up. But you must realize that in those days we were novices, and our organization was very loose, although quite large. We learned hard lessons.

"Arkadi began recruiting among his and Michael's old friends when he traveled to Moscow and other major cities on military business. The old Moscow group was spread around the country by then, but most had important positions and were open to the idea of trying to stop Stalin's return to paranoia. The organization grew, and information started flowing West almost immediately. Too fast. We hadn't made up lists for them, asked them for specific things, so, in their exuberance, they began sending everything they could get their hands on. It was foolish endangerment, and we were very quick to put a stop to it and get them organized and trained at being careful as well as productive. Michael made a number of dangerous liaisons with our new operatives by traveling through Geneva, then Istanbul, then into the Crimea and on into the Soviet Union. His tireless dedication kept the whole thing from collapsing at that early point."

That explained the passport under the name of Koniev.

Hainey continued. "Michael trained them as best as he could and arranged for codes, drops, transmissions by those given radios, everything to give them at least a small degree of protection. They were even given a false set of papers in case they had to get out of the country quickly. Unfortunately, travel documents and passports changed so frequently in those early days that this was of little use. So Michael smuggled in a printing press, and they made their own."

"How long did his organization last?" Alex asked.

Hainey smiled. "Vestiges of it lasted until the fall of the Union in 1992. Even though Grachev found a number of our people, most were left inside, undiscovered, and they enlisted the help of others. Some had to be brought out when Grachev caught on to what was happening, and Michael did that with exceptional efficiency, but Grachev's inroads into the organization your father established were mi.ior, even though the Soviet propaganda machine tried to say otherwise. We owe those agents a great debt of gratitude. They reported to us, for instance, that the Soviets were intent on amassing offensive nuclear weapons with the intent of controlling Europe and forcing us out of European affairs. Information like that could never be gleaned from one source but was so important it set American policy for years to come. The information coming through the remnants of your father's beginnings gave us the ability to take appropriate countermeasures.

"But in your father's mind, his greatest victory was in the number of Jews they continued to bring out of Russia through his underground network, at least in the early years right after the war. He saved many lives, Alex. Thousands."

"When did the underground stop functioning?"

"It still functions to some degree, but with the establishment of the state of Israel in 1948, it became a governmental thing, and Michael began moving it into their new intelligence organization."

It struck Alex that his father's real business in Israel wasn't banking.

"There must have been casualties. An operation of this kind and apparent size—"

"If you mean in the intelligence ring, yes. The first was one of Arkadi's recruits who was caught using a radio to send information to us from Moscow. We had a receiving station set up in

Finland and had been getting things from him for some time—very good information because he was an aid of S. M. Shtemenko, chief of operations of the Soviet General Staff. Our man was tortured and gave up another name before dying from the beating."

"Just one?"

"We were careful to insulate cell members, but it is very much like dominoes. Once one name is given, more are going to fall."

"He revealed Arkadi?"

"No, another man. These things always work from the bottom up. But the second was also a part of our former cooperative group in Moscow—the ones who worked together for the trade of information during the war. Pavel Grachev, who was in the East Berlin office of the NKVD at the time, received the usual report on the events that led to the capture of both these men. We believe he saw pieces of the puzzle even at that early date and began watching others, especially Arkadi."

"He found others before Arkadi, though."

"Several, but the most unsettling was when he caught Stenka Pushkarev in 1950. Pushkarev was passing information through a drop to one of our people in East Berlin. Grachev was moved to Moscow to head the investigation of Pushkarev. We believe it was at Grachev's own request."

"And he led them to Arkadi."

"Arkadi was close to Stenka in the command chain. When he fell, we knew we had to get Arkadi and Nadia out because Grachev was close, and they knew more than just a few names."

Alex remembered the name *Pushkarev* from the letters in the deposit box.

"Michael knew the other cells were safe unless Arkadi was captured and forced to talk. He made arrangements to go in through East Europe and warn Arkadi and Nadia personally and bring them out. Grachev moved more quickly than we thought and had them imprisoned before Michael could get to them." There was a pained look of remembrance on Hainey's face. "Before Grachev could begin serious interrogations, Arkadi hung himself. He had much to live for but knew he endangered many others."

"But Grachev made the connection to Michael Poltoron."

"And enjoyed letting Michael know that Arkadi was dead— that he knew of others and would see them all imprisoned and shot."

"What happened to Nadia and the children?"

"They were held in protective custody—under guard at Nadia's apartment."

"She never revealed further members of Michael's organization?" Alex said. "Surely, torture—"

"Grachev would never allow the torture of Nadia. He was in love with her, had been from the first time they met." Hainey smiled. "Both Arkadi and Pavel loved Nadia, and both had courted her, but she chose Arkadi. Michael was happy for them, even helped Arkadi pay a dowry that was expected for Nadia. She was from a very old family, a family with royal lines attached to it—Prussian, I think. They held a very strong tradition about dowries, and Arkadi could not pay what he knew he should. Michael gave him that and much more. I don't think Pavel ever forgave either of them. It was a strange thing, all of that, almost as if they were playing a serious game of nineteenth-century matchmaking. I was not privy to most of it, but it was quite important to Arkadi and Michael. Even more so to Pavel."

"Then part of Grachev's hunting of Arkadi was to get her back."

"I believe so, and so did Michael."

"What did Michael do?"

"When Michael received Grachev's note about Arkadi's death, he sent an immediate reply offering Grachev a deal based on Nadia's absolute safety. Then he left for Russia personally."

"Under the name of Michael Koniev."

"Yes, that was his Russian identity. He was taking a horrible chance but seemed confident Grachev would accept a deal. At that point, Grachev still had the power necessary to free Nadia and the children if he wanted to. The two men met secretly. Michael told me later that Grachev had taken the deal but kept putting things off, claiming it was dangerous for him, for all of them at that point, because Beria had become personally interested in the case. I was worried, afraid they were setting Michael up, but he said there was no need for concern. He had everything under control, said that Grachev wouldn't harm him, that the offer had him hooked."

"What did he mean, hooked? Why was Michael so confident?"

"He never said. The only thing I could figure out is that Michael offered him a sizable portion of his personal fortune. Grachev did have a weakness for money. Sweetened with an offer of asylum in this country where he could spend it, I suppose it was enough, although I remained skeptical. Grachev had greater lusts, power and Michael's death most prominent among them."

"It seems plenty sweet to me."

Hainey didn't answer.

Alex sat back. "It all came unraveled didn't it. What happened?"

"Comrade Beria's popularity was waning in the party. Some think Stalin was on the verge of removing him. He needed a propaganda event that would shake up the West and bolster his own value in the party, and especially with the butcher, Stalin. Among others, some innocent, Beria decided to use Arkadi and Nadia to show his strength and make the average Soviet along with the general party membership believe that without him they were all in danger from a United States attempt to overthrow their government."

Alex remembered the newspaper clipping. "The propaganda statement in your letter to Michael. It was in the safety deposit box—Beria's congratulations to Grachev through the newspaper *Pravda*."

"Beria made Grachev look the hero, but he also removed Nadia and the boys from Grachev's influence and sent them to Siberia," Hainey said.

"Then Grachev was trying to make a deal he couldn't deliver on."

"No, they were still under Grachev's care and, therefore, still accessible to us, but the unimaginable happened. They died en route."

"How? With so much at stake surely Grachev would have taken extra precautions!"

"According to Grachev, Nadia poisoned the children, then took her own life, afraid of what would happen to all of them in the mines of Karaganda. I have heard stories of those places, and believe me, they were horrible for women and children. It would have been worse for her because she was considered a traitor. The depression, the loneliness of losing Arkadi, the dread of the treatment to her and the boys . . . " He shrugged. "Apparently it was more than she was willing to put them all through."

"Knowing what the conditions were, knowing her state of mind, surely Grachev would have given her some knowledge of what was going on!" Alex said.

"You are forgetting something, Alex. He was selling the woman he purported to love, for money. How could he explain that to her?" He sighed. "We may never know exactly what happened. Grachev alone knew."

Alex took a deep breath. "Michael was sure they were dead?"

"Yes. Michael said Grachev showed him pictures of the three of them."

"It was over. It must have been hard for Michael . . . "

"The news was devastating, but it was far from over. You forget Grachev's greed. With Nadia dead, his prospects for riches had taken a sudden turn for the worse. Whatever it was Michael had offered him was no longer available."

"He tried taking Michael captive," Alex said.

"He was nearly successful. Fortunately, Michael had taken precautions and was able to escape by a route set up earlier, but Grachev swore vengeance. Michael was never safe after that."

"So you started making plans for a change in identity."

"Michael was never the same after coming back from the Soviet Union. Arkadi's death changed him, but it was when Nadia and the children died that Michael had no more enthusiasm for intelligence work. Yes, we started thinking about alternatives, but a new identity wasn't one of them, not then. We didn't realize how sincere Grachev was in his determination to have vengeance on your father, and to what extent he would go to bring it about. Only after a nearly fatal attempt did we decide it was time for Michael Poltoron to disappear."

"Near fatal?"

Hainey nodded. "Actually, Grachev gave us the perfect chance to give Michael a new identity." He emptied his glass of water, then refilled it from a pitcher on the table by his chair. "Grachev sent two men to kidnap Michael and take him back to Russia. Michael escaped the initial contact at his New York apartment and ran for his life. There was a car chase. Both vehicles crashed, but your father's exploded. The circumstances didn't allow the kidnappers the chance to verify Michael's death. If they had, they would have discovered he had been thrown clear and escaped. As it was, we declared him dead."

"And he becomes Charles Barrett."

Hainey put his head against the back of the chair. "Yes."

Alex sat back, feeling how awful all of it had been for Michael Poltoron, how much the losses meant to him. Alex was beginning to understand why he had left it all behind, a part of his life he had simply wanted to forget.

"In my father's papers was an article stating that Grachev had disappeared in the Khrushchev purges. Did you get a positive verification? Could he still be alive?"

Hainey smiled. "And the one after your father? Beria and Khrushchev vied for power after Stalin's death. Grachev took Beria's side. It was the wrong one, and anyone found on that side was sent to Siberia or shot outright. Sources close to what was happening then verified Grachev's death."

"But Michael never believed it, did he."

"Not at first. That is why he continued taking precautions, but as time passed without any word of Grachev, both of us began to relax, then to believe that the enemy was dead and buried."

The room went quiet. After long minutes, Alex picked up his briefcase and opened it.

"Who else would have known about Arkadi and Grachev?

Who else would have used their names in an attempt to blackmail my father?" Alex asked.

"I'm not sure, but I think all those directly involved are dead by now. Your father and I were the last." He paused. "What else was in the safety deposit box belonging to your father?"

"These." Alex removed the copies of the material in the box, extending them toward Hainey, who made no move to take them.

"You will have to tell me about them. My illness comes from a serious case of sugar diabetes. I am blind."

Now Alex understood the darkened room. He went through the information and read the letters to Hainey, who smiled with recognition at his own. Alex finished by reading the blackmail notes they had only briefly discussed earlier.

"They indicate the kidnapper wanted something Charles has, and they expected his cooperation in getting it," Alex said. "As you can tell, the first two notes are pressure, the third a threat— something to do with a shipment of some kind. Do you know of anything of value Father was responsible for? Anything he took from Russia or Berlin at the end of the war?"

There was an extended silence, Hainey scratching his bristled chin, thinking through the past.

"Arkadi and Grachev are the only ones mentioned in the notes. Whatever happened had to involve them along with your father," Hainey said. "No, I can think of nothing."

"There was a map in the safety deposit box," Alex said.

"A map? Of what?"

"Hitler's new Germany. It had military markings on it and a red line drawn that worked a route to Switzerland."

Hainey sat back, a look of relief on his face. "I know a lot of soldiers who took such a trip through the Alps and into Switzerland after the end of the war. It was the only place where you could see Europe as it was before the war. And the food, compared to military fare, was wonderful. Your father went there several times."

"The line starts in Breslau, Poland, Mr. Hainey. Breslau was never occupied by the Allies, and the Russians weren't allowed to go to Switzerland for R and R. You stated that Breslau was the city from which the mission to save the Russian pilots was launched, and to which all of you eventually returned. Could there have been something there? Something Father and Arkadi removed and sent west? Wouldn't that explain the markings on the map?"

Hainey scratched his chin again. "As I told you, I had been reassigned by the time Michael and Arkadi returned from Germany to Breslau. So had Pavel Grachev. We were not there at the time." He paused. "There was something a bit strange, though . . . "

Alex leaned forward.

"When your father and Arkadi returned, they immediately asked for leave. They were gone for two weeks, yet when I questioned them about what they had done, both would change the subject. I didn't press them." He leaned forward, his eyes staring blankly into the fire but his mind alert, anxious, as if suddenly remembering something important. "When we went in to rescue the imprisoned pilots, our orders were explicit—get in and get out. But Michael put off leaving, getting extensions from command in Breslau by offering all kinds of excuses. It was almost . . . almost as if Michael were waiting for something to happen." He rubbed his thin and slightly shaking hand across his mouth as he coughed lightly. "There were reconnaissance missions—he and Arkadi, Pavel and I paired off—always the same. It was after one of these missions, one that took Michael and Arkadi northwest to a place called Gorlitz, that Michael gave Pavel and me orders to return to Breslau. He said he had important information that must be taken back to command personally."

"And did he?"

Hainey shrugged. "It could have been handled by radio, but ours had come up broken, and it was sufficiently important, yes. They found a German weapons stash in Gorlitz, defended only by a small garrison. He wanted permission to capture it." He paused. "By the time Grachev and I arrived in Breslau, they had the radio working again or we would have had to return with an answer. As it was, command radioed for them to use the local underground and go ahead."

He paused, wrinkling his brow. "There is one other thing. Gorlitz was only a short distance from where we were, yet it took them three days to reconnoiter." He shook his head adamantly. "No. There was nothing in Gorlitz but a weapons stash."

"You're sure? Did they return with the weapons? Bring them back to Breslau? Is there any record of what they did bring back?" Alex asked.

Hainey thought a moment. "I don't know. Maybe. There would have been a debriefing on their return with both American and Soviet leaders in attendance. A record would have been kept."

"Would the record still exist?"

Hainey nodded. "But it would tell us only what Michael wanted told. If he removed something without approval . . . "

"It is that something that I'm interested in, Mr. Hainey. If Father kept it out of the military record, is there any other way we could find out what it was he and Arkadi might have removed from that area of Germany?"

Hainey thought a moment. "The Historical Archives. War records. Possibly, yes. But your father wasn't a thief, Alex. What you're suggesting . . . "

"No one knows that better than I do, Mr. Hainey. I'm only suggesting they removed something of value. They must have had good reason. When we find out what it was, we will know the reason as well.

"I see what you mean. I still have important contacts in the intelligence community. I can have them do some research, but it will take time—at least a full day, maybe two." He paused. "But that will not tell us who is after your father."

"When we discover the *why*, Mr. Hainey, the *who* should become much more clear."

With a shaky hand Hainey tried to pour himself another drink but spilled most of it. Alex stood and poured him half a glass, then sat down again. "If you are too tired . . . I think we should call it quits. We can continue tomorrow . . . "

"What are you feeling Alex? About your discovery, about your father?" Hainey asked.

Alex was a bit surprised at the question and thought a

moment before answering. "Sad. Disappointed. Empty. Bitter."
He stood and walked through the near darkness to the window,
staring out into the dim light of the street lamp cascading off the
trees, casting dark shadows against the wall in front of the house
and on its small lawn and gardens.

He had a feeling of loss. There was so much he didn't know
and wanted to know—so much he hadn't experienced and wanted
to experience. How would his life have been different if he had
known who his father was? If he had been the son of a Russian
Jew instead of an American Mormon? What had he missed?
What would he have felt when the two of them stood atop the
walls of Jerusalem if he had known he were Jewish?

"I deserved to know," he said. "He shouldn't have kept it from
me. From any of us."

"He anguished over it, Alex. He decided it was best."

Alex turned, a little miffed at the answer. "Best? For whom?
When is it best to deceive your family? How could it be right to
hold back something as important as who you are?" He shook his
head sadly while collapsing into the chair again. "No. He was
wrong. What he did was wrong. How can I ever have what he
took from me by denying me the chance to know who he really
was, and . . . and in so doing depriving me of becoming who I
should have been?"

"Then you are not pleased with what you have become?
What he has given you?"

Alex was jolted but unwilling to let his frustration with his
father be redirected.

"That is not the point. He . . . "

"It is exactly the point. You feel deprived when you should
feel gratitude. You let your anger at a perceived loss rule your
judgment about what has been gained. Michael had the most to
lose, Alex. Not you. Not your mother or sister. And he decided
the trade-off was worth it. You have to trust that decision, even if
you don't know all the reasons it was made and feel a bit deprived
because you weren't asked for your opinion. What if he had
decided the other way, made it easy for his enemies to find him—
and his family? What if he had lost one of you because of it, or

what if you had lost him? Would you be challenging his decision then, Alex?"

There was a long silence between them.

"You must trust his instincts," Hainey said. "And you must believe in him."

There was another long silence, and Alex knew the conversation was over. Both of them were exhausted. Both needed time to think, to recover. Alex returned to his chair and picked up his case, placing the papers inside. He glanced at Hainey, who had his eyes closed but was not asleep. As Alex turned the knob, the old man spoke.

"When your father found his new faith, he found a new life. It wasn't hard to leave the old one behind after that. Maybe this, more than everything else, affected his decision to be Charles Barrett for the rest of his life." He sighed. "I hope you find Michael Poltoron. It is clear he intends you to do so. In finding him, you will find part of yourself. It is an important discovery, but not one in which Michael would want to challenge the identity of the son he decided to raise. Good night, Alex Barrett. And God speed."

Alex closed the door behind him.

Later he would wish he had thanked Arthur Hainey. They would never meet again.

11

ALEX LAY AWAKE IN HAINEY'S GUEST ROOM. Jet lag, combined with the revelations of the day, just wouldn't let him get some sleep. His body ached for it, yet his eyes were wide open. A few years ago he would have taken some sort of sleeping tablet, but lately they seemed to upset his system, make him nervous, anxious. His doctor said he had developed some sort of chemical allergy.

He illuminated the dial on his watch. Nearly three. He turned on his side, thinking about what Hainey had told him. Alex had a gut feeling he was on the right track. It was obvious to him that Michael had deceived Hainey about what had happened after the freeing of the Russian pilots, but for what reason? What had they found at Gorlitz? His mind searched for possible options. There weren't many, and what there were all dealt in monetary value. But Hainey was right—Charles Barrett was not a thief. In fact, his honesty was legendary. It wasn't about money.

He turned to his other side.

A lot of artwork had disappeared during the war. Masterpieces, one-of-a-kind items that had never been recovered.

Alex smiled. If Michael Poltoron was Charles Barrett, the idea that he would steal a masterpiece was ludicrous. Charles wouldn't even cross the street to *view* a masterpiece. In his mind, they were overpriced, and he saw no value in a picture hanging on the wall unless it was of something he had seen and wanted to be reminded of again and again. Alex felt the same way.

Alex pounded his pillow, then flopped on top of it, chest to the sheets.

Jewish. A Russian Jew!

So many unanswered questions, hidden mysteries. It was as if his father wasn't really his father at all but someone distant—someone he didn't really know. And now, with his father . . .

Would he ever know?

He closed his eyes, willing himself to fall into slumber. Not a chance. Tossing the covers aside, he went to the bathroom and removed a couple of Tylenol from the plastic container in the medicine cabinet. His system tolerated them, and they might help. He filled a glass with water and gulped them down, then turned off the light and started back to bed.

The shock of the blow shook him clear to his toes and knocked him to his knees. He tried to control his arms, put them out in front of him, but they didn't work. He did a face plant into the carpet and felt rough hands yanking him about, tying his wrists and ankles. The slight pinch in his upper arm was followed by a warm sensation that drifted up through his neck to his head. He fought the drug, tried to stay conscious by forcing his eyes to focus on the dark figure moving through the haze above him. His mind started to blacken, wanted to sleep.

Not now! he screamed inside. I can't sleep now! I have to . . .

Have to what?

He couldn't remember. A cloudy, dark haze filled his mind. He felt himself being lifted, his body limp. The darkness was too much, coming at him with such force that he simply couldn't fight it. His mind went black—blacker than anything he had ever known.

Then there was nothing.

Thompson let himself out through the front door, used the key pirated from the unconscious chauffeur to open the trunk of the limousine, then tossed Alex inside.

It had been almost too simple. Going over the wall, he had disarmed the house's alarm system, then used a crowbar to snap open a window and lower himself into the basement. The chauffeur that looked like a transplant from the San Francisco Forty-Niners defensive backfield had been his biggest worry, so he had taken care of him first, then found the old man asleep in the wing-back chair in front of the fireplace. The .22 bullet had entered Hainey's forehead, putting an end to a suffering man's life.

Thompson had left plenty of evidence that Alex Barrett committed the crime—fingerprints on a glass next to the body, for example. The chauffeur along with some of Barrett's clothing and a little of Hainey's blood on the sheets would do the rest. Alex Barrett was about to become one of the federal government's most wanted.

Thompson climbed into the limo, pushed on the opener button for the gate leading to the street, and exited the property. Turning right, he worked his way back to the freeway, then headed for the airport, where a charter plane was waiting. Barrett would soon be on his way. From then on, it would be someone else's responsibility. He had only to return to Salt Lake and finish business there and he'd be home free, a million dollars richer.

The work still left in Salt Lake would be simple but necessary. Even though the chances that Charles Barrett would ever regain consciousness were slim to none, Thompson took no chances. The old man had no further usefulness; he was a loose end. Thompson knew loose ends were what caught up to men like him, so he would be careful to make sure there weren't any.

Using one hand, he pulled the tape from his small recorder and slipped it into Barrett's carry-on. His employer would want it as evidence that Alex Barrett had the information they were after. Recorded by use of a laser device invented for the American CIA that measures and translates reverberations of sound on glass, the conversation between Alex and Arthur Hainey was of high quality. He had recorded it by using a device created for the Russian KGB only five years ago. Getting his hands on it had been expensive, but money purchased almost anything in Russia these days. The device measured sound waves and turned them into recordable voices in some manner that completely baffled Thompson. But how it worked didn't matter to him—only success mattered, and it had proven successful often enough to pay for itself more than half a dozen times.

His employer's request that Alex Barrett be shipped directly to them for interrogation had complicated things for Thompson.

Barrett's disappearance had to be explained, or a manhunt might follow—a manhunt for Thompson. He decided Hainey's death and the framing of Barrett for his murder would keep investigators busy hunting the young Salt Lake attorney long enough for Thompson to cover his own tracks and disappear. It was unfortunate the old man had to die, but survival was the name of the game, and Thompson intended to survive.

Thompson was feeling better about things—much better. Although the first of his assignment had nearly been a disaster, things had come together again, and his employers should be happy. He was happy. He would get paid.

He relaxed a little in the limo's plush seat. In years past, Thompson had worked for the old Soviet system as a freelance operative who took care of sensitive threats to the KGB's rather intensive operations in the United States, England, and parts of Western Europe. Soviet agents often got into hot water, and outside help was needed to extricate them, or to resolve the issue some other way. Sometimes that meant simply whisking them away by use of a predetermined exit plan. Sometimes it meant eliminating someone who was a threat to them or their cover. And sometimes it meant elimination of the agent, simply because he had turned double or endangered other operatives in a larger plan. In those years William Thompson did his job well, lived well, and was content with his role in the world domination by Communism, which he felt was a better system than capitalism because it gave the strong an advantage. But after the collapse of the cold war, business went into a slump, and the strong were forced to fend for themselves. He had a family. He needed money. He had taken up freelancing.

He turned onto the freeway going west.

"Killer for hire" wasn't something you advertised in the local newspaper, but William had contacts and used them to keep himself busy. Most of them were in the former Soviet countries, and he did a little work for the Mafia there and in Ukraine and Latvia. Some corporate work was available, and, of course, drug bosses were always looking for someone outside the clan to whack a brother. He liked those best. He felt he was ridding society of something that might hurt his kids.

He turned through the gate leading into the private airport, took a left, and drove to the hangar at the end of the row. After he had pulled the car inside, the attendant closed the door. Thompson shut off the car, got out, and removed Alex from the trunk, slinging him over one shoulder. He picked up the briefcase and overnight bag with the other hand, went the short distance to the private jet, and climbed the steps. Once inside, he deposited the luggage in one seat, then put Alex in another, strapping him in tightly. Using some rope, he tied Alex securely even though he was still unconscious and probably would be for the entire trip. No sense taking any chances.

The pilot approached, and Thompson returned to the limo, removed an athletic travel bag, counted out the twenty thousand from the pile of hundred-dollar bills inside, then handed it to the pilot. Plenty to guarantee delivery and a closed mouth.

Ten minutes later, he watched the plane taxi from the hangar and onto the tarmac, then move into position at the end of the runway. After it took off, he drove Hainey's limousine to the parking lot of the small airport and placed it where it would be found when the search for Hainey's killer got started in the morning. Thompson knew they'd check the flights out of the airport. It didn't matter. By the time they discovered which flight Barrett actually was on, the pilot would have delivered his goods. He'd return two days later with a story that he'd been forced by Barrett to fly him out of the country. Even if things went poorly and the cops refused to believe the pilot's story, it would delay things long enough that Thompson would be out of the picture. If things went well, the police would believe that Alex Barrett was on the run, hiding with friends or business contacts in the countries of the former Soviet Union. They would try finding him but with no luck. He would be a fugitive, one of the United States' ten most wanted. He would never be found, of course, because Thompson knew that his employers didn't intend to let Alex Barrett live once they had what they wanted. Not that he knew what they were up to—he just knew the kind of men they were.

Alex Barrett might be breathing, his heart still pumping blood to his vital organs, but in reality the young attorney was a dead man.

Thompson walked to the phone booth near the main office and called for a cab that could take him to the Dulles Airport. He had a flight back to Salt Lake City he needed to catch.

12

CLAIRE HEARD THE KNOCKING and was suddenly awake. She struggled to throw off the covers and get into her slippers and robe before stumbling from Alex's spare bedroom and down the hall to the front door. She stepped into the small alcove housing the TV monitor and could see Detective Logan standing under the camera's eye on the outside steps. She opened the door.

"Good morning," he said, looking past her. "Where's your brother?" He stepped forward as if to enter, and she backed into the wall, closing the door behind them.

"What's wrong?" she asked, forcing the haze from her mind and regretting the medication given her for sleep.

Logan handed her a paper, the *Washington Post.* Her eyes open a little wider when she saw the headlines: "Arthur Hainey Murdered by Utah Attorney."

"Who is Arthur Hainey?" she asked.

"Read the article," Logan replied.

"Wanted in the murder for questioning is Alexander Barrett, an attorney for Ivanov and Associates of Salt Lake City. Barrett's clothes were found on the premises and, according to informed sources, his fingerprints were found on the murder weapon."

Claire felt weakness in her knees and went to the couch to sit down.

"The feds called me this morning," Logan said. "I picked up a copy of the paper and came directly here. Have you heard from him?"

She shook her head. "He called and told me he was going to Washington but didn't say what for. What's going on? Why would they suspect Alex?"

"Like the article says, his fingerprints are all over the place, and they found his clothing in Hainey's guest room. The shirt had blood on it. When they find him, they intend to charge him with murder."

Claire kept searching the story in the paper. No witnesses. Limo missing. Found at the airport. Barrett's fingerprints inside. Suspected of taking a flight out of the country. A charter. The pilot was still missing, and police feared for his life. The investigation was being handled by federal investigators who were seeking the cooperation of international police forces in Europe, where the plane was said to have been headed.

"Alex couldn't kill anyone." She glanced at the clock on the wall. Nearly seven. She had overslept—always easy when Melissa stayed with friends. A last-minute decision, but now she was grateful. Her daughter had an uncanny talent for understanding too much and then asking questions. This wasn't something Claire could even begin to explain.

"Have you heard from him?" Logan asked.

"Do I look like it?" she said, her voice rising an octave.

Logan smiled. "No, I guess not. Where's Melissa?"

"At Della's house. She wanted to spend the night. I wanted to spend the evening at the hospital, then get a good night's sleep." She took a deep breath, tossing the paper onto the table. Logan picked it up, rolling it in his thick hands.

"In answer to your question," Logan said, "Arthur Hainey is a former director of the CIA and one of the top three people responsible for its creation after World War II." He lifted the paper. "It's all in here. Article in the back. A very big man in Washington. The president has promised a complete investigation. Your brother is in it up to here." He waved his hand above his hairline. "Why did he go to Hainey's?"

"I didn't know he did. He said he had to go to Washington but wouldn't tell me why."

"The local media picked up on it early. They called and wanted to know if there was any connection to the kidnapping."

"And?" Claire asked.

"I told them I had no comment. But you and I both know there is. We have to find Alex. If we can't do that, we have to find out why he went to Washington." He sat down across from Claire.

"What can we do?" Claire asked.

"We start by making a commitment to be up front with each other. If he contacts you, you contact me. I'll keep you informed on the investigation. We work together. Deal?"

"Deal. Why are you doing this? He looks guilty."

"As someone said, looks can be deceiving. Someone is up to no good, but it isn't your brother. Get dressed. We have to get you out of here before the press swarms all over this place."

Standing, she left the room, then came back. "What did you find out about the notes from Dad's safe?"

"There was some Russian writing on one of them. Numbers—six-four-six. Did your father know Russian?"

Claire shook her head. "Not that I know of."

"We'd better get moving. We need to go back to the house. I think those numbers had something to do with why Alex went to Washington, but I've got to take another look in your father's safe to be sure."

She had already disappeared.

Logan began a cursory search of Alex's house. His gut feeling was that Alex Barrett wasn't guilty, but it was his nature to be snoopy. Alex might have left something important lying around— something that he had discovered and that had driven him to Washington, then landed him aboard a charter headed for some yet-unknown destination in Europe.

Logan had nagging fears about that plane and about the murder—fears born of his belief that Alex hadn't killed Hainey. That meant he was being framed. And if that were true, Alex was aboard that plane as a prisoner, not as a murderer fleeing prosecution. And his life was in danger.

It made Logan's stomach churn.

There was a chance Alex had discovered the body, knew he was being framed, and was trying to stay free long enough to prove his innocence. But Logan didn't think so. From what had happened to Charles Barrett, it was obvious someone wanted information. They weren't going to get it from Charles any longer, and they probably knew that. Did the kidnappers think Alex could give it to them? Had they kidnapped him, killing

Arthur Hainey to cover their tracks? For Logan it fit. And it was working. The FBI was hunting Alex, and the murderer was getting enough time to get away.

He walked into the study and searched the desk, the files, the trash, and the bookshelves. Nothing. He went down the hall and into the garage. It was massive and would take a long time to search alone—a waste of time. Besides, the feds would be all over it by noon, and he could glean any pertinent discoveries from Carnahan of the FBI later.

He took a deep breath. It was going to be a very long day.

He went back into the apartment. The bedroom door was open, and Claire stood in front of the mirror finishing her hair. Logan noticed pretty ladies. He didn't stare, he didn't gawk, and he didn't covet, but he noticed. Claire Barrett wasn't particularly beautiful, but he had taken note of her just the same. There was something special about her that had caught his eye. He hadn't known what it was the first time he saw her, but he knew now. Claire Barrett had a quiet strength and determination most women never attain. It showed in the way she stood, the way she walked, and even the way she combed her hair. Since his wife's death a few years earlier, Logan hadn't seen what he was seeing in Claire in many other women.

"Find anything?" She was staring at him in the mirror, her brush stopping in mid-stroke. She had a slight smile on her lips and in her eyes.

He shook his head, unsure of why he couldn't respond verbally before clearing his throat. "No, I thought he might have left something behind. A note . . . something. No luck."

She turned to face him with her arms, brush in one hand, folded across her midsection. "You *don't* think he's guilty, do you?"

He shook his head. "Your brother isn't the type to kill an old man by putting a bullet through his head." The sudden change in her face made Logan regret his words. "Sorry."

She turned back to the mirror and started brushing again. "It's all right, Detective Logan." She lay the brush down and faced him again. "You must see some horrible things."

"Yeah." He looked at the floor, remembering the condition in which he had found Claire's late husband. He changed the subject. "Someone is setting Alex up, Miss Barrett, and they're good at it." Logan told her what had been going through his mind while doing his search.

"Then you think the kidnappers—"

"They want something bad enough to kill for it, Miss Barrett. They didn't get it from your father and have accepted the fact that they probably never will. They must believe that Alex can give it to them."

"And if they're wrong?"

Logan hesitated only a moment. "He's a liability. They'll kill him."

"You're very direct, detective."

"You don't strike me as a woman who would want to dance around the truth."

She smiled. "You're also a good judge of character." She picked up her purse. "I'm ready." They headed down the hall. Once outside, they climbed into Logan's car, riding in silence most of the way to Park City, both involved in their own thoughts. As they drove through the canyon, it seemed to Logan that she started turning a little pale. He thought about saying something, then decided to keep quiet, but by the time they reached the Park City turnoff he could see she was very uncomfortable.

"Are you okay?" Logan asked.

"My stomach. I'm a little carsick." She was beginning to turn a little green, and Logan slowed the car.

"I can pull over."

She shook her head vigorously. "No, I'm okay." She paused, setting her jaw. "I can handle it." She kept her eyes on the horizon, her hand gripping the arm rest as a sign of her determination to keep her food down.

"Do you know who the kidnapper is yet? The one in the picture?" Claire asked, trying to divert her mind from her stomach.

"The resort gave us a name, some background, but we think it's all false. At least it doesn't lead anywhere. The name we have is William Thompson—not even a traffic ticket."

"The resort didn't actually hire him, did they?"

"Not to put in snowmakers. He was hired as a groundskeeper and lasted only one day. It gave him a chance to steal those uniforms." He paused. "The glasses turned out to be German, but, so far we haven't been able to trace them to any particular person. The eyeglass company is big in Germany, and the prescription is not an unusual one. They didn't sell any to a William Thompson, but all that tells me is what I already knew. Thompson has another identity. I think the guy is a professional, and that makes him a lot harder to catch."

"And a lot more dangerous," Claire added. "Have you found anything from canvassing hotels with the picture?"

Logan shook his head. "Hotels, short-term rentals, recently purchased homes. With the help of a few of Salt Lake City's finest, we're trying to get to all of them. It's going to take some time. Nothing yet." They came to an intersection. Logan took the lower road.

"The other one goes to Dad's house."

"I know. We're going to your friend's place. The press, remember."

A few minutes later he pulled into Della's driveway.

Claire opened the door and ran up Della's front walk in a crouch. She didn't make the front door, depositing what little was in her stomach in the bushes to the left of a flower box with a few pansies that looked even worse off than she did. When she was finished, Logan got out of the car. As he had expected, she waved him away, gave up one more deposit, then moved toward the house. Logan stepped to her side.

"That was impressive," Claire said.

Logan smiled. "But necessary."

She wiped her mouth with the back of her hand and chuckled. "Yes, I guess it was."

She looked weak, and Logan took her arm, giving support.

"Thanks."

"You're welcome."

He opened the door, and both of them went inside.

13

ALEX EASED BACK TO CONSCIOUSNESS, greeted by a terrible headache. His hands and feet were tied, and he was prostrate, the rough feel of a blanket against his arms. He was still in his pajamas, and a gag ran through his mouth so tightly that it cut into the outer edges of his frown.

It was dark. No mask, no blindfold. Just pitch black darkness.

He was moving, rolling really, from left to right, right to left. Left to right. A boat. He could hear waves lapping against the sides and smell seawater mixed with fuel. Diesel. Maybe that was what was giving him the headache. He must be near the engine room.

He tried freeing his hands. The cords cut into his wrists, and he felt them bleed. He kept at it until the pain was unbearable and forced him to accept his efforts as futile. He felt with his feet, moving about a bit to seek the edges of his confinement. He was lying on a cot of some kind with a board along the outside to prevent the occupant from falling out. The sides of the boat were rounded and made of wood, and the ceiling was not reachable even when he raised his legs as high as he could. The compartment, or hold, or whatever it was, was small in width—he could touch the opposite wall with his shoeless feet—but he found no door. That meant a hatch, probably overhead.

He lay still a moment, catching his breath, putting the pieces together. He couldn't hear any wind, yet the boat was tossing quite a bit. He must be on the ocean. That didn't make sense unless they had moved him to the coast and out of D.C. He shoved the *where* aside and concentrated on the *why*. Obviously he had been followed from Salt Lake to Washington. The kidnapper. The professional. The one who had killed Steve Navarro as if he were no more than a bug to be stomped on. Now it seemed to be Alex's turn—kidnapped, held hostage. Was he using Alex as leverage, blackmailing the bank? Was it about money after all?

Alex didn't think so.

The notes. His father's past. Something in his father's past.

The kidnapper knew by now that Charles wasn't going to give him what he wanted. Obviously he thought Alex could. He must have been watching the house, followed Alex to the bank, then to Hainey's. He must have heard the conversation, thought something Hainey said was important.

Alex racked his brain but found nothing.

He shook it off. If they thought he had something . . .

Interrogation was bound to follow.

Who was it, anyway? How many? It was frustrating not knowing the face of the enemy.

And frightening.

He had to get free.

He focused his hearing. Nothing but the gentle lap of the water and an occasional knock of something against wood above and forward—at least he thought of it as forward—on the main deck. No voices. The boat must be docked.

He felt weak, probably from the drug they had used, and from the lack of food. He had kept fasting, even aboard the direct flight to Washington. After Hainey's talk, he hadn't had an appetite, his mind too filled with what he had learned to be concerned about food.

He began his fight against the numbing pain in his arms and legs, pain from being tied so long. He worked his way into a sitting position, then pushed against the board that acted as a rail. It gave way and toppled to the floor. He listened for the sound of someone coming. Nothing. He dangled his legs over the edge of the bed and felt for the floor. It wasn't there, at least not where he could reach it. Must be a top bunk.

He tried thinking about other things than the pain, but it was hard. Long minutes that seemed like hours passed. Then he heard the soft sound of rubber sneakers against wood—overhead—then the rattle of chains and the removal of a lock. Light came through the crack in the hatch and cascaded into the room. Alex did a quick once-over of the place, of his own condition, as well as he could in the dim light. The hatch was opened a little more, and the silhouette of a man appeared against the brighter background. He dropped something into the hold and shut it again. Alex quickly realized it was a gas capsule of some kind and that it was knocking him out—again. He fought the cords, hoping the pain would help him stay conscious, but managed only to dig a deep cut into his already bleeding wrists. The last sound he heard was his own voice uttering a prayer.

Alex woke up sitting in a chair in the middle of a small room. At one side stood a table with a quart of bottled water and a cup on it. In his groggy mind, he saw the door of the room at his right—an old beat-up thing with panels in it that reminded him of the ones in the first house his father had purchased for their family. This one was in worse condition.

As he shook the cobwebs aside, the door opened, and a man walked in. He was wearing a gray tweed jacket with a black turtleneck and black slacks. His shoes were expensive. To Alex, he looked like someone straight out of a men's clothing magazine. Alex shook his head to make sure he wasn't dreaming. The man didn't go away. Instead, he walked to the table and placed a small box there, then picked up a bucket of water and proceeded to pour it over Alex. The cold liquid had its intended effect. Spitting and shivering, Alex was much more alert.

"Hello, Mr. Barrett. Nice to meet you." The man said it with a cordial smile. Alex was still shaking water from his hair and didn't look at him.

"I am here to ask you a few questions, Mr. Barrett. You will give simple, direct answers, always remembering to be honest with me. If I sense you are lying, I will punish you. If you tell me the truth, I will feed you, clothe you, and set you free at the earliest possible moment. Do you understand the rules?"

Alex was feeling like a half-drowned rat and didn't respond.

Instead he focused on the beat-up door. The man walked to a position in front of him, grabbed Alex by the hair, and jerked his head around and up so that their eyes met. He twisted the hair until Alex grimaced. "I asked you a question. I'll ask it again. Do you understand?"

The voice was hard and cold as a silver spoon in an icebox, and Alex began to understand the depth of the trouble he was in. It was all he could do to keep his fear from showing.

He nodded. "I hear you. Who are you and what do you want?"

The interrogator smiled. "A natural question, but I must insist that we do this my way."

Alex shrugged, trying to control the fear his captor was causing him. He took a deep breath and asked another question just to keep his mind off his churning stomach. "Where am I?"

"At the moment where we are is not important."

"You're Russian. The accent—"

"I speak Russian, but I am Ukrainian." The interrogator said it as though the difference was important. Alex knew that to most nationalist Ukrainians, it was.

Alex was fully awake now, felt the danger, but tried to look passive. His eyes went to the ropes that were binding him so tight he could hardly breathe. They were wrapped around his arms above the cut in his wrist made by his earlier attempt at freeing himself. The blood had dried, but the stiffness and sting were still with him. He was bound to the chair with another rope that wound its way tightly around his chest. A third rope secured his bare feet to the legs of his chair.

He looked up when the door opened and another man entered the room. Dressed in a dark brown T-shirt and jeans, the man's stocky frame looked solid enough to stop a truck, with all the damage coming to the truck. He was flexing his fingers and cracking his knuckles. The noise made Alex grit his teeth. The knuckle-cracking giant leaned against the wall in front of Alex, his cold eyes searching those of his prey. It was getting hot in the room now, stuffy. Sweat started gathering on Alex's face.

Alex was beginning to understand how deeply into this mess

he had fallen. Even when his father was hurt and Steve's body discovered, the enemy hadn't seemed a threat. But that was before they had become faces—flesh and blood with empty eyes and cold hearts.

The interrogator stood in front but a little left of Alex, the bouncer still visible and intimidating. Alex noticed the difference in size immediately, and the interrogator was no small man. One blow from the bouncer's huge hand and Alex would be sitting across the room against the far wall. Sweat rolled down both sides of his head.

"I don't have any idea what you want." Alex felt the nervous shake in his voice but knew there was nothing he could do about it. He was afraid, and he couldn't hide it, at least not all of it.

"We will get to that in a moment. First, let me introduce you to my associate." He turned to the man against the wall. "This is Yegor. Yegor is a very talented man." The interrogator was by the ape's side now and lifted one of the huge paws for Alex to see. "He was a national champion heavyweight boxer for the USSR in 1988. He gave two men concussions and nearly killed another." He flashed another sadistic smile at Alex that revealed how much he was enjoying this. "You can see why."

Alex sensed what was coming, and it made his skin crawl.

"Why the physical abuse?" Alex asked.

The interrogator smiled. "Would you answer my questions, honestly, with just a plea for your cooperation?"

Alex didn't answer.

The interrogator smiled. "I thought not. It is important that you understand the ground rules, Mr. Barrett. I find it saves time in the long run." He nodded at Yegor. The boxer stepped forward and took what seemed to Alex a gentle swing with the back of his hand. The blow snapped Alex's head backward and to the right. His body followed, upending the chair and slamming him to the floor. While he was picking away the cobwebs, Yegor lifted him and the chair and set them upright, ramming the legs against the floor hard enough to jar Alex's teeth. Alex could taste blood. It was certain now—this was not just a bad dream. He was alive, awake, and in very deep trouble.

He looked up at Yegor's cold, mechanical eyes, trying to find some kind of compassion there, some hope he was finished using his face as a punching bag. Hope didn't exist in those eyes, and Yegor wasn't finished.

The fist hit came against Alex's cheekbone and nose, once, twice, then a third time. Alex heard each blow as he felt it, a loud cracking noise inside his ears. He thought his nose was surely broken, then his cheekbone and jaw. The fourth blow came to his solar plexus, knocking all the air from his lungs. It sent the chair reeling backward, and the last thing he felt was his head denting the hard wooden floor.

Semiconscious, with pain coursing the length of his body, he felt Yegor pick up the chair with him still attached and plant both back in the center of the room for the second time. He tried opening his eyes, but when he did the room was spinning so violently he closed them again. The interrogator's voice seemed far away, and it was all he could do to pay attention.

He felt something against his lips. Liquid. He drank through his cut, the taste of blood mingling with the bottled water. The interrogator poured it over his face, cooling the bruised flesh around his eyes, nose, and mouth.

The interrogator's voice seemed clearer. "Do you see why you must not play games with me, Mr. Barrett?"

The interrogator removed a straight-backed chair from a dark corner of the room and placed it in front of Alex so that he could straddle the chair with his arms atop the back. "Now you see, Mr. Barrett. You cannot win except by telling me what I wish to know. Now, Yegor has given you a lesson in what will come if you do not cooperate. Let it be enough."

Alex looked away through the thinning slits of his swollen eyes, trying to keep himself calm. He was experiencing emotions he hadn't known existed. Fear, hate, anger—all of a kind he hadn't realized could be felt. But he knew he had to keep control, to fight the intimidation. His life, not just his face and ribs were at risk; his answers had to be careful ones.

"I don't know anything."

"You know that your father was once a man named Michael

Poltoron and that he was a member of the American OSS during World War II, correct?"

Alex nodded with a slowness born of pain and exhaustion. "But that means nothing."

"Do you know what he did during the war?"

"Only what Hainey told me." He coughed, bloody saliva scattering across his pajamas and the front of the interrogator's turtleneck. The man jumped back, cursing.

Alex found it a bit funny and smiled inadvertently.

The interrogator slapped him, adding bruise to bruise. Alex marveled that he really felt no additional pain. What he did feel was disgust and a bit of belligerence. He spat the foul blood in his mouth onto the floor to his left.

The interrogator grabbed him by the hair and lifted it until Alex could see him.

"Do not push me, Mr. Barrett. I have used my considerable talents on men much stronger and better trained than you. Few have succeeded in standing up to me." He let go of Alex. "Now, shall we begin?" He sat down in the chair again.

"One of our people followed you to your father's bank. What was in the safety deposit box?"

Alex felt tired, his resistance so low that he knew he wouldn't hold back anything if they gave him another beating. But he also knew that if he did give them everything they were after, they'd kill him. Carefully, almost calculatedly, he began speaking about the pictures, the passport, things he thought they must already know. He then talked about the letters, leaving out several items but emphasizing his discovery of his father's past identity and Arthur Hainey's name. He left out the key and the map. A gut feeling told him that to reveal them would only get him killed, even though he wasn't sure himself what they meant. "I went to see Hainey because I thought he might fill in some of the blanks."

"We had the conversation between you and Hainey monitored—a special microphone that uses laser beams and sound waves. Modern technology is a wonderful thing, don't you agree?" He smiled. "According to what was recorded, Hainey accurately described your father's past. Our viewpoint of his successes and failures is somewhat different, but that is a philosophical position, not a historical one. Nothing else in the safety deposit box?"

Alex knew he had to lie. "No, nothing." He tried to direct them away from the box. "I went to Hainey because I needed to know if I was right about Poltoron being my father, if I could link it to the attempt to blackmail him. Hainey verified the first but had no idea about the second." Alex hesitated but only for a moment. If they had heard the conversation, they would know anyway, and this might be a way to get some information of his own. "He . . . Hainey told me about a place called Gorlitz. He wasn't sure what it meant. He was going to make a call and let me know in the morning."

"Your conversation with Hainey is no longer of importance to us." The interrogator said it with renewed stiffness.

"It was everything to me. Without his help I was at a dead end. It's Hainey you should be questioning about my father. He knows more—"

"Hainey knew nothing!" It was a sharp, definitive response. Alex couldn't understand why.

"No, you're wrong. Hainey is the key. He knows . . . can find out . . . "

"No. It is your father who held the secret. Hainey was not there! Only your father and Lutria! And Lutria is dead." He put his face next to Alex's. "And now your father is as close to that same condition as a man can be, and all we have is you." He leaned back. "And you will tell us what we want to know."

Alex tried to keep his voice even. "After the mission to free the pilots—something happened then, didn't it." He paused. He was right, at least about that. "I'm sorry, but I can't help you. I don't know what happened during that time. Hainey was going to try to find out; ask him."

The interrogator's face turned hard. "Arthur Hainey knew nothing."

Alex caught the past tense use of the word. "Knew? What do you mean?" Hot anger rolled through Alex as he realized what it meant. "You killed him? Why! You fool! If you heard the con-versation—"

"I told you, Hainey knew nothing we didn't already know." He pulled a cigarette package from his pocket and started ner-vously fishing for one through the small opening in the top. "The entire American intelligence apparatus is looking for you by now." He struck a match.

It took Alex another minute to understand what the inter-rogator had said. "You blamed me for the murder."

"A last-minute decision, but one we can stand." The inter-rogator sat down. "With your father nothing more than a veg-etable, a most unfortunate event even our talented associate could not foresee, you are our only hope, Mr. Barrett. We had to have some time with you, and it was decided the best way to give us that time without fear of interruption from the authorities was to have them hunting for you as a fugitive." The interrogator was lying. He was still finding it hard to believe that Thompson had fouled up so badly. Hainey might have helped if Thompson had given him time.

"Framing me was a mistake. They'll never believe it."

"That is yet to be seen."

"It was stupid. I told you what was in the safety deposit box. There is nothing there that can tell either of us what you're after. Hainey was the only chance. Whoever made the decision to elim-inate him was a fool."

The insipid smile returned. "You are forgetting—we moni-tored your conversation."

Alex's heart skipped a beat, but he kept his cool. "Then you should know I am telling you the truth. I have no idea what you're after or where it is."

"You may not know the what, but we believe you know where, although you may not be completely aware of it. What of the map?"

Alex's breath caught, but he tried to keep it from showing. "If you heard the conversation, you know everything I do about the map. Hainey said it was not unusual for soldiers to go to Switzerland on leave. He said my father went there several times."

Alex was praying they had missed his own challenge to Hainey's remarks.

The interrogator stood and walked to the door, left for a minute, then returned with Alex's briefcase. He opened it and removed the papers. "There is no map here, Mr. Barrett. You copied the pictures of your father, the letters from Lutria and the other documents, but not the map. Why? Did you realize it was of greater significance and that you could not take the chance that it would be confiscated? And if you held back one thing, is it not fair to assume you may have held back others?"

"The map was large. I had no way of copying it without a lot of trouble. I didn't think it was worth the time."

"I think you are lying."

Alex didn't answer, tried to keep his eyes impassive. It was difficult because the boxer was beginning to crack his knuckles again. Alex decided he would never let anyone tell him, ever, that intimidation didn't work.

"In your conversation with Hainey, you said that the map was marked, that your father designated a route that went from Breslau to Vienna and then to Switzerland. The items we are looking for were stolen by way of Breslau, Mr. Barrett."

Alex felt everything slipping away, felt the panic, fought to keep control.

"What is it you're after? Gold? Artwork? The spoils of war? You know Michael's background. He had no need for money." Alex said it as a diversion, buying time to think. "If it is money you're after, why didn't you just ask for it? Charles has plenty. He could have paid your little blackmail."

The interrogator smiled. "I did not say it was money, only that it is of great value. It is of greater value to us than all of your father's money, and we intend to have it."

"What is it, and what makes you so sure it still exists?"

"You have asked enough questions, Mr. Barrett. These I will not answer, but rest assured, we know your father stole from us, and we intend to have what he has taken." He slammed the briefcase closed. "The map! What was the final destination of the markings?"

"There wasn't one. The markings went only as far as the Swiss border," Alex lied.

The interrogator didn't say anything, measuring Alex, weighing the answer. "I do not believe you."

Alex sensed a tinge of doubt in the statement and saw what he had to do if he wanted to survive. It was taking a chance, but he couldn't see anything else to do. "Check for yourself. The key to the safety deposit box is in the glove compartment of my car. It's parked at Salt Lake International Airport. Get the map for yourself, look at it." Alex didn't like giving them anything, but he knew he had no other choice. If he wanted to survive, he had to buy time.

The interrogator seemed to brighten, as if the thought of such an action had never occurred to him.

"It's parked in long-term parking just southeast of the Delta terminal. A black '68 Corvette. You can check out the rest of the safety deposit boxes while you're at it. There will be personal items in two of the three; an envelope containing the originals of the letters and photographs along with the map will be in 646. There is nothing else." His tone was calculated to dare.

The interrogator stood. Alex could see he was in a dilemma. He watched the man pace, glancing at Alex now and again as if attempting to see something that would help him make a decision. Alex kept his face as impassive as he could, even though his stomach was churning with hope swallowed with a healthy portion of anxiety. It would take time to get the keys and use them, time to discover that the key to box number 646 would give them nothing, that Alex had removed everything and put it all in another box—a box in which his mother's jewelry and papers had been stored under her maiden name while she was alive, and which he had inherited at her death.

The interrogator finally stopped in front of Alex and smiled. "You know, Mr. Barrett, there is a chance you are telling the truth. Then again, there is the chance you are lying. To discover which it is will take two, maybe three days." He smiled. "I think we will try something else first." He went to his little case and retrieved a small vial. Removing a hypodermic needle, he filled it with the liquid and came toward Alex. Alex's mouth went dry, and he felt the sweat break out on his forehead like a late summer rainstorm.

"This vial is what laymen might call truth serum. However, it is not completely foolproof, and professionals have been known to fight it and keep the most critical of information back. For that reason, I have added something to it. It is a simple drug. When it enters the bloodstream, it heightens anxiety and gives one suicidal tendencies he will have to deal with for a minimum of two, maybe three hours. Nothing permanent, but extremely unpleasant. And the great value is that it also enhances the strength of the drug. Only a very few men have been successful in resisting it." He gave Alex a knowing smile. "As weak as you are, Mr. Barrett, I think we will get results."

Alex tried to keep his eyes off the hypodermic needle. He had always hated needles, but this one seemed particularly ominous. He knew his fear was showing now, but he couldn't help it. He *was* afraid—afraid of this monster and his truth serum, afraid of the unknown, and afraid he wouldn't be able to keep Michael Poltoron's secret while knowing that he must try. He knew now that Michael had done what he did for good reason—not for money, not for self, but to keep whatever he had taken from Germany from men like these.

"I've told you everything." Alex was surprised at the calm in his own voice. "Using that stuff won't do any good."

The interrogator's face turned to granite as he saw Alex stiffen in defiance. He jammed the needle into Alex's arm and pushed on the plunger.

The sudden pain made Alex grimace, the hot liquid flowing through his veins and reaching his brain almost immediately. He started losing his bearings. The room began spinning, and he felt sick, weak, his thinking hard to control. He tried focusing on the faces of his father and Arthur Hainey, to steel himself against the questions he knew would come. But his mind weakened, and he felt mentally limp, unable to resist. The floating sensation came next, and he felt strangely at peace. He tried pulling up Claire's face from memory but couldn't find it. He panicked, felt like crying.

Then came the despondency, the fear.

It climbed inside his soul like a tiger in the black night, an evil presence that ripped at his mind and left him afraid, screaming for fear. He closed his eyes so tightly they hurt. Then he began jerking his body from left to right, forcing his mind to overcome the desire to give up, to let the interrogator loose in his head. He bit his lip, hard, hoping the pain would keep his mind alert, responsive to his pleas to resist.

"Now, Mr. Barrett, let's start again. And remember, if I don't get what I want, there is always Yegor. What is the value of the map?"

Alex pushed the question aside. Others came. He shoved them away. Sweating. Drops of it everywhere, stinging his cut, pouring into his clothing. He kept using pain as something on which to focus and resist. More questions. More resistance. He was floating again, his breath coming in great gasps.

Then the fear attacked him. He screamed against it, flexed every muscle in his body as if to fend off a very real and very physical enemy. The muscles in his legs went taut with such sudden power that he broke the leg of the chair. He toppled to the floor and lay there, his mind bracing itself against the enemy, his muscles ready to explode.

He heard a curse.

Someone screaming at him.

He didn't care. He was too tired to care.

Rough hands grabbed him, lifted him, then brutally pounded his flesh, like a butcher tenderizing a tough piece of meat.

Yegor was back.

And Alex was relieved.

After Logan helped Claire into Della's house, where she could lie down for a few minutes, Claire gave him the key to her father's house, explained where she had put the combination to the safe, and sent him on his way.

Logan left Della's and walked across the ski run to the Charles Barrett residence, grateful he couldn't be seen from the road in front, where the press was probably camped out by now. He entered through the back door of the basement level, then went upstairs to the main level and on to the second-floor suite and den.

He found the combination where Claire had put it, slid back the panel, and began turning the dial to the appropriate numbers in the appropriate sequence.

Something had sent Alex to Washington. Logan thought he knew what it was but needed to make sure. The number six-four-six was jotted on one of the blackmail notes. The numbers were written in Russian, so it wasn't until the lab had brought them to his attention that he realized what they might be: the three-digit number of a safety deposit box.

Logan's theory was that Alex had removed some things from the safe, that they had led him to something that in turn had led him to Arthur Hainey. He found himself wishing he had paid closer attention, confiscated the keys. If he had, Alex might still be in Salt Lake City, and Arthur Hainey would still be alive.

He pulled on the handle and opened the heavy steel door. Doing a quick but thorough search, he found the keys missing.

Logan started shoving papers back into the safe when one fell to the floor. He glanced at it. It was written on the letterhead of the bank of Geneva. His eye scanned it briefly. Just bank business. It wasn't unusual for international bankers like Charles Barrett to do business in Geneva, Switzerland.

Then his eye caught hold on the date. He read the letter more carefully. An account opened in 1944 had been closed in 1985, and the bank thanked him, Charles Barrett, for his business. At the bottom was a personal note from the bank's president to Charles, asking after his health and hoping they would see him soon.

Logan stared at the letter. It seemed ridiculous for a soldier to be opening a Swiss bank account while the war was still being fought. Soldiers didn't have enough money to buy cigarettes, let alone open Swiss bank accounts. At least he never did. There were those who managed to smuggle contraband or sell things on the black market, but somehow Logan had a hard time seeing Charles Barrett as one of those.

He stuck the letter into his blazer pocket and closed the safe, then pushed the button so the panel would slide back into place.

As he turned to walk from behind the desk, his toe caught on a cord and pulled the phone off the small table next to the desk. It hit against the wall hard enough to leave an indentation before it came to rest on the floor. As he picked it up, he noticed the small, round piece of metal on the carpet near the leg of the table. He picked it up between his thumb and forefinger. A listening device.

It must have been attached to the phone. He removed a three-by-three plastic bag from his back pocket, then placed the item inside.

"What is it?" The voice startled him, and he turned to see Claire Barrett standing in the doorway between the den and the bedroom.

"A listening device. In television vernacular, a bug. Someone has tapped your father's phone. And, from the looks of this one, the whole room."

"Then someone heard us in here yesterday," Claire said.

Logan nodded. "You're looking better, Miss Barrett." He smiled.

"My stomach would argue the point. So would my ego. I don't make a habit of upchucking in front of strangers." She smiled. Logan tried to keep his mind on his business this time.

"Your father's assailant followed Alex from the house. Then to the bank."

"Alex went to the bank? How do you know—"

"The deposit box keys are missing." He paused. "After that, he called you and said he was leaving town."

"Why would the kidnapper be watching this place? With Father in the hospital—"

"He couldn't tell the bad guys what they wanted to know. They looked for someone else. You and Alex were the most likely candidates." He lifted the plastic bag with the bug in it. "I'd bet we'll find one of these little gems on every phone you and Alex have used in the past two days. The man who killed your husband followed Alex when he left here yesterday, Miss Barrett—followed him all the way to Washington."

"But why kill Hainey?"

"I told you my theory. Once the kidnapper knew Alex had the information he wanted, or could get it, he banged him over the head and flew him out of the country where they could have a more intimate conversation about what Alex had found out. To keep the police hunting in the wrong places, he set up the murder."

"You mean Hainey died just so this . . . this killer could buy time?"

Logan nodded, his face filled with deep concern. "If what they wanted was in the safety deposit box and Alex removed it, they would have killed him once they had it."

"But instead they set him up. Which means he didn't take it with him, at least didn't have it on him?"

"Yeah, maybe it's still in the box. I can get a court order to open that box, but it will take some time. Have you got any connections that might speed things up a little?" He grinned.

Claire laughed, then picked up the phone and dialed the number she knew by heart. "I think I can arrange something."

"Barrett Bank. Central Branch. May I direct your call."

"Let me speak with Hal, Milly. This is Claire Barrett."

"Hi, Miss Barrett. Just a moment, please." She was connected, and Frost's phone rang.

"Hal Frost's office."

"Is he in? This is Claire."

"Just a moment please, Miss Barrett."

"Claire. How are you?" Hal Frost asked in a businesslike tone.

"Fine. I need a favor, Hal. How fast can you get us into Dad's safety deposit boxes, without keys?"

There was a pause.

"Hal, this is important."

"I'm right in the middle of the merger meeting with the people from that bank in Nevada, Claire. I—"

"How soon?"

"It will take a little time to get an approved locksmith in here. Can you give me two hours? That will give me time to set things up."

Claire had forgotten federal banking rules about opening boxes that no longer had keys, or people to open them. She looked at her watch, then covered the phone and spoke to Logan. "He says he needs two hours."

Logan shrugged. "It'll take at least twenty-four hours to get a court order, and we're an hour away from the bank anyway. Good enough."

She gave Hal the go-ahead and hung up the phone.

Logan had removed a folded piece of paper from his pocket and handed it to her. "What do you make of that?"

She looked at it, then at him with a quizzical stare. "Father is a banker, Logan. He—"

"Note the date the account was opened."

"1944."

"Correct me if I'm wrong, but there was still a war on, and your father didn't get into banking for at least another ten years— not in this state."

She looked at the letter more carefully. "It says the account was closed in 1985. They thanked him for his business."

"The blackmail notes mention a shipment. As near as I can tell, Pavel and Arkadi come from that period of your father's life. At least no one in recent years seems to know anything about them. They were Russians. The number of one of the safety deposit boxes was written in Russian." He lifted the bag with the listening device in it. "I'd be willing to bet a month's wages that this is Russian." He paused as he put the bag back into his pocket. "What if he shipped something valuable to Geneva, from Russia, for safekeeping, and somebody over there wants it back?"

"To my knowledge, my father was never in Russia."

"How much do you know about his war years?"

She had to think a minute. "Very little. I see what you mean." She picked up the phone and dialed the bank number listed at the upper right-hand corner of the letterhead. After identifying herself as Charles Barrett's daughter with important business and a request to talk to the bank's president, she was put through. She punched the speaker so Logan could hear the conversation.

"Miss Barrett. This is Jacques Montreux. I am president of the bank. How may I help you?" He spoke very good English.

Claire looked at the account number, also written in the letter. "In 1944 my father opened an account with your bank." She gave him the number. "He closed it in 1985. Can you tell me anything about it?"

There was a slight pause as Montreux seemed to be making a decision. Claire knew what it was. Swiss banks had very strict rules about accounts and didn't ordinarily give out information of any kind. But the strictest rules applied to open accounts, not closed ones.

"Normally our policy is not to reveal to a member of the family the contents of any account until after the account-holder's death."

Claire quickly explained the condition of her father. "If you wish to verify—"

"No, no, that is quite all right. Under these circumstances, and because you have the account number, I think we can help you, especially so on a closed account. Can you give me the number again, please?"

She did. There was a long pause. She could hear him rustling papers.

"Strange."

"What?"

"This account was originally opened for someone else. Your father's name doesn't appear on the account until 1975." More rustling of papers.

"Most strange." He seemed flustered.

"Who actually owned the account?"

"I . . . I don't know. The name has been blacked out! This is most unusual."

"Who made the change on the account?" Claire asked. "Shouldn't there be some sort of paperwork or something?"

There was an embarrassed pause.

"Mr. Montreux?"

"I am most apologetic, Ms. Barrett. My father . . . " He gulped. "My father, who was president of this bank from 1925 until his death five years ago, made the change." Another pause. "But the usual paperwork is missing. And the blacked-out name . . . My father must have had good reason. He . . . "

Claire sensed the banker's embarrassment. "No indication of who originally opened it, then?"

"None. I am sorry."

"What kind of account is it?"

"Safety deposit box only."

"You're sure?"

"Yes, of that I am sure."

"Thank you, Mr. Montreux. You have been most helpful."

Montreux said a relieved good-bye and hung up. Claire clicked off the phone.

"We have another mystery," Claire said.

"So it seems. Let's talk about your father's military career. Did your mother ever say anything about those years?"

"Very little. He was out of the service long before my parents met. He didn't talk about it much. Mom said he had a rough time, that it was a part of his life he wanted to forget."

Logan removed a small planner from his pocket, turned to the section containing phone numbers, then picked up the phone and dialed. Claire noticed the call was long distance.

"Leave a quarter on the desk." She smiled.

Logan returned it, deciding he liked her smile very much.

"Give me Denton Harker's office, please," he said when the receptionist answered.

Claire remembered hearing the name somewhere but couldn't place it.

"Hello, Denton. Brig Logan."

Small talk. Claire remembered. Denton Harker was director of the Federal Bureau of Investigation. Logan was on a first-name basis with a powerful man in Washington. No wonder he had been one of the first to hear about Arthur Hainey.

"Denton, what's happening on the Arthur Hainey murder? Anything new?"

A pause to listen. "Nothing." Another pause. "I think Alex Barrett is being set up." Another pause and a deep breath. "I can't explain it yet. Right now I need a favor. Dig up all the information you can on Charles Barrett. Send it to Jack Carnahan's office in Salt Lake City. I'm particularly interested in his military history prior to . . . " He paused, looking at Claire while covering the receiver. "What year did your father leave the military?"

"Middle fifties." She shrugged. "I can't remember off the top of my head."

Logan repeated it to Harker. "I owe you." He hung up.

"My father's military history?"

"Yeah, just another part of the mystery."

The interrogator wiped away the sweat coursing down his forehead. He got up from the chair and walked to the table, taking a hefty swig of water from the bottle there. He looked back at the unconscious American. He had been stronger than expected. There was a map, and there was something else in the deposit box, but Barrett wasn't going to give it to him easily.

"Take him back to the boat. Don't tie him up, but make sure the hold is secure. He'll need to move around a little, get his blood going in preparation for further interrogations. We must be careful." He left the room and went down the short hall to the living area. Picking up the phone, he listened for the dial tone. It was there for a change, and he started dialing the numbers he knew by heart.

The first attempt failed, and he cursed his country's long-distance service, then tried again. Still the line failed. He dialed an international operator and gave her the number. After about ten minutes of trying, the call rang through.

There was no sense taking chances. If there was something in the safety deposit box, if Barrett was telling the truth . . .

"'Lo." The voice was half asleep.

"Have you taken care of Charles Barrett yet?"

"No. It was a long trip. I've been sleeping. Barrett isn't going anywhere," William Thompson said.

"You know we want him dead."

"He's dead now. I just have to shut off his machines. It'll be done by evening."

"I have another opportunity for you—a fairly easy matter."

"The usual fee."

"You messed things up very badly, my friend. Killing Hainey was a mistake. The kidnapping was a mistake. The only thing you have done right is to get Alex Barrett here as instructed. If you want the retainer for those already negotiated, you will do this for me."

"I don't like being blackmailed, Andrei. I've earned my—"

"I will decide what you have earned, my friend. Your reputation is at stake here. Your success will determine my recommendations for work in the future."

"All right, but this it. And Andrei, my retainer had better be in my account by the time I'm finished."

Andrei smiled. "It will be there." He told Thompson about the keys to the safety deposit box. "Get them and obtain whatever is in the box. When you have them, call the appropriate numbers. We will give you instructions about delivery." He hung up.

Thompson lay back on the bed, thinking. It was obvious Andrei had never dealt with an American bank. They didn't let you into just anyone's box, even if you had a key, and if the woman at the bank knew he was opening one belonging to her boss . . .

But there had to be a way. Obviously he wasn't going to get his money until he found that way, so he'd find it.

He mulled it over in his mind as he went to the shower, deciding he'd have to take a look at things, then decide just how to handle it. As he toweled himself off, he looked at the clock on the nightstand. It was nearly one in the afternoon. He could go to the airport, break into the Corvette and get the keys, then be at the main branch by three. Then tonight he'd finish business at the hospital and be ready to leave for L.A. sometime tomorrow.

As soon as he finished shaving, he'd check times and flights, make the arrangements. He was looking forward to seeing his little family again.

He'd earn his fee. And then some—give his employers their money's worth. It was all part of public relations.

It made for good business.

But he was worried about having to rob a bank.

14

T HEY TURNED INTO THE BANK PARKING LOT at 2:50, and Logan pulled the car into a shady spot under a row of trees on the far side. He used the cellular phone to call his office and tell them what he'd be doing for the next little while. Then he got out of the car and helped Claire and Melissa do the same. He was pleased when Melissa took his hand.

Claire had called the woman responsible for safety deposit boxes from her cellular, making sure everything had been done by Hal Frost. Frost was still conducting some sort of merger meeting with a bank in Nevada, and Logan wondered if the guy would even make himself available for the actual opening of the box. In Logan's mind, Hal Frost had his priorities screwed up.

"Natalie says Alex came here yesterday. He made copies of some papers out of a deposit box and left with them in his brief-case. As near as I can tell, it was just before he booked a flight to Washington," Claire said.

"Then the originals are probably still here." There was a hopeful tone in Logan's voice.

Logan opened the second, inner door for them.

Melissa pulled on his pantleg. "Your horn is honking."

Logan gave her a quick smile. "I'll join you in a minute. I had the cellular hooked to the horn in case I'm out of normal range. Probably nothing." He jogged back the way they had come. Claire took Melissa's hand and continued into the bank. They walked to the elevators that led to Frost's office on the second floor and pushed a button.

As the door opened, Hal stood there with a broad smile on his face. "I saw you from my office window," he said.

"You look pleased with yourself, Hal."

"I am. The bank at Battle Mountain, Nevada, is now part of the Barrett organization. I think your father would be pleased."

"Yes, I'm sure he would. Congratulations," Claire said as sincerely as she could. Somehow such things just didn't matter right now.

He took her arm and Melissa's hand and moved toward the chairs near the stairway leading to the safety deposit boxes.

"Are you ready?" Hal asked.

"Is the locksmith here?"

"Downstairs."

Claire glanced at the door. "We have to wait for Logan. He'll just be a minute."

Hal nodded, pointing to a couch.

They sat, Melissa between them. "Have you heard from Alex?" Hal asked.

"No. The ones who attacked Father . . . Logan and I both believe they have Alex. They are framing him for Hainey's murder."

"Do you have proof?"

"That's one of the reasons we need to see inside that box, Hal. But you know as well as I do that Alex couldn't kill anyone—especially in cold-blooded murder."

There was a prolonged silence in which Hal seemed a bit nervous.

"Spit it out, Hal."

He looked away. "The doctors have called my attention to the clause in the will that all your father's organs are to be donated to the hospital organ bank," Hal said. "His . . . his kidneys are in very good condition. They have a patient who needs one of them very badly."

Claire bit her lip. "Alex has to decide . . . "

"No, he doesn't. Especially now. His disappearance . . . The will is clear—if Alex is not available, you can make the necessary choices."

Melissa stood and went to a nearby desk, fiddling with the stapler. The secretary wasn't annoyed but took Melissa on her lap and showed her how it worked. Claire lay her head against the seat as Logan came through the door and approached them.

He could see something was wrong and asked. Frost looked at Claire, then away again. Claire explained to Logan what they were discussing.

Logan sat down in the chair to her left. "Tough decision. No signs of life?" He asked Frost.

"None the machines aren't creating."

It struck Claire that they were talking about her father as if he were nothing but livestock brought to auction. Organs to be bought and sold. She closed her eyes against it, hoping it and everything that had happened over the past few days would just go away, that her father and Alex would somehow appear at the door to the bank, smiling at each other the way they used to. She wanted it so much she could taste it and opened her eyes and stared at the doorway as if to wish it would make it come true.

They weren't there. Another man was. Tall, with a strong face, a familiar face.

She glanced quickly at Melissa, who was also staring at the man, her thumb in her mouth, sucking for all she was worth. Her eyes were wide, and fear was etched in them. Claire sat bolt upright.

"Logan!" Claire stood and went to her daughter, picking her up, shielding her from the man still coming toward them.

Logan saw the fear in Claire's face, then Melissa's. His eyes went to the man they both seemed to be staring at, and his heart leaped into his throat.

"It's him, Mommy," Melissa said in a quiet, frightened tone. "He hurt Grandpa."

Logan was out of his chair and moving toward the man the photograph said was William Thompson. Thompson saw his movement and stopped in his tracks, suddenly aware, drawn out of deep thought. They were still separated by fifty feet of plush carpet and a dozen onlookers when Thompson reached behind his back and pulled the revolver.

Logan pulled his own and held his ground. "Police! Everybody down!"

The place exploded in chaos, people screaming, ducking, jumping through open doors and behind any tables and desks that were available. Logan lifted his gun. "Stop right there, Thompson!" He said.

The man only smiled, then fired. Logan reacted at the smile, moving fast enough to save his life even though the bullet creased his neck, causing it to burn and bleed. He picked himself up as a uniformed security guard rounded the corner where he had been stationed near the front entrance. Logan flashed his badge, pointing at the door through which Thompson had just gone, even while running toward it. The officer bolted through the double glass doors side by side with Logan but was stopped there when a bullet exploded through the glass of the outer doors and hit him in the chest. Logan hit the deck as two more bullets shattered the remaining glass, scattering small pieces over him like snow. He came to his knees and grabbed the guard's shirt, pulling him aside and out of the line of fire. He tried finding a pulse. The guard was only barely alive. He picked up the man's revolver and stuck it into his belt as he backed himself into the bank. He couldn't see Thompson but knew he was waiting in ambush. He would be signing his own death warrant to take him on through the shattered entry.

Logan decided on another exit, one around the side. As he returned through the main area, he yelled at Frost, now watching things from behind the couch, telling him to call for backup and to get an ambulance for the downed guard. Bursting through the side entrance, Logan ran cautiously down the outside wall of the building, feeling vulnerable. A row of cars was parked there, probably belonging to bank employees. He ducked behind them, keeping low, moving toward the rear of the bank and its parking lot.

Reaching the end of the row, he lifted his head just enough to see over the last car without being a target. The bullet slammed into the car's window, changed trajectory a few inches, and exited near Logan's side. He hit the pavement as two additional bullets did more damage to the car, each one closer to the rear of the vehicle. When Logan realized what Thompson was doing, he got to his feet and dove over the next car just as the gas tank of the first exploded and sent a fireball in all directions. He scrambled away, keeping only inches ahead of the hot flames and diving for cover behind another automobile as the sky rained down parts of the destroyed Lincoln. After a curse and a second's chance to catch his breath, Logan raised himself over the car, pistol ready. He saw the assailant running between vehicles. He aimed and fired but missed as Thompson threw himself to the ground between cars. Logan ran, keeping low, covering the ground between him and the first row of cars in the back parking lot in less than three seconds. Thompson raised above a car only twenty feet away, gun aimed at the bridge of Logan's nose for the second time.

Without hesitating, Logan dove for cover, ripping holes in his slacks and scuffing up his knees as they came in contact with the rough pavement. He gritted his teeth against the pain as several bullets scarred the surface of the hood and fenders of the car next to him. Logan heard the slap of leather against pavement and knew Thompson was on the move again. He quickly stood, saw the killer, and fired but missed again as Thompson zigzagged between cars. He had to get closer. He went to one knee, grabbing for half a dozen bullets he kept in his pants pocket, and reloaded. As he stood, ready to fire, he saw Thompson bolt for a car coming into the lot. Logan aimed, but Thompson shoved his gun through the window of the vehicle and placed it against the head of the driver, with an eye on Logan that told him he'd kill the innocent patron before Logan had a chance to pull off a round to stop him.

Logan lowered his gun, stood still. Thompson, a victorious smirk on his murderous face, said something to the driver, and the man slid into the passenger seat. Thompson pulled on the latch to the driver's side door. A bit surprised that it didn't open, he glanced away from Logan and at the door handle. It was enough. Logan raised his pistol and fired. Thompson's quick reflexes were all that saved him as he flung himself backward, the bullet hitting him in the arm that held his weapon and knocking it out of his hand to clatter on the pavement and slide under the car.

Logan moved forward now, knowing he had Thompson cornered, watching the driver of the car take advantage and launch himself out his own door and run for his life.

The second gun appeared in Thompson's hand if by magic. Logan reacted, firing, but wide. He launched himself to the ground for the third time as Thompson's shot warmed the air around him. When he came up, the killer was behind the wheel of the vehicle and shifting into gear.

Logan had never been in a battle like this one! Didn't this guy know when to quit, know how to die gracefully? He stood, aimed, and fired as the blue Pontiac bolted away from him in reverse. Logan's next two bullets shattered the front windshield. The car went left, then right, then straight again, moving away, heading for the entrance to the lot. Logan started to run after it when another car came out of the street, directly in the path of the fleeing killer. The Pontiac rammed it, disabling it. It blocked the exit. Thompson, frustrated, angry, rammed the gearshift into forward and jammed his foot on the gas feed. The tires squealed on the hot pavement, but the car bolted toward Logan, who steadied himself, preparing to fire. It was he or Thompson now, bullets against speeding steel, will against will.

Logan waited, sweat pouring down the side of his face, his jaw set with firm determination. Thompson aimed the car at him, his only weapon, knowing that Logan was all that stood between him and the exit at the far end of the lot. He hunkered down in the seat, making himself as small a target as possible, his face and arms granite, his heart set with the same determination he could see in the enemy in front of him.

Seventy-five feet. Sixty. Only seconds had passed. Fifty. Forty.

Logan emptied his service revolver, threw it aside, and pulled the guard's pistol. The car kept coming. He emptied the second weapon at the small target slumped behind the wheel, then dove between two parked cars as the Pontiac came to claim his life.

The Pontiac slammed a fender into one of the cars, just missing Logan's leg. The impact closed the gap between the two cars, and Logan found himself glad to be flat on the ground instead of smashed between fenders of hardened steel. He watched from beneath the vehicles as the Pontiac careened across the lot, then hit another car with such impact that it went airborne. He couldn't see it for a second. Then it hit the pavement on its top and slid toward the bank, spinning, turning, the sound of the metal against pavement nearly deafening. The rear of the Pontiac slammed into a large oak tree a few feet from the bank's rear door and came to a sudden stop.

Logan crawled from beneath one of the vehicles that had him trapped and stood up. The Pontiac was sitting very still—the driver wasn't moving. Logan leaned against one of the cars for strength.

It was over.

It was nearly five o'clock; the bank was closed. The Pontiac was loaded aboard a trailer now and was being removed. The other wrecked vehicles had already been removed, except for the burned-out Lincoln. Several workmen stood near its carcass, waiting for another truck with a lift to haul it away. A couple of Salt Lake City cops were doing a once-over on a red Ford Taurus near the end of the lot. It was the one Thompson used to get to the bank.

Logan had done all he could outside, so he headed for the doors to the bank. He showed the officer stationed there his badge and was let in. Carnahan from the FBI stood nearby and smiled at Logan when he saw him. Logan could see Claire and Melissa sitting with Frost on the same couch where the battle had started.

"You finished with them?" He asked Carnahan.

"Yeah." He glanced out through the shattered windows. "Messy, Logan. You're very messy," Carnahan said.

"Any word on the security guard?" Logan asked.

"Just heard. He died in the emergency room at University Hospital about fifteen minutes ago."

Logan took a deep breath. Sometimes he hated this business. "What about the killer?"

"He's in bad shape, but I've asked that his room be watched day and night."

"You put him in under a John Doe like I asked?"

"Yeah. Nobody has even heard this guy's name. We're taking every precaution, Logan. You're sure this is the guy who killed Arthur Hainey?"

Logan handed him a brown envelope, then a gun. "This is the same caliber of gun you said killed Hainey. Dig the bullet out of the security guard and match it up to the one you dug out of Hainey. I think they'll match."

Carnahan took the weapon. "What's in the envelope?"

"A driver's license and some credit cards—the usual stuff you find on a guy like this. The license has the same phony address we found for him earlier." Logan handed Carnahan the envelope. " Almost everything we found is in there. See what you can get, will you?"

"What do you mean, almost everything?"

"I kept a set of keys that belong to Charles Barrett. They fit deposit boxes downstairs. Don't worry, I had them dusted for prints by the on-sight team while they were here. Somehow Thompson got them from Alex Barrett and was headed here to get whatever is in one of the boxes downstairs. Our being here put a cramp in his plans."

"Do you think he took them off Barrett at Hainey's place?"

"Possibly, but I don't think so. Alex doesn't strike me as the stupid type. I think they forced him to give them the location."

"They? Got any idea who *they* are?" Carnahan asked.

"None, but they come out of Charles Barrett's past, and they have Alex Barrett. I'm sure of that now. They've had time to interrogate him. He sent them after the keys, and Thompson showed up to use them."

"Do you think Barrett is still alive?"

"Yeah, he's still alive. They think he can give them what they want, and they would want to make sure he wasn't sending them on a wild goose chase before they eliminate him."

"But you think they will eliminate him?"

Logan nodded while watching Claire and Melissa. He had

been concerned about them from the moment he had recognized Thompson, and it wasn't just cop concern, either.

Carnahan noticed the look. "Does she know how serious this is getting?"

"Yeah, she knows."

"How come SLPD let you have this stuff?" Carnahan was looking at the evidence in his hands. "You're out of your jurisdiction, you know."

"But not out of yours." Logan gave him a smile. "I told them you were taking control of the case. Orders of the president."

"You don't know how close to the truth that is, but I haven't received orders to take charge yet."

"You will. I assume you've been out to Alex Barrett's place by now, done a search?"

"I hate it when you're one step ahead of me, Logan. Yeah, we searched the place, but we came up empty. The guy's a neatness freak and has some woman living in his spare bedroom."

"You've got a dirty mind, Carnahan. His sister is staying with him." Logan looked at Claire again. "As long as Thompson was on the loose, Alex told her to stay away from the place up at Deer Valley." He paused. "I think she can go back now. One other thing, Carny. Can you put a couple of guys to work for me?"

"Doing what?"

"Thompson's been here for several weeks, near as I can tell. He'd have to stay somewhere. We're covering the hotels and short-term rental places, but so far we've come up empty. We need to find his place."

"And quick. From the sound of it, Alex Barrett's life may depend on it." Carnahan paused, thinking. "Long-term rental is more likely, but this is a lot of city. It will take some time."

"I'll send some photographs over." Logan smiled.

"You're a big help." He sighed. "All right. We'll start with a phone campaign and check out anyone that fits this guy's description or looks suspicious, but by the time we get finished, Thompson will either have died from the accident or he'll be well enough that you can ask him all the questions you want."

"Yeah, but will he answer them?"

"From what you've told me, and if this gun checks out as the weapon that killed Hainey, we'll have enough to put him away for a mighty long time. Maybe we can get him to deal."

"Let's hope he survives so we can find out. By the way, you'll be getting some stuff by fax from Denton Harker. Let me know when it comes."

Carnahan nodded. He knew Denton and Logan went back a ways—some federal narcotics case. "What's Harker sending you?"

"A background check on Charles Barrett."

"Makes sense."

One of Carnahan's agents came toward them, and Logan broke away, anxious to get to Claire and Melissa. Claire stood as he came near, looking at the bandage on his neck. She stepped close enough that she could touch it.

"How bad?" She asked.

"Nothing to worry about. Just stings like the dickens." Logan was grateful he could feel it. Another couple of inches and he would have been in the rack next to the security guard. He stooped down in front of Melissa, and she let him pick her up. "You were a brave girl, Melissa."

Melissa gave a smile with her thumb still in her mouth.

Hal stood. He had a worried look on his face.

"Sorry about the mess," Logan said.

Claire smiled. "The Lincoln was Hal's—well, it was the bank's, and Hal drove it." She laughed lightly. "Quit worrying, Hal. The board isn't going to fire you for something out of your control. You need a new car anyway; that one was fifteen years old."

"Has the locksmith showed up yet?" Logan asked.

"He's waiting for us downstairs with Natalie Stevens, the young woman responsible for our safety deposit program here and the one who saw Alex last." They started for the stairway, and Logan withdrew the set of Charles Barrett's deposit box keys from his pocket. "We found these on Thompson." He handed them to Frost, who checked them over and matched them to the list of Charles Barrett's personal boxes.

"Yes, these are the ones belonging to Charles," he said.

"But that means . . . Alex must have given them to Thompson."

"Or told someone where to find them. Thompson is a messenger boy. He was sent to pick something up."

"But if they have the keys, they don't need Alex. They must have killed him." Claire was pale with concern.

"I don't think so. They'd want to check out the boxes before doing anything to Alex," Logan said.

Claire still looked worried.

"He's alive, Claire. They won't do anything until they hear from Thompson."

"But Thompson—"

"Isn't telling anyone anything."

"That gives us time, doesn't it?" Claire asked hopefully.

"Yes, it does. They'll wait for Thompson to report back. When he doesn't they'll investigate, because they'll suspect he ran away with what they're after. It will give us time and a chance they'll come looking. We'll be waiting for them."

"And if they don't come?" Hal asked.

Logan gave him a frosted look. "If they want what's in the deposit box, and we have it, we have something to bargain with, don't we, Hal. Maybe even something that will lead us to them." Hal got the message, and Logan turned to Claire. "Alex is still alive and will be until they get what they want. Now, Let's go downstairs." They started down. "Frost, you can send the locksmith home."

Carnahan had caught up by the time they reached the safety deposit boxes.

After dismissing the irritated locksmith, who swore he'd bill Frost for overtime, the bank president stood ready to put the bank key into the key slot. Claire used the one belonging to Charles, and Logan gave them the go-ahead. Box 646 was opened.

Logan could tell it was empty by the disappointed look on Claire's face. Still holding Melissa, he stepped forward and checked for himself. He then had the others opened. All of them revealed only personal items belonging to Charles Barrett—nothing out of the ordinary or of enough value to cause the mess confronting them. So much for anything that might lead them to Alex. William Thompson's importance suddenly loomed impressive for Logan. He turned to Natalie Stevens. "You said he made copies of the items in 646."

She nodded.

"And he never took the envelope out of the building?"

She shook her head. "No, he didn't leave the building with it, I'm sure of it.

"Did you see him return down here?" Logan asked.

She nodded again.

"And he didn't come back upstairs with the envelope?"

"No. It has to be down here somewhere."

"What did he do when he came back upstairs?"

"He put the copies in his briefcase, said good-bye, and left the bank."

"How big was the envelope?"

"A nine by twelve. Bulky, filled with items. It was barely closeable it was so full."

"Does Alex have a box here?"

"No," she said. "Alex didn't do business . . . "

"Then he *must* have taken it with him," Frost remarked with some irritation.

"It was too large to hide under his jacket without my noticing. He didn't leave with it," Natalie said defensively. Logan could see she knew what she was talking about.

"Then it's in one of these boxes," Logan said.

"It can't be. It takes two keys to open them. I never . . . " She seemed to hesitate.

"What is it?" Logan asked.

She glanced at Frost. "I left Alex at my desk, alone, while I returned some phone books he had been using to the back room. When I returned, he was just coming upstairs. He made an effort to beat me to my desk. The keys . . . They were on the desk. He may have . . . but I don't think . . . He doesn't have a box. He has to have two keys!" Her face was red with anxiety, and she turned slightly to keep from looking at Frost.

"Natalie, you're doing fine," Claire said, glaring at Frost. "It is all right."

Frost changed the look of irritation on his face quickly.

"Do you have a complete list of box holders?" Logan asked, trying not to sound threatening.

"Yes, upstairs in the computer." Natalie glanced at Frost for only a second, then at Claire. She was beginning to see who was really in charge. Logan couldn't help but smile.

"Show Logan," Claire said.

Logan followed Natalie upstairs. She quickly had the list on the screen. They read down through it, but none of the names was familiar to him, or any possibility to her. They double-checked the B's. It took nearly fifteen minutes, but Logan saw nothing he could use.

He turned to Hal Frost. "I want you to call everyone on that list, verify who they are and if they have any connection to Alex Barrett. He may have had a client's key. I'll get a court order for every one of them we can't verify." He knew he had probable cause now, but a judge wasn't going to let him open every box, only those they could show might in some way be connected to this case.

"It will take several days," Frost said.

"We don't have several days!" Claire said. "Close the bank down, Hal. I want everyone working on this, do you understand?"

Frost nodded.

Logan estimated it would still take at least until morning.

Logan steered Claire toward the car while carrying Melissa. A few minutes later they were leaving the back parking lot and heading for Foothill Boulevard.

Claire looked pale and tired. She rested her head against the seat. Melissa was belted in the back, still sucking her thumb. They rode in silence until they left Foothill and entered the I-80 freeway going west.

"Are you sure they haven't killed Alex?" Claire asked softly.

He took a deep breath. "Yes, I'm sure. Think it through,

Claire. Alex is buying time. He sent them to the box, knowing it was already empty."

"And hoping he could escape before they got word back." She paused. "If he doesn't get away . . . "

Neither one of them wanted to finish the sentence.

"He has also given us some time, Claire. We have a chance now, a chance to catch up to them."

"If only Thompson could talk."

"Yeah. I blew that part," Logan said.

She reached over and touched his arm. "Oh, Logan, I'm sorry. I didn't mean . . . it wasn't your fault. You had no choice!"

"I should have shot him in the leg the moment I saw him."

She laughed lightly. "You don't strike me as the type to shoot first and ask questions later."

Logan turned onto I-15 going north.

"How much time do you think his little ruse will buy him?" Claire asked.

"I don't know. Maybe twenty-four hours."

"Will what is in the safety deposit box help find him?" Claire asked.

Logan had asked himself the same question. It had led Alex to Arthur Hainey. Hainey was dead now, and that route would lead nowhere. If there had been anything else, anything more pertinent . . .

It was just another sign that all of this had to do with the past—with Charles Barrett's years as a soldier. If the safety deposit box could tell them more about that part of Charles Barrett's life, maybe it would help.

Logan picked up the phone and called Carnahan's office, then asked the secretary if a fax had come for him from Denton Harker. It hadn't.

"You're convinced this has something to do with my father's past, aren't you." Claire said.

Logan nodded. "I'm convinced your father removed something from the war zone, Claire. Something of value. Alex may have discovered what it was. At the very least he was on the right track because of what he found in your father's safety deposit box."

"Then the same information could lead us to Alex."

"You're forgetting Hainey's death."

"And if Alex went to him first . . . "

"It was the best direction to go."

"But if Denton Harker can get us something about the connection between Hainey and Father, and if we have the rest of what is in the envelope, we might find out who has Alex?"

Logan nodded.

Claire closed her eyes. It was a lot of ifs.

And it would take a lot of time—more time than Alex could afford.

"There is one other possibility," Logan said. "Alex might get away."

15

As the haze in his mind dissipated, Alex felt as if someone had been playing tic-tac-toe on the back of his head with a sledge-hammer. He rolled over, changing his position, trying to escape the pain coursing through his body like hot liquid. He was one big bruise that had acquired a bad case of rigor mortis. He opened his eyes as best he could, only to find himself surrounded by darkness and the foul smell of diesel again. He was back in the hold of the boat. He realized his hands were no longer tied and used the index finger of his left one to poke himself, trying to discover what was broken and what was not. All his bones seemed to work, but his face and midsection were so tender they hurt even when touched. The puffiness around his eyes and nose felt as though someone had shoved enough cotton under his skin to fill inventory for the University of Utah medical center. His eyes were nearly shut with swelling, and his lips were cracked and bleeding.

He had been awake before, a number of times since the beatings, but now was the first time he had had enough strength to stay that way.

With some effort Alex pushed himself up. The throbbing worsened for a moment, then eased a little. He let himself down from the bunk gently, reaching for the floor with the tips of his bare toes.

He felt around the room, then above his head for a light switch or pull cord. Nothing. No light. No table. No chairs. Nothing but the double bunk against the wall two steps away. Nothing in his cell had seemed to change.

Alex was in a cubicle about six by ten. The double bunk ran along one end, the end he thought must be the front of the small boat. The ceiling was nine to ten feet above his head. He soon discovered that his first opinion was correct—there was no floor-level entrance into his new home, only the overhead hatch.

He sat down carefully on the lower bunk. The stiff ache was incessant, and his face hurt clear to the bone. He checked his scalp and face for cuts, measuring each and trying to determine how badly scarred he was going to be. All in all, after the beating he had taken, he was encouraged.

He could hear nothing but the lap of water against the sides of the boat, the wood creaking when it came in contact with what must be some kind of dock, and the occasional sound of a sea gull over head.

So, he was tethered on a body of water that smelled of sea salt, imprisoned in an old wooden vessel that had the distinct odor of mold and diesel. But where? He had few clues. His interrogator was Ukrainian, but that didn't mean the butcher hadn't come to Washington. He had no idea of how long he had been unconscious before waking up on the boat the first time, so they could have brought him a great distance, or no distance at all.

Possibly he was on the Atlantic Coast. Possibly not. The interrogation room had no windows, no pictures, nothing that might reveal his whereabouts. He simply didn't know where he was or how close help might be. He had to find out.

Alex tried listening harder, tried to hear something—the sound of traffic, even distant, would be some relief, but there was nothing but the sound of his cell bumping against the dock.

He climbed into the top bunk and tried reaching the hatch. No use. It wasn't that he wasn't high enough but that the hatch was too far away from the bunk, near the other wall. The bunk couldn't be moved because it was built right into the wall, a part of the boat. His extended fingertips fell a good foot short of the spot around which he could see just a tinge of light. And even if he could reach it, what then? He knew it was locked from the outside.

He sat down and waited, hating the darkness and the pain that left him no comfortable position. The hold was cool, even chilly, and he pulled the blanket over him. He dozed fitfully, the pain

waking him with even the slightest movement. His head ached
severely, and he wondered if he had a concussion. He didn't think
so.

He lost track of time as he moved in and out of sleep.

Alex woke up as the chains overhead rattled and the hatch
was opened. Something was dropped inside and the hatch closed.
At first Alex was afraid it was another pellet, but when nothing
happened, he slipped from the bed and checked the floor. He
found a tin can, probably for using the bathroom, and a package
that felt warm. He unwrapped it to find hot bread and what
smelled like cooked meat and thick slices of cheese.

Odd. His first reaction was to remember an event from
Church history—Joseph Smith's captivity in Liberty jail. For the
first time he was beginning to relate.

He sat down, smelled the meat one more time, then began
nibbling. It tasted good, and he finished it quickly.

He felt better, stronger. He thought of using the can but then
had an idea. Carefully he knelt down, feeling the floorboards, and
they were boards, about four or five inches wide, that made the
bottom of a boat flat so it could be walked on. He wondered . . .

Taking the can, he carefully and quietly pushed its tin sides
together, giving him a stiff point with which to work. He tried
forcing this between the planks but had no success, not at first.
He moved around the floor, pushing and shoving, trying to force
the sharp edge of the tin between the boards. It was more than
another hour before he finally wedged the makeshift pick
between two boards in a small crack near the interior wall of the
boat. The can slipped between the two planks, and he was able to
force it along for about a foot. He pushed and wiggled it deeper
into the crack and tried using it like a pry bar, but the tin was too
weak and the wood too well fastened, bending the can. He pulled
it free and decided on another approach. He picked at the wood
with the point, chipping away small slivers of it a little at a time.
It worked but was slow and tedious.

Alex didn't know how much time passed, but his shoulders
and arms ached as badly as his face. It took a lot of chipping
before he had made a wide enough opening that he could get a

finger past and under the board. He pulled. Not enough strength with one finger. He again used the can to widen the hole, then tried two fingers. It gave enough that he could get three under, picking up a dozen slivers for his trouble.

Alex pulled up on the board. It bowed a little but didn't give. He moved to the side of the board, giving himself a better position of leverage and tried one more time.

His breath caught as the board gave a little! He pulled harder, putting his back into it, forgetting the pain in his bruised muscles.

It gave, then tore free. He stood there, the board in his hand, a dark hole in the floor in front of him.

16

YEGOR KAMANEV SHUT THE DOOR BEHIND HIM and walked down the path toward his father's old fishing boat. It had been some time since the rotting vessel had been on the waters of the Black Sea. It wasn't fit for such things anymore. After his father's death ten years ago, there had been no one left to operate it, and Yegor had found no buyers. The decks had rotted somewhat, and the motor was ruined with rust and poor care. Now it had finally found some use again.

He stopped long enough to light an American cigarette. While he smoked, he looked back at the house. He had been raised there, had lived there all his life, still lived there, would probably die there. He stayed alive by selling his services as a bodyguard to the new rich class who came to the Crimea for rest and relaxation but felt in need of some protection. It was that way nowadays. Everyone needed protection. Such things paid well and gave Yegor contacts that were beginning to pay off. The man who paid him now had come that way—a nameless contact who expected him to do what he was told and paid him well for it.

The house was dark. The interrogator had gone to town to use the phone because Yegor's had gone bad again. It was bad most of the time. Although the country was doing its best to make things better, new phone lines were not high on the list of priorities, especially out here, away from the city.

Yegor knew his boss would be back any time. It had been nearly thirty-six hours since the first beating, and his employer would want the American ready for his next session. Yegor flipped the cigarette into the wet grass and heard it sizzle as he started toward the boat.

He slipped on the path and nearly fell. It had started raining about midnight, stopping at about three, leaving everything soaking wet and chilled. He pulled his jacket around his ears against the cool air and continued on. Rain was starting again, and he could hear the deep resonance of thunder out to sea.

He didn't understand the interrogator. The prisoner could be kept in the locked room in the house just as well as in the boat where the damp and cold would endanger even a strong man's health. But the man had an idiot's belief that the stranger the confinement, the more frightened the prisoner might become. Yegor thought it was hogwash but hadn't said so. He needed the money.

Yegor was paid in dollars, not kupons—a thousand of them for a job like this one, ten times more than even the best wages his friends could muster in a month at the nearby resorts. And dollars were worth so much more, the Kupon nearly worthless. This money would pay for much-needed repairs on the house before he brought Yena there to live.

Yena, his new wife in a little less than three weeks. He wanted to have the place looking nice for her.

He crossed the plank that led from the shore to what was left of the dock. It used to be a nice dock—concrete pilings driven into the sea floor, with more steel-reinforced concrete running from piling to piling and covered with thick wood planks. Now the wood was gone, stolen when he was away as a boxer trying to make the national team for the Soviet Union, stolen because lumber was nearly impossible to get unless you were rich with dollars. Wood, like blocks and bricks, was a black-market item now. You had to have money to get them—American money.

The rain came, beating hard against him. He deftly worked his way along the concrete, careful not to step on one of the protruding pieces of metal that once held the wood in place. They were rusted dark by the salt sea air and would give a man blood poisoning if he injured himself on them. A friend of his had fallen on another dock just like this, the piece of metal rebar driving itself through the calf of his leg. A week later they amputated his leg. He was lucky to have survived at all.

He hadn't liked hitting the American as much as he'd thought he would. The interrogator was a cruel man, hard and determined.

Yegor didn't know what his game was, didn't even know who he was, but he had seen the type before. Most of them had been members of the former KGB, heartless men looking for information and willing to do almost anything to get it. He had steered clear of them all through his military years and was careful not to confront any during the time he was training for Olympic competition in the mid-eighties. They had always been evil men who could ruin your life with a word or, worse, see you in Siberia ending your life at hard labor.

This time he needed the money. For Yena.

He quietly approached the boat, slipped aboard, and walked to the hatch. Removing the chains and padlock, he lifted the lid and dropped the capsule inside, quickly stepping away. The canister contained a type of sleeping gas used in military cartridges. He had used it against the Afghani warriors holing up in mountain caves. He would throw the gas inside, wait ten minutes, then enter to find the enemy fast asleep. The rest was easy.

It still gave him nightmares.

Yegor had served in Afghanistan after his hopes of becoming an Olympian were dashed by a broken hand gained when punching a wall while drunk. His inability to fight had sent him back to the military ranks and eventually to active duty. After six months of training he had gone to Afghanistan, where he had learned how to kill in order to save his own life. But the war had taken its toll on him, as it had on every other soldier. He had left a part of himself behind, a little of his soul dying with each man he had been forced to kill. Only Yena had given him hope again.

Strange that the few canisters he had brought back with him should be used in this way.

After ten minutes he lifted the hatch lid. From experience he knew it would take another five for the gas to leave the hold before he could enter. He waited.

Donning his gas mask as an added precaution, he lowered the wooden ladder and removed a flashlight from his pocket. Flipping it on, he descended into the darkness. When his feet were firmly planted on the floor, he flashed the light into the top bunk.

The American wasn't there.

The ray of light jumped to the other bunk. Gone!

But how?

He flashed the light around the room, under the bed. Nothing! The American had disappeared!

Yegor panicked. Grabbing hold of the ladder, he began climbing to the hatch. As he reached for the last rung, he felt the sudden shock of a tight grip around his ankle. He was yanked downward with such force and surprise that he lost his grip and fell, the flashlight flying against the wall, its light disappearing in an instant. He saw the dark form over him, heard the swish of something moving through the air, and felt the shudder in his body as the plank met his skull. His mind melted into darkness, his limbs nothing but useless appendages.

His last thought was of shame; he had been outwitted.

Alex felt the body relax, the hard muscles turn suddenly to putty. He brought his arm back for another blow but didn't have the strength. He fell to the side grateful, gasping for air through the cloth he had wrapped around his mouth and nose, knowing that another minute and he would not have had enough strength to win. He had hoped the gas would rise, not settle through the floorboards, and for the most part it had done so, escaping through the hatch after Yegor opened it. But some of the noxious substance had arrived in his little coffin of a hiding chamber and weakened him.

He lay next to his captor, taking deep breaths.

His plan had been to dig a hole through the boat's hull, but after removing a few planks, he realized it was impossible. He decided surprising the boxer was his only chance—a desperate idea considering their difference in size. It was a thin strand of hope that had worked, and he was grateful for the element of surprise along with the sturdy two-foot plank that had given him an advantage.

With a lot of effort Alex lifted himself into a sitting position. He had to get moving. Now.

Pushing against the floor, he got himself to the bed. Searching in the back corner of the lower bunk, Alex removed the thin strips of cloth he had already made from the food bag. Kneeling next to the unconscious Yegor, he tied the boxer's feet, then forced his hands behind his back and tied them as tightly as his strength would allow. He could only hope his knots would do as much damage to Yegor as Yegor's had done to him.

The last piece was used to gag his enemy. He then rolled the body under the lower bunk and covered it with a blanket.

Alex knew a careful search would reveal Yegor, especially once he was conscious and able to make noise, but by then Alex hoped to be out of reach of any further torment at the boxer's hands or the interrogator's needle.

He put the last of the planks back in place.

He had lain beneath the floor for what seemed like an eternity. The drug injected by the interrogator had made him listless, afraid, even a bit schizophrenic, even though he knew it had been some time since he had received it. Twice he had come to tears as his state had overwhelmed him. Twice he had cried out to God for the strength to get past the crisis. Both times the calm, the control had come.

It had been a long time since Alex had prayed like that. His mother's death was the last time. He had felt so alone, despondent. Even though he had great trust in the plan of salvation and God's decision not to intervene in his mother's illness, she had been everything to him, and it had hurt when she left. But God had come then, too, and the strength to make all the arrangements, to help with the final preparations of the body for burial, had been there when he had needed it.

Now he was getting that strength again, and his heart felt gratitude because of it.

He felt the rain as he positioned himself at the foot of the ladder. It cooled him, and he stuck his tongue out to catch a little as he started the climb. Peering cautiously into the rain-filled blackness from just above the top of the hatch, Alex could see the dock and the shoreline with trees shrouded in haze and pouring rain, gray masses more than distinct objects. Descending the ladder, he searched for the flashlight, found it, and clicked the switch several times, slapping it against the palm of his hand before giving up. The lens and bulb inside must be shattered.

Before going up the ladder, he thought of something else; kneeling down, he reached under the bed and pulled Yegor's feet out so he could remove the shoes and socks. They were a little big on Alex, but he knew he'd be grateful he had them.

He ascended the ladder again and exited the hatch. Keeping as low as possible, he worked his way across the deck and jumped to the concrete. He could actually see better there than in the hold, probably because his eyes had learned to adjust to the extreme darkness of his prison. He moved from slab to slab while avoiding the sharp pieces of metal that seemed to jut from every angle through the concrete, then crossed the plank to the rocky shore and quickly worked his way up to higher ground along the path. A few minutes later he found himself facing a small house built of rough, porous blocks and roofed with what he thought must be steel or tin. The construction was definitely not American.

The place was silent and dark, a spooky hovel that gave goosebumps to his goosebumps. He quickly worked his way around the house, glancing over his shoulder, afraid someone might be watching through the dark windows. He found a beat-up old truck on the other side and checked for keys but found none. Just as well. Starting it would alert anyone sleeping, and if that happened to be the interrogator, Alex knew he would have little chance of escape. Even now his chances were slim.

He squinted through the wet air, shivering a little against the cool night and soaking rain. He was stronger than he had been when first awakening from his beating, but his bruised and healing body was sapping his strength, making any prolonged movement nearly impossible. He bent over, hands on knees to catch his breath while looking for lights through the trees. Nothing.

He walked up the lane, away from the house. Somewhere nearby there had to be other people, a road, help.

He had gone nearly half a mile, his mind searching for some clue as to where he was, when he saw the lights coming toward him. A car. He immediately moved off the road and buried himself in the thick underbrush, watching as the Russian Zhiguili bumped and rattled past him, slipping on the muddy lane but working its way quickly downhill. As it passed directly by him, Alex lifted his head cautiously and peered at the profile of the man inside. He held his breath when he saw the interrogator. When the taillights disappeared around the corner leading to the house, Alex picked himself up from the wet grass and began running up the road. It wouldn't be long now until the enemy found that he was gone and came after him.

Alex found himself stopping constantly to catch his breath. On the fifth stop, he looked back toward the house. His spirits sagged when he saw how short the distance was he had covered. He was weaker than he had thought—moving but getting nowhere fast. He sat, taking deep breaths, fighting the pain of breathing, the desire to lie down and quit.

He wondered if he should cut through the woods, away from the road, but decided against it. He could get lost in the dark and give his enemies more time to get help and find him.

He thought about the Zhiguili. No one shipped them out of Russia. They were a lousy little car even the Russians despised. He stared at the dark expanse of water that spread before him. He was sure it was the Black Sea—all the pieces fit. He had been brought to southern Ukraine, to Crimea. But why so far?

He had to get moving.

He climbed the narrow brush- and tree-lined road through three more turns and two more stops before coming to the narrow strip of highway. He looked both directions. He could see for some distance now, the first rays of morning light forcing their way through the gray, dismal mist and clouds. The road had posts along it with electrical wires hanging from them—trolley bus lines, a good sign that civilization was close by.

At his left was a high mountain that looked like the hump of a camel and culminated in cliffs at the water's edge. The sea itself went on for as far as the clouds and rain would allow him to look. To his right, the road led in an undulating manner over a series of hills. Directly in front of him were fields of grapevines. Further in that direction stood high, steep cliffs that seemed to thrust themselves up and through the low cloud cover. It was Crimea all right, and he was a long way from home.

He limped quickly up the road, the sea to his right, the mountains to his left. The thin band of asphalt went upward, and when he reached the peak of a hill, he could see into a valley that extended from the cliffs to his left, under a bridge on the road, and down to the sea. It was getting light enough now that he could see the dark line of the seashore until the rim of the next ridge and heavy rain interfered. He could make out the outline of buildings by the sea. Dark still, but there would be people there. He could only hope they would have the desire and ability to help him.

He pressed on, putting one tired foot in front of the other. It was when he reached the rise of the next hill that he noticed the pain in the heel of his foot—a blister from the boots, which were two sizes too big.

He heard the noise and turned quickly to look the way he had come. The lights were just coming over the first hill. The truck! He was completely visible in the early, gray morning. He plunged down the side of the road and into the trees and underbrush, working his way down the steep hill and in the general direction of the buildings he had seen. He was afraid now, panicky, knowing what was in store if they caught him. As he turned to look over his shoulder, his foot caught on the thick undergrowth, and he tripped. Grabbing for the underbrush, he tried to break his fall, but his hands came up empty. He did a nose dive down the steep incline of the hill and began an uncontrollable roll, his body finally coming to a halt as his head and shoulders slammed into the trunk of a wide tree. The pain to his bruised body nearly made him cry out, but he bit his tongue.

Lying there in the wet underbrush, covered with mud, out of breath, struggling to keep the pain from sending him under, Alex heard voices from the way he had come. They had seen him.

Gritting his teeth, he forced himself deeper into the undergrowth, his eyes peering back between branches and left through the early morning light at the steep hill above. Through the growth he could see two men silhouetted against the gray clouds. Yegor's large build stood next to the smaller interrogator, who shouted an order and pointed in the direction Alex had just come. The boxer, reshoed and shirted, came downhill at a fast pace, the angry interrogator following.

Alex got up, his eyes darting right and left, looking for a hiding place. Feeling like a cornered rabbit, he kept trees and heavy underbrush between him and his pursuers and worked his away across the hill as quickly as he could without leaving an obvious trail.

But the voices were getting closer.

Alex saw an outcropping of stone and thick underbrush twenty yards ahead. It was a heavy clump of scrub oak brush so thick Alex wondered if even a rabbit could wiggle its way in. If he could do it . . .

Moving low and being extra cautious about leaving any trail, he worked his way to the edge of the outcrop. Looking over his shoulder, he checked his back trail, then got on his belly and carefully pushed himself forward, underneath the low branches and into the thicket. The limbs tore at his clothing and ripped at his flesh, but he forced his way further in, desperate, afraid.

He held his breath as the last of him slid under the blanket of brush and into the darkness. The voices were close now. He pulled his feet up to his chest, trying to make himself an invisible ball in the darkness.

He waited. His breathing sounded like wind blowing through the brush. He tried to silence it, but the thump of his heart was even worse.

A small hole in the underbrush gave both light to his dark cavern and visibility to see a small portion of the woods directly in front of him. He nearly fainted as Yegor came into view so close that Alex could see each bristle of his unshaven beard. The boxer turned left, then right. He looked down the hill for a long time. Then he turned and looked directly into the bushes.

Alex knew his heart stopped. It seemed to him as if their eyes met, as if Yegor knew he was there. He wanted to run for his life but forced his body to remain as still as the rock he was resting against.

Then the boxer disappeared.

Alex waited a long time. His heart finally started again but he felt weak, nauseous, exhausted. Now he could only wait. He pulled his knees up to his chin, the cold and wet chilling him to the bone. He put his head on his arms and closed his eyes, the exhaustion rippling over him like a morning tide.

By the time the interrogator stumbled onto the road another three hundred feet away, yelling at Kamanev to follow, Alex had blacked out from pain and exhaustion.

They continued their search clear to the health spa by the seashore, spreading out through the trees, looking for tracks or some other evidence of the game they hunted. It took nearly an hour before they gave up and the interrogator dispatched himself and Yegor back toward the main road. As they reached Yegor's truck, the boxer received his final orders.

"Get help, Yegor; search these hills," the interrogator said coldly. "Find the American before he finds help. If you do not, I will personally kill you."

Yegor, frustrated and angry, only nodded before climbing into the driver's seat of the beat-up truck.

The interrogator got in on the passenger's side but kept his eyes searching the mountain as if somehow they would latch onto some sign of where Alex Barrett had hidden himself. Nothing.

The truck turned and went back the way it had come. "You have lived here all your life, Yegor. Put out the word we are looking for a dangerous man. Let the people be your eyes and ears, but find him!" The interrogator's square jaw was set firmly in his long face, his short, graying hair bristling with controlled anger. "Tell them I offer a five-thousand-dollar reward for him— American money. I will put the word out in Yalta and have the authorities alerted." He took a deep breath. "It was stupid, Yegor. How could you have been so stupid?"

Yegor clenched his teeth. "You pay five thousand dollars for him now. If I find him I also get the money!"

The interrogator gave a loud laugh. "You stupid fool! You let him get away, and now you expect me to pay you to get him back?" He laughed a second time, then his face turned to stone. "If you wish to ever see the thousand I promised you, you will find the American, and quickly! And if you don't, I will kill you with my bare hands!"

Yegor didn't answer, his cold, dark eyes staring at the muddy road. He was tired of this little man and his promises. Yegor had seen his money, knew he kept several thousand on him in a money belt. It was time to collect his fee.

He shifted down to make the corner, his heavy hand driving the shift stick forward hard enough that he put a dent into the rusted metal dash. His eyes turned neither right nor left, and there was a firm determination in the set of his jaw.

"I think you will pay me now," he said coldly.

The interrogator gave Yegor a hard stare when he saw that the boxer was serious. Deftly he pulled a 9mm Makarov from under his jacket, jammed it under Yegor's chin, and shoved upward.

"I think not, my big and very dumb friend. And if you are smart—!" He jammed harder with the Makarov.

Yegor grabbed an arm and threw the smaller man against the door. The gun went off, and Yegor was hit in the side of the head, a dead man. The truck jerked right, then left on the muddy surface of the steep lane, turning it sideways. The front wheel broke, and the axle dug deep into the earth, caught, and flipped the vehicle.

The truck did half a dozen somersaults down the lane, its doors swinging open and throwing both men mercilessly through thin air. The vehicle came to a rest another hundred yards further downhill as it disappeared from view and got entangled in the underbrush. Yegor was lying very still. The left side of his face was missing, and his blood mingled freely with the mud and grass around his head.

In three days Yena would mourn his passing.

The interrogator was lying a few feet further down hill on the opposite side of the road, his leg bent under him at an obscene angle, his skull crushed from contact with an unforgiving rock outcropping near the road's edge.

They would trouble Alex no more.

17

As THE LINE DWINDLED and the door was closed, Claire wondered how long they had been standing there, greeting the Navarros' family and friends. She glanced at her watch—two hours. It had seemed like an eternity. She belittled herself for the hundredth time for agreeing to come at all.

She shook another hand. "So sorry," the woman said. "He was such a fine man—so much promise." Claire forced a smile and turned to the next mourner. It amazed her how few people had been able to look her straight in the eye when they spoke to her. She wondered if it was because they had seen all the press on Steve's involvement in the attempted kidnapping of his own stepdaughter and didn't really believe what they were saying, or because they simply had a hard time confronting another person's grief. She didn't know. All she wanted was for it to end.

The last man in line, a latecomer, was a familiar face.

"Detective Logan." She said it with a real smile, the first of the day for Claire. "A pleasant surprise. You're the last person I thought I would see here."

"Umm." He gave a smile and leaned forward. "You're a bit of a surprise too, Claire. What the devil are you doing here?" The question was the first genuine one she had heard all morning.

"I don't know," she said. "Can you stay for the services? I want to talk to you, and I can't—"

He nodded. "I'll be at the cemetery for the dedication of the grave." He moved down the line, shaking the hands of Steve's two brothers and three sisters before disappearing out the side door that led to the hallway.

Logan had found nothing new. The man they still knew only as William Thompson had died last night, the night of his capture, of massive head injuries. He was now under a John Doe at the morgue awaiting a decision by Logan about when to give information to the press. Logan believed that something might still turn up, some connection to Alex's whereabouts could be made, as long as the enemy still thought William Thompson was doing his job. Claire agreed and was thankful he was still hanging on to the thin thread of hope that Alex was alive—a thin thread that was holding her up as well.

For the same reason, Alex's name still headed the list of suspects in Hainey's murder. Although the gun used by Thompson to kill the guard at the bank had been found to be the same gun used to kill Arthur Hainey, and the rest of the evidence substantiated that Thompson was the murderer and not Alex, both Logan and Denton Harker of the FBI felt that any change in the investigation would close all doors by which they might find Alex and the people behind the whole mess.

But even though they had Thompson, it all seemed to end there. They hadn't found his apartment yet, and Logan had little to nothing on him that pointed to where they should look next. They had nothing more than they had eighteen hours ago, and with each passing hour Claire felt more desperate, frustrated, and out of control. Her life had been turned completely upside down over the past few days, and she wondered how so much could go so wrong in so short a time! At first Alex had been her anchor in a rough sea, and now he was gone. She needed him back, and their father needed him. Melissa needed him. And they didn't even know if he was still alive.

If it hadn't been for Logan . . .

Claire and Melissa had returned to the house the previous night. The evening had been long, lonely, and frightening. By nine o'clock, Claire wondered if she could stay in the house any longer when Logan had showed up on their doorstep. The three of them had shared a wonderful time until Melissa had fallen asleep. Logan had tucked her into a makeshift bed in the small reading room next to the living area, then Claire and Logan had spent several hours talking and fixing a late dinner. The loneliness and fear had returned when he left but lasted only until she saw his car still parked out front with him in it. In the morning, he was gone.

The mortician and his assistant approached the casket and closed the bottom half, then asked members of the family to say their final good-byes. Claire hadn't looked at Steve since coming into the room and didn't intend to do so now. She stepped back into the crowd, knowing that all eyes were watching her. She didn't care. She had come only as a favor to Steve's dad, a man she admired and respected and who had begged her to do it. She wasn't about to give credence to the belief everyone seemed to have that Steve was a saint already back in the presence of his God because of his many good works and a merciful atonement. That was one thing about the gospel plan she understood well—unrepentant sinners didn't get mercy until justice had been paid. The principle had been a source of discontent in Claire's life for years. It was one of the things that had made her face her own life and start her way back.

Steve's uncle, a returned mission president, gave the family prayer. He was Hank Navarro's brother, and from what he said in the prayer he understood Steve had a few problems to answer for. Claire was grateful for an honest plea to save a wayward son's soul instead of praise for good deeds.

Plenty of that came later.

Over the next hour and a half, Claire sat with the family and listened to selected speakers give their appraisal of Steve's life. When the eulogizers had finished, she wondered if she was in the right services. She was glad it was nearly over.

Then there were the looks and whispers from the extended family, most of whom hadn't the slightest idea what Steve had been like, why he and Claire had divorced. All were well aware of what the papers were saying about Steve's role in the attempted kidnapping of Melissa, but she could tell all of them refused to believe it was anything more than a father's attempt at reclaiming his child, or some other foolish rationalization. Claire wasn't sure they would ever believe Steve was what he was, an abuser, a hypocrite, about as far away from a Christ-like life as an everyday Mormon who attended church regularly could be. Steve was the fair-haired boy with the athletic body and toothpaste smile, the kid in the family who could do no wrong and was surely destined for greatness. To his family, there was some sort of mistake. The police were wrong, had to be, and they looked to her for some sort of verification of their judgment. All during the viewing and services, they had whispered and watched her, waiting. She never gave them the satisfaction, couldn't give them the satisfaction, of believing their icon was still holy.

Claire shivered to think how little everyone really knew Steve. But then, he had always been the consummate liar and con man. She had fallen for it just as hard as all of them had. The only difference was that when he had shown her his true colors, she had had enough sense to admit she had been wrong and get out.

Now she knew that some of them had also come to know Steve, but they had never admitted that what they knew might be true.

Steve's younger brother stood to give the closing prayer. Claire bowed her head and closed her eyes, grateful to have all those of the family closed as well. Something nudged her hand, and she opened her eyes to see a parchment envelope with her name on it. She grasped it and looked at Steve's dad, who was sitting next to her. He gave her a slight smile, tears cascading down his cheeks. She closed her eyes, knowing she would never forget that look. His eyes were filled with sadness and understanding— and thanks. She felt an ache in her chest, tears working their way into the corners of her eyes, not for Steve but for Hank, for the part of him his son had killed by his actions. Then she cried for her own father, and for Alex, and for the mess she had made of her life.

The prayer was over, the mortician gave his little speech, and the pallbearers moved into position. She stood with the others, her white handkerchief quickly dabbing at her eyes, her head lowered. She knew others would believe the tears were for Steve. It didn't matter. In a way she supposed they were.

They left by the side entrance and were escorted to limousines parked along the tree-lined street of one of the city's older neighborhoods. She sat by herself until the door opened and

Steve's uncle, the one who had said the family prayer, asked if he and his wife could ride with her. She nodded, grateful. A few moments later, the procession of cars was moving in the direction of the cemetery.

He leaned forward, offering his hand. "My name is Will. I'm Hank's brother. This is my wife Margerie." The tall slender woman in the black dress smiled.

"How are you doing?" Hank asked in genuine concern.

"All right," Claire responded. "Actually, lousy. I shouldn't have come."

William smiled. "Hank will be eternally grateful. He thinks a lot of you, of anyone who would put up with his son the way you did."

She looked at him, then remembered the note still clutched in her hand. Her eyes went back to Will's, searching for an explanation of his statement.

"Steve gave Hank fits all his life, Claire. Hank kept him out of jail on two occasions by using influence with friends in the police force. He regrets it now—thinks all of this could have been avoided if he hadn't covered for Steve, had made him face his mistakes back then. Being covered for, Steve just learned to keep his dark side out of sight." He sighed. "He knows some of how Steve treated you, how he treated others. Your being here helps remove some of the guilt from Hank's shoulders while giving him the opportunity to honor you for sticking it out with Steve as long as you did."

"Steve lied his way through life," Margerie added. "Unlike Hank, Steve's mother has never admitted that Steve was a violent personality who lived two lives—the one he wanted the public to see and the real one—the one you had to deal with. Because of that, she wouldn't let Hank deal with Steve the way he should have." She glanced out the window. "Steve could do no wrong in her eyes, and when that happens, a child has a hard time believing his conduct is anything but proper."

"But how could she . . . " Claire sat back. "No, I know the answer. Steve was a Jekyll and Hyde. She would only see what he wanted her to see."

"All of us saw Steve's real self more than once, Claire. His mother was no exception, but she believed what she wanted to believe," Margerie said. "Too many mothers are like that. Then they wonder why their children turn out the way they do."

They rode through several intersections, policemen directing traffic at each. It was noon, a hot day outside, and Claire was grateful for the air conditioning.

"Have they found your brother yet?" Will asked.

Claire shook her head. "Alex couldn't kill anyone." She realized it sounded like she was trying to protect him, make excuses for him. She felt embarrassed. Innocent people didn't need that kind of apologetic justification.

They turned into the cemetery and drove between rows of tombstones. When they stopped, Claire could see the mound of dirt next to the hole that awaited Steve's casket. The small hill was covered with green outdoor carpet, and a number of chairs were set up under the trees near the grave. Getting out first, Will helped Margerie and Claire. They walked to their places and sat down. Steve's mother was having a harder time now, her tears turning to sobs, and she was refusing to let her husband comfort her.

Claire felt numb, the thought of death hanging over her like a thick cloud. Was this all there was—a hole in the ground in which a body was placed to rot into nothingness? She looked down at her arms and hands, the sudden realization of how fragile and important life was washing over her. When she finished with this life, what did the future hold? She knew there was an afterlife, a place where the spirit continued. She believed in paradise. And in hell. What was it like for Steve now? What would it be like for her? She rubbed her arms, trying to make the cold go away. Was her rejection of the gospel so much better than his? Her mouth was dry, and she felt weak as she stared into the vault at her feet. Death had never frightened her like this before, but it frightened her now. She started to get up, to walk away, but the crowd had gathered, and she could see no escape. She sat back down, staring into the chasm in front of her and praying they would get the burial over quickly.

The Navarros' bishop stepped forward and started the dedicatory prayer. It was a lot like Will's and seemed to make Steve's mother even worse. When he closed it, Claire stood, her heart racing to get away. She moved through the crowd, shoving, excusing herself. She'd had enough.

Someone grabbed her arm and pulled on it hard, flipping her around. Mrs. Navarro stood there, her face contorted with so many emotions Claire didn't recognize who it was at first.

"You are responsible for all this!" She hissed. "Steve . . . " Her voice raised an octave. "Steve would still be alive if he hadn't met you!" She dug her fingers into Claire's arm, and Claire grimaced, trying to jerk it free. Hank Navarro grabbed his wife by the shoulders and pulled back hard enough to make her let go. She turned into him, and he wrapped his arms around her to try to make the pain go away. She was beating against his chest with her hand when Claire turned and walked through a crowd that seemed to separate as if Moses were parting a second Red Sea. The looks she got were mostly of the wilting kind, and it was all she could do to keep going. Someone stepped from the crowd and put an arm around her shoulder. It was Logan. He took her to his car and opened the passenger door for her. She glanced toward the crowd. All eyes were on her now. Will and Margerie stood in front of the others and waved lightly, the look of thanks on their faces enough to keep her from completely going to pieces. Logan started the car and pulled into the lane. A moment later, they were leaving the cemetery.

"You've got a lot of guts, Claire," Logan said.

She put her head against the back of the seat and closed her eyes. She felt weak, exhausted. "Just dumb, that's all," she said.

Logan laughed. "I could use a cold drink. How about you?"

She laughed lightly. "The kind I need right now I gave up when I left Steve."

"Two good decisions in the same day," Logan said. "I admire that. How about a fresh lime?"

"With lots of ice," she agreed.

"You got it." He turned left and stopped at the next red light. "Why did you go?" he asked.

"I'm a masochist. And Steve's father—I always liked him—

he asked," she said, her eyes still closed. "It's over. Thank the Lord, it's over."

They pulled into an Arctic Circle. Logan left the car running while he went in and got them each a large fresh lime. Claire was feeling a little better when he returned, and she was thirsty. The cool liquid burned her dry throat a little but tasted wonderful.

"Why were you there?" She asked.

He shrugged. "How is your father today?"

"The same."

"Maybe you should unplug the machines, Claire. Alex—"

"Is coming back. And what happens to Father is his decision, not mine. Besides, I'm in no condition to handle another funeral. Not now. Not alone."

"Are the doctors still applying pressure?"

"Through Dad's attorney, and through Hal Frost at the bank."

"What's happening at the bank? This morning's papers say the board wants to get rid of Frost."

"Until Father is actually gone, they can't do anything to Frost." She shrugged. "Then it will be up to Alex and me."

"And?"

"And we'll keep Frost. Dad liked him; why shouldn't we? He may be a bit pompous but he's done great things at the bank. He deserves to stay." She smiled. "But Alex will be chairman."

"I didn't think he had any desire to take over your father's empire."

"He doesn't, but it's in Dad's will that way. I think Alex will accept the challenge once he faces a few things." She paused. "He *is* coming back! He has to! Do you know anything?" She asked, pleading.

"Nothing more than we discussed last night, Claire. I'm sorry, but it's a street filled with dead ends. All we can do is keep hoping for a break."

There was a long silence.

Logan slurped from the bottom of his drink. "Oops." He blushed.

"Still a kid at heart, aren't you," Claire remarked, her smile finally returning. "Logan, thanks. You have saved my bacon more than I care to think about in the past twenty-four hours. I hope the car wasn't too uncomfortable last night."

Logan laughed lightly. "You get used to it in this profession."

Claire remembered their conversation of the previous night. Logan's wife had died about ten years ago. She could tell by the way he spoke about Julie Logan that they had been happy, that it had been a good marriage. But there hadn't been any children. Julie had lost their first child and found out she had cancer at the same time. It had been a temple marriage, and Claire had been able to tell that fact had pulled Logan through some pretty tough times.

"What's it like, Logan? In the temple I mean. I hear so many things," Claire asked.

Logan was surprised by the question.

"Special. Very. No place as beautiful. No mistaking the commitment. You know you're in it for more than a lifetime, and you'd better give it your best shot."

"My parents were married in the temple, but they divorced. They taught us about the sacredness of the covenant when we were young, but they broke their promises to each other. I've had a hard time with that."

"It happens a lot in the Church these days. People don't take their covenants as seriously as they should. Too many becoming too much like the world, slipping in and out of sacred things the way they do a change of clothing." He paused. "What was it that caused your parents' breakup?"

"At first I blamed the Church, and God. Back then I didn't have enough knowledge to figure out what the real problem was. But I'm not sure. They both suffered, they both loved each other, even after the divorce. Dad was accused of adultery, but he claimed he didn't do it. Mom didn't believe him, and neither did Alex. I did. When the Church held a court and excommunicated him, I grew bitter. It festered like a boil until it drove me further away." She sighed. "Mom has always had a hard time forgiving others; I know that from personal experience. Dad tried to hold it together, to get her to accept his innocence, but she just couldn't. When they both refused to give, it drove them apart. The tension was unbearable, the arguing frightening, especially after the Church court." She shrugged. "I can't blame Mom. The evidence was very convincing. Dad had a lot of pride, especially when someone was challenging his word. I don't think the man ever told a lie in his life. He expected to be believed, and he wasn't. Neither would give. Mom left so angry I knew it was the end. She had forced me out of her life in the same way." Tears sprang to her eyes. "I know she never stopped loving either one of us, and in the end it hurt her more than it did us."

"Is that when you left the Church?"

"No, I did that years earlier. It just gave me another excuse, justified my past actions. All I did was ruin my life further."

"You have a lot of life left, Claire. I wouldn't say it's ruined, not yet." Logan said it with a smile. "Besides, you seem to be softening a little. Trouble does that. The Lord knocks you around to see if you're ready to wake up." He said it with a feeling of experience.

She didn't answer, her mind reflecting on how far downhill she had really come—two horrible marriages with losers, the immorality. She had done more than Logan could ever imagine, more than God could ever forgive. Going to a temple, being married, was something she knew she would never do. Those doors simply wouldn't open for her. She was no better than Steve Navarro—not in the Lord's view. The thought crushed her.

She glanced at the letter in her lap, noticing for the first time it had something bulky inside. She picked it up and pulled the sealed flap open. A Schlage key dropped into her lap. She removed the note and quickly read it.

"Dear Claire,

"This is the key to Steve's apartment. We'll be moving things out of there tomorrow. Please go and take anything you like.

"Claire, I wish I could make it all right, but I can't. Steve will have to answer to a higher authority than I am for what he's done. I hope you can forgive him, forgive us all."

It was signed Hank Navarro.

"What's the key for?" Logan asked.

She handed him the note. When he was finished and handed

it back, she spoke. "Have the police finished their investigation? Are you finished with Steve's belongings?"

"Yeah."

"Then I'd like to go there. Will you take me?"

He nodded, then took the half-empty cup she offered, got out of the car, and deposited both in the garbage can a few steps away. Fifteen minutes later, they were in front of Steve's apartment.

––––––––––––––

Claire had never been to Steve's place. When he moved out, their separation had been complete, and it was left for attorneys to work out the details. As she stood on the landing staring at the plain metal door, she wasn't sure she wanted to be there now. Logan inserted the key and opened the door, then ripped away the black and yellow police ribbon. "It should be gone already." He said it almost apologetically.

The place was dark, with the smell of pine-scented cleaner. Stepping inside, they closed the door.

"Someone has come in and cleaned up," Logan said.

A few boxes were stacked near the bar that separated the living area from the kitchen. On the bar itself, a number of Steve's personal items sat as if waiting for their owner to make use of them again. A laundry basket full of dirty clothes stood next to the boxes, and Claire caught herself thinking she ought to wash them, then reminded herself Steve wouldn't need them again. They'd probably all end up at a charity store, or in the closets of half a dozen of Steve's cousins or nephews.

When it came to clothes, Steve had spared no expense. He had worn the best, and Claire had paid for it. It was something about him she hadn't minded. She liked him looking nice, was proud to be by his side in public, a vain side of her that had made her overlook his quick and often brutal temper. She had paid for it.

"It's gruesome."

"Yeah, like invading someone's tomb," Logan said.

"It's hard to believe that through this whole ordeal I haven't felt the least bit of remorse for Steve's death—just pity."

Logan didn't answer. Claire walked to the laundry basket and picked up the shirt that lay half folded on top. It was one of his favorites, a teal canvas short sleeve that looked like it had been professionally cleaned and ironed. She held it up, staring at the front of it, trying to picture Steve in it. He had worn it when they were still married, hadn't he? But where? Where had they gone the last time she had seen him in it? Was it day or night? She couldn't remember. It seemed so long ago. She tossed it back onto the stack.

"What happened between you and Navarro, Claire?" Logan asked.

She glanced at him, wondering why she wanted to tell him.

"Steve was smooth and handsome, and I was trying to escape the turmoil of my mother's death. I should have seen it coming, but from where I stood it all looked wonderful. Steve represented a dream I could get hold of that would make my miserable experience with my first husband go away." She leaned against the bar. "Steve was worse."

"Worse?"

"My first husband used me for my father's money, was a worthless bum, but at least he treated Melissa and me with a degree of civility. He was an empty-headed laugher who didn't see the world as anything but his personal Disneyland, but he never beat me. Steve did—regularly."

"And your daughter?"

The fact that she didn't answer told Logan what he wanted to know.

"You were married for three years. Why did you stick with him so long? Abuse is more than ample reason for divorce— especially in the Church."

Claire wasn't sure herself. Her brow wrinkled as she thought about it. "I suppose because I had failed once, I didn't want it to happen again."

"But it wasn't your fault," Logan said.

"I said yes to marriage. It was my fault."

"Navarro was a respected attorney," Logan said. "He must have seemed like a good choice."

"I had some idea of what he was like, and he hit me once before we were married. His impatience with Melissa was obvious, but I ignored it. A friend of mine who had dated him for quite a while before she broke it off warned me. I ignored the warning—even called her names for it. Besides, he was reputed to be a good Mormon."

"You placed stock in that?" Logan asked.

"I turned from the Church out of anger and bitterness born of misunderstanding, not because I wasn't taught what the Church stood for. I had believed since I was a child that the Church put out good people. I learned a lesson. Just because they're born in the Church and go on a mission doesn't mean they'll make good husbands or stick to their beliefs. Steve took me to church once in a while, but usually it was to keep up appearances more than because he had any firm roots in the gospel."

"But it doesn't mean they won't either."

"No, it doesn't. But I knew it was all show, that he was all show. When I put that with what I knew and had been told, quietly, about his abusive nature, I have no one to blame but myself."

Logan couldn't argue with her logic. His eyes fell on Steve's briefcase on top of the counter. "Nice," he said stepping forward, hitting the latches and popping it open. It was empty.

"Steve went first class. There are probably tons of clothes in the closet in the bedroom, all tailor-made. Even the ties were made for him."

"On a prosecutor's salary."

She laughed. "My father gave me a healthy allowance, and Steve wasn't shy about asking me for a clothing budget."

Logan closed the lid.

She stepped to his side, opened it again, and pressed on the back side of one of the latches. Something gave in the bottom of the case, and she lifted the panel Logan had thought was just the inside of the case. There were some papers and credit cards inside.

"Steve was robbed once. He was in New York, and the thief entered his room while he was taking a shower and cleaned him out. He bought this the same day. When he showed it to me I thought the cost far outweighed the losses."

She lifted the papers and started looking at them.

"How much did it cost him?"

"Two thousand dollars."

Logan laughed, then saw she was serious.

"The latches are fourteen-karat gold, and the leather is some kind of exotic stuff that made another species extinct." She said it in a matter-of-fact tone, then smiled. "Any thief in his right mind would steal it as well. Kind of a kick to think about, isn't it? He buys a briefcase to hide his valuables in that is more valuable than what he's hiding, and he's stupid enough to believe thieves would just ignore it."

The tears came suddenly, and Logan found himself taking her into his arms but feeling unsure of what to do or say. So he just held her close. After a few minutes she pulled slowly away, her head lowered with embarrassment as she dried her eyes with a hanky.

"Sorry. This whole thing has messed me up. I cry when I shouldn't and don't cry when I should." She forced a smile.

"No apologies necessary. I'm impressed with the way you've held up. Having your former husband attempt . . . "

"Yeah, its the pits when you think about it. Makes you wonder about a girl like me—how dumb I have to be to pick the likes of Steve Navarro. But he had his good side; he just didn't show it often." She felt as if she was making lame excuses again and picked up the papers as a way of ending the subject.

She looked at each receipt and handed them to Logan— Murdock Travel receipt for a round-trip ticket to New York City, itinerary attached; hotel, same city, more than a week earlier. Probably business. She unfolded another one. It was from an apartment complex on 7th South—single bedroom, bath, laundry facilities, access to pool and sauna. It was signed by Steve and marked paid in cash. Two weeks old, a single payment of five hundred dollars for one month.

"What would he want with a second apartment?" Logan asked.

She shrugged. "Maybe he was moving."

Logan picked up the phone and dialed the number under the name at the top of the receipt.

"Ridgewood Apartments."

"Hi. A friend of mine recently passed away. I understand he paid a month's rent for an apartment there, and I wondered if he might have already moved his things in. His family—"

"What's his name?" the voice asked dryly.

"Steve Navarro."

A pause. "Nope. No Navarro."

"But I have a receipt, dated . . . August 1."

"Does it have a number?" The voice was half irritated.

Logan looked it over. "Yes. 410."

"Just a minute." A long time passed, and Logan could hear the shuffle of papers in the background. "Yeah, I found it. I remember now. This Navarro guy isn't living there. It's another guy. Navarro just rented the place for him."

"Do you have a name?"

Silence. Then the voice came again. "What's going on? Why all the questions?"

"This is Captain Logan of the Park City police. Mr. Navarro is involved in an attempted kidnapping. Possibly you've seen the write-ups in the paper."

"Don't read the paper. Read books."

Logan couldn't help but wonder on what level. "He had an accomplice—a man by the name of William Thompson."

"Don't know no Thompson. Navarro's name is on the documents, but I know he never lived in the place. This other guy . . . I never knew his name. A very private guy. Never had any guests that I knew of, except Navarro. Minded his own business."

"Have you seen him in the past twenty-four hours?" Logan asked.

"Now that you mention it, no, but his apartment isn't by mine."

"All right. I'm going to come over. If no one is there I'll want you to let me in."

"Can't. Not without a warrant."

"You can if the police think the man may be involved in a murder. I'll be there in about fifteen minutes. I'll expect you to be available." Logan hung up, waited a second, picked up the receiver, and dialed a second number.

"Federal Bureau of Investigation, Salt Lake Office."

"Give me Carnahan. This is Captain Logan, Park City Police. It's an emergency."

A short wait.

"Logan. What's up?"

"I think we may have found our friend's hiding place." He gave Carnahan the address.

"It'll take me about twenty minutes," Carnahan said.

"We'll meet you there. Make arrangements for forensics, will you?"

"You'll need a search warrant, Logan."

"Probable cause, Carny. Besides, Thompson's dead. He won't sue."

"But if it's the wrong guy . . . "

"Then I'll apologize. You'd better get moving. I want that place gone over with a fine tooth comb. And stop worrying—it's Thompson's." He hung up. They finally had a break.

———————

Logan parked several spaces away from apartment 2D. The parking area was empty except for a young man and his apparent girlfriend who were washing a blue Geo. Logan checked the time on the digital dash clock. It had been twenty-five minutes and still no sign of Carnahan. But then, he was known for being less than punctual.

"Wait here," Logan told Claire. He got out, walked over to the two young people, and showed them his ID.

"Have you seen the guy in 2D today?"

They shook their heads. "Naw," the boy said. "Haven't seen him for several days."

"Do you know what he was driving the last time you saw him?"

They glanced at each other. The girl answered. "It was red, but I don't know what kind."

"Do you see the car here now?"

The boy and his girlfriend both shook their heads. Logan thanked them and went back to the car. He opened the passenger door and pushed the button on the jockey box, then removed his revolver and shoved it into his belt under his sport jacket.

Two cars pulled into the parking lot at the far end and pulled up next to Logan. Carnahan got out of the first and approached.

"Anything?"

Logan shook his head. "You and I go. Have your men get those kids out of sight, just in case I'm wrong about someone else being around."

Carnahan gave the orders and distributed the rest of his men around the complex.

"Claire, stay put." Logan closed the door.

Logan loosened his tie, then he and Carnahan went to the manager's place, retrieved the keys, and headed for 2D.

They removed their revolvers and took position on each side of the door. Logan tried the knob. Locked. He knocked. No response. He knocked again. "Police. Open up." Nothing.

Logan used the key and turned the lock. Opening the door, he shoved it aside and peered around the edge of the frame. It was dark with the drapes closed, but his eyes quickly adjusted. No one inside. He stepped in as Carnahan followed, revolvers ready, checking each room. A closet with half a dozen hangers filled with clothes. A couple of drawers full of clothes in the four-drawer dresser. Shaving gear in the bathroom. Groceries in the kitchen that made Logan think the guy must have been a gourmet cook. A half-eaten orange sat on the counter, collecting mold.

They came together in the living area and put their guns away. Carnahan went to the door and gave the okay while Logan started a more thorough search.

Under the bed he found a metal suitcase. Using his handkerchief, he withdrew the case and put it on the bed.

"Carnahan," he said. The agent joined him.

Logan flipped the latches. Inside he found the pieces for a

sniper's rifle and two boxes of shells. One box contained the
ammo for the rifle; the other was half full of hand-loaded .22 hollow points. The pistol itself was missing from its slot in the
molded foam of the case's interior.

"Eureka," Carnahan said. "The missing gun is probably the
one you turned over to me at the bank."

Logan agreed. As he closed it, Claire appeared at the bedroom door, her face full of question.

"You should have stayed in the car, Claire," he said firmly.

She didn't answer, and he could see saying anything else was
a waste of time. If Claire was anything, it was independent.
Carnahan only shrugged, lifted the case from the bed, and took it
into the kitchen.

"This is our guy," Logan told Claire.

"What's in the case?"

He told her. Claire sat on the bed and watched him, appreci-
ating his concentration and expertise as he continued searching.
"You're good at this."

He flipped the switch on a new answering machine by the
bed, rewinding the tape, then pushing play.

"It's Thursday morning at eight, Mr. Randolph. This is John
at Hertz Auto Lease. The Honda has been delivered to the ZCMI
parking garage, level two, the first slot nearest the door into the
store, as you requested yesterday. It's maroon. The keys are in the
magnetic box under the front fender, driver's side. You said you
would drop it off at the airport. If that is no longer your plan,
please let me know. Thanks." The machine gave the date and
time, then went to the next message—nothing but a few seconds'
time and another beep, then the time again.

Carnahan stepped back into the room. "What was that?"

Logan ignored him.

"Thompson, now Randolph, rents a car for today, but he did it
yesterday, the day he was killed. Why?"

There were half a dozen more pauses with beeps on the
machine, indicating that others had called but had left no message. Finally a second voice came through. It was accented, male,
and brief. "Your plans for delivery are acceptable. Ticket under

your name at Asian destination per your request. Someone will meet you. Wear those ridiculous snakeskin boots." The machine gave the date and time, then clicked off.

"Just an hour ago," Claire said.

"Did you recognize the accent?"

Claire smiled. "It sounded Russian."

Logan nodded. "That's my guess."

"What is going on?" Carnahan asked.

They ignored him. "Do you think the delivery was the envelope from the safety deposit box?" Claire asked.

Logan nodded. "The timing fits. Thompson must have called in a plan before going to the bank. My guess is the other beeps represent attempts by this same caller to talk to Thompson personally. He finally left the message. Not very professional. But then, the people who hire professionals usually aren't."

He stepped to the closet and did a search of the clothing. They hadn't found any indication of any identity for a Randolph. He found the wallet in a brown tweed sport coat. Inside were several credit cards, a calling card from AT&T, several hundred dollars in cash, a driver's license, and a picture of a woman with a baby. Logan couldn't help but wonder if it was Thompson's/Randolph's wife and child. He turned to Carnahan and handed him the wallet.

"Check out everything in it, Carny. The calling card should give us something. This guy is the man we're after."

Carnahan thumbed through the stuff as he left the room.

"From the sound of the messages on the machine, Thompson was planning on leaving town today," Claire said to Logan.

"Yeah," Logan said as he picked up the phone book. He turned to the Yellow Pages under airlines and started dialing. Ten minutes later he had what he wanted and hung up, a big grin across his face.

Carnahan had turned the items over to one of his men and returned, closing the door to the room. He had an envelope in his hand. Logan didn't notice.

"I think we finally have our break, Claire. Randolph has tickets aboard Delta. The first leg takes him to Istanbul, Turkey, via

Cincinnati and Frankfurt, Germany. He returns on the second leg
two days later, from Istanbul back through Cincinnati with a final
destination of Los Angeles International. Both tickets are paid in
full with American Express. The flight is for today at 3:00 P.M."
He paused, thinking. "He finishes business here, closes down this
apartment, drives to the parking garage at ZCMI, and switches
cars and identities. Leaving all vestige of William Thompson
behind, he becomes Randolph, drives to the airport, and catches
his flight to Istanbul."

"To deliver the package."

Logan nodded. "In Istanbul, according to the message on the
machine, he has tickets waiting for him."

"Where to?"

"If the man who left the message is Russian, it has to be
somewhere in the former Soviet Union. Thompson is met there
and delivers the package."

"Then he returns to Istanbul in time for his flight back to
L.A.," Claire said.

Logan nodded, glancing at his watch. "Too late to catch
Thompson's flight, but I still think he should keep his appointment."

Carnahan spoke up. "Before you make a rash decision, I think
you should take a look at these." He handed Logan the envelope.

Logan removed the contents and thumbed through them, a
quizzical look on his face.

"They're Charles Barrett's military records. Denton Harker
sent them and several other things by special courier. That's the
reason I was late getting here—I was right in the middle of a
briefing over the hotline. It was directly from Harker in
Washington." He turned to Claire. "What do you know about
your father's military years?"

Claire had never tried to put it into words before, and now
that she was being asked, she realized she didn't know very much.

Carnahan saw the empty look and smiled. "Don't worry, neither does the United States government." He pointed at the papers
Logan was holding. "The file includes a lot about your father.

Harker says it will make interesting reading. Just one catch—
everything before 1953 is made up."

Claire's mouth fell open. "What?"

"Your father is what we call a "deep cover." For some reason,
he was given a new identity in 1953 and became Charles Barrett.
We don't know who he was before that. He did such a job for
Charles that even we can't find him!" He smiled.

"Who did a job for Charles?" Logan asked.

Carnahan smiled. "Denton Harker got hold of the files
belonging to Arthur Hainey when he was one of the top guns in
the early development of the CIA. Your father was created by his
department in 1953 as a cover for one of their agents who needed
to disappear."

"Then Barrett was an agent during the war?"

"Probably with OSS. We have no record of him during that
time, but apparently Hainey knew exactly who he was. There
were probably others who knew him as well, but they wouldn't
be involved in the change of identity. That was all Hainey's
doing."

"Then Alex may have known!" Claire said.

"Yes. Harker says Hainey wouldn't have told him if your
father were well enough to do it himself, but under the conditions
I'd say Alex knows."

"What is Harker's theory about the reason for killing
Hainey?"

"Same as yours, Logan. Hainey was killed to cover the kidnapper's tracks and make Alex look like a man fleeing from prosecution." Carnahan smiled.

"The safety deposit box contained information about my
father's former life, didn't it." Claire said. She looked like someone in shock.

Logan sat next to her. "Are you all right?"

She nodded, a wan smile on her face. "This is crazy, Logan.
You can't live with a man and call him Father for as long as I
have, then suddenly discover you didn't know him at all without
having the distinct feeling you are living in a bad dream."

Logan tried to smile. "Are you ready for more?"

She laughed lightly. "Why not? It certainly couldn't get any more ridiculous than this."

"Your father took something valuable out of the war zone in 1944—probably delivered it to Geneva for safekeeping."

"The safety deposit box account at the bank of Geneva that was closed in 1985?"

He nodded. "The envelope in your father's box that Alex saw held information about what that item was, or where it is."

"Then Thompson was sent to put pressure on Father to give it up. That means whoever sent Thompson knew about Father, possibly even knew him during the war years," Claire said.

Logan nodded.

"When Charles could no longer give it to them, they decided the son could," Carnahan said.

"Thompson was watching Alex and Claire. When Alex went to the bank to open the safety deposit box, he followed. Once he knew Alex had something important, Thompson kidnapped him and sent him to the man in charge somewhere in Russia."

"The guy on the answering machine." Claire said.

"We find him, we find Alex." Logan said. "I'm going to replace him. It's our only chance of getting close enough to help Alex."

"You're betting they'll keep him alive, at least until the package arrives," Carnahan said. "A package you never found and can't deliver."

"Therein lies the risk, but the package does exist. Alex knows where. It can still be used as a bargaining tool." He glanced at Claire. "For both Alex and me if I find him but can't get us out."

"You're out of your league, Logan—and your jurisdiction. You'll do nothing but get you both killed," Carnahan said.

Logan glanced at his watch. "By my calculations, whoever has Alex is expecting delivery of that package in the time it takes to make the flight booked by Randolph, alias William Thompson. That flight left fifteen minutes ago, so we're already running behind schedule. If that package doesn't arrive, they'll realize that someone has intercepted Thompson. That will tell them they have no chance at the package. It will also tell them they have only one source to turn to. That source is Alex Barrett, and they will torture him. If he knows what they want to know and he tells them, they will kill him. If he doesn't know and can't tell them, they will kill him trying to get something he doesn't have. Either way Alex is dead." He looked at his watch again. "We're falling further behind by the second."

"I get your message, Logan, but throwing your life away—"

"He's right, Logan," Claire said. "Alex wouldn't want you to try to save him if there was a chance you might both get killed."

"Then give me some help, Carnahan, some backup."

"We can't be involved in affairs of this kind anywhere in the former Soviet Union, Logan. You know that. I can't help you, and neither can Denton Harker. The president would have both our hides for it, and the Republicans, ever mindful of embarrassing our illustrious organization, would have a heyday."

Logan was smiling. "I have another option, Carnahan. And it won't cost you and the American taxpayer a single dime."

Carnahan was afraid to ask.

18

Alex awoke with a start, and the attempt to sit up in the darkness caused his body to tense up with pain. He lay back instantly, gritting his teeth. It was then he realized he was in a bed.

He tried to focus his eyes in the dim light. The room was not the prison from which he had so recently escaped, and it was a far cry from the damp undergrowth he last remembered. It had a window, covered with a blanket so that only a small amount of light entered around the edges. The bed was made double by sliding two singles together. Each mattress was made of thick foam-rubber pads, probably lying across a woven rope mat from the feel of it. He was covered with thick blankets placed inside sheet coverlets.

His pajamas were a few feet away, neatly folded on a chair. Clean and dry. The assailant's borrowed shoes were underneath the same chair, scuffed but clean.

He lifted the covers, grateful to find he still had his garments on, then a little concerned when he realized they were clean.

He had bandages wrapped around his midsection and a type of Band-Aid on the cuts on his arms and face. His whole body gave off a dull ache, but the pain was sharper in his ribs, which were wrapped in cloth bandages. He wondered how many the boxer had broken.

The room was rather large and yet seemed crowded, a bookcase covering one entire wall. It was filled with books whose titles he couldn't read very well in the dim light. Against the opposite wall stood two small wardrobes that looked to be of good workmanship, their tops stacked high with more books. Closer to the window, he could see that the titles were in Russian and Arabic.

To his left, next to the bed, was an end table with a lamp of

1920s vintage and a mechanical alarm clock with a loud tick. It showed a time of 1:00. From the looks of the light coming around the edges of the blanket hung over the window, he knew it must be in the afternoon.

He tried sitting again and was successful this time. Next he moved the heavy covers aside and slid his feet over the edge of the bed, then stood. He took several steps to the window and gingerly moved the blanket to one side. The view took his breath away.

The house stood on the sloping side of a hill that fell quickly down to the sea. Trees clung to the ground, but the slope was so steep that he had a clear view of the deep blue of the water that extended before him as far as his eyes could see. The sky was a cloudless blue, and the midday sun glistened off the surface like a mirror, hurting his eyes. He leaned forward, trying to see to his right and left. Trees near the house prevented him from seeing much, but farther down toward the water he could follow the curving shoreline for some distance. Far enough away that he couldn't make out much detail, a town sat on the seashore and meandered into the steep hills around it. Concrete docks jutted out from the shoreline along a wide road that ran for some distance. Multicolored dots of sunbathers covered the shore like ants, soaking up the midday sun. From this distance it looked like an idyllic tourist town along the coast of the Black Sea.

He noticed a path that led from the house and worked its way down the steep slope toward the water. At its end he could see the outward stretch of a dock. His heart skipped a beat as he thought of the house and dock from which he had run, a painful memory.

He turned back to his pajamas. Sitting on the edge of his bed, he pulled them on, careful about quick movements. His muscles were stiff, tender, and painful. He couldn't raise his arms much higher than his shoulder. He finished by doing up the buttons on the top, noticing that even the tips of his fingers were scraped raw, probably from trying to get into the undergrowth. But all in all, he felt pretty good. At least he was safe.

The door opened behind him, and he glanced over his shoulder. A middle-aged woman of round figure, a scarf tied around her oval face, stood in the doorway. She didn't notice him in the dark and hung up her sweater and scarf as if she had just come in from out of doors.

"Zdravsvetya," he said, glad he had his pajamas on.

She squinted in the darkness, then turned and said something to someone in the next room. A moment later, a man joined her and switched on the light.

"Good, you are awake," the man said in Russian. He stood a little taller than his wife, almost as round but solid, and had a bald pate totally devoid of any hair. He had a homemade pipe in his hand.

"Where am I?" Alex asked in Russian.

The man seemed surprised. "You speak Russian well, but you are not Russian."

"No, I'm American. I figure I'm in the Crimea." He nodded toward the window. "And that's the Black Sea."

"Yes, that is right." He stuck his thumb into the bowl of his pipe and crushed the fire out. Alex thought it must surely have burned a little but then noticed that the man's hands were calloused and rough enough that he probably hadn't even felt the change in temperature. The man gave his wife instructions to put some food on the table, then closed the door when she left.

"You are in my home. The city you see in the distance is Alushta, a resort town."

"How long have I been taking advantage of your hospitality?" Alex asked.

"Since this time yesterday. You had a slight concussion and slept a good deal. Do you remember anything?"

Alex nodded. "I was kidnapped, beaten. I escaped. After that, no. I don't remember anything. How did you find me?"

"My usual walk with Ivan." He smiled. "Ivan is my dog. A Borzoi—Russian wolfhound. You groaned a little, and he found you deep in the underbrush. With some difficulty I removed you and brought you here."

"The place . . . I was near a group of buildings."

"The sanatorium where I do odd jobs when I can." He

motioned with his hand to the left of the house. "It is in that direction, just over the hill."

"Do you have a phone?"

"No, but they have one there." He paused, putting his pipe into his mouth and relighting it.

"May I ask your name?" Alex said as he sat back on the bed.

"Isjet Yazhul. The woman is my wife."

"I thank you for your help."

"You are welcome. You say you were kidnapped?"

Alex nodded.

"Do you know who—"

"Only one of them. A man named Yegor. Big, a former boxer with a very mean punch." He checked his jaw.

"Yes, your body and face tell me so."

"Have you contacted the authorities about me?" Alex asked.

Isjet shook his head gently. "No."

"Why not?"

Isjet ignored the question, making Alex uncomfortable. "Yegor Kamanev. A neighbor. He is doing things his father would have been very ashamed of. But then, many do the same. Our economy is doing very badly, and money is hard to come by," Isjet said. "You wear pajamas and have no identity papers. We did not know what problems you might be having. We weren't sure you would want us to contact the authorities."

Alex smiled. "I appreciate your concern, but I'd like to talk to them as quickly as you can arrange it."

"As you wish. Where did they take you from?"

"From the home of a friend in the United States. Washington, D.C. They may have killed him as well."

"A long way from Crimea," Isjet said. "You must be of great value."

"Who does Yegor work for?"

"Many who wish to hire a bodyguard—mostly our new rich class who come here to vacation but fear their enemies. I hear being a bodyguard is good business these days."

"The new rich class? You mean the mafia?"

"All of them are not mafia, but most. Yes, I believe it is so.

You were hurt badly. Several ribs are broken. Your face was a mass of swelling. Your eyes are black. Not very becoming." He smiled.

"I have to get to a phone."

"All in good time. I will make the arrangements to have you taken to Alushta. It would be better to speak to the authorities in person, I think." He paused. "It is strange that I have heard of no one looking for you."

Alex looked up. "How close are you to Yegor's house?"

"Only a mile through the woods, maybe less."

"And they haven't knocked on your door?"

"Nor anyone else's that I know of."

Alex thought a moment, then shrugged it off. "They may have thought it best to disappear, afraid I might contact the authorities."

"Yes, I suppose it is possible." Yazhul agreed but without conviction. "Still, they may be waiting for you to come out of hiding. It would be wise for us to use caution."

Alex knew Yazhul was right but didn't say so.

"What is your name?" Yazhul asked.

"Alex, Alex Barrett."

"Well, Mr. Barrett, you are very weak, and your injuries are still very bad. You must take things slowly."

"You don't understand. People back home . . . they need to know I'm all right."

"Soon, Mr. Barrett. Another hour or two won't make any difference."

Alex saw that he was getting nowhere and felt too weak to argue. "No, I don't suppose it will."

A quiet knock came at the door. "My wife has prepared food. You must eat." He paused. "And you must trust me, Mr. Barrett."

Alex looked at the large eyes set in the broad face. What choice did he have?

He stood. Isjet reached for and opened the door. Alex left the bedroom to find a table sitting against the wall of a room that served as a kitchen, a large iron cooking stove standing in one corner that also heated the house. Russian bread, fresh vegetables, and borscht sat on the table. He sat down, said a quiet prayer of thanksgiving, and began eating.

"You are Christian?" Yazhul asked.

Alex nodded. "And you are Islamic."

Isjet nodded. "Crimean Tartar. My family was converted to Islam generations ago."

"I heard your people were returning to Crimea but that your reception hasn't been very good."

The woman stood by the table and served the two men. She filled their bowl and plate and buttered bread. When she smiled, she showed a row of half a dozen gold teeth. Alex knew she wouldn't eat until later, but there was another place setting. He decided not to ask.

Isjet frowned. "I will explain something to you, Mr. Barrett."

"Call me Alex, will you? My father is Mr. Barrett. I think."

Isjet gave him a quizzical smile, then let it go. "Before, we were controlled by the Communists; now we are controlled both by Ukraine and Russia."

"But Russians are the majority."

"Yes, and recently the pro-Russian majority decided to have elections and declare Crimea independent from Ukraine. They elected a man by the name of Meshkov as president—a man who wants Crimea to become a Russian protectorate, as do most of the majority."

"The Ukrainians won't allow it." Alex pushed away the thin layer of grease that covered the borscht and spooned a mouthful. It was hot, good. He took another, his appetite picking up.

"No, and that is why they keep a strong military presence here." Isjet took another piece of bread. "Crimea is a strategic land, Alex. The Black Sea gives military and economic strength to both Russia and Ukraine. Much tension builds between these two great powers over the Black Sea Fleet, based only a few kilometers from here at Sevastopol. Although some treaties have been signed to ease tensions, war between Russia and Ukraine could break out over difficulties that may develop here. Many Russians want to use force to take back the fleet and the Crimea. The Ukrainian response is to hold onto their nuclear weapons just in case they need them. And they hang onto Crimea because it gives them access to the sea. We Tartars are caught in the middle, with little to say about how things should be done and no real power to control our destiny." He dipped the bread in his borscht before taking a bite. "Do you know our history, Alex? The history of the Tartars?"

"A little," Alex said. "Descendants of the Mongols known as the Golden Horde ruled the Crimea and much more around the year 1400. When the Horde began losing territory to Russia, you came under the protection of the Ottoman Turks in Istanbul. Then as they were overcome, Catherine the Great annexed the Crimea as part of Russia. Your people lived as a part of her empire until World War II."

"Stalin deported most Tartars from Crimea in 1944. My parents were among them. Fifty percent or nearly two hundred thousand of my people died on their way to the deserts east of here, or in labor camps. But our people never gave up hope, and we continued to have large families and plan for the day when we could return to this land again. Under Gorbachev there began a slow trickle back to these mountains, a trickle that turned into a stream. Now there are nearly three hundred thousand of us again. We have not been well received by the Russian majority, and they discriminate against us and filch the aid from other nations that we are to receive for our settlement here. They have leveled several of our settlements with bulldozers, and some of my people have been killed."

Isjet finished his borscht and drank heavily from a glass before continuing. "We know that the only way the Tartars will ever be safe in Crimea is if it becomes a Tartar state. We work to that end against both Russians and Ukrainians. But we do it diplomatically, at least for now, even though there is an element among us that wants to use violence. Violence I fear. It will destroy our people forever."

Isjet's wife poured her husband a cup of tea. "Would you care for some, Alex?" Isjet asked.

"No, thanks."

The door to his left opened, and a woman entered. She was

taller than Isjet and his wife by several inches, her hair dark, thick, and straight. It was tied at the back in a sort of ponytail with her bangs seeming to head in every direction. Her face was thin with high cheekbones and an aquiline nose. Two pretty eyes, dark enough to be coal, forced a smile at him as did her full lips.

"Zdravsvetya," she said.

"Hello," Alex said in English. She was wearing a Western-style windbreaker over faded jeans, and several of her toes could be seen through the holes in her old pair of tennis shoes. Her figure was slim but well proportioned. Alex guessed her age at late twenties.

"I am Vilinia. Isjet and Lenta are my father and mother," she said in adequate English. Alex noticed the stiff edge to her voice.

"Alex Barrett," he responded.

She seemed to hesitate in the removal of her jacket, then tossed it aside and sat down, eyeing him as she spoke to her father. She put a folded newspaper next to her still-empty plate.

"A mile down the road, at the lane leading to Yegor Kamanev's house, there is a roadblock. I talked to a policeman I know who was there. He came on the bus and checked our passengers very thoroughly."

"For what reason?" Isjet asked.

Vilinia's eyes stayed on Alex, making him quite uncomfortable.

"Two men were found dead down the lane early this morning. Yegor Kamanev was one of them; the other has not yet been identified—at least they are not giving his name."

Isjet and Alex looked at one another, surprise registering on both faces.

"That explains why you haven't heard about them looking for me," Alex said. He turned to Vilinia. "How did they die?"

She kept her eyes on Alex. "They say it is murder, by a foreigner." She stared at Alex. "My friend with the police said that Lazar Kherensky is heading the investigation personally and that he is being very secretive."

"Kherensky!" Isjet sat back.

Alex was confused. "Are you saying I did this?"

"Did you?" Vilinia asked.

Alex didn't answer.

Vilinia tossed the paper beside his plate. He opened it and, although it was printed in Russian, the headlines jumped off the page at him. He quickly reread them, then the story beneath.

"What is this story?" Isjet asked his daughter.

"Alex Barrett is wanted on another matter, Papa. It seems he killed a very important man in the United States."

19

E<small>VEN THOUGH</small> A<small>LEX HAD BEEN TOLD</small> by the interrogator that they had blamed him for Arthur Hainey's murder, he was stunned by the article and could only put it aside slowly. "I told your father—another man was killed when I was kidnapped. They made it look as though I was responsible."

"It isn't often that our small paper carries such news from your country. This man you killed must have been a hero to your people," Vilinia said.

"I didn't kill him."

Isjet picked up the paper and began reading.

"I need to get to a telephone," Alex said.

"Do you know how the phone system works in this country?" Vilinia asked. "All of the calls in a given district must be placed through that district's central exchange. It was set up that way under the old Soviet system, and it hasn't been changed here. Kherensky can use that to his advantage now. He will give instructions for the exchange to monitor all calls carefully, especially those placed by a foreigner or going to a foreign country."

"They can't possibly watch all calls. It is an impossible task."

"We made it a fine art under Communism. It is one of the reasons our phone systems are so archaic. The government refused to update them because they could no longer keep their oppressive thumb on the freedoms of the people."

Alex could remember television documentaries about the early U.S. system where an operator could listen in on calls placed through them. But on this scale?

Isjet lay the paper aside. "She is right. You do not want to take this chance. It is the reason we still have no phone. We do not trust our Russian keepers." He paused. "This is most confusing."

"All I can do is tell you I didn't do it and hope you will help me get safely out of here and back to my country where I can defend myself." He looked into Vilinia's dark eyes. "And I didn't kill your neighbor; he nearly killed me."

"You expect us to believe you are innocent?" Vilinia said.

"Yes! How do you think I got all these bruises?"

"Tell her what you told me," Isjet said. Alex did. She still seemed skeptical. She and her father exchanged looks.

"You make our life very difficult, American," Vilinia said. "My father and Lazar Kherensky are at odds with one another. It is another reason we must be very careful. If you should be found in this house, or if our involvement with you is discovered and proven, Kherensky will use it as an excuse to put my father in prison."

Alex looked at Isjet for an explanation.

Isjet was frowning. "I belong to the Milli Mejlis."

Alex had heard of the Tartar ruling body set up to speak out for Tartar rights. An assembly of officials elected by Crimean Tartars, and those yet to come from lands to which they had been sent by Stalin, the Mejlis represented Tartar attempts to maintain their rights through peaceful means.

"Kherensky and I butted heads over the bulldozing of one of our settlements. I did it in such a way as to protect myself while making sure he knew that if such an event were to happen again he would lose his life. He plots to kill me but would look upon this as a better way."

"Why?"

"He knows that my people would retaliate if any of the Mejlis were found murdered. This way everything is legal, and we could do little but let the law run its course, archaic as it may be."

"You have endangered yourself to save me."

Isjet shrugged. "As your Bible says, a good Samaritan does not cross to the other side of the road. My Koran is in full agreement. Besides, no one could foresee the events that would bring us to this point." He paused. "For the good of everyone, we must get you out of the country as quickly and quietly as we can."

"No, you're out of this," Alex said. "I'll leave now, turn myself in. Kherensky has to let me contact the American consulate, and I can get help from there." Alex got up from the table.

"Your decision is honorable but stupid and very naive." Vilinia's words were almost offensive.

Isjet gave his daughter a glaring look. She ignored it. Alex knew it wasn't the first time and wouldn't be the last. Vilinia was obviously a woman with a strong personality and mind of her own.

"Sit down, American; there is something else you should know."

Alex sat.

"The soldier at the roadblock tells me Kherensky knows you are involved in this. It seems your passport was found in luggage at Yegor's house. He is also aware of the search for you because of Hainey's murder. Lazar Kherensky would kill for a chance like this one—a chance to be in the national and international news as the man who caught such a noted thief and killer. Yet he is keeping things very tight. Does that not surprise you?"

Alex gave her an understanding smile. "He has a better offer."

Her eyebrows lift slightly. It was the closest to a real smile Alex had seen since she walked in the door.

"Kherensky is also known for his willingness to take bribes, especially lucrative ones." She paused. "His actions almost convince me you are telling the truth."

"Almost?"

"We have only your word that you are not a fugitive, that you did not kill this man Hainey. There are still many unanswered questions, but for now your guilt or innocence is not important to me. You endanger us, especially my father, and my first concern is for his safety. If we do not help you, we are very bad off."

She turned to her father. "Kherensky will search these hills carefully, and time is against us. I took the liberty of sending for Tazbir. His neighbor was on the bus with me."

She looked at her watch. "He should be here soon."

Alex felt dizzy, out of control, tired, confused, and half a dozen other things all at once.

"If you were kidnapped, what was the reason?" The question brought Alex out of his thoughts. "You are rich?"

"It isn't about money. They want information they think I have." He paused, wondering how much he should say. He was going to need their friendship, their trust. He had better be completely up front. He told them about the interrogation, the envelope, and what had happened in Salt Lake City.

"Do you believe your father has what they want?" Isjet asked. Alex nodded.

"And you believe you can find out what it is, that you have enough information to do so?" Vilinia's questions were warming up a little.

"Yes, given enough time."

"We will give you your chance very soon, American," Vilinia said.

Alex was about to ask her how when the door opened and a man entered the room. He was dark in complexion, had a heavy moustache and beard, and was tall, thin, and wiry. Alex guessed his age at about thirty.

Vilinia stood and hugged him.

"This is Tazbir. He will help us get you away from here."

Tazbir looked at Alex in such a way as to make him feel like nothing more than a boil that needed lancing.

"What have you found out? What are they doing, Tazbir?" Isjet asked.

"A reward has been offered for information about him, Isjet— one thousand American dollars. Many people can use that kind of money and are already coming to search the hills. I saw several small groups congregating near the main road and at the sanatorium."

"What are they being told?" Isjet asked.

"Only that they are looking for a stranger, an Englander, the man who murdered Yegor and his friend. Also that this man killed others and is very dangerous—that he is a crazy man. Even the description is not a very good one."

"Have they made any effort to connect Kamanev's killer to this?" Isjet handed Tazbir the paper. Tazbir quickly scanned the story.

"None."

Isjet turned to Alex. "Then Kherensky is keeping your true identity a secret. It is as we thought—he is being paid by others, and if he finds you he will give you to them," Isjet said. He seemed relieved, even though the news gave Alex heartburn.

Tazbir spoke to Alex. "Your innocence or guilt is of no consequence to me. You endanger Isjet and Vilinia now, and you must go from the country as soon as we can arrange transport to Istanbul. For now we must get you away from here."

"Where can he go? It may be several days before we complete arrangements to get him to Turkey," Vilinia said.

"We will take him to Alushta, to the children's camp that my aunt runs," Tazbir said. "I can protect him there."

"How do we move him, Tazbir?" Vilinia asked. "In broad daylight—people searching the woods and the police watching the roads."

"There is only the sea," Tazbir said. "We move him by boat."

"You have fuel, Papa?" Vilinia asked. "The boat can be used?"

"Yes, enough fuel, and I just finished overhauling the motor yesterday. It is getting him from here to the dock unseen that concerns me. If it were dark—"

"We cannot wait," Tazbir said anxiously. "They could come to the house at any time. If they find him here, Kherensky will destroy your house and put you in prison. You know how they feel about what you are doing."

Isjet's frown deepened. He saw things now, things he had not seen when he had decided to bring Alex into his house. But the look quickly disappeared. Allah would help them.

"Hook the horse to the wagon, Vilinia. We will have to take him down the road to the sea. It is longer, but we have no choice. Make a place for him to lie using blocks and planks, then cover them with the fish nets from the shed and the bait I have been saving. It is in the tank."

Vilinia looked at Alex with a smile that said *poor fool* all through it, making Alex wonder what he was in for.

"Tazbir, check the road to the sea. Make sure it is clear enough for us to take this chance."

Tazbir and Vilinia left.

"Tazbir is a quiet one," Alex said.

"Moody."

"He has many problems, that one. His brother committed suicide a month ago, and he left a wife and four children without any way to support themselves. Tazbir is doing his best to keep them from starving, along with helping Marina financially at the children's sanatorium." He shrugged. "He works his fingers to the bone."

"A thousand dollars would make a difference."

"And he has probably considered it," Isjet said. "But he knows that our people would disown him if he were to take money from Lazar Kherensky." He stood, looking through the window as Tazbir walked down the path.

Alex wondered if the fear of sanction would be enough. Isjet seemed to shrug off the worry he had about his friend and went into the other room. When he returned, he had Yegor's stolen shoes, a shirt, and a pair of pants. "The shirt is a bit big but clean and warm. The pants belong to my son; you are about the same size."

"You have a son?"

"No, he is dead. May Allah take his soul. Remove the pajamas and dress in these. My wife will burn what you leave behind in the cooking stove." Alex could see that his host didn't want to talk about the past and let it alone. He had enough to do anyway as he struggled with the change. He finally finished getting into the cotton pants, wool shirt, and wool socks; then Isjet helped him slip on the shoes.

Tazbir returned. To Alex he seemed a bit agitated and out of breath. "No one on the lower road. I think we can make it all right."

"Good," Isjet said.

Tazbir tossed Alex a knit cap. "Pull it down to your eyebrows."

Isjet smiled. "Yes, it changes you significantly, but you still look very ill. Possibly we should wait a day."

Tazbir spoke. "No! It is too dangerous. They are sure to come here. We must move him now."

Alex agreed. "He's right. Let's get moving."

Vilinia came in, smiled, then frowned at Alex's appearance. "You look very pale, American, and very funny at the same time."

"Thanks a million."

She handed him a set of plastic rain gear. "You will need these." She smiled.

Alex shrugged, then put them on as Tazbir checked the roads again. When Alex was ready, Vilinia opened the door and walked quickly to the back of the wagon outside. She lowered the back gate.

Alex went quickly to her side as Tazbir pointed and told him to get inside.

Alex couldn't believe the smell. The heavy netting was covered by a thick layer of rancid fish bait. Tazbir pushed him slightly.

"Now! We will be seen."

Alex held his breath and with painful difficulty slid into the small pocket beneath the nets Vilinia had made with boards and yellow rakushkas, rough sandstone bricks used in building homes. They covered the openings with the net and bait, then closed the tailgate. Alex immediately believed he would die of suffocation, the stench so strong in his nostrils he wanted to choke. He wiggled forward and placed his nose and mouth near a thin crack in the boards that formed the wagon's front, trying to get enough fresh air to survive. Through the slit he saw the rump of the horse, then the legs of Isjet and Tazbir as they climbed aboard and drove the old nag forward.

The road immediately steepened, forcing his head against the planks. The jostling of the wagon on the rough, rutted road made his ribs throb and his whole body break out in a sweat as he struggled with the pain.

At the moment he thought he must scream, the wagon came to a halt. He heard voices and squinted through the slit between boards. Two men, both middle aged, both armed with what looked to Alex like World War II vintage rifles, stood by the side of the horse and were talking to Isjet. Alex held his breath as they discussed the reward they hoped to retrieve by finding the murderer the police were looking for.

"Murder? Who did he murder?" Isjet questioned innocently.

"This English is a bad one. He killed a woman and child in Sevastopol and escaped from the police there. It is thought that he caught a ride with Yegor and his friend and must have tried to steal their truck. He is in these hills somewhere. It is only a matter of time until he is found."

Murder was bad enough, but of a woman and child? Alex understood Kherensky a little better. He was not only greedy but also demented. Alex listened. From the tone in the voices, he knew the two would give him a good beating before turning him over to Kherensky. The police chief's disinformation was working, and Alex wondered how many innocent people would be pummeled before the day was over.

"Going fishing, eh, Yazhul? I didn't know Tartars could fish—especially those from the desert."

Isjet ignored the dig, preferring to answer the question and get moving. "Soon. We have to prepare the nets first."

"And this one, who is he?" The second man said in a challenging tone.

"He works for me sometimes."

"You are not Russian either, are you?" the second man said.

Tazbir said nothing, but even Alex could feel the tension in the man's body.

"You should hire Russians, Yazhul." The first said. "They are better workers and might teach you desert people something about fishing." The laugh that followed was loud and boisterous. Alex thought the remark must have come right out of the Deep South—a conversation between bigoted whites, a black man, and his black employee. But then, racial discrimination wasn't geographical.

Getting no response to their question but a whip to Isjet's nag, the two started up the road, still mumbling about Tartars and pigs. Alex could feel the air let out of everyone's lungs, including his own, as they distanced themselves from the two bounty hunters. Soon they arrived at the bottom of the hill, next to Isjet's boat.

After walking up the narrow road and making sure they hadn't been followed, Tazbir opened the tailgate. Isjet pulled a sweating Alex Barrett from his hiding place and was helping him move to the boat when the two men came from the trees and underbrush to their left.

Alex found himself looking at the old rifles from a different angle this time—straight down the barrels.

Tazbir felt the steel of the gun dig deep into his flesh as the man prodded him with it, moving them back up the road from which they had just come. He glanced over his shoulder at Isjet and the American and could see that Barrett was struggling, in a lot of pain, and would be of little help if an opportunity to overpower these two snakes should come. And a time must come. For Tazbir there was too much to lose.

"You're a fool, Yazhul," the captor nearest Isjet said. "You cannot defy Lazar Kherensky and get away with it. We will ruin you for it! You Tartars think you are a law unto yourselves. Well, you're not, and this will teach you! They will throw you in prison and let you rot!"

"Your home will make a nice place for my son's family," the second man said.

The first laughed. "And we pick up a thousand American dollars at the same time. You will make us rich, Tartar, you and this murdering Englander you try to hide from the police!" The voice was cold and malicious.

"I would do it for five American dollars, Yazhul," the other man said, spitting in the road. "Seeing you in prison is all the reward I need. You, and all like you, must be driven from our land!" He jabbed the gun into Tazbir's back, making him wince with pain. "And you! Shooting is too good for both of you!" He

spit, the wad covering Tazbir's boots. It was all the mustachioed
Tartar could do to keep himself in control, but he knew that the
man had his finger on the trigger, waiting for him to react so that
he could put a hole through him. When the Russian saw that
Tazbir wasn't going to respond, he cursed and prodded him
harder with the rifle. Tazbir felt the pain and jumped a little,
bringing a laugh to his captor.

They were nearing a fork in the road. One path led to Isjet's
house, the other to the sanatorium. Suddenly Alex slumped to the
ground, moaning in pain, his eyes clenched shut. His muscles
seemed to relax, and the air went out of his lungs. Then he fell
silent.

"Get him up, Yazhul." The man closest to Alex said it in
anger, his gun aimed at Isjet's midsection. Isjet went to Alex and
knelt down, hesitating, then standing. "He's dead. His wound . . .
it was very serious. He must have been bleeding internally."

The man stepped forward to get a closer look. The second
prodded Tazbir back toward them, his face contorted with anger.

"He's playing games with us, Boris! Stick him with that gun
and get him moving!"

The one called Boris took another step, jamming the rifle into
Alex's arm. Both men were surprised when the rifle made its
mark but Alex didn't move. They came closer, their eyes wide,
searching for some kind of life.

It was then that Boris felt the sharp blow to the back of his
head that drove him to his knees, then flat on his face as the lights
went out. A second later his partner, who had barely lifted his gun
against the onslaught coming from behind, lay beside him. Vilinia
stood over them, the heavy piece of Crimean pine dangling from
her hand. She poked her last victim but received no response. "I
think I killed him," she said, her eyes wide.

Isjet stooped down. "No, you just knocked him very cold."

"The other?"

Isjet checked him as well. "Nasty tempered, this one.
Deserved to have his head split open. But, still alive."

She seemed relieved.

Alex rolled over and got slowly to his feet, rubbing the spot where Boris had poked him. He smiled at Vilinia. "I saw you in the trees and knew you'd need a diversion." Vilinia smiled back appreciatively.

"You die well, American," Tazbir said. "Let's get moving before it becomes more than play."

Tazbir took the rifles, emptied them, then tossed bullets and weapons into the thick underbrush. Isjet hoisted one of the men over a shoulder. Tazbir did the same with the other one, and they headed back to the boat. Alex was surprised at the older man's strength.

Isjet spoke to his daughter. "How did you know we were in trouble?"

"Mother made some food. I was bringing it to you, hoping I would catch up before you left. I took the steep trail and nearly bumped into them working their way down. When I saw them capture you, I followed, hoping for a chance to help but afraid I wasn't going to get one. Then the American—how do you say in English . . ." She glanced at Alex.

Alex smiled. "Took a dive."

"Yes, took a dive. It was my chance." She looked at the man over her father's shoulder. "Why do we take them with us?"

"We must keep them out of trouble until we can get the American away from here. After that, it is their word against ours," Tazbir said a little impatiently.

Isjet sighed. "I have no doubt which of us the police will believe my friend, but you are right. We must take them with us. Once the American is gone, the police will have no proof."

"I have seen both these men at the rallies against our building homes and fighting for our rights. The one will cause us all the trouble he can," Tazbir said, the hate and disgust evident in his voice.

They were soon at the boat and on their way. Alex felt tired and a bit chilled. He sat on the floor of the hold and put his head on his knees. Something nudged him, and he looked up. Vilinia had a bottle of water in her hand. "Drink. You will need liquids. Your body overheats as it tries to heal itself."

He took the bottle and drank. She handed him a blanket, then started up the ladder out of the hold. She stopped and looked back at him. "I believe you, Alex Barrett. I am not sure all of the reasons why, but I will help you all I can."

As the boat moved along the shore in the direction of Alushta, a man who had been standing near the dock belonging to Yegor Kamanev lowered a set of binoculars from his eyes. He had watched the boarding carefully, relieved that Tazbir had found a way to extricate himself from the two overzealous locals looking to get rich.

The boat now safely at sea, Lazar Kherensky walked back up the hill toward Yegor's house. Tazbir had approached him only briefly in the woods, and they had struck a deal. But the Tartar wanted more than just money, as did Kherensky, and it would take a little time to bring their plan to fruition.

What had been needed immediately was time for Tazbir to spirit the American away for safekeeping, and Kherensky had given instructions to move the search west, away from Yazhul's house. But apparently not everyone had gotten the message, and it had nearly cost them.

Not that Kherensky cared that much. He would still have the money he was to be paid for the return of the American, and he would have Yazhul to bring to trial. But he wanted more. Why settle for little when a lot was available with only a bit more effort? Working with Tazbir would get it all.

He walked around to the front of the house and gave orders to his second in command before climbing into his car and driving up the lane. One had to keep up appearances.

It had begun when he had discovered who the second victim was and reported his gruesome knowledge to the victim's brother, Sergei Davidov, in Kiev. Sergei had then told him about the American and that he must be recaptured quickly, without knowledge of his identity being given to the press. Kherensky didn't ask questions after Davidov promised him twenty thousand American dollars and asked if Kherensky thought he could find the man by the end of the day. He had worked with Davidov and his family long enough to know that successful completion of a request could mean additional American dollars. He had set to his task with enthusiasm.

But things had not gone well—until Tazbir had appeared and changed the direction of fate.

Kherensky knew that Tazbir was power hungry, and poor, as yet unmarried and with no children, with a lot of demand on him by others. In the oppressed Tartar community, it was a dangerous combination, one that had finally produced a traitor.

Kherensky understood Tazbir's position. The Tartar saw getting rid of the American as profitable, while getting rid of Yazhul would put him in position to move up in the Mejlis where he felt he belonged, where he could attain more prominence and power—at least if he could do it discreetly. His new position in the Tartar community would give him a chance to marry well and secure his future. In his mind, all it would take was this one betrayal.

Kherensky had other plans for him.

Yes, he wanted the American and would gain a good profit from him. A part of that profit, a few thousand dollars, would go to pay Tazbir for his betrayal of Yazhul. He would then have Yazhul thrown in prison and make an example of him that the Tartars would not soon forget, nor be able to do anything about. But, more important to Kherensky, Tazbir would be his, a spy within the Tartar camp who would bring him a good deal of information on a segment of the Crimean population that needed close scrutiny. It was a great opportunity, one he would relish.

Kherensky had his driver turn onto the highway and head east. There were several things to be done now. Davidov would have arrived from Kiev, and he must meet with him. A good deal more money could be gained from this venture, but he must secure it quickly. Then he must meet with Tazbir and arrange for the capture of Yazhul and the American. Indeed, there was much to do.

Kherensky didn't know why Davidov and his brother had brought the American here, but it didn't matter. Opportunity had strange ways of presenting itself in his newborn country and, if Lazar Kherensky was anything, he was an opportunist.

He looked at the sea to his right. Clouds were gathering, but they were moving east as well. It was going to be a beautiful day for the tourists along the beaches.

And a profitable one for him.

20

THE LEAR CHARTER WAS IMPRESSIVE and not of the ordinary variety. The seats were wide, with plenty of leg room, and there was a small galley in the corner, near a door that led to a small bedroom and dressing area. The bathroom was much larger than those found on public airline jets, and it included a large shower. They had found blankets and pillows in the overhead storage compartments, and each curled up, Logan in the chair and Claire in the bedroom, to get what sleep they could. They both dozed until the copilot told them they were about an hour away from refueling in Paris. Claire had taken the first shower; then Logan had taken his turn and added a shave. Now the Lear was beginning its descent, and Logan was staring out the window at a city he had never seen but had always wanted to, wishing it wasn't a business trip.

He lifted his watch to check the time—9:00 A.M.

"It's three in the afternoon here," Claire said. "As soon as we land, I'm going to fix something to eat. Do you want anything?"

He was hungry, but he wasn't sure for what. "I don't know whether to want a sandwich or eggs and sausage."

"Eggs and sausage sounds good, but we don't have any. There are some bagels, cream cheese, orange juice, cinnamon rolls, milk, and premade sandwiches with chips."

"Juice, maybe some bagels."

"We have orange, grape, and tomato."

"Grape, thanks." He stood, folding the blanket he had used during the night while he watched out the small window. The plane came to a stop in front of a private terminal. A fuel truck moved next to them, and a man climbed onto the wing and fiddled with something until it lifted. He shoved the fuel hose inside.

The door at the front opened, and the pilot came in, or the copilot, Logan wasn't sure which. "About thirty minutes and we'll be back in the air. Need anything from the terminal, Miss Barrett?"

Claire looked at Logan, who shook his head and shrugged. "Souvenirs for our friends. Postcards, that sort of thing." There was a teasing tone in his voice. "French pastries would be nice. Just as well get some of the atmosphere, don't you think?"

Claire gave him an "I don't believe you" look.

"Just kidding," Logan said.

"No, nothing," Claire told the pilot.

"I suppose this thing has a phone I can use to call back to the States?" Logan questioned.

The pilot pointed at a box on the wall between the galley and the passenger areas. "Instructions are clearly printed on the inside of the door."

"How long before we get to Athens?" Claire asked.

"Four hours, a little more. If it's all right, Miss Barrett, the other pilot and I are going to stretch our legs and grab a bite to eat in the terminal." She smiled her assent, and he closed the door behind him.

"The lifestyles of the rich and famous," Logan said.

"You're the one who needed fast transportation, remember? Next to an Air Force F-16 or something, this is one of the few planes that can get you to Istanbul before Thompson's flight shows up."

"An expensive part of pulling off this little shindig. It's nice to have rich friends, though. You're the only one I know who can charter an airliner on a Visa card."

"It's not an airliner." She smiled, handing him a grape juice.

"True. The stewardess with this outfit is much better looking."

"Thank you." She took a sip.

Their eyes met, and he marveled at how green Claire's were. His arm was on the small of her back drawing her to him before he could stop himself. Their lips came together, and she pulled him close, one hand around his waist, the other still holding her juice. Her touch made his hair tingle and his heart race, the kiss melting him into a tall pile of soft putty. He pulled away a little, but her arms told him otherwise, prolonging the kiss and making him weak in the knees.

Slowly they parted. He looked into those green eyes again, glad he had finally worked up the guts to do what he'd wanted to do for several days now.

"You're full of surprises, Logan," she said with a pleasant look.

He kissed her again, more gently, sharing with her what he was feeling inside. She put her head on his shoulder and held him close. It had been a long time since he had felt so good. It was then he noticed he had dropped his juice. It had splattered on the couch, the thick rug, and his pant leg.

He looked down at it with a red blush running up through his neck into his face. What a klutz he'd been. "There goes your cleaning deposit," he said to her.

She laughed lightly, kissed him, then went to the sink for a wet cloth.

"Sit," she said. He did, and she tried removing the stain from his pants. It wasn't going to happen.

"I don't suppose this flying hotel has a washer and dryer," Logan said.

She sat in the chair next to him. "It costs extra."

"Umm. Any recommendations?"

"I'll go inside the terminal and buy you something while you try cleaning up your mess. Sizes?"

He told her.

She knelt beside him on the couch and put her arms around his neck, then kissed him lightly again, making him tingle all over. "I'll change and be back in a few minutes." She got up and went into the bedroom. She left as he was filling a pan with soap and water. A feeble attempt at getting grape juice out of the carpet followed.

After doing the best he could, he dumped his cleaning water

into the sink. Drying off his hands, he went to the phone. Following the instructions, he dialed and waited while the connections were made. Carnahan answered on his private line.

"This is Logan. Anything new?"

"Where are you?"

"Paris. We're refueling. Did Gerondi make connections to Athens all right?"

"Yeah. He'll be there." A rustling of papers. "A couple of things you should know. We found Thompson/Randolph has a third identity—his real one. His name is Henderson, Roy William. He dropped out of sight about fifteen years ago. Not much in the way of a life before that—graduated from high school, served a couple of years in the military, disappeared."

"Anything on his other identity—Randolph?"

"He has a wife and kid in L.A."

"What about the calling card?"

"I thought you'd never ask. A dozen calls to Ukraine. Two numbers. One in Kiev, one in Yalta, on the Black Sea."

Logan sat up. "Any names?"

"The Kiev number belongs to an assistant minister in the government. I called and got a direct line into his office—a guy by the name of Davidov. And get this, he's the guy who's been dealing directly with Alex Barrett on a big computer deal. I called Barrett's boss, and he says the whole thing fell through, that some kind of deal was going on under the table between Davidov and Dick Samson, the president of one of the companies bidding for the business. You don't suppose this could be a vendetta do you?"

"No, I don't. More like Davidov set the whole thing up to get next to the Barretts. Get me what you can on him, will you?"

"Gerondi has his people working on it. They're better situated, and seeing as how you two are going to be seeing a lot of each other over the next few days, I thought Gerondi should handle it."

"Yeah, good idea. What about the number in Yalta?"

"I called, but there isn't any answer. We're working on it. The Ukrainian authorities aren't real cooperative, and even when they do cooperate, it takes forever to get anything done. The Soviet regime may be out of style, but the bureaucracy is still in place."

"Anything else?"

"I still don't like this, Logan. Neither does Denton, even with Gerondi along. You're a fish out of water."

"Your confidence in my considerable talents is overwhelming. Thanks."

"You're welcome. And what about Ms. Barrett. She shouldn't . . . "

"She gets off before we get to Istanbul. I'll call you before leaving Turkey." He paused. "If I come back in a pine box, I want you to speak at the funeral. And tell Harker I expect him to be there."

"Nice way to end a conversation, Logan."

They hung up. Logan thought things over for a minute before beginning a raid on the refrigerator, a sudden appetite flaring up.

When Claire returned, he had the table set for both of them with warmed bagels, more juice, and sliced fruit in a bowl. He took the package she offered him, pulled out the receipt for 472 francs, then his wallet. "How much is that in American dollars?"

"Ninety-five." She smiled.

He removed a hundred-dollar bill and handed it to her.

"Keep the change." The smile was a bit pained. He could have bought a pair at Penney's for forty. "The service is worth something."

"The usual tip is fifteen percent. You owe me ten bucks."

She put the five-dollar bill into her pants pocket.

He was already at the bedroom door. "I made breakfast. Call it even." He closed the door behind him, quickly changed into the new pants, pulled off the tags, and was pleased with the good fit. Carrying his shoes in his hand, he joined her at the small table. He felt famished but told her about the pertinent parts of the conversation with Carnahan first.

"Davidov came to the house!" Claire said. "It was after that Father began acting upset."

"It sounds like we've found our man." He smiled. He poured

juice and started on his first bagel. Claire was thinking, her brow wrinkled.

"This is stupid, you know," she said.

She was glaring at him. He looked at the bagel, then back at her.

"Not the bagel, Logan—this posing as William Thompson. If we know it's Davidov . . . "

He sat back, placing the bagel on his plate. "We don't *know* it is, and more important, we don't know where he's holding Alex if it is. Do you think we can just walk into his office and he'll hand over your brother, apologizing for the inconvenience? Nothing's changed, Claire. This is still the only way."

He picked up the bagel and nibbled at it, his appetite waning. He smiled. "Besides, no one ever accused my mother of raising smart kids."

She was still frowning. "What happened a while ago . . . between us . . . it complicates things," she said.

He put the bagel aside. "I'll be all right, Claire. I know what I'm doing, and I won't take any unnecessary chances."

"You will, I know it! It's just the way you are! I saw what you did when Thompson came into the bank, Logan! You're a cop, a good cop, willing to put his life on the line! It'll get you killed! You can't just waltz into a foreign country, having no clue about the people you're dealing with, unfamiliar with the language, no one there to help you—"

"I'm in love with you," Logan said.

Claire was visibly jolted. "What?"

"You heard me, Claire. I have a lot of reason to live, and I intend to take care of myself. And I'm not just waltzing in there without help."

Claire was in shock, speechless, and didn't even hear the last part.

"But I also have a problem," Logan went on.

Speechless turned to confused, then exasperated.

Leaning forward, he took her hand, squeezing it gently. It made him tingle. Just looking into her eyes made him feel good. He started sweating a little, started getting nervous. He had never had anything like this happen before. Usually it took him months to rake up the courage to kiss a woman he'd dated dozens of times. For him this was crazy behavior. But it it felt right. He'd spent the whole night tossing and turning, figuring that out. Now he just had to say it—and that was even harder.

"I am not sure I'm worth having. I'm a cop, I have bad habits. I watch too much television, especially on big sports days, and my feet smell. I hate yard work and pizza, and I never go to concerts where they play nothing but classical music. I've never been a father, and with a daughter like yours that worries me. I might ruin her. And you! You've got a great figure and a beautiful face, and I'm scared you won't want to be seen with this boxer's mug and growing midsection." He sighed. "And worse still, my mother says I'm insufferable and I snore some."

He sat back in the chair. "If you're still interested after knowing all that, I'll try to bring myself back in one piece so you'll at least have everything you bargained for." He smiled.

She slugged him on the shoulder, her face turning red. "This is nothing to joke about, Logan!"

"I'm not joking. What makes you think I'm joking? Can't you see I'm sweating like I just ran from New York to Paris? I want to marry you, but I'm no pretty package. When I'm with you, I feel like I'm whole again, alive, and I'm not about to go out there and throw it all away by letting somebody shoot a hole in me."

"You *are* insufferable."

"I told you that already. Question is, are you willing to put up with me?"

Claire took his hand, a worried look on her face. "I'm carrying a lot of baggage, Logan. I've done a lot of things I'm not proud of, and I'm not sure the Lord could ever forgive me for all of them. I'm even less of a bargain than you think you are. You haven't known . . . don't know me . . . "

"No, you're right, I don't. I'm banking on my heart this time—just like I did the first time. It worked once, it will work again. If you're carrying baggage, so be it. We deserve one another." He smiled. "You're selling yourself short, Claire. The

Lord isn't nearly as displeased with you as you are, and I'm not displeased at all. I understand baggage, and I know it can be unpacked and put away. We'll do it together, if you want."

She sat back, her eyes filling with tears. "I'm expecting Steve's child."

Logan blinked, then smiled. "Boy or girl?"

"I haven't checked! What kind of question is that? This isn't your child, Logan, it's Steve's!"

"No, it's God's, and it can be ours. I got a late start at being a dad, Claire; this just speeds things up some."

A tear cascaded down her cheeks. "You want to marry me for my money, don't you," she said, trying to lighten her own heart.

He grinned. "Didn't I mention that? Must have slipped my mind."

She leaned over and put her arms around his neck, and they kissed again. When she drew away slightly to look into his eyes, she had a question. "Does this mean we're engaged?"

"I'd like to make it more formal when we get back to Salt Lake. Candlelight dinner, a ring, silly stuff like that, but, yes, I think it does."

She kissed him again.

From the other side of the living-area wall, they heard the outer door being closed; then the engines were fired.

They separated their hands and cleared away their glasses and breakfast leftovers in preparation for takeoff. When they finished, they sat on the couch and fastened their seat belts. She took his hand again and leaned into him. Logan put an arm around her shoulders and held her tight, kissing her hair and gently stroking her arm.

When his wife had died, something inside had died with her. He had felt empty, dislocated, lost. He had stopped feeling anything about anything, a zombie who had come into contact with other people but never really felt anything about it. Over time he had gotten used to being alone and had learned to deal with the emptiness, but it had never gone away because there hadn't been anyone to fill it. Now he was beginning to feel whole again.

He looked down at Claire. Her eyes were closed and her

breathing shallow. She was asleep. She felt good against him. He closed his eyes. He hadn't slept much since leaving Salt Lake City, and he was tired.

Now was a good time to catch a little sleep.

21

SERGEI DAVIDOV POURED HIMSELF A THIRD DRINK and downed the hot liquid in three swallows. The past twenty-four hours had been filled with bad news. Charles Barrett, now a vegetable unable to give them what they wanted; Hainey's involvement and unnecessary elimination; Andrei, dead; and the American gone. Everything was in jeopardy.

He had made immediate arrangements with Lazar Kherensky, now standing only a few feet away, to keep Andrei's death under wraps. Then he had requisitioned one of the government's small jets to fly south and take charge of things himself. With Andrei gone, there had been no other choice. How could so much go so wrong so quickly?

It had been Minister Antonov's idea to fix the bid. He had tried to avoid it, wanted nothing but to use the opportunity to get close to the Barretts, but he had been forced to go along or lose that chance and his position. Not that he didn't have a share in the proceeds. Everyone had been going to get a cut, but more important things were at stake, and Walden's discovery had ruined more than an attempt at a few American dollars.

He poured another drink. There *was* hope. Andrei had enlisted Thompson's help in getting the envelope and had reported it to him. Although Davidov hadn't been able to get hold of Thompson since his brother's death, he was sure there was no problem or they would have heard by now. Thompson was good—Andrei had used him before in his former work with the KGB and had guaranteed the man's success. Davidov had no reason to doubt.

He glanced at the clock on the wall. Thompson would arrive soon, and if the envelope contained what was needed, Alex

Barrett wouldn't matter, even though he must be found. They couldn't complete their task with him still alive to witness against their sudden good fortune and discovery—and the attempted kidnapping of Charles Barrett's granddaughter, the killing of Hainey, and the treatment of Alex Barrett himself. Davidov didn't relish spending the rest of his life in some prison, American or Ukrainian.

He took another swallow of his drink, then turned to Kherensky, commandant for the Yalta region. Lazar Kherensky was of medium height and slight build, with brown hair cropped short. His face was round, with gray bulges under small eyes, which were magnified through the heavy lenses of his wire-rimmed glasses. To Davidov he looked more like a schoolteacher modeling a military uniform than a man of considerable power.

"You are sure of the time of death?" Davidov asked.

Kherensky nodded.

"The same hour I talked to him by phone." Davidov's remark was under his breath; Kherensky couldn't hear it. He was thinking how strange it was that at one minute his brother was excited about the progress of his interrogation and the next hour he was dead. Life was fragile.

"You took care of Andrei's body?" Davidov snapped out of his thoughts.

Kherensky nodded again. "I will see it is delivered wherever you like."

"And you are sure of the cause of death?"

Kherensky was sipping only a small amount from the drink he had poured himself while waiting for Davidov to appear. "I am sure, Sergei. The big one, Yegor Kamanev, must have given Andrei some trouble while they were going down the muddy road. Yegor's head is half missing—a bullet from Andrei's gun, which we found in the bushes near his body."

"You have kept his name out of the papers?"

Another nod.

"And you have not given anyone the American's name?"

"Nor his true nationality. And we have given a sketchy

description. People think they are looking for a crazy man—a murderer of women and children, a man from England."

Sergei was thoughtful, pacing. "Our first concern must be to find the American. And he must be alive, Lazar—at least until I make sure I have what I want. Once I am finished with him, we can arrange his death, and you can announce to the world that you have captured a double murderer," Davidov said. He knew it would work out well. The American, fleeing from justice, kills and then was killed—more convincing for the world press while still getting rid of the last man who could keep them from enjoying the fruits of their labors.

"We believe he has left the area of the accident. It is my opinion that he had help," Kherensky said.

"Help? From whom?"

Kherensky shrugged—time to play the game. "We believe it is the Milli Mejlis." He placed his glass on the table, feigning a frown.

Sergei felt the pressure that was coming. Kherensky had been playing these games all his career, had done it well, becoming one of the most powerful men along the Black Sea Coast of Crimea—and one of the most corrupt. Davidov knew the policeman, knew his feelings about the Tartars, and knew he was about to make a pitch for more money, ostensibly because the Tartars would not cooperate otherwise. Davidov also knew that most of what Kherensky would ask for would end up in the policeman's Swiss bank account. But what choice did he have? Besides, Kherensky had been protecting them for years, even though they had never involved him deeply in their affairs. In the matter of Alex Barrett, Davidov had no one else to turn to, and Kherensky knew it. The thought gave Davidov gas, but it was not life threatening. He disliked playing in muddy waters, but in his business, that was the usual state of things.

Davidov took several sips of the hot liquid in his glass, emptying it for the third time, biding his time, acting casual.

"The Tartars are a tight group, very private," Kherensky went on. "It will be extremely difficult to get information from them about the American's whereabouts." His face feigned concern.

Davidov was trying to reflect that concern, even though he had the urge to laugh. He suppressed it, knowing it would be unwise. Kherensky liked believing he was good at deception; bursting his bubble would only antagonize him.

"Even then," Kherensky said, "we will have to take Barrett away from them. You know how the Tartars feel about our authority here."

Davidov forced a frown and a nod, letting Kherensky believe he was understanding about the problem.

"Try to understand my position, Sergei," Kherensky said in a solicitous voice. "Even though the Tartars may be harboring a criminal, and that gives me justification to take armed action against them, they will not let this go unanswered. There will be a violent response and much bloodshed. I must do it quietly. In order to do that, I must buy help inside the Tartar brotherhood. This does not come cheap." Kherensky paused for effect. "I know a man who will give us the American, Sergei, and quickly, but he is expensive."

"How much?"

Kherensky shrugged. "Two hundred thousand American dollars."

Davidov didn't blink, even though he wanted to gasp. He forced himself only to sip from his glass evenly while wanting to down the whole thing in one gulp. He could not believe his ears but knew instantly Kherensky was completely serious. "It is too much. Out of reason, Lazar, and you know it." Davidov said it evenly.

Kherensky shrugged again, rubbing his index finger around the lip of his glass. "They have the American, Sergei." He smiled. "The man who is responsible for Andrei's death. I cannot go among them with my men. There will be a bloodbath and an international commotion none of us can afford. We must have a Judas."

"Even Judas never commanded such figures."

Kherensky smiled. "If you want the American, you really have no choice."

Davidov remained outwardly passive even as he boiled

inside. Kherensky had overstepped the bounds, even for a consummate opportunist. Davidov's family had paid him well for his
services, were willing to continue doing so. For him to take
advantage of them at a time like this was unconscionable.

Davidov twirled the last bit of liquid in his glass even as he
made a decision. It was an amazing decision really. Not because
of the enormity of it. Not because it meant that Kherensky's life
was involved. It amazed Davidov only because he felt nothing as
he made it. No remorse, no guilt. Nothing. He remembered the
first time he had given such an order. There had been guilt then,
fear as well. Fear of reprisals, fear of being caught and summarily
shot. Even some fear of God. But these did not exist for him anymore. He walked to the bar and put his glass down. The decision
was made. Kherensky would never live to collect the money.

"Very well, Lazar. But the American must be delivered here,
alive," Davidov said.

Hardly able to contain his excitement at his victory,
Kherensky leaned forward and placed his glass on the table
before standing. "It is agreed, then. You will have the money at
the time of delivery?"

But it was an expected victory. Kherensky did not feel threatened by Sergei Davidov because the man was in his territory now,
and it was Kherensky who allowed Davidov the use of the house
once used only by the Soviet elite. It was Kherensky's men who
guarded it. It was by his efforts that Davidov's family had the
anonymity they desired. Their association was years old. He had
provided good services, never asked questions, cleaned up messes
when necessary. Such services made him invaluable, and he had
no concern that Davidov might physically harm him.

Davidov moved to the window, drinking lightly from his
refilled glass. "The money will be here, Lazar," he said.

Kherensky, a bit uncomfortable with the apparent dismissal,
pulled at the bottom of his uniform jacket as if to straighten it,
then went to the door and left.

Davidov stood motionless at the window, watching
Kherensky leave the house and go to his chauffeur-driven Chaika,
stopping only long enough to talk with the member of his guard

who was responsible for watching the dacha. When he finished giving orders, Kherensky entered the open door of the car. Sergei watched it go to the gate, wait for the iron barrier to be moved, then drive through and into the road to the valley.

"Good-bye, Lazar," he said. He placed his empty glass on the bar and walked to the door on the far side of the room that led to the rear hall. He removed the card key from his pocket and placed it into the slot on the left of the solid oak door. The lock clicked open, and he entered the hallway. Kherensky's men didn't come there when Davidov was using the house, were never allowed beyond the first locked door. Only Davidov's people administered affairs in this part of the main house, because it was where his family had come over the past few years to meet and conduct their preparations.

The second door was also locked, but this time he knocked lightly on the reinforced bulletproof window and was let in by a man with an automatic rifle slung over one shoulder, a precaution and preparation for the return of Alex Barrett to their possession.

Turning left, he entered another door into a comfortable office. There was a large cherrywood desk and an adequate leather couch Davidov found uncomfortable but was supposed to have been purchased by Leonid Brezhnev for his own use. It sat against the wall opposite a few bookcases filled with books from around the world. Half a dozen pictures by Russian and Ukrainian artists were the only decorations.

Sitting at the desk, he punched a button fastened to its underside before sitting back to contemplate his decision to eliminate Kherensky.

Once Barrett and the envelope were in their hands, once they had the information he was sure both had, Kherensky would be needed no longer. They would not need his protection, nor his influence. In fact, he would become a liability. It was a good decision, one that would please many people, especially the Tartars. The fact that Kherensky felt he was safe enough to pull such an outrageous stunt only made the decision a more important one, and easier to complete.

The door opened and Maxim entered. Maxim was an impos-
ing figure, his six-foot frame and hardened muscles formidable.

Davidov called him the Giant. He had square shoulders and
a round face with the almond eyes of the Chinese mother who
had borne him. But Maxim was totally Russian in language and
culture. Sergei and Andrei had raised him since he was eight, and
they had seen to that. Maxim was their half brother and completely dedicated to them.

Maxim's only fault was not his own—an accident had
reduced his mental capacity.

Andrei and Sergei were full brothers, together since Andrei's
birth one year after Sergei's. Their mother had died young, but
their father had made sure they were taken care of, properly
schooled and trained, and given every advantage his money and
connections could get them in the Soviet system, even after he
had been forced from the country by political forces out of his
control.

Their father had been a man of great foresight, a man aware
of how fickle Stalin, the party, and the Soviet system could be. As
a precaution that the tentacles of that system would never reach
them, Sergei and Andrei had been raised by their father's sister.
They had been given different names, different identities, but they
had been taught the truth about who they really were, and they
had been educated in such a way as to prepare themselves for the
future. Even when their father had been forced to flee the country,
he had taken care of them, sending the necessary funds, provid-
ing the contacts, giving instructions for their research and continued preparation, and finally guiding them in the attempt at
reclaiming their heritage.

Davidov's chin lifted a little with pride. He had been the one
to find the first clues necessary to get back what was rightfully
theirs. As a researcher in the Historical Archives in Moscow, he
had used his position to search the World War II records thoroughly and had come up with the railway and shipping papers
showing how Michael Poltoron and Arkadi Lutria had managed
to steal eighty crates of contraband from southern Germany—

contraband their father had been sure was stolen from the family by the Germans at the beginning of the war.

But after discovering Poltoron's theft, they had reached a dead end. The American had performed the impossible, the stolen crates disappearing into thin air in the countries west of Poland.

But Sergei had refused to give up. Relentlessly he had searched. Using German war records made public in 1964, he had discovered that the contraband he had thought Poltoron was responsible for stealing had contained more than just possessions belonging to Sergei's progenitors. Among these there had been six paintings and two valuable icons stolen from a small museum in Kiev that had once belonged to a number of prominent families under the Tsars. As he had researched these, their history, who they had belonged to before their disappearance during the war, he had discovered they had all been returned to the descendants of the original owners, all of whom were living outside the Soviet Union. In every case the returns had been carried out anonymously after 1953, the year Poltoron was to have died.

At first it had confused Davidov. Lutria and Poltoron were both dead, yet works they had stolen had been returned. Had Poltoron given them to his government? Had the Americans then returned the works to the families who had owned them prior to the revolution?

Davidov hadn't thought so—not without fanfare and extensive press coverage. And even if they had, why hadn't the most important items, and the largest part of the stash taken by Poltoron and Lutria, found their way into daylight? No, the only real conclusion for Davidov was that Michael Poltoron was still alive.

That had brought Sergei a dilemma. His father would never believe Poltoron was alive without substantial proof. Sergei had never gone behind his father's back before but decided to pursue his evidence without his father's knowledge. He enlisted Andrei's help, and they began a search born of bitter hatred for the man they believed had stolen everything from them. For Michael Poltoron. Their search began in 1985. They found him two years later.

The only surprise had been their father's reaction when they revealed what they had found. There was only a smile.

"What about Mr. Thompson, Maxim? You have made arrangements to meet his plane?"

Maxim nodded. "I and Dimitri will go."

"When he arrives, bring him directly to me. I have another job for him."

Maxim didn't answer. It was not uncommon. Maxim's mind had a tendency to wander. Even though Sergei had dealt with his brother's limitations for years, it still took a good deal of patience sometimes. Maxim hadn't always been this way. The doctors had said that the concussion from a fall as a child had caused trauma. He would never think very clearly again even though his motor skills would remain effective.

"Did you hear me, Maxim?"

"We don't need him here. I have always . . . "

"He is not a threat to you, Maxim. He brings us something very important, and the job I have for him is something we can have nothing to do with. Do you understand?"

Maxim didn't respond to the question. Instead he asked another. "Where is Andrei? He is supposed to be here."

Andrei and Maxim had always been close. Andrei was sadistic and used their younger brother's physical talents to carry out his malignant interrogations. Sergei had to admit, they worked well as a team. It was only because Maxim had been with him, and not with Andrei, as was usually the case, that Andrei had been forced to use Yegor Kamanev. It was apparent that had led to Andrei's death. Davidov grieved. If he had sent Maxim with Andrei . . . but he hadn't. There were dangers in Kiev at the time. Antonov was looking for a scapegoat for Cynthia Walden's discovery. In such instances, men had been known to be thrown out of their offices or their homes and even killed. The Giant was always a good deterrent against any physical harm.

"I have bad news, Maxim. Andrei is dead."

Maxim stiffened, his face turning pale and hard as oak.

"The American. In his escape," Davidov added. It was only partly true, but Davidov wanted Maxim to perceive Alex Barrett as his enemy. It would be easier for him to stay focused.

"No! Andrei was too smart. No American . . . " His voice trailed off.

"Andrei is dead, but when we find the American, we will have our revenge. For now we must concentrate on bringing him here. Do you understand?"

Maxim slowly nodded, a faraway look in his eye.

"The police commander, Kherensky, will find the American for us. When he does, I want you to be there. Kherensky is a friend of the American, and I don't trust him. I want you to kill Kherensky and bring the American to me."

"No, I will kill them both."

Sergei bit back the desire to scream at his oversized little brother. "No," he said calmly. "Until we are sure we have what we are after, the American must be kept alive." He slowed down, emphasizing each word. "He must be brought to me." He leaned forward. "Look at me, Maxim." Maxim looked up. "Do you understand? He must be brought here. When we are finished with him, you can kill him."

Maxim's face didn't change except for the eyes. The look there gave Sergei goosebumps, but he knew Maxim would do it now. That was the way it was. Once he understood what must be done he became focused, and nothing would keep him from his appointed task. Kherensky was a dead man.

Maxim stood. "All right."

Sergei leaned back and made one last point. "Kherensky is not to know you are following him. Do you understand my orders concerning Kherensky?"

"I understand." Maxim said it with a little irritation.

"And bring the American to me."

"I am not stupid, Sergei. I told you I understand."

"Send Dimitri to the airport for Thompson." Dimitri was Davidov's regular driver and had seen Thompson before. He was, next to Maxim, Sergei's most dependable guard and a familiar face to the American assassin. Maxim was unknown to William Thompson and vice versa. The ox might have difficulty locating him at the airport anyway.

"Take a driver with you, Maxim."

"I drive, Sergei," Maxim said stiffly. "No one else."

Sergei shrugged. "This is not Kiev. The streets are not familiar. You will need someone who knows the town." Sergei tried to
look nonchalant. Maxim had a thing for driving, as if it told the
world he was as smart as the rest of them, and he did drive fairly
well as long as it didn't take much thinking ahead.

Maxim hesitated. "I will drive. He will only tell me where to
go." He left the room without waiting for an answer. Sergei
accepted the compromise.

After a few moments in which Sergei thought about his decisions, he opened the drawer and pulled out a bottle of American
whiskey. Leaning back in the chair, he put his feet up on the desk,
unscrewed the lid, and took a healthy swallow. What he had to do
next had to be thought through, the right words chosen. The
whiskey was needed to bolster his strength.

After fifteen minutes he screwed the lid back on snug, placed
the bottle on the desk, and reached for the phone. It was a special
phone, scrambled, with a direct line to several locations. Unlike
the regular phones across the Soviet Union, which had the quality
of two cans hooked together with string, there would be no operator, no static, and no chance of being interrupted or misunderstood.

This call would be one of his most difficult. Andrei's death
would be the subject of discussion.

He would miss Andrei. He had been a good brother. They
had worked hard for this, and now he would not be there to share
their final victory. Putting the phone down, he took the bottle
again and removed the lid. He hoisted the bottle high in a salute to
his little brother. Then he downed a generous portion.

Finished, he put the lid back on, picked up the phone, and
dialed the number of the ship-to-shore operator in Sevastopol. He
pulled the small book from under the phone, checked the number
on the back of it, then put it back in its hiding place. He then gave
the number to the operator and was connected.

He took a deep breath. He had never liked giving bad news
to their father.

22

LOGAN WATCHED MAX GERONDI EXIT the Athens terminal and head toward the plane. Gerondi had changed some, aged, but then so had he. Now he was taller and with more girth, in fact, with a little paunch that hung atop his belt. Logan checked his. Nothing yet.

His old friend was dressed in a pair of tan summer shorts and a white polo shirt, his hair still dark but thin, and his round face covered with a heavy beard and moustache streaked with gray. His small eyes were shadows created by bushy brows and high cheek bones. Logan estimated he had probably put on at least twenty pounds.

For the average person on the street, Gerondi would hardly have matched the idea of an Israeli agent. But then there was nothing typical about Max Gerondi. He smiled.

Gerondi boarded and was greeted with a healthy hug from Logan as the exterior door was sealed shut. Logan's old friend, sweating a bit, removed a wide handkerchief, then wiped his forehead, face, arms, and thinning hair. Then he turned his attention to Claire.

"Max Gerondi," he said in his baritone voice. "Logan's friends are usually less than interesting, and quite ugly, but you . . . "

"Control your hormones, Max; the beautiful lady and I are engaged."

Max kept his eyes on Claire but gave her a "do I feel for you" look.

"So sorry. As soon as I return, I will go to the synagogue and pray for you!" He smiled.

"I'm Claire Barrett." She looked at Logan. "I've never met

any of Logan's friends, but if you're a sample it should be interesting."

Gerondi laughed. The sound filled the interior of the plane and resonated off the walls. "Yes, well, don't get your hopes up. I'm one of a kind."

"He's also married and has ten kids," Logan said, smiling. "How are they, by the way?"

"Expensive." He took ten minutes to give Logan the rundown on each of his kids, then talked about his wife for another ten. Claire hoped Logan would talk that way about her someday.

"Now tell me, my friend, what is going on?" Gerondi asked.

It took Logan nearly twenty minutes to tell him what had happened over the past few days and where it was leading them. By the time he had finished, Max's heavy eyebrows had come together in one worried bunch. Logan went on to explain their belief that this was somehow related to Charles Barrett's war years, about which no one seemed to know much, then told him what Carnahan had learned about Sergei Davidov.

"Sergei Davidov, the assistant minister to Leonid Antonov of the Ukrainian government?"

Logan nodded.

"Umm. The next leg of your trip will take you into Crimea," Max said matter-of-factly.

"How do you know that?" Claire asked.

Gerondi smiled, then looked at Logan.

"I haven't told her anything. I wasn't sure what you'd want me to say, what you wouldn't," Logan said.

He nodded at Logan, then looked at Claire. "Israeli intelligence has a very long arm, Claire. I am a part of that arm." He smiled. "Somewhere near the shoulder."

"He heads the European branch. I know of only one man who ranks higher," Logan said.

Gerondi grinned. "Modesty prevents my saying so, but thank you for building my worth in the eyes of this beautiful lady.

"To answer your question, Claire, my country has agents in both Istanbul and Yalta. The ticket Logan will pick up at Ataturk airport in Istanbul, the one for Mr. Randolph, is at the Ukraina airlines desk and will get him aboard a small aircraft that flies directly to Yalta. Thus, I know to what city he will be going and have made plans accordingly. Second, my government keeps track of men like Davidov. He flew to Crimea earlier today. It is my guess that the two events are related."

Claire nodded. She was already impressed. "How did an Israeli intelligence agent meet a cop from Park City, Utah? I don't suppose you were on a ski vacation."

"If it had been my choice, skiing would have been much more to my liking," Max said with a slight laugh. He glanced at Logan. "Unlike myself, Logan is much too modest to beat his own drum, so I will do it for him." He grinned.

He looked at Claire. "Your fiancé was involved with a rather big drug investigation several years ago as an undercover agent. His path led him into Syria, where I, also, was working under-cover but on another matter, one that dealt with Israel's security. It seems the man he was seeking—you know his kind as a drug lord—was selling his product to amass money for a nuclear war-head he wanted dropped on Tel Aviv. To make a long story very short, Logan stopped him and saved my life. We have been in touch since, watching each other climb our chosen ladders of success."

"My, my. You *are* full of surprises, Logan," Claire said.

Logan blushed. "He makes it sound better than it was."

"Hardly, but to tell more will make it impossible for your enormous head to disembark from this plane." They enjoyed a laugh together, then Gerondi grew serious, looking directly into Claire's eyes.

"I also know your father, Charles Barrett."

Claire had a confused, quizzical look on her face.

"How? What do you mean?"

"Your father made a number of trips to our country."

"Yes, I know. I went with him on most of them. We vaca-tioned there, even lived there several summers. Dad had business with Leumi Bank."

"The bank was a minor affair—important but often just a front for his more important business. He spent a fair amount of time in the private offices of the Israeli intelligence service. He was a consultant on the Soviet Union and was highly regarded by our early organizers. I met him while attending some of the meetings on Soviet affairs a few years ago. He was more an interested onlooker by then but still had a good grasp of things, although his role had diminished over the years."

"Are you telling us that Charles Barrett was an intelligence operative?" Logan asked.

Max smiled. "I knew him as only a consultant, but it was rumored that he had been one of the best operatives the OSS, or CIA, as you call it now, ever had. At one time in his former career, he operated one of the first anti-Soviet intelligence organizations inside the Soviet Union—or so the rumor mill says."

"My father?" Claire's voice had the sound of disbelief.

"No wonder his records before 1953 are as clean as the driven snow," Logan said.

"Do you know anything about those years? Anything at all?"

"Only what I have told you. You have to understand, Claire, your father was a mysterious figure in our organization. Few people ever met him personally, and even fewer knew his name. The one man he dealt with in Israel was rumored to be a former member of your father's organization in the Soviet Union. Your father managed to get him out just hours before the KGB, known as the NKVD then, was to pick him up. Your father helped him relocate in Israel, where he was among the first members of our intelligence community. But, other than these rumors, we were never informed of your father's past history—not officially. But you have to understand that such things are not unusual. Most people in the Mossad don't even know my history. Or my name. It has to be that way in order to prevent fallout if one of us is caught."

"But you must have gleaned something," Claire said.

Max smiled. "Yes, a few things. Your father helped develop the present Israeli intelligence organization, and he was a Jew of Russian descent. I also believe that he was, and still is, responsible for funding a trust used to help settle Jews of Russian heritage. Millions of dollars have been filtering through it for decades."

Max sat back. "I'm sure there is more to your father's past than just these things, but he is a revered man in Israeli intelligence."

Logan looked at Claire. "You look like you've seen a ghost."

"You live with someone most of your life, you'd think you might get some idea of who they are. If *any* of this is true, I haven't the slightest idea who Charles Barrett really is!"

Max glanced at his watch as the plane engines cut back and the front tipped down slightly.

"Time to get to business. We are going to land in a few minutes and pick up a few items we will need. Then Claire and I will catch a plane of our own and fly directly to Yalta. You, Logan, will play out your little charade. Go to Istanbul, pick up your ticket, and take the flight to Yalta. I assume someone is going to meet you there?"

"Yes." He glanced over at the snakeskin cowboy boots standing against the wall. "I'm supposed to wear those as identification."

"A bit amateurish, but a good sign you will not be met by someone who knows you. At least let us hope this is the way it will be." He paused, thinking, then let whatever thought he was having pass by. "Whoever meets you must be taken prisoner, and it must be done quickly."

Claire looked surprised. "If Logan is supposed to lead us to Alex—"

Max held up a hand, cutting her off. " Even though the people who meet Logan at the airport will not know him, the next person to see him will. Logan will immediately be taken prisoner, and that complicates everything, don't you think?"

She nodded. "You then have two men to free."

"The charade is good only to a point; after that it becomes a liability."

"Then why send him at all?"

"Two reasons. First, they will know if he picks up the ticket, because they will want to know he is on his way. That gives them a false sense of confidence and us enough time to make plans. Second, I want to have a short conversation with the people who do pick him up to verify what I already know." He removed a map from his case.

"What you already know?"

Max smiled. "That I have found the place where they are keeping Alex."

ᴀLEX DIDN'T LIKE IT. The long pier looked deserted, but there was something . . . was it just the darkness, the shadows across the row of boats along the pier? Or was there something else—something his eyes couldn't see but his brain was reading?

He tried to relax. He felt better, stronger, even though his face was still somewhat swollen and quite black and blue and his ribs still kept him from laughing. Vilinia had been stuffing him full of food for the past twelve hours, and his body was healing pretty well.

Alex had come to like Vilinia. Since leaving Isjet's, they had spent their time together, discussing and arguing about everything from politics to religion. Strong willed, opinionated, proud—that was Vilinia. Her long fingers were as much a part of her speech as her soft lips. When he set her off, she raised her voice and became as animated as any preacher trying to save a stadium full of potential believers, and Alex enjoyed every minute of it. Her almond eyes came alive, and she flushed with the passion she put into everything she did. She could make him laugh one minute and be completely exasperating the next. Alex didn't think she knew the first thing about playing games to impress a man, and if she did, she had no intention of doing so. She was her own woman, genuine, full of life and strong willed. He found himself wishing he had more time.

The truck sat with its backside looking across the wide expanse between the single pier and the place where Alex and Vilinia waited. It sat in the shadows of tall trees near the northeast end of the embankment, its tarp-covered bed making them invisible to anyone moving through the streets.

Vilinia had told him that in the daytime the space before them was filled with people, a large boardwalk of sorts that ran the length of the central part of Yalta and along the Black Sea. Called Lenin's Embankment, the concrete waterfront had an upper and lower section. The lower part was built right on the water and had tie-ups at several locations for boats. Directly in front of them a tug was harbored, its running lights trimmed for the night.

To their right, a half-mile distant, a pier of wood and concrete jutted into the sea. Half a dozen boats were docked there, silhouetted against the light of a moon intermittently snuffed out by floating clouds. It was along that part of the embankment that the main shopping district sat, busy with tourists during the day and until the place shut down at night. From this distance Alex saw few people around, and the evening air carried only an occasional voice. At two o'clock in the morning, Yalta was asleep.

In front of them but fifty yards to their left were a number of larger ships docked against the embankment where it turned out to sea. Vilinia said most of them were tourist ships that ran people from place to place along the Crimean coast and charged for port tours, but there were some private yachts as well. She told him that one large one was the *Professor Zubov,* which belonged to a Russian scientific institute but no longer made research voyages for lack of money. When she did operate, it was under lease to entrepreneurs who took her to Turkey to buy goods they brought back to Crimea for sale to tourists along the coast and on the black market in the rest of Ukraine.

The embankment itself was covered with small vessels dry-docked atop it, along with a clutter of crates, barrels, and boxes that made it look like a maze, a maze made more frightening by the near total lack of light.

Isjet Yazhul had disappeared into that maze nearly ten minutes ago and hadn't returned.

"It doesn't feel right, Vilinia," Alex said. He stared intently into the darkness, searching the shadows. There were so many. His mind reluctantly went back to the beatings he had been given, the threats and interrogation. Were his enemies out there, waiting?

Alex glanced at his watch. "Your father has had plenty of time to check things out," he said.

"The place where your ship is to come is very near the end of the embankment. It will take some time, Alex. Father must meet with the captain and make the payment. Then he will return."

Vilinia's voice was even, but Alex sensed apprehension. She had a tight grip on the wooden seat hinged between the sides of the truck behind the cab, her body stiff.

After another five minutes, a dark figure appeared at the beginning of the maze and waved an arm. The darkness prevented them from seeing Isjet clearly, but the signal was properly given, and they started out of the truck. Once on the pavement, they walked quickly toward the maze of the embankment. As they neared the halfway mark, Vilinia put her arm through Alex's and slowed him down.

"How are you feeling?" she asked with genuine concern.

"Like I've been in a fight with a very large truck."

She grinned slightly. "Yes, this is a good description. But you are beginning to heal I think."

There was a pause.

"I must tell you something, Alex Barrett." They kept walking toward the maze. "I hope you will come back to us. I would like to see you again."

Alex stopped, then started walking again, a bit stunned.

"This surprises you?" Vilinia asked.

"Yeah, a little."

"Why? Americans do not express how they feel?"

He smiled. "Americans play games—dumb games."

"This game—it has a name?"

"Playing it cool. I've always hated it."

"Our way of life does not give us time for, as you say, playing it cool. Will you come back?"

"I would bet my last dollar on it."

"Bet? Your last dollar? I do not understand this . . . "

Alex was far from impulsive. Everything he did was thought out carefully, planned, in detail—especially when it came to women. For that reason he could never understand why he kissed Vilinia right there, in the middle of the boardwalk. Maybe it was the moon. The moon was supposed to make people do strange things. But he couldn't blame it on the moon this time. It was just impulse—impulse born of the heart.

He placed his arm around her back and pulled her tight, kissing her with a passion he had never before felt toward a woman. When their lips parted, she looked stunned. He took her arm and started toward the pier.

"Why did you kiss me?" she asked, stopping. Before he could answer, she pulled him to her and kissed him.

They pulled away. "You hated me twelve hours ago," Alex said.

"Yes. You were an arrogant American then." She said it with a fake scowl that lifted her dark eyebrows and made him laugh.

"And now?"

"You are still an arrogant American, but I have decided I must save you," she said. "You didn't answer my question. Why did you kiss me?"

He looked up at the cloud-covered orb above them. "Full moon. Men go crazy under a full moon."

She smiled. "You will come back, won't you?"

Her kissed her again as his answer, wondering how something so good could happen so fast. Was it real or an aberration? The analytical side of him said what he was feeling was impossible, the heat of the moment, and would go away when circumstances changed. The other side didn't care, didn't want to be analyzed or to look at things logically, wanted only to feel what he was feeling and hold on to it because he had never felt it before and was afraid he'd never feel it again.

She pulled away and took his hand. "Come, Father will be waiting. Your safety depends on our getting you aboard the boat to Istanbul." They started into the shadows again, Alex trying to get his head out of the clouds. They had passed the first two ships on their left and were approaching the third when someone stepped onto its deck. Lights went on, filling the shadows, blinding them enough that they reacted instinctively, placing a hand up to ward off the offending light.

"Well, well, what have we here?" said the man on the deck. "Two lovers trying to find a place to be alone?"

Laughter at the remark came from at least two other people. He wondered how many hadn't found the joke funny, what the odds really were.

"Where is my father, Kherensky?" Vilinia said. Her voice was angry, full of hatred while still tinged with fear. "What have you done with him?"

"He is further down the dock. You will join him shortly." Alex's eyes adjusted, and he lowered his hand a little. The light stood to the side of the man Vilinia called Kherensky and cast him in shadow.

"Let them go. It's me you're after," Alex said.

Kherensky laughed. "You take too much upon yourself, Mr. Barrett. I wanted Yazhul as much or more than you. He and his people are nothing but a plague to me. You have simply given me full opportunity to be rid of him and deal them a hard blow." The shadow stiffened as another appeared behind it, shoving the light aside like a small toy and sending it crashing to the dock far below.

Alex sensed some confusion in the movement to his right and left but didn't take the time to ask questions. Grabbing for the dark shadow to his left, he filled his hand with shirt and punched where he thought the face would be. His hand felt the impact of solid bone; then the body went limp and fell to the ground, the weapon clattering at Alex's feet. He stooped, picking it up, his eyes adjusting to the darkness. A second man came from the darkness, a glint of metal setting off a warning in Alex's head. The gun barrel seemed to grow into a dark hole, and Alex took a deep breath as he waited for the flame that would come from it and end his life.

A shot.

Alex opened his eyes.

The man was falling to the ground, then lay in a heap on the concrete. Alex didn't understand. Why was he still alive? What had happened?

He stared at the lifeless body with an amazed look on his face.

"Do not move, Mr. Barrett." The voice was chillingly familiar to Alex, and he froze.

"Toss the weapon aside." Alex did.

"Tazbir?" Vilinia said.

Tazbir came out of the darkness, Isjet in front of him.

"Father!" She started toward Isjet. Tazbir lifted the gun, pointing it at her midsection. She stopped.

"What are you doing?" Vilinia asked in amazement.

"He betrayed us, Vilinia," Isjet said. "He alone knew about our plans. I told no one else. Now he has betrayed Kherensky himself."

"Who is your new partner, Tazbir? Who pays your blood money?"

Vilinia stared at Tazbir, hatred in the firm set of her jaw.

"Let them go, Tazbir." Alex knew even as he said it that the man had no intention of doing so. If anyone was left alive to testify of his betrayal, he would be hung by his own people.

Tazbir waved Alex toward the sea side of the embankment. "A small boat is waiting. You will find a ladder near the front of the large ship directly ahead. Go, and if you do anything foolish, I will kill Isjet and Vilinia."

Alex started walking, his mind working out what he could do only to find there wasn't anything. If he ran, he'd be killed. If he ran and escaped, Tazbir had nothing to lose. He would kill Vilinia and Isjet. The young Tartar had crossed the line, and there was no return.

When they were all at the same spot, Alex could see the thirty-foot fishing boat below. A large outboard hung on the rear. No one else was on board, but Alex knew there had to be at least one accomplice. There hadn't been time for Tazbir to take out Kherensky without a shot, then get to the embankment and take out the guard who had his mind set on killing Alex.

"From what has just happened, I'd say you're not going to wait for Kherensky," Alex said.

"Kherensky is dead. It is the first service I will do for my people this night!"

Tazbir looked into the darkness and was getting a bit nervous.

"And my death is the other," Isjet said calmly. "You have always wanted to tip the scales toward more radical methods of dealing with the people who persecute us. With me gone, you have your voice, your power."

Tazbir's eyes lit up like hot coals. "They killed my mother and my sister, these Russians! They are a plague on us, and all you do is call for calm, for common sense! We need none of your common sense, Yazhul! We need to drive them from this land!"

"You're outnumbered twenty to one," Alex said.

"More for each of us to kill, American!" Tazbir responded. He leaned further forward as if to make his point. "Our people turn to nations like yours for help! You ignore us, pretend we don't exist! We know you will never help us! We must help ourselves before another purging of our people takes place! It is better to fight now than to let them come when they are ready, when they want to slaughter us!" The hatred in Tazbir's voice made the hair on the back of Alex's neck stand on end.

Tazbir forced himself under control. "I do what I do for my people." He spoke in a soft tone but between clenched teeth.

"*We* are your people, Tazbir. My father is a great leader among them whom they admire and love, and you betray him! How can you say you do this for them?" Vilinia's voice was cold and hard. "You are a liar, Tazbir. You do this out of greed and hunger for power. Do not try to justify what you do by telling us you do it for them! It shows the coward in you!" Vilinia's voice cracked as she took a threatening step toward her new enemy.

Tazbir pointed the gun at Vilinia's heart, and Alex held his breath. "Isjet, tell your meddlesome daughter to shut up or I will kill her."

"I do not believe you can kill my daughter, Tazbir. You are friends. I do not believe you can kill either of us. It is why you have not done so yet. You wait for someone else, someone willing to do your dirty work so you will not feel responsible."

Tazbir's face turned to sweating granite, and Alex could see he was about to break under the pressure. If that happened, he might kill, if for no other reason than to prove Isjet wrong.

"Back off, Tazbir," Alex said. He pulled Vilinia back a step, trying to defuse the situation.

"I do not like you, American, but you are smart." He motioned toward the ladder with the gun. They started down, Isjet first. As he reached the boat, Tazbir demanded that Isjet move to the front and sit down with his hands on his head, then turned to Alex while pulling a length of rope from his pocket. "You're next, American. When you're in the boat, tie up Yazhul, then sit by his side. If you try anything, I will kill Vilinia."

Alex tried to stay calm, his fists clenched tightly around the rope, turning his knuckles white. Now it was his turn to keep cool, and it was all he could do to move to the ladder and start down. The throb in his injured ribs increased his heat level, but he worked his way down the ladder.

"Hurry up, American," Tazbir said.

Alex ignored him as he stepped into the wooden boat and began tying up Isjet.

"At least one other person is helping Tazbir," Alex said in a whisper. "Any idea who it is?"

Isjet shook his head.

"Okay. We'll just have to play this thing out. And Isjet, I know you don't believe he'll kill you, but don't push him. Under this kind of pressure, anything can happen."

Isjet nodded. "You are right, Alex. He is crazy with fear, but we must escape. Our fate is sealed now. He cannot let us live and survive himself."

"Agreed. Possibly when he boards—"

"No talking!" Tazbir said from above. Alex finished tying Isjet.

"Be ready, but we must be sure we have the upper hand," Alex said.

"If I find you have not done an adequate job, American, I will break Yazhul's hands instead of tying them a second time."

Alex glared up at his adversary, checked the ropes, and tightened them.

Tazbir gave Vilinia a second piece of rope and told her to join them. Alex positioned himself as close to the ladder as he could without raising suspicion. When Vilinia was in the boat, she began tying Alex's hands.

"Take your time. I have an idea," Alex whispered. "Be ready to move when I tell you."

She nodded. "I am sorry, Alex; you were right about Tazbir." Alex wasn't gloating.

"I will kill him." Vilinia said it through clenched teeth.

Alex felt the acid in his stomach. He knew her well enough now to know she meant it, and her impulsive, passionate nature, as much as he loved it, might be dangerous.

"Losing control will get us all killed, Vilinia. Just do as I tell you, all right?"

The anger still burned hot in her eyes, and he could tell he wasn't getting through.

"Vilinia, I think I'm in love with you, and if you do something stupid—"

"What?" The look in her eyes changed from hatred to shock.

He smiled. "Shock therapy. Promise you'll do only what I tell you."

Tazbir was starting down the ladder.

She nodded, her eyes showing a curious kind of tenderness.

"I do love you." Alex looked up at Tazbir. "I'd like to get out of here with what few pieces of me are left so I can say it properly. Work with me, will you?"

She nodded, still in shock.

As Tazbir stepped for the boat, his eyes mechanically glanced down to make sure his footing was secure.

"Now!"

Vilinia jumped to one side, and Alex took the step needed, grabbing the weapon and pushing upward, throwing his weight into Tazbir. The Tartar lost his footing, slipped, and fell backward.

The weapon fired, but Alex had redirected it, and the bullets bounced harmlessly off the hull of the boat. Tazbir was trying to get his footing, hold onto the gun, and fight off the aggressive attack of Alex but lost all three battles. As he went over the edge of the boat and into the water, Alex tried to wrest the weapon free but was only partly successful. It flew from Tazbir's hands and landed in the water five feet farther out, disappearing quickly in the dark waters of the Black Sea.

Vilinia had already jumped for the motor and started it as Alex untied the boat from the dock. She turned the throttle, and the boat lurched away from the ladder as Alex slammed a shoe against Tazbir's fingers, now desperately fastened onto the boat. The Tartar screamed but hung on as Vilinia turned the boat out to sea, dragging Tazbir with it. Alex was about to nail Tazbir's hand again when he decided to let him hang on. The farther out to sea they got, the farther Tazbir would have to swim.

Suddenly another boat, larger by half, came from behind the other end of the *Zubov*. Its speed was carrying it across the short distance so fast that Alex had time only to grab Vilinia by the arm and jump.

The boat rammed their small vessel and split it in half. The driver of the larger boat swung it around and came back in time to see it sink beneath the waves of the Black Sea. He shined a spotlight on the water. Alex Barrett was swimming to the struggling old man with his hands tied in an attempt to keep him from drowning. The driver of the boat pulled his vessel next to them and began helping them aboard.

Tazbir was first and Alex was last. When he boarded, he was helped up by the strong arm of a Oriental man who had the strength of a gorilla. He tossed Alex forward with such force that he nearly went over the front and into the water again. He fell to the deck and found himself staring into the blank eyes of a very dead Lazar Kherensky. The gorilla picked Alex up and placed him rather firmly in the seat next to Vilinia as the driver throttled the boat and they headed out to sea.

The gorilla sat across from Alex and stared at him with cold eyes. The boat slipped through the water, its loud noise filling the air and making it impossible to talk. Shivering, Alex watched the lights of the city move into the distance as they went farther out to sea, the lights finally becoming nothing but dots on the horizon. The gorilla stopped watching Alex only long enough to tie Kherensky's feet to an anchor rope and toss him over the side. Alex knew he would never be seen again with flesh still attached to bone.

Alex watched Tazbir dry himself off with a towel as he talked with the driver of the boat. The sound of the dual engines didn't allow Alex to hear what they said, but he could tell the driver wasn't pleased with Tazbir's performance.

Alex focused on the man behind the wheel. The darkness kept him from seeing his fine features, but he estimated he was about the same age as his father, well tanned, with silver hair combed straight back from his forehead. The man was over-dressed, the double-breasted blazer and light tan slacks a bit much for a kidnapping.

Alex saw lights on the horizon. Another boat? The speed of the boat and the cool night made him cold clear to the bone. Vilinia moved closer against the wind, and he put his arm around her while still trying to control his own shaking body. His ribs throbbed, and he was exhausted, willing to give them anything they wanted if they'd just let the three of them walk away to a steaming shower and hot meal.

They stared ahead as the lights of the larger boat rushed toward them. It was a medium-sized cabin cruiser with two decks above the waterline and a large captain's bridge. Alex figured it to be fifty to sixty feet long, maybe more. Several men with rifles walked the well-lit deck, leaning into the night as they heard the speeding boat approaching through the darkness.

The blazered gentleman slowed the inboard motor, and the front of the boat fell into the water as he deftly pulled the speed-boat alongside the yacht. The gorilla stepped to Isjet, knife in hand, leaned over the older man's shoulder, and cut the ropes that bound him. He stared down at Alex with such coldness that Alex was afraid the knife would be used to cut out his heart and feed it to the sharks.

"You killed Andrei," The gorilla said. He placed the smooth blade against Alex's throat.

"Maxim!" The man in the blazer said it evenly, like a father calling to a small child. "Get them aboard. You can play with Mr. Barrett later."

Maxim grabbed Alex and shoved him toward the ladder.

Coming on deck, Alex saw Isjet being searched by one of the ship's guards, and Alex had the funny thought of wondering what the man thought he was going to find. Fish maybe, who knew. Another stepped toward Vilinia to do the same but hesitated when she gave him a look that could kill.

"It's all right." The voice came from the man in the blazer who stood near the entrance to the main cabin. "Let her be." He turned to go inside. Alex was searched, then all three were herded in. Inside it was warm, bright, and comfortable, and Alex felt his teeth slow their chatter. The well-dressed man stood at the bar, pouring himself a drink.

The vessel was old, well built, with expensive wood paneling on the walls. The rugs were Oriental, as was most of the furniture. Pieces of beautifully carved ivory in a glass case adorned the far wall, and a five-foot, intricately molded Buddha stood near the door. The pictures on the wall were silk paintings, some of the finest Alex had ever seen.

The man in the blazer turned directly to Alex. "You have cost me a great deal over the past few days, Mr. Barrett. It makes me very unhappy."

"You drag me halfway around the world, have your goons beat half the life out of me, and you're inconvenienced? Interesting twist," Alex said blandly.

"Your father could have saved us all a good deal of trouble if he had been more cooperative," the man said.

"I always told him he was stubborn." Alex had stopped shivering, but his clothes still hung wet, dripping on the rugs.

"His stubbornness and yours have cost me one of my sons."

"The interrogator. I think your gorilla called him Andrei. I can't see the physical resemblance, but there is the same cold heart."

A slight smile creased the man's lips. "Your flippant attitude is commendable, Mr. Barrett, especially under such conditions. Or is it just a cover—a way of hiding your fear?"

Alex didn't answer. The man turned to the window. "Other lives now rely on your good sense, Mr. Barrett. A less flippant attitude would be in order."

Alex bit his tongue, cutting off what he wanted to say, selecting instead a more important question. "What do you want?"

"Before his death, Andrei sent one of our people to look for an envelope your father promised to give us." He turned, staring at Alex.

Alex stared back; something about the face suddenly seemed familiar.

"Thompson will deliver the envelope in the next few hours. Then your usefulness will be over, Mr. Barrett, as will the usefulness of this woman and her father. If you give me the information I want now, your friends will suffer less."

He motioned to the gorilla, who turned and slammed a fist into Isjet Yazhul's ribs. The older man went down moaning. From the force of the blow, Alex guessed at least two ribs had been broken. Vilinia attempted to go to Isjet's side, but another guard restrained her. She glanced at Alex. His eyes told her to calm down, so she stopped resisting the guard's firm grip. Instead, she gave the man in the blazer a melting look.

"A woman with passion," he said. "It would be a shame to kill something as wild and full of life as she is. Her life is in your hands, Mr. Barrett—as is that of Mr. Yazhul. You see, I am tired of waiting and out of patience, but I am also a realist. I will give you their lives for your information."

Tazbir, until now standing quietly near the door, stepped forward to say something when the gorilla grabbed him by the throat and lifted. The traitor's feet were an inch off the floor and his eyes had begun to bulge when he stopped struggling and was allowed to fall in a heap on the floor. He choked, grabbing his throat as if to make sure it hadn't been crushed. Alex found himself sorry it was only a "sit down and be quiet" kind of lesson.

"Earlier today Tazbir met with Kherensky to make plans for

the Tartar's betrayal of you and these two. Maxim," he said, looking at the huge man, "saw the meeting and reported it to my other
son, who reported it to me. I made contact with the Tartar and
made him an offer he couldn't refuse. I even offered my assistance. As you have proven tonight, he needed it. I owe him nothing, because in actual fact he gave me nothing. I took it for
myself."

"Then you don't intend to keep your deal with him," Alex
said.

"I will kill your two friends for him only if you let me down,
Mr. Barrett."

Alex knew what he had to do. "We talk, alone."

The man saw that Alex was serious and made a decision. He
waved his hand at the gorilla, who helped Isjet to his feet, then
pushed him toward the door at the far end of the cabin. The second guard motioned for Vilinia to go with him, but she hesitated.
Alex gave a nod, and she walked after her father, anger in her
eyes.

"Get them some dry clothes," Alex said.

The gorilla looked at the man in the suit, who nodded. "When
you are finished, Maxim, you must take the launch and go for
Sergei. He will have Thompson by then. Tell your brother Mr.
Barrett is our guest and bring them both here." The Giant stared a
moment, then nodded, a little slow in catching the order. Alex
realized the man wasn't mentally sound.

A third guard put a gun in Tazbir's ribs and herded him
through the door to the outside deck. Alex was pleased that he
looked frightened.

Once they were alone, Alex spoke his mind. "I am the only
one who can give you what you want. I think it's worth the lives
of my friends *and* myself."

"There is the envelope from your father's safety deposit box.
I can wait."

"You'll wait in vain. The box is empty. I put the envelope
somewhere else."

The man faced Alex. "You lied to Andrei in order to buy

time. I thought as much, but Andrei wouldn't listen to me." He smiled. "You are smart, like your father."

Alex was pleased with the compliment. "From what I have learned about my father over the past few days, I owe you a thank-you."

The man stared at Alex long enough to make him uncomfortable. "You look very much like him." He went to the bar. "We were good friends once, your father and I, but then he and Lutria betrayed me."

Alex thought so. Ever since his conversation with Arthur Hainey, he had believed that Pavel Grachev must have escaped somehow. For Alex there simply had been no other explanation. "Everyone thought you died in the Khrushchev purges, a Beria man." His voice showed his lack of surprise.

"But since your discovery of your father's past, you have not believed."

"Father never believed it either."

"No, I suppose not. Why else keep his identity hidden even after my apparent death?" Pavel Grachev finished pouring himself a drink. "Would you like something?" he asked calmly.

"You took a page out of my father's book, staged your own death."

Grachev smiled. "Possibly an orange juice?"

Alex didn't want anything but thought the juice might help dissipate the dryness in his mouth, the knots in his stomach, and the lack of energy in the rest of his body. He nodded.

Grachev removed a carton from the small refrigerator, poured the juice, and handed it to Alex. Then he walked to the intercom and gave his captain orders to weigh anchor and put out to sea. He pointed at a chair. Alex sat down, grateful to have something that would keep him from falling. Several pictures of Grachev with children sat on the end table. The first was quite old— Grachev as a young man, two boys standing in front of him. The other was of a later time, when the boys were teenagers. A younger Maxim had joined them in front of what looked like a statue of Buddha. Alex sipped the juice, pondering the revelations thrusting themselves upon him.

"You went to China. From the look of it, they paid you well," Alex said.

"Mao was tired of paying Stalin and his Soviet machine billions of yen and getting so little in return. He saw my knowledge and secrets as something of great value. I lived quite comfortably, married, and carried on my affairs from foreign shores. Better than from the Gulag, don't you agree? Far better than the bullet they wanted to put through my head."

"Then the gorilla is yours."

"Yes, he's mine, by my second wife. She was Chinese. He's been in Russia since he was eight years old. I sent him there to be raised by his brothers. Andrei was one of them."

"And Sergei Davidov is the other."

"Very perceptive, Mr. Barrett. You are aware, then, that we used you to get to your father."

"The pieces are beginning to come together. You are responsible for his condition. He still had good years in him, Grachev," Alex said stiffly.

"You are going to hold me accountable?" Grachev smiled. "You have your eye for an eye, Mr. Barrett. My son—"

"It must be something of great value." Alex cut him off.

"You mean what your father stole from us? Yes, of great value." Grachev placed his empty glass on the table. "Have you ever heard of Grigorii Orlov?"

"Catherine the Great's lover. They had a child, but she sent Orlov packing when she saw a younger face she liked. I understand he died in debt. His purchase of the Orlov Diamond for Catherine at a cost of four hundred thousand rubles took most of his fortune."

Grachev waved his hand dismissively. "Giving the diamond to Catherine was an attempt at getting back into Catherine's good graces. She controlled important strings of continued power and wealth for him. But Orlov's finances went much deeper than the diamond. When Catherine was in love with him, she showered him with works of art and other gifts, gave him land and serfs that stayed in the family for generations and generated great wealth.

He lived like a king, Mr. Barrett. The only problem was that he didn't sleep in the queen's bed."

"Must have been a real comedown when she dropped him," Alex said evenly.

Grachev picked up his glass, saw it was empty, and returned to the bar, his back to Alex.

"Count Orlov went into a deep depression. Several years later he died in an asylum—1793. The diamond he purchased for Catherine was nearly 200 carats, Mr. Barrett, one of the largest in the world—even bigger than the Hope Diamond that sits in the crown of the queen of England. And the Tsarina snubbed Orlov—the height of snobbery, don't you think? She took the diamond, had it put in the royal scepter, where it still resides, but didn't give Grigorii the time of day." He chuckled at this irony as he faced Alex. "Orlov was my great-grandfather, Mr. Barrett. I inherited what remained of his legacy."

"Umm. I suppose you have proof."

Grachev faced him. "At present, no, but you are going to help me with that. Your father has the family papers and much more belonging to the Orlovs. He stole the legacy at the end of the war."

Alex smiled. "That's what you're after?"

"Hard to believe such a wealth of treasure could survive the Communist revolution, isn't it. But such is the case." He took another pull on his drink. "Lenin was outsmarted by the Orlovs' descendants. They were shrewd men and took precautions." Grachev seated himself. "The year before the revolution broke out, they brought everything to Crimea, to a new property, secretly, and hid all of it."

"But the Nazis found it."

Grachev nodded. "When the war began and it looked like the Germans would take all of western and southern Russia, the heirs, my family that is, attempted to ship the Orlov possessions to a safer place. The proper people were bribed, and the treasure went north. Unfortunately, it was captured at the Swiss-Austrian border by the Nazis. I found out later that Himmler was the recipient of the legacy, and that he housed it an estate near Fribourg. As you know, the German hierarchy had a insatiable passion for great art."

"It's apparent you think my father found the Orlov legacy. Where, and how?"

"Your father and Lutria knew about the loss of the legacy; I told them. I don't know how but they discovered its where-abouts—I assume through intelligence work." He smiled. "After all, it was their business. Then they set out, successfully, to recover it. They had everything sent to the West. As I told you, they betrayed me."

"A part of the operation to save the Russian pilots—after they used Hainey to get you out of the way."

"They told command in Breslau there was a stash of weapons in Gorlitz and asked for time and permission to use the resistance to capture them. It was only an excuse. What they were really after was in Himmler's palace in Fribourg, north of Gorlitz."

Fribourg. Alex remembered Hainey's telling him about the lengthy reconnaissance by Michael and Arkadi. "Surely Himmler had the place guarded," Alex said.

"A small garrison. Most were pulled back to Berlin to make their final stand and save the city from the Russian onslaught. Michael and Arkadi used partisans to take Himmler's palace, commandeer a train, and ship two carloads of material east. At a crossing near Breslau, one of the cars was detached and hidden in a bombed-out factory with a rail head that ran directly inside. The other one was sent on to Breslau with what was purported to be the weapons stash captured at Gorlitz."

"Then the weapons did show up."

Another nod. "Arkadi and Michael had them stored in a ware-house at the train station, and eventually they were used in the war effort. It made the story plausible and aided in their deception."

He leaned forward. "My two friends then took leave to recover from their exploits. According to war records, Arkadi stayed in Breslau, and Michael went to Vienna, Austria. Two days later, a Captain Yergin requested a pickup of the train car outside Breslau for delivery to Prague. It was listed as munitions to be used in the war effort."

"But according to war records, which I assume you searched diligently to verify all this, no Yergin was stationed in Breslau."

"That is correct. The Soviet Union controlled Prague at the time, and station logs housed in historical archives in Moscow show the car was reassigned for Allied use in the Austrian theater and went from Prague to Vienna. The phony Captain Yergin accompanied the cars and saw that they were delivered to the station at Vienna, where the contents were placed aboard American transport trucks. At that point they disappeared, and so did Yergin."

"And you think Yergin was Arkadi Lutria, and my father the person who took delivery in Vienna."

"I don't think, Mr. Barrett, I know. The method of removing the legacy from Fribourg has been documented by excellent research done by Sergei. Before the split of Russia and Ukraine, he worked in the Historical Archives in Moscow for many years. Once I told him where to look, he was highly effective in his findings. In combination with firsthand testimony of the existence and capture of the legacy from Himmler, it is sure that the legacy was stolen by your father."

"Firsthand testimony? From whom?"

Grachev smiled. "Your father, Mr. Barrett. Michael Poltoron."

Alex sat back, a question answered. "His offering for the freedom of Nadia and the boys."

"Then you know of that unfortunate part of our history."

"Arthur Hainey."

"An old friend. It was not my wish that he die. Thompson . . ."

"Blew it."

Grachev nodded.

Alex picked up the picture of the boys in front of the Buddha. "The two boys with Maxim, older, but they're Nadia's children, aren't they."

Grachev nodded again.

"When your father came to make a deal for Nadia and the boys, he offered me that which he had stolen—the Orlov legacy."

Alex thought it quite an offer for a man who had gone to so much trouble to steal it in the first place.

"You hoped Nadia would marry you, let you raise the children," Alex said.

"I was angry as well, stunned when your father told me he and Lutria had found the Orlov legacy and retrieved it for themselves. But trading even that for Nadia and the children was out of the question."

"Honorable." Alex downed the last of his juice.

"No, foolish. I thought I could have all of it."

"So you put off Michael with excuses while trying to work out a way you could force him to deliver the legacy and still keep Nadia and the boys."

He nodded. "I delayed too long, and Beria did the unpredictable." He sipped his drink. "Beria was struggling with Khrushchev for leadership, Stalin all but out of the picture with failing health. Beria needed all the propaganda he could muster. He released the story about Arkadi and Nadia and sent her and the boys to Siberia. She died on the way."

In Alex's way of thinking, only part of it fit. "But the children survived."

"Yes, but I knew Michael would demand the children's release, so I told him all of them had been killed."

"And he believed you?"

"I gave him convincing evidence—pictures of Nadia after death, two children at her side. Michael had never seen them in person, and the dead children buried with her were very close likenesses. I had the boys taken care of and finally released, then provided for. In essence I became their father. I had their names changed and put them with someone I trusted to take care of them, then kept our relationship as private as possible. The action proved correct."

"When Beria was purged, you were forced to flee to China, leaving them behind. You planned for just such an event."

"In those days you planned for all kinds of contingencies. When I was forced to flee, they could not go with me; I did not want them to go. They were Russians and deserved to be raised in Russia. But if I had not taken this precaution, the government would have imprisoned them. As it was, Khrushchev knew nothing of them, and they were safe to continue their education and development. After Khrushchev's death I was able to return, privately and under a false identity. I told them of my heritage as an Orlov and my wishes to include them as my heirs. We have worked to that end ever since."

"And you think this is your chance to get back your family's heritage."

"The boys have searched for many years, tried to find where those trucks deposited their treasure, but your father covered his tracks very well. We never found it."

"How do you know it still exists?"

"The items have never surfaced on either the black or real market. They are hidden, and your father knows where. He hides them because he blames me for the death of Nadia and, he thinks, the boys." He shrugged. "What other reason would he keep them hidden?"

Alex could think of several other reasons but didn't say so. He didn't think Grachev would appreciate his candor.

"How did you find out Father was still alive?"

Grachev smiled. "I have always known. Finding him was the difficulty. As I have told you, China was my place of residence after fleeing Russia, but I managed to travel to other areas of the world, under an alias, of course. In 1985 I made my first visit to your United States. On my way from Los Angeles to Las Vegas, we had a layover in Salt Lake City. I stayed in a hotel across from your Temple Square—very nice, just remodeled, the Temple View, I believe it was called. Anyway, there was an article in the paper about Barrett Bank's purchase of a small bank in Southern Utah. There was a small photograph of the group involved. Although it was not a very clear picture and your father's appearance had been altered somewhat, I recognized him, or thought I did. Needless to say, I was quite excited. I stayed in the city for several days, visited the bank—just the parking lot. I wanted to get a better look at him. Once I saw him in person, I was sure. I flew back to Eastern Europe immediately and met with Andrei.

He was in the KGB at the time, and he used his position to get other photos and information. Everything verified that Charles Barrett was Michael Poltoron."

One chance in a million, and yet Alex remembered the picture, remembered how upset his father had become when he saw it in the papers. At the time, Alex had attributed it to his father's eccentric attitude about such things. Now he saw it for what it was, a matter of survival. It was ironic that the one picture that had slipped past his father's fanatic avoidance of such things was the very thing that had given away his whereabouts.

If Grachev's story were true. Other parts of it weren't, but Alex wasn't sure about this part. He still had one question: if Grachev found his father in 1985, why wait eight years before doing something about it? Or had he?

Alex wanted to ask but was impressed to bite his tongue. It was important that Grachev think Alex was becoming a believer. It was an edge Alex felt he needed.

"You know the rest, Mr. Barrett. Now you know why you are here. I want the information you have, the place where my family's treasure is hidden."

"Set us free and I'll give you what you want," Alex said.

"I am sorry, Mr. Barrett, but you will never be free. Any conditions you set must not include yourself."

Hearing his death sentence stated so coldly made him feel faint. He fought it off.

"Not a very appetizing bargain. I suppose you'll explain."

"It is obvious. You know too much about what I have done to get what belongs to me. The international community frowns on kidnapping and murder, especially if there are witnesses. You are a witness. I and my sons cannot enjoy the fruits of our labors if you are around to have me thrown in prison."

"I don't suppose you would accept my word of silence."

"You have the same sense of honor and justice as your father. I do not think you could make such a promise in the first place, and if you did, it would be a false promise. No, Mr. Barrett, I cannot take that chance."

"Sorry, no deal." Alex said.

"You have your two friends to worry about, Mr. Barrett; do not forget that. At present they are no risk to me. They do not know me, do not know about the legacy, and have no proof of my involvement. And if they do pursue us, Sergei will quiet them through government channels. I do not fear them; therefore I have no reason to kill them. But if you give me reason, if you force me to use one of them as leverage so that you come to your senses to save the other, I will do so."

There was a long pause in which Alex tried to rub away the cold. Being in Pavel Grachev's presence was like being in the way of a chilling wind that froze clear to the bone.

But Alex had no intention of freezing up. Or of letting this enemy kill him. Not without a fight. He had to buy some time.

"They go free before I lead you to what you want."

"Arrangements can be made, but how do I know you will give me what I want if I let them go?" Grachev asked.

Alex knew that two must play at the game of half truths and outright lies when dealing with a man like Grachev, but for the briefest of moments he wondered how God viewed such lies. Then he let it go; more than his life was at risk. He had no right to forfeit the existence of Isjet and Vilinia and felt justified in doing whatever was necessary.

"There was a map in my father's safety deposit box—a World War II map with red marking the route of the shipment from Breslau to Vienna, then west. I know where that line ends. I also know the name of the place where what you're after is hidden. I have other information you will need to actually get what you want."

Grachev gave it some thought, then picked up his glass and took down the last of the liquid. He checked the time by the clock on the wall. "We will dock in Sevastopol in a couple of hours. I will tell you if I am willing to trust you before we do. For now, change into dry clothes and rest." He motioned to the guard near the door.

Alex got up from the couch and headed for the door, the guard behind him.

Grachev watched after him. Michael's boy was sharp, but,

like his father, he had a weakness—he cared. Grachev would exploit that.

He was sure Alex Barrett hadn't believed all of his story, even though much of it was true. Eventually Grachev intended to tell him the truth anyway. For now he had the leverage he needed to keep Barrett going in the right direction.

He looked at the clock again. Thompson had arrived at the airport by now unless the plane was late. He would be at Sergei's soon. There was the chance that Alex Barrett was lying about the envelope, that Thompson had it in his possession. If so, that would give him even more leverage against Barrett, possibly even do away with his usefulness. Then he could be eliminated.

He took his glass to the bar and placed it in the sink.

Barrett didn't know that the Chinese no longer paid Grachev for his services, that he was close to running out of the kind of money to which he was accustomed, that the family business needed new capital to move to the next step where real money could be made. But, now with a little patience, those problems would soon be resolved.

He thought back to all the times Michael Poltoron had defeated him. He thought of Arkadi, Nadia, and all their friends who became traitors to Russia and the new order. Then Michael had wanted to take Nadia and the boys away from him a second time. It had been more than anyone should have had to bear at the hands of another. And the legacy—it did belong to the boys. He was their father. Michael did not deserve it, nor did Alex Barrett. He was not a true Russian. He would only bring disgrace to it.

Finally! Finally he would have his revenge! It would be complete this time, and Michael would lose everything.

He walked to the windows and looked across the dark water to the distant lights of Yalta. He had waited so long.

24

LOGAN WAS STANDING ON THE SIDEWALK near the exit, the snake-skin boots pinching his feet enough to make him want to rip them off and give them to the beggar just down the walk. And what was he doing out this time of night anyway? Logan supposed he thought the late plane from Istanbul a good time to pick up on rich travelers.

He checked his watch again. Had they missed him? He looked down at the boots, then at the footwear of others waiting for rides into the city. It was ridiculous to think there could be a mistake about identity. He leaned against the wall.

Where was Max? He hadn't shown his face since they had parted ways on Samos island off the coast of Turkey.

It hit him. He looked back at the beggar. Same height, same weight, a beard that was dirtier, longer. And the face—what an ugly face! Add to that the dirty hat and scarf tied around his ears and under his chin, the old coat with its collar up . . . Logan nearly laughed; Max had outdone himself this time.

The beggar glanced at him, then turned back to the business at hand.

Logan watched the street, the cars, the faces. Better not watch Max; if anyone noticed, was watching him . . .

He looked around again, watching for even a hint of anything out of the ordinary, for someone else who didn't fit—someone watching him, waiting—someone with a bulge under a jacket. There were a couple of tourist types. One couple looked as if they came from Russia but were a terrible mismatch, the woman twice the size of her husband and expecting as well. She carried the lug-gage and almost bullied him out of the building and onto the sidewalk, yelling at him in Russian and pointing toward the city. Definitely a beleaguered husband.

Logan looked at his watch again and broke out in a bit of a sweat. It had been too long. They must be on to him. So much for buying time for Alex.

He removed a handkerchief from his pocket and wiped away the moisture collecting on his neck and face in spite of the cool evening.

A black Chaika pulled up to the curb. Logan felt his mouth go dry as a man of slight build stepped out of the back door and approached him. The beggar launched himself toward them, but the woman shoved her husband into his path, then grabbed Logan by the collar and threw him against the door.

Before Logan realized what had happened, the man from the Chaika had shoved a gun into his face and told him to get into the car. Logan glanced over his shoulder and saw the woman smashing the beggar against the wall, then fighting to get free. The woman wasn't a woman at all. The beggar hung on, tripping her as she tried to get away, and they went down. Logan was on his own.

He was pushed into the car, his carry-on tossed in after him, and the man with gun followed, the weapon still shoved firmly into the side of Logan's face. Seconds later the driver was pulling away from the curb and into traffic. Logan didn't see Max running after the car because the gun kept his face forward until they were well down the street.

"My name is Dimitri Bugalov, and you are not William Thompson."

"Your weapon, please." The small man spoke it in fair English as he lowered the gun.

Logan was flustered, unsure of what to say, of *how* to say it, but he thought a direct approach was probably his only option.

"Point that gun another direction or I'll ram it down your throat," he said, looking as nonchalantly as possible over his shoulder. He could only wonder if Max had recovered yet.

"Your friend will not be coming. Your weapon, please."

Logan looked at his captor with empty eyes. "I don't have a gun. Customs doesn't allow it."

"I believe you made arrangements on arrival. Remove it."

Logan lifted his coat to show he didn't have a weapon. Max was supposed to take care of things so he didn't need one. "Check for yourself, shorty," he said.

The man patted him down good. "The name is Dimitri. Where is Thompson?"

Logan decided the truth wouldn't hurt—under the circumstances, might even help.

"Dead. A car accident."

"And who are you?"

Logan looked out the window. They were climbing up a hill. The city looked fairly large but not very well lit. "I have an envelope that I expect to be paid for."

Dimitri tried taking Logan's carry-on. Logan resisted, then shrugged and let go. "You won't find it in there. I may not be Thompson, but I'm not stupid either."

"That is yet to be seen," Dimitri said. He spoke something hurriedly in Russian to the driver in the front seat. Logan didn't understand a word but sensed he was in deeper trouble than he had thought. The Chaika turned sharply down a side road that led into a ravine. The envelope actually was in his carry-on. At least *an* envelope was in it—an envelope stuffed with yesterday's *Deseret News*. There was nothing he could do about that. Since there wasn't a sign of any car lights behind them, he decided it was time to try getting out of this mess on his own.

"I want to see Davidov," Logan said.

Dimitri looked startled at the use of the name.

"How do you know—"

"I know a lot more than you think I do. I know about the American, Alex Barrett. I know Thompson kidnapped him and had him sent here. I know you interrogated him and sent Thompson looking for the contents of the envelope at a bank in Salt Lake City. I was there; Thompson was killed and I wasn't."

He paused. "If your boss wants the envelope, he'll have to deal with me now."

"How do we know you're not a policeman?" Dimitri asked.

Logan decided to gamble. "I am a cop, but that doesn't change anything. I'm willing to sell him the envelope." All Russians thought American policemen were corrupt, just as all Americans thought all KGB agents were corrupt. Each country could thank television for the misconception. Logan thanked television for the idea.

"And what is the price?"

Logan faced the smaller man with anger in his eyes. "Listen, you! You're nothing but a small-time hit man with the intellect of a snail! This has nothing to do with you, so lay off the questions!"

The man jammed the gun into Logan's ribs. It felt like a hypodermic needle, but Logan refused to flinch, his eyes boring into those of his captor, who leaned forward to speak, his foul breath reeking of garlic and half a dozen other repulsive smells.

"And back there, at the airport, what was that? Your American idea of softening up the opposition to get a better deal. You are lying, American, and I am going to kill you!"

Logan was slammed into the back of the front seat by the force of whatever hit them from behind. Then he was slammed back into the seat as the driver overcorrected. The car behind them had no lights on, but the second time it smashed the Chaika, the lights were shattered anyway. This time the driver of Logan's car jerked left, and the car hit the soft shoulder of the narrow road. The mushy dirt pulled hard at the wheel, and the driver pulled hard to the left to keep the vehicle from being dragged into the gutter. When the wheel snapped free and the car swerved back onto the highway, Logan grabbed for Dimitri's hand and shoved it forward. The gun fired, putting a hole through the front of the windshield, shattering it. The driver's natural reaction to the unexpected was to jerk the wheel again, knocking Dimitri further off balance and sending the car out of control. Driving a fist into Dimitri's chin, Logan opened the door behind him and shoved. Dimitri spun out of the car and onto the pavement, bouncing twice and coming to a stop at the side of the road as the car hit a rut and flipped. Logan felt the vehicle turning under him and snatched anything available to keep from being thrown out. When the vehicle stopped, he was lying on the ceiling, the driver next to him, unconscious.

Logan shook his head, trying to rid himself of the cobwebs muddling his brain.

He didn't think anything was broken and tried sliding out through the hole where the back window had been. The space was narrow, the top of the car pancaked, and he didn't fit. He could smell gasoline; he knew he didn't have much time. He shifted his position and wiggled his way to the front of the car. As he struggled past the seat toward the windshield, he sensed another presence and glanced to his right. A pair of large, hairy, muscled legs in flats the size of small boats greeted him.

"Late again, Max," Logan said.

This woman who was a man stooped, lowering the rest of his body to a position where he could reach through the broken window and give Logan the benefit of a strong hand. Between the two of them, Logan wriggled free of the wreck, grabbing his carry-on as he exited. Then the two of them pulled the unconscious driver free and into the grass at the side of the road. While Logan caught his breath, Max ran back down the road and checked Dimitri, who was sprawled like a beached jellyfish in the grass. When he returned, he was shaking his head. "Broken neck," Max said.

Max was not only missing his blond wig but his dark moustache and beard as well. He stood before Logan in a flower-print dress with what Logan estimated must be a size forty-eight bustline. The makeup was so thick Logan figured it must have been painted on with a standard paint roller.

"You're looking lovely today," Logan said.

"I like to dress up for my men," Max said.

"Where's your husband?"

"Him? Some poor sap who just got off the plane. He thought I was crazy."

"I thought you were the beggar."

"I knew they were on to you when I saw him hanging about.

No beggar in his right mind is on the street at this time of night, not even in this country. I took him out because I thought you could handle the little fella on your own."

"He had a gun in my face, Max. What happened to your beard?"

"It wasn't mine." He shrugged. "I'm not deep cover anymore, Logan. My face is well known by enemy and friend. I use the beard when I want to travel in peace."

They had both been watching the car, fascinated as the gas ran from the punctured gas tank onto the road, wondering what would finally set it off. As the car settled on its roof, a spark ignited the fuel, and the explosion threw metal heavenward to come hurtling back onto the pavement with a tumultuous clatter. The fireball reached into the dark night, illuminating the trees around them. Logan could see several beat-up houses set back away from the road.

The driver moaned, pulling himself back to consciousness.

"Anything seriously wrong with this guy?" Max asked.

"Broken leg, maybe a bit of a concussion." As the fire died down, Logan was hit with the ridiculous notion that it wouldn't be long before they could roast a hot dog on it.

Max pulled the man to a sitting position by grabbing his shirt. His eyes widened when he saw the half man–half woman staring at him through fake eyelashes. Max said something in Russian, shook him a little, then pointed to his leg. The man shook his hand vigorously in the negative, speaking in a mumbled fury. Max said something else that sounded to Logan like a threat, then let go of his shirt as he fell back in the grass.

Max stood up. "Come on. The locals will get him help." He moved toward a car further down the road that had its front end bashed in. Logan picked up his carry-on and stepped to Max's side.

"That thing will run?"

"Chaikas are like tanks, Logan. It takes more than a little tail-bashing to put one under. Although, lights we don't have."

"What did you tell the driver?"

"You don't want to know, Logan, but it had something to do with his good leg." Max smiled.

"And what did he tell you?"

Max opened the door on the driver's side and got in. Logan joined him through the passenger's-side door after tossing his carry-on onto the back seat.

Max was fastening his seat belt but didn't start the car, his eyes on the glowing flames in the middle of the road. A half dozen people from homes in the surrounding trees were gathering, admiring their handiwork. "I think we'd better move on before the regional police start asking questions." Max put the car in gear. He drove the Chaika into a driveway and turned around. Logan was surprised at how well they could see with only the light of the moon.

"Bless a merciful God for a full moon, Logan. Without it I would never have gotten close enough to help."

"You didn't answer my question. The driver—"

"He said Davidov is exactly where I thought he was and that an American was being delivered there tonight." Max turned left at an intersection.

"Where did you get the car?"

"It belongs to the American consulate here. A friend of a friend gave me permission to use it." He shifted as they hit the main highway and headed right. Logan glanced at his hands; they were shaking. He rubbed them together, realized he felt sweaty but cold. After-battle jitters. He'd had them before.

"Where is Davidov?" Logan asked.

"Housed at a rather large estate in the hills north of here." Max was squinting into the night, the car going at a pretty good clip, when he suddenly jerked right and slammed on the brakes. They turned off the main road, and Logan picked up his stomach from the floor.

"You should warn a guy before you do that," Logan said.

"Sorry. I forgot you have a weak stomach." Max grinned.

Max slowed down as he came up behind a car, then passed it on the narrow road. Logan held his breath and noticed the driver of the other car suddenly go pale when they appeared at his side.

Max pulled on the wheel of his car and nearly went off the edge of the road before recorrecting. Logan looked over his shoulder as the car pulled up and stopped in the middle of the road.

"You probably gave the guy a heart attack."

"Too young."

"Not so. You're giving me one, and I'm only in my thirties. Slow down, Max, before you kill us both."

Max lifted on the pedal a little—Logan figured about two miles an hour. He wanted to look at the speedometer but decided against it—better not to know.

"Davidov spends a lot of time down here. But then, that's not unusual for a man in a government position. They usually have money—bribes. But we think his reasons for coming here run deeper than that."

"Entrepreneurs of the lower kind."

"Rumor has it that he and his brother tried to get in big, involve themselves in the selling of a few warheads of the nuclear type to a nation near my own."

"Syria?"

Max nodded.

Logan remembered what they had gone through to stop something like that from happening only a few years earlier. He supposed it was only a matter of time, but he knew what it meant to Max's country, and to Max. "But they weren't successful."

"People in the military already had a corner on that market and weren't about to share in the profits, so the Davidovs moved into black-market goods. They make a fair living by smuggling them in here and selling them through kiosks in Kiev, Kharkov, Donetsk—all the larger cities. They also smuggle a few things out, although in Ukraine there isn't much to sell."

"Small-time mafia."

"With dreams of expanding. For that they need capital."

"Kidnap a rich man's granddaughter." Logan wondered if it was that simple.

Max nodded. "Davidov's brother, Andrei, lives in Yalta and is probably responsible for the smuggling operations. He is also former KGB and likes to dabble in the finer arts, such as fileting people alive and using drugs as a tool for interrogation. He was an advisor in Syria for a couple of years, and I ran into his work once or twice."

"Nice."

"Alex has probably had talks with both of them by now."

It wasn't a pleasant thought.

"We're going to pay Davidov a visit," Max said. "Alex has to be there, but if he isn't, we'll have a talk with Sergei or Andrei, or both if we catch them together. They'll know where to find Alex."

They were high in the hills now on a road that traversed a deep ravine, a stone wall on one side defined by the moon's rays. Logan could see that a fall from this point would be fatal and hung onto the door handle as Max pushed the Chaika beyond a reasonable speed.

"How do you know where this place is?" Logan asked the question to keep his mind off his own mortality.

"I was here once. When Brezhnev lived here and my government was negotiating an end to conflicts between Israel and Egypt, he called a private meeting. I came along as an aide to our intelligence chief."

They were high up the side of the ravine now. When the car came to an opening in the trees, Logan could see only the dark canopy of the forest accentuated by moonlight below them.

"How much further?"

"Shouldn't be far. The fences are tall, unmistakable, even in the dark."

They went another mile; then Logan saw high walls anchoring a main gate about a hundred feet off the road. The canyon dropped off to the right, the stone wall the only barrier between the road and a three-hundred-foot landing. Max turned left with the road and followed the estate wall until it ended, then kept going another mile before turning right and climbing higher into the hills. Ten minutes later he pulled the vehicle down a dirt road through trees and into a clearing. He stopped the car next to a snub-nosed, dark-blue van.

A stocky man dressed in black was removing items from the back of the vehicle. Logan was shocked to see Claire helping him.

"What the . . . "

"Watch your language, Logan." Max smiled. "As you can see, your little lady is not one to take orders."

Logan looked miffed. "Yeah, I know, but you should have tied her up—put her on a plane or something."

Max laughed. "I tried—putting her on a plane, I mean. Relax; be glad she loves you this much. And don't forget, it is her brother we're trying to save." He opened the door and got out as Logan did the same. Claire met him at the door, put her arms unashamedly around Logan's neck, and kissed him. Logan decided having her there wasn't so bad after all.

The stocky man finished his task and joined them. He extended a hand and introduced himself as Ilya in good English. Apparently he had no last name. Max told Logan he was one of Israel's best-trained people but that he was scared to death of heights. Logan didn't understand the joke, but all of them were laughing.

Max opened the back of the van and stepped in, followed by Ilya, then Claire and Logan. Once the doors were closed, Max turned on a light and pulled a map from his case. He put it on the floor before them, using a pencil to point at a set of boxes near the center of the picture. Logan couldn't get over how odd he looked in a dress and war paint.

"Quit staring, Logan," Claire said. "You're making me jealous."

"And you're making me nervous," Max said.

"Just get on with it, Max," Logan said.

"Ilya was kind enough to provide this schematic of our objective. He used to work inside the house until Davidov started using it and Kherensky's people began running the place for profit." He pointed at the center, at a large building. "The house. It is a hundred yards from any side of the outer walls, with nothing but open grass and a few small trees in between. My information tells me there will be plenty of guards, dogs, cameras, and a dozen other obstacles between us and the front door." He smiled at Logan. "So we will not go to the front door."

"I'm counting my blessings already," Logan said flatly.

"We passed the main and only gate. At one time the place was considered impenetrable, but that was when a garrison of the Soviet's most elite troops were housed here to protect Brezhnev and the other leaders using the place. We're lucky; we won't have to deal with them." He wasn't smiling anymore, and Logan held back the wisecrack scratching at his lips.

Max removed a large pair of binoculars from his case. "Ilya, you and Claire keep watch, will you? Logan, you join me." All of them got out of the van, and Logan went with Max.

The breeze was brisk. They walked through the trees and underbrush until they came to an open spot overlooking the hills below. In the distance Logan could see the moonlight glinting off the Black Sea, the lights of several large boats dotting its surface. Max flipped a switch on the binoculars, then put them to his eyes.

"Night vision," he said, moving them, searching, finally finding his target. After a few minutes he handed them to Logan. "Take a look."

Logan was amazed by the quality of vision. He picked out the complex wall and followed it until he was nearly blinded by a light. He jerked the binoculars away from his eyes.

"They don't work well against bright light," Max said with a smile.

Placing them back to his eyes, Logan found the wall again, then searched for the house. It stood in the open, flat roofed, expansive, with balconies, stairways, sidewalks, shrubbery, and a few trees, including a stately Crimean pine on the back side of the house. There were at least a dozen guards with nasty-looking weapons.

He handed the binoculars back to Max. "I think we should call the police."

"They are the police, Logan, remember?"

"It's impossible. No way in, and even if you do get in, you're dead before you reach the house."

"We can't wait until Davidov brings Alex out, can we. Because Alex may never come out. And we do have some time restraints. The guy we left back at the burned-out Chaika will get to a phone before long, and then we'll have no chance at all."

"Are you sure Alex is in there?"

"We think so."

"You think so?"

"I'm not your American Superman, Logan; I can't see through walls. All our intelligence indicates Davidov is there, and Alex should be as well. You heard the driver—a delivery was to be made. Ilya says a car came here about an hour ago. I can only assume Alex was on board."

"But you didn't see him."

"The car went directly into the garage. The windows were so dark Ilya couldn't see anything. And don't forget—if Alex isn't there, Davidov still knows where he is."

All was silent as Logan took one last look; then they started back through the woods. "I get the impression you have a plan," Logan said.

"As you will see, getting in will be the easy part. Getting out is another matter." Max smiled. "We'll have to convince Davidov it is in his best interest to give us safe passage."

"Gentle persuasion."

"Whatever it takes to get out the front door standing straight up."

"And if he's uncooperative?"

"You've been in the situation before, Logan. You know the drill."

"Retreat under fire. I remember. We were lucky that day, Max."

"A charmed life is a long life."

They reached the clearing.

"Turn on the car lights, Logan, so we can see what we're doing while we finish putting this contraption together."

Going to the car, Logan found the switch and pulled it on. On the ground was a large pile of black nylon and several short pieces of stainless-steel pipe.

"What's this stuff?" Logan asked.

Max grinned at him as he started unfolding the cloth.

"Wings, Logan. Wings."

25

I SUPPOSE YOU'VE DONE THIS BEFORE." Logan said as he pulled his part of the double harness tighter.

"Many times. At night, only once. Our special operations program has studied the use of such conveyance for insertion purposes. My interest in the sport instilled a natural curiosity, and I involved myself in training. I had just accomplished my first successful night flight when you pulled me away for this day in the sun," Max said. He had changed from the dress into dark clothes and had removed the paint from his face, replacing it with dark camouflage paint. Now he looked as though he had been washing in mud. But then, so did Logan.

"Great." Logan looked at the silk above them as it caught gusts of the brisk wind coming up the mountain. The stainless-steel pipe had been connected in less than half an hour, then Claire and Ilya had applied the silk and attached the guy wires and harness while Max gave Logan a crash course in weapons he hadn't seen before.

"You carry this thing in your suitcase, I suppose."

Max laughed. "No, this one isn't mine. Ilya provided it when we figured we had Davidov cornered. We knew we'd need an unusual way in."

"Borrowed?" Logan said it with a smirk.

"These mountains offer some of the best winds in the world for gliding. It's becoming a hot spot for the sport—cheap hotels, fair food, good weather, and winds that can carry you for hours. A new shop was recently opened in Yalta by an American woman by the name of Jensen and a Crimean partner. They had everything we needed." Max smiled. "Ilya is one of their instructors."

Logan looked at the automatic rifle lying in the grass near his feet; it had several clips with it. It was an American-made M-16A. He wore a bullet-proof vest from which half a dozen grenades hung by small hooks. Tucked inside was a standard army-issue .45 caliber handgun. Max had similar weapons and a very large vest.

"Where did you get this kind of armament inside Crimea?"

"We picked it up in Samos."

"And smuggled it in."

"You can get anything into Crimea for the right number of dollars, Logan. Since the dissolution of the Soviet Union, weapons flow back and forth across the borders as easily as your American-made Snickers candy bar. Which, I might add, is very popular here. If I told you why I was able to get American weapons on a Greek island only a stone's throw away from the conflicts in Turkey and the Middle East, you would develop an extreme dislike for your country's weapons industry."

Max handed him a pair of night-vision goggles. He saw the worried look on Logan's face. "Just remember what I told you, and you'll be fine."

Logan didn't smile, the crash course in weapons operation cascading through his mind like a waterfall at flood season. He'd never pull this off.

But he'd try. They were out of options, and Alex was running out of time.

They slipped the black stocking caps over their heads, then the night goggles. Clicking on the switch, Logan tried getting used to them. It was no use. He took his off.

"Too much. These will get me killed."

"You only use them while you are in the air."

"Uh-uh. I trust you'll handle that part. I'll have my eyes closed anyway." He handed them to Claire. "The moon is good enough."

In fact, what had given them light coming up the mountain was now their worst enemy. They would be sitting ducks against the light sky unless clouds suddenly appeared. Their only hope was to stay low, just above the trees, which brought to mind other possibilities Logan didn't want to think about.

They adjusted their harnesses one last time. Max was in the rear, with Logan strapped in a second harness in front. Logan would dangle below Max once they were in the air. The harness had been altered to release easily—the Velcro didn't give Logan a lot of confidence.

"Ready," Logan said, drawing a deep breath.

"Remember, from here it's straight along the ridge. Once the wind catches under the wings, relax and let me do the flying."

Logan nodded, his heart racing, his stomach in knots, and his lips and throat too dry to say anything more.

Claire stepped up and kissed him. "See you at the main gate." She looked pale in the dim moonlight. Claire was smart enough to understand the odds, but she knew they were worse for Alex if they sat around and waited for Davidov to cough him up. For Logan, nothing had changed but method. He had started this whole thing to free Alex; that was still his purpose.

Logan and Max picked up the frame and balanced the huge bird above their heads. It wasn't easy; the wingspan was a good thirty feet to each side.

"Go!" Max said.

They started their run. The strong wind coming up the ridge caught the wings, pummeled them, then flowed under and lifted them after only fifty feet. Logan felt his feet leave the ground and his muscles tighten. He tried to relax. "Just dangle," he told himself. "Let Max . . . "

The wind caught the wing—Logan's breath caught in his throat as Max adjusted, and the large black bird soared to an even keel again. Logan choked down the bile that had flooded into his throat while having visions about his legs being snapped off by solid objects such as trees and hard ground.

He tried concentrating on the lights far below, but the black of the mountain, the sudden appearance of trees grasping at him like the dark hands of the devil himself, kept his eyes wide and on the immediate space in front of him.

Max pulled on the guide wires, working the air currents, moving the sleek, quiet glider toward their destination while maintaining a close proximity to the treetops. Logan was amazed at his calm, and at his talent.

"The wind is good tonight. We could stay aloft for an hour, maybe more," Max said.

"Maybe another time," Logan answered evenly. He was beginning to like the feeling of it while still fearing for his life. "Do you ever stop being afraid?"

"No, that's part of the challenge, dealing with the fear," Max said.

They were nearing the estate.

"This is the tricky part," Max said. He manipulated the lines, and they did a hard left turn that sent Logan's stomach into his throat. They started down fast, heading into the mountain, the sound of the wind rushing past, growing louder.

"The mountain—" Logan started to say.

Max pulled hard on the lines, and the glider turned sharply again at tree level, then soared toward the estate. They were coming in low—too low. Logan saw the buildings coming at them, saw the side of the big house. They were going to crash, to splatter themselves all over the northern wall! Logan closed his eyes, then felt a sudden lift. He opened his eyes as they came even with, then rose just above the flat roof.

They settled to the landing, and Logan's feet churned. He tripped but caught himself, and they pulled back on the glider, stopping ten feet from the edge of the flat roof. Quickly they undid their harnesses and left the glider sitting. The sound of the Velcro opening was so loud that Logan cringed.

Going to the edge of the roof, they gazed into the compound below. Logan had been fearful he'd be staring into the upraised barrels of a dozen weapons, but he was relieved to find this side of the compound empty. He could hear chatter and laughing—normal stuff. Their luck was holding.

Logan handed Max his rifle, grabbed the edge of the roof, and let himself over. Swinging his weight back and forth, he dropped himself over the edge of the balcony railing and onto solid wood. He reached up, took the weapons from Max, and waited for him to use the same method. They worked their way quietly toward the rear of the building, checking each door until they found one open. Letting themselves in, they closed it.

It was a large bedroom with a large bed. No one was there. They checked the bath—black tub, black tile, gold-plated taps, large mirror. Lots of space but no people. Everything looked expensive, European and American.

They went to the hall door. Logan checked his watch. They had been down two minutes.

Nothing in the hall. Logan let himself out, Max behind him. Twenty feet to the stairs, the open railing looking down into an entryway. They stopped in shadows as a door slammed.

They could hear leather heels on a hard floor, a door opening and closing, then silence.

They moved. Max checked the entry below before going down the stairs with Logan covering him. Once Max was down, Logan quickly joined him.

A voice—behind the door to the left, the sound of muffled talking. They positioned themselves at each side of the door, then glanced at each other, ready.

A door opened down the hall directly opposite them, and a man stepped in. He pulled his gun up to fire, but Max beat him to it. The assailant went down screaming as the wall and door next to Max were shredded. It had been close.

So much for stealth.

Davidov was closing his briefcase when he heard the gunfire and looked at Maxim standing near the door. He gave the Giant a hard look, and Maxim turned to check it out.

The door opened fast and hard, hitting Maxim in the mouth and knocking him back a step. A man dressed in black was standing in the doorway, a ski mask hiding his face. He drove the rifle into Maxim's midsection with little effect, then swung the butt into the Giant's chin, knocking him onto the table.

"Kill him, Maxim." Davidov was out of his chair and through the side door, depending on his brother to give him time. He pulled a gun from his shoulder holster as he scampered down the hall to the kitchen. He needed to get to the garage.

Logan saw only the man's back as he fled out the door. He was starting after him when the gorilla grabbed his shoulder, turned him, and put a fist to his jaw. Logan landed on the floor several feet away, dazed, shaking his head to get rid of the cotton. The gorilla jumped at him again, lifting him off the floor for launching. Max used the butt of his rifle to cave in the assailant's kidneys, but the Giant didn't seemed to register much pain. He turned just enough that he could latch onto Max's gun. He wrenched it free, throwing Logan across the couch and into a table, dazing him. Then the gorilla turned on Max.

He threw Max's weapon against the wall ten feet away, then hit Max with an earth-shattering right that made Logan cringe. Then Max was flattened against the wall when he got a left to his stomach that sent all the air in his lungs into the room, and he melted to the floor. The Giant turned to Logan, who started backing away, then to Max, who wasn't going anywhere or doing anything but sucking air. Then he left the room the same way Davidov had gone.

Logan gathered himself up and locked the door as the sound of yelling and running feet came from the entry. He retrieved his weapon, then helped Max to his feet.

"What was *that?*" Max asked, still fighting for air.

"A one-man wrecking crew. Are you all right?"

Max nodded. "Go after them. Don't let Davidov get away. He's our ticket out of here, remember? I'll check the house for Alex."

There was pounding on the solid-oak, reinforced door.

"Thirty seconds and they'll be in here. Keep moving."

Logan moved quickly to the door leading into a hallway. Through years of police experience, he had learned to use caution and revealed only a small part of his shoulder to the man he knew might be at the bottom of the stairs. As he pulled it back, a gun fired. The bullet planted itself in the frame, and Logan closed his eyes in a long blink, grateful for experience. He hated gunplay. Making sure his safety was off, he tried again. No shot. He closed the hall door behind him and locked it against pursuers, then went quickly down the hall and into the kitchen. He saw the open door to the cellar. Grabbing a pan from the counter, he waved it quickly across the open doorway. The bullet knocked it out of his hand and sent it clattering to the floor. He stuck the automatic around the corner and fired, then stood straight while Davidov answered with another couple of shots from his handgun.

Logan ripped off the black mask. It was stifling hot; he could hardly breathe and was sweating buckets of salt. The air felt good, the pressure lousy.

He fired again, just to let Davidov know he was still there, then took a deep breath and started down the stairs.

———————

Max had moved from the living area into the den by a connecting door, which he locked. The pursuers were having a hard time breaking the first door down, and Max was grateful that a paranoid Brezhnev had ordered good, solid doors. From the den he had gone through a door with a security lock on it by blowing the lock away with his weapon. He had been forced to take down a guard there who had fired at him but missed. Now he was standing over that guard, his rifle barrel placed between his eyes.

"The American," he said in Russian.

"I know of no—"

Max pressed on the gun while glancing through the window in the door he had just entered and locked. No one.

"Don't lie to me."

"He . . . he was coming but did not. I don't know anything else. Please, my family—"

Max pressed on the gun while taking a quick survey of his surroundings. It looked like a suite with several large bedrooms, a living area, and an office. A hallway ran to the back of the building. Obviously Alex wasn't there—which meant it was time to leave.

He pulled his gun away as he saw the armed man on the other

side of the window at the far end of the hall. The man fired. Max jumped back but knew he was too late. The bullets hit the glass, making spiderwebs with small, lead centers. Max mentally thanked Brezhnev a second time, this time for the shatterproof glass.

He ran left down a hall between rooms, then right through an atrium with windows on one side. Too late he noticed several guards in the yard. They could see him through the wall of windows. Now knowing Brezhnev's penchant for safety and betting the glass was bulletproof, Max just gave them a smile and walked nonchalantly across to the far door.

The guards stared at each other in disbelief for long seconds before one raised his gun and fired.

When the glass shattered, Max dove for cover. This time Brezhnev had failed him.

He gathered himself up and ran for the door, praying it was open, knowing he had only seconds before a bullet caught up with him.

He grabbed the knob as bullets ripped up the plaster to his left. Yanking the door open, he jumped through and slammed it behind him only to find himself on the outside of the house in full view of the same guards.

He fired and they scattered. Removing a grenade from his pocket, he pulled the pin and threw it into the yard between the scattering guards, then ran for the door thirty feet away. By the time he arrived, he was being followed by a hail of bullets that failed to end his life only because he managed to get on the other side of a bulletproof door as they caught up with him.

Sweating and weak, he leaned against a wall long enough to catch his breath, then locked the door.

He was in an equipment room. To the left was a large furnace with the word "Lennox" written on it; he wondered if anything in this place was Russian.

The reinforced door was being fired on, but no bullets broke through. Max had seen such doors often; they were on every office in his office building and had Kevlar centers.

He heard something from beyond the door on the far side of

the equipment room—the starting of a motor. His mind ran through the schematic, and he realized he was on the back of the garage, Davidov's escape route.

He crossed the room quickly as he heard a garage door opener click on. He opened the door and saw the Chaika, Davidov sitting behind the wheel, the gorilla in the passenger seat.

The Russian saw him at the same time, fear mixed with anger and hard determination in his eyes. He jammed on the gas feed, and the Chaika leapt forward. Max fired, his bullets planting themselves in the Chaika's windows and side but without compromising them. Bulletproof.

The car hit the door, top high, bulging it out, then splitting it before breaking free with Max staring after it.

Davidov was gone.

Max saw the flashes of light in the darkness outside and dove for cover as bullets planted themselves all around him. Someone appeared at the far door. It was Logan.

"The car!" Logan yelled, pointing at the second vehicle in the garage.

Max nodded.

Logan fired at the opening, giving Max enough time to cover the ground and get into the driver's seat. Logan put in another clip, then lay his gun down and used his teeth to pull the clips on his grenades. Tossing them out the door, he picked up the gun and waited for the explosions. The impact shook the building and threw a cloud of dust over the doorway. Logan dashed to the back door of the car, opened by Max, and threw himself in. Max pushed on the gas feed, and the car bolted into a mess of startled guards. One knelt to fire. By aiming the car at him, Max informed the gunman he had better get out of the way. He lunged into the bushes to the left as the Chaika hit the spot he had occupied.

Another guard fired as they sped by him, and Logan thanked a merciful heaven that the glass was bulletproof. Max redirected the car again and again, forcing guard after guard to run for his life. The glass in the window opposite Max was hit twice but held; hit again, started to bow; three more shots and it was lying on the seat.

Logan leaned forward over the seat, keeping as low as he could, and fired back. Another window was hit, shattered, fell.

Logan ducked, and Max hunkered down in the seat. Logan came up again, a new clip in his gun. He stuck the weapon out the window and fired at anything that moved. It was survival now. And freedom was still three hundred yards away.

After Max and Logan had flown into the night, Claire had moved the van into the shadow of trees along the road near the front gate. Then she and Ilya had climbed onto the roof of their vehicle so they could watch through the night-vision binoculars and give help if needed. Claire could see the glider atop the roof and knew Max and Logan had landed without breaking half their bones. She also knew they had gone inside.

"Please, God, get them out!" The prayer had been said under her breath even as her hands shook with the tension.

The first gunshots came from inside. There was momentary confusion; then guards converged on the house from every direction. Claire had gripped the binoculars so tightly her knuckles had gone white. She had watched the gate, could see it beginning to open, and knew the world was falling in around Logan's ears.

Moving the binoculars back to the house, she could see everyone in the yard running toward the front entrance. Then a group broke away and went left, another right. They disappeared around the sides of the house.

Her heart was pounding. The numbers looked overwhelming! How could Logan and Max possibly get free?

Minutes passed. No sign of them. Gunfire in back. An explosion. A few minutes later the garage door began to open.

A car exploded from the opening, splitting the half-open door. Claire focused the binoculars on the vehicle. Two men. Logan and Max? Davidov and Alex? They were too far away, and the binoculars were not good with detail.

Claire jumped from the roof of the van and placed herself behind the wheel. She rammed it in gear as Ilya belted himself into the passenger seat, then released the safety on his automatic.

They both knew they had to meet that car, stop it if it was Davidov. They had to get to the road coming out of the compound first, had to block it.

Sweat ran down the sides of Claire's face, the adrenaline running hot through her system. She pushed on the gas feed and prayed she would get there first.

To the surprise of both drivers, their vehicles arrived at the intersection at the same time. Davidov saw the van only a few feet away just as Claire slammed on her brakes. He tried to swerve but was too late to avoid a collision. The blue snubnose of the van hit the door of his car on the passenger's side and drove the Chaika toward the wall running alongside the mountain road. He tried giving the vehicle more gas, but the motion of the car had been drastically changed, and his tires couldn't correct it.

He watched in horror as the side of the mountain suddenly appeared, nothing but a two-foot rock wall dividing them from a three-hundred-foot drop to their graves.

Desperately Davidov slammed on the brakes, but the car still hit the wall, driving through it and sending broken rocks flying into the thin air of the Crimean night, the car finally stopping only inches from pitching over the edge. Davidov froze, got control, and slowly moved across the seat toward Maxim and the passenger's door. He reached across his brother and clawed for the door handle, still looking at the abyss of the canyon he was trying to escape. The car teetered as if playing with them before passing final judgment. Davidov glanced toward the passenger's door and viewed the front of the van planted solidly against the smashed-in door and bowing window. Then his eyes looked higher to see a woman behind the wheel.

Claire couldn't move, her body and mind frozen in shock. The van motor had died, and steam was rolling from the snubnose grill stuffed into the side of the car. All was quiet. She could hear popping sounds in the distance, the squeaking of the car scraping against rock as it teetered on the wrong side of disaster. Her eyes first met those of a large man in the passenger's side of the car. He seemed confused, frightened. The second man was next to him. His eyes were desperate, pleading. Sergei Davidov.

Alex was not with them.

Claire searched for a way out for them, but there didn't seem to be any. There was a shifting of weight, and the black car tilted further away from her. The only thing keeping it from going over the edge was the van. She gripped the steering wheel tightly, afraid to adjust her weight, afraid the car would free itself and topple over the edge.

Ilya had other concerns. Ripping off his seat belt and ejecting himself from the seat, he went for the back of the van, exited, and placed himself behind the closest tree, aiming at the guards standing near the gate. They stood there for several seconds before realizing the danger imposed by his automatic weapon, then ran for cover. Ilya could see the second car coming down the drive in the distance, bullet riddled and practically windowless. He held his fire. His time would come.

Another shift in weight, another slippage. Claire could see the car was just seconds away from becoming airborne. Davidov seemed to sense it and said something to the larger, Oriental-looking man. He nodded, then doubled up his fist and drove it into the window, once, twice, three times. It cracked, bowed, but didn't break. He kept pounding, his hand bleeding with the effort. Finally the window weakened, then bowed further out and fell into the gnarled mass of the attached vehicles. Davidov scrambled over the Giant like a child scooting from its mother's lap. He squeezed his way through what little of the opening wasn't filled with the front of the van.

He was free.

Claire watched as the Giant positioned himself to do the same. He worked his head through the opening without trouble, but his shoulders simply weren't going to fit. Davidov tried to pull him through while looking anxiously over his shoulder at the gate. He seemed to grow impatient, then afraid. Jumping from the wreckage, he had the driver's side door open before Claire could think to lock it. Grabbing her arm, he pulled her from the vehicle, throwing her to the side. She fell to the ground as he replaced her in the van. She scrambled to her feet, yelling.

"Stop! Don't move! You'll kill him! The car—"

Davidov looked toward the gate, seemed to panic. He looked into the eyes of the Giant as if pleading for forgiveness, sweat rolling down his face, fear in the set of his jaw.

He turned the key. Miraculously the motor started. It had a high-pitched sound, the fan screaming against the radiator. Claire covered her ears, her eyes riveted to the two men.

Davidov looked one more time at the Giant, yelling at him to get free! The Giant struggled but was caught, frustrated, confused. Davidov cursed, then rammed the van into reverse and pulled away.

Claire screamed as the two vehicles separated and the car began its fall. She ran to the car, grabbing the large man by the hand and trying to free him, trying to keep him from going with the car. He pushed and she tugged, his fear so thick between them she was choking on it. The car slipped further, lifted, ripping him from her grasp. He looked at the fleeing van in disbelief, then down at the canyon, then at Claire. The fear, the anguish, the confusion on his face made Claire scream for him as the car fell and he disappeared.

The sound of scraping metal filled the canyon, echoing from its walls as the car crashed against the sides of the cliff on its way to annihilation.

The explosion jolted Claire's teeth, and flames lit up the trees and forest like the flash of a camera as the car hit the solid rock of the canyon floor.

Claire closed her eyes in anguish, then heard someone scream.

Max had seen the gate closing, the taillights of Davidov's car on the other side. He had seen the van come out of nowhere, then the collision. He had felt his stomach lurch upward, afraid for Claire and Ilya.

He had pushed on the gas feed, the Chaika plummeting down the hill; had watched the guards at the gate turn on him, about to fire. Then he had watched them flee, looking over their shoulders and toward the van. Max had seen the flame of gunfire in the darkness by the van and had known Ilya was clearing the way. Now, his hope renewed, he concentrated on getting past the gate. It was still partially open when they hit the wrought iron.

The car caught, hesitated, then tore free and continued its course for another hundred feet before he came opposite Ilya. The van was fleeing down the road ahead of them as Max hit the brakes, bringing the car to a stop in the middle of the road. He watched, paralyzed by the scene of the limo reaching high in the air, a man the size of a large tree desperately trying to free himself from the window of a mangled door. Then he watched it disappear over the edge of the precipice to its inevitable disintegration.

Logan saw Claire and ejected himself from the car. When he reached her she was screaming, staring down at the fire and rubble of the car, tears rolling down her cheeks. He picked her up in his arms and walked briskly back to the Chaika, placing her in the back seat while Ilya and Max kept an eye on the gates. He slid in next to her and closed the door.

It was then he noticed how quiet the night air was. No one was firing, not even talking. He glanced over his shoulder and out the bullet-riddled back window. The guards were standing near the gate next to the wall, staring down into the chasm.

It was over.

Davidov wiped his mouth with the back of his hand. He had to do it. It was survival! There was no way to free Maxim! He had to leave! Everything would have been ruined!

He cursed, slamming his hand against the steering wheel. The van's radiator was pouring out steam, but he pushed on the gas feed anyway. He had to hurry! They'd come after him! He had to get to the launch, to the boat! Had to get to Pavel!

He had to make Alex Barrett pay!

The car, the windows blown out or masked with cobwebs, one headlight shattered, and steam now rolling from its bullet-vented radiator, limped down the hill toward Yalta. Twice it killed, threatened to quit completely, but Max nursed it on toward the valley floor.

Claire pulled her knees up, placing her head on them. She felt sick but was too tired to even throw up. So much death! So much destruction! And for what?

Alex was still missing.

26

ALEX FELT BETTER AFTER CHANGING into dry clothes. He stared at himself in the mirror. The flesh around his eyes was less swollen but still black and blue, matching the color of the shirt he'd been given to wear.

He walked to the small portal and stared at the distant shore. They were sitting at anchor, a city at a good distance opposite them. The sun was giving its first morning light, and the scene seemed tranquil, even picturesque, making him wonder if he had dreamed everything that had transpired over the past few hours. The reality made him shudder, the scenery before him taking on a pale quality that marred its beauty.

Alex had tried to work things out in his mind—divide the truth from the lie. He had more pieces of the puzzle now, was beginning to see the whole picture, but he was still a few pieces shy of being absolutely sure.

Obviously Michael and Lutria had taken something from Germany; that part of Grachev's story held true. Alex also knew Grachev thought Alex had that something, calling it the Orlov legacy—items of art, precious gems, gold, and silver. The actual value? Alex didn't know, but if Grachev was speaking the truth, it was considerable.

Alex could live with Grachev's "what," even though it seemed a bit farfetched; he just hadn't come to grips with the "why."

There were only two possibilities. The obvious answer was that Arkadi and Michael had removed the legacy for its value, but Alex knew Michael hadn't needed the money, and Arkadi had gone back to Russia, putting himself in a position where he could never spend the fruits of his efforts. That made no sense.

The less obvious answer was that Arkadi and Michael had wanted to protect whatever was taken, to get it out of the hands of the Nazis and keep it out of the hands of the Soviets. The problem was, if they thought that much of what they had taken, if they felt the things should be preserved and displayed, why hadn't the items surfaced after the war? Why keep them hidden? Wouldn't they see that the items got into a national museum where they could be properly cared for? They would. The only thing that might have prevented them from doing so was the destruction of the items in transit. It was a possibility. A bomb, fire, loss at a river crossing—all were possibilities. But not the only ones.

Alex was still deciding. He needed one more piece of the puzzle.

Alex *was* sure that Grachev was lying about Nadia's death. She wouldn't have committed suicide to escape Karaganda herself while leaving the children behind to suffer its atrocities on their own. Possibly she had poisoned all of them, and Grachev was lying about Andrei and Sergei. But why the elaborate deception? Why create children to replace them? You would have to take care of them, brainwash them, teach them, prepare them for your great ruse. And on whom would you pull this ruse if you weren't even sure Michael was alive?

Alex didn't suppose it was beyond the realm of possibility, but it left him with a lot of unanswered questions.

A second possibility was that Grachev had killed Nadia—a fit of rage born of jealousy or her refusal to marry him. Accidental? Probably, but Alex knew it could have been more than that in Grachev's case. If Nadia were fighting him, refusing him, telling him she would rather die at Karaganda than be his wife and have him raise her children, he might have murdered her.

The thought made Alex shiver. It meant their own lives were of little value to Pavel Grachev. If he had killed Nadia, whom he was supposed to have loved, he would certainly kill Vilinia. And if Grachev wanted to destroy Michael Poltoron as badly as Alex thought he did, he would most likely want to destroy Alex as well. The man was filled with hatred.

Where did the hatred come from? Alex supposed that if Grachev's story about the legacy were true, that Michael and Arkadi had taken it from him, that would warrant some of it. But Alex didn't think the story was true—at least not all of it. The hatred had developed much earlier, during the war. Part of it came from the fact that Grachev held Michael responsible for Nadia's rejection of him as her husband, and for her acceptance of Arkadi's proposal of marriage. Had jealousy, could jealousy, fill a man with that much hatred?

That was at least part of it, but Grachev also held Michael responsible for Arkadi's decision to betray Stalin and the Soviet system, along with all the others Arkadi had recruited in that cause. Grachev probably also held Michael responsible for his forced removal from Russia and having to live outside his country for more than forty-five years.

In fact, as near as Alex could tell, Michael was a convenient scapegoat for Pavel Grachev, carrying all the sins of the past on his shoulders, and Grachev wanted revenge for every one of them. His lust for that revenge accounted for a lot of things, including keeping the children's survival a secret and infecting them with the same hatred that poisoned his own life. Alex couldn't help but wonder what other atrocities had and would be committed in the name of that hatred before this was all over.

Alex went back to the window and stared at the deep blue of the sea. Did the Orlov legacy really exist? Had Michael taken it out of Germany? Had he then offered it to Grachev to buy freedom for Nadia and the children?

In reality, it didn't matter if the legacy existed or not. Grachev believed it did, and he wouldn't be satisfied until he proved it to himself one way or another. Michael could have fed him the story, made Grachev a believer, in order to free Nadia and the children. What greater temptation for a man of Grachev's degenerate nature?

But whether the legacy was truth or fiction, Michael's story had its down side. Once Grachev believed the legacy existed, he wasn't about to let it slip away. After Nadia's death and Grachev's vengeful decision to keep the children, Grachev had gone after

Michael, had tried to capture him, to bring him back and force him to lead Grachev to the promised wealth of the legacy. It must have been a bitter pill when Grachev's henchmen returned with word that their carelessness had caused Michael's death and that the offered treasure was out of reach.

Alex now knew that was the point at which his father had made the decision to let Michael Poltoron die. Michael had known he would never be safe from Grachev's greed and hatred, and neither would any of his family. He had made a new life, a good life, one that had offered even more than his life as Michael Poltoron, but he had never stopped looking over his shoulder—not even when word had come to him that Grachev was dead. There was no body, no physical evidence, only a small write-up in the Soviet papers. Michael understood the system, knew it could be circumvented, and knew Grachev had a talent for doing so. He was smart enough to stay hidden.

Alex was coming to a complete understanding of why Grachev had made the decision not to let him live. Grachev wasn't just afraid Alex might ruin things for him; in fact, Alex doubted that Grachev feared him at all. The man had to kill Alex because Alex was Michael Poltoron's flesh and blood. He wanted to take everything from Michael, eliminate every vestige of Michael's existence, and the moment he had discovered Michael was still alive, his goal had become single. He wanted to eliminate everything Michael had created—his empire, his reputation, his family. That was why it had been so easy to make a decision to kidnap Melissa. There had never been any intent of letting her go. All of them were scheduled to die, sooner or later.

A picture flashed through Alex's mind of his father fighting for Melissa's life. Grachev had found him. Charles had known it, had known Grachev was after everything that was important to him. He had defended it with his life. Now Alex deeply regretted his stupid pride, which had kept him from being there for his father.

He thought about his father's excommunication—not so much the fact of it but about why he had been so quick to judge his father as guilty. Yes, there was evidence; the woman had

walked into the court and personally accused Charles Barrett. But
with all that his father had been, all that Alex knew of him even
then, why had he judged so quickly?

He supposed part of it might have been his reliance on the
Church leaders, some of it his reliance on his mother, the rest his
own stubbornness, his willingness to accept the outward evidence
instead of the inward feeling as proof of guilt. Thinking of it made
Alex hurt inside.

A knock came at the door, and a guard came in, weapon in
hand. He used it to motion toward the stairs. Alex closed the door
and started for the main cabin. As he entered the room, Grachev
was standing near the windows, the light from the early morning
accentuating his gray and somber face. He held a telephone at the
end of a long cord and was carrying on a conversation. When he
saw Alex, he gave a curt motion for him to sit down. Alex walked
to the couch where Vilinia sat and took a place next to her.

"How are your ribs?" she asked.

Alex nodded an okay. "What's up?"

"I haven't been able to hear what he is talking about, but it
seems serious. What are you planning, Alex? What did you tell
him when you made all of us leave the room? And what does he
intend to do with us?"

"You're leaving the ship, Vilinia—you and your father. I'm
staying."

"No!" she said. "I refuse to leave you with this lunatic!" She
pronounced it a bit loudly. Their host, involved in other problems,
didn't notice.

"He'll use you as leverage, Vilinia. He'll torture you or your
father until I tell him what he knows, then kill all of us anyway.
This way there is at least a chance." He glanced at Grachev, the
guards. Preoccupied. Then Alex talked to both Vilinia and Isjet,
who was sitting next to her. "I will take Grachev to a town called
Voltaire, near Geneva, Switzerland." He sat back. Isjet nodded.
Vilinia took Alex's hand and held it tight. Alex wondered if
they'd ever have a chance for more.

He glanced over at Grachev. His posture, sagging shoulders,

and pale color made Alex cold. Something had happened. Something had changed.

Grachev faced Alex with a cold stare, speaking into the phone mechanically. "You know what to do. Have them clean it out, completely. Be sure you take care of the body." Grachev hung up the phone.

Alex knew what was coming and felt fear grip the lining of his stomach. He could see it in the blank eyes, the iron set of the jaw. Alex's mind tumbled, righted itself, tried to figure out what to do to stop Grachev from doing what was clearly etched in his dark eyes.

"You have cost me another son, Mr. Barrett. For that I must ask payment." He motioned to one of the guards, who walked to Isjet. "Mr. Yazhul will be the eye-for-an-eye this time."

Alex felt the cold knot in his stomach. He had only one bargaining chip, and he wasn't sure it amounted to much now—not with the hatred he felt from across the room. But he had to try.

"Touch him and you'll never get what you want," Alex said firmly.

The guard moved Yazhul toward the door that led to the rear deck. Isjet grimaced with pain from his broken ribs but had a defiant look on his face.

"Do not tell him anything, Alexander!" Isjet said. "I go to Allah with a clear conscience!"

"But you go to Allah just the same," Grachev said. The guard had reached the door.

"I warn you, Grachev. Nothing!" Alex said. "This legacy you claim is yours will be lost again!"

Grachev motioned to the guard, who seemed disappointed, at least for the moment.

"Who has found us, Mr. Barrett? Who and how?" The questions were cold and flat, like something from the lips of a dead man. A chill blew through Alex. It was all he could do to keep from panicking, but to show fear or be indecisive now would cost Isjet his life.

"There are only two possibilities. My government seems the

most likely. They would have investigated Arthur Hainey's murder. Their investigation may have led them here."

"No, not this quickly, and they would use proper channels, not attack Sergei's home. There is someone else, Mr. Barrett. Who?"

"Logan. Captain of the Park City police. Logan is investigating the kidnapping and must have found the man your son sent after the envelope. It is the only other possibility."

"A more likely candidate, but without the connections to accomplish the disaster this morning."

"It may be a combination of the two," Alex said flatly. "Either way, your little can of worms has been opened. It won't be long until they find you."

"I agree that speed is of the utmost importance. Therefore, I advise your complete cooperation."

"Not until you set Vilinia and her father free." Alex saw a man enter from the hallway, a man he recognized—Sergei Davidov. Then it was the Chinese-born son that had been killed. He was disappointed.

Davidov looked worn, tired, and afraid, but the hatred in his eyes was as real as Grachev's. Alex was glad the man was unarmed and tried to ignore him as Davidov went to the bar and poured himself a drink. He and his so-called father seemed to have the same appetite for American whiskey. Another worry—whiskey invited boldness and induced poor judgment. That, with the captors' already unstable minds, meant things were bound to become explosive.

"I will get the information from you or your friend will be shot and thrown overboard!" Grachev said.

"Do not tell him!" Isjet spoke in calm defiance. At Grachev's nod, the guard hit him across the mouth and told him to shut up. Isjet spit in his face. The guard sent Isjet to the floor with three successive blows. Isjet didn't move. The guard stepped back, aiming a foot at Isjet's midsection.

"Grachev! Stop him, or I'll give you nothing!"

"Wait!" Grachev said, a wicked smile on his face.

The guard's booted foot stopped in midair.

"Let Mr. Barrett decide," Grachev said.

Alex knew he had to call the man's bluff but didn't like doing it with someone else's life. He prayed for calm.

"I'll give you what you want, but I have terms."

Grachev's laugh turned Alex cold. The man was nearly over the edge—Alex could feel it.

"Do you hear, Sergei? Mr. Barrett has terms." He downed his glass of whiskey as he took the gun from the guard next to Alex and shoved it under Alex's chin with such force that it broke the skin. Alex winced and pulled away, but Grachev kept the gun against his skin.

"If you kill me, your sons will have died for nothing." Even Alex was surprised at the calm in his voice. "I hold the key that can make this all mean something. All it takes is a decision that will set my friends free."

"You will die, Alex Barrett. One way or the other, *you* will pay for what you have done to my sons!" He pushed harder on the gun, making Alex flinch again.

He spoke to the guard standing over Isjet while keeping his eyes on those of Alex. "Take the old man downstairs and lock him up! Only Mr. Barrett and the woman will go with us." Grachev pulled back on the gun, and Alex started breathing again. He glanced at Isjet, who was lying on the floor, partially conscious. Alex thought of forcing the issue, of making them bring Isjet along, but something told him to let it go. The guard helped Isjet to his feet and practically carried him to the door leading to the stairs. Alex feared for Isjet because of the lust for brutality he saw in the guard's eyes.

Alex . . . please . . . "

"He'll be all right, Vilinia." The tone was even, confident. He wanted to go to her, take her in his arms, and give her reassurance, but he knew it would be unwise. Grachev would perceive it as a weakness and exploit it. "Won't he, Grachev."

Without answering, Grachev went to the bar and retrieved a clean glass. He seemed calmer now. What he put in the glass he downed with one motion.

"Yazhul will remain here as security. If we run into any problems and do not return, he will be killed. You, Mr. Barrett, and the woman, will go with us. She will act as a deterrent as well—leverage to assure your fullest cooperation. If I sense that you are stalling or leading us astray, she will suffer. If you give us what we want quickly, I will set her free, then her father on my return."

"What guarantees do I have?" Alex asked.

"None, Mr. Barrett, but it is an offer you had better not refuse. I don't believe that a few extra hours to make you talk will hurt my chances as you would like me to believe. Push me, and I will kill Yazhul in front of you, then torture the woman until you talk."

Alex had hope. Everyone was still alive; he had bought time. His instincts told him to take what was offered.

"I accept the terms."

Grachev gave a condescending laugh. "These are not terms, Mr. Barrett! I dictate them to you, and you will do what you are told." He downed another whiskey. "You are not dealing; you are surrendering. You have no choice because I deal from the position of strength, and yours is one of weakness. You will always deal from such a position, even if you hold a gun to my head! Do you know why, Alex Barrett? Because you are weak. You care about people, and that gives me the advantage." He smiled wickedly. "You are a godfearing man, Alex Barrett; I am a godless one. In this physical world, my kind rule your kind, because we have only one law—survival, at all costs. Even human life is of no concern to us. We defeat you because you hold life too dear."

The words were full of hatred, spewed forth like acid.

Grachev signaled, and the guard took Alex by the arm to remove him from the room. Alex held back, staring at his captor with determination.

"You think of yourself as godless. You do not worship the same supreme being as I do, Grachev, but you have gods, just the same. You worship at the feet of greed and hatred. They rule you, control you, more than my God would ever control one of his creations. You consider me in bondage while you see yourself as free when just the opposite is true. You are bound, Grachev, controlled by your gods. They tell you to hurt people, and you obey. When their insatiable appetites cry to be fed, you present human flesh at their altar. How many lives have you sacrificed to your gods, Grachev? Arkadi, Nadia, my father, Arthur Hainey, and now your sons! All because of your gods! The life of my father bears witness to your weakness, Pavel Grachev. Nadia and Arkadi bear witness. Now, even the lives of your so-called sons bear witness as well. Your gods make you vulnerable, Grachev. They make *you* weak! It is because of them I know I can defeat you, even as my father defeated you!"

Leaving Grachev cold and silent, Alex walked from the room. It was life or death now, and Alex knew it.

His intentions were to live.

Logan glanced at his watch—nearly eight in the morning. Claire was at the airport, aboard the plane, two of Max's men with her. The evening had taken its toll. Logan worried about both her and the baby. He insisted that she stay and get some rest, knowing she wouldn't but content to have her where further pressure wouldn't make things worse. It had been a frightening night for both of them. He was on the edge, and she simply couldn't take any more. Both of them knew if they didn't find Alex soon, they wouldn't find him at all, and it haunted them. It was a nightmare that wouldn't seem to end, or that would only end badly. Logan knew if it did, they'd both be ready to check in to the appropriate ward at LDS hospital.

He stared out the window anxious, depressed. After everything that had happened last night, it was obvious that Sergei Davidov had a number of accomplices, including the regional police chief, Lazar Kherensky. Kherensky was a powerful man in Crimea, and no one questioned his authority or his demands while he was in a position to have them shot for doing so. But Kherensky was missing, had been since the killing of two of his top aides on the embankment sometime during the early morning when Logan and Max were busy at Davidov's. Janos Lopukhin, second in command under Kherensky and visibly pleased that his boss's body had been found about sunrise by fisherman who had gathered the former commandant up in one of their nets, was now in a talkative mood. His description of Kherensky's years as commandant were the stuff bad movies were made of, and Max quickly moved him to a discussion of the past few days. It was about those days that Lopukhin was presently filling them in as they drove toward the Brezhnev house and last night's battleground with Davidov. Lopukhin was taking them back to the house where they had so nearly died. It seemed like the only place available to get back on track and find Alex.

"He ordered us to keep this very quiet. To the commandant it was a matter of national security," Lopukhin said.

"And you believed him?" Max asked.

Lopukhin only shrugged, shifting down a gear to make the corner.

"What were you to keep quiet?" Max asked.

"The fact that we were hunting an American for the killings of two men."

"Did he tell you the American's name?"

"No, but he gave us a description." Lopukhin repeated it.

"That's Alex," Logan said.

"Who was he supposed to have killed?" Max asked.

"That is what I find of great interest. You say that Sergei Davidov is responsible for the kidnapping of this American friend of yours. Sergei's brother, Andrei, was one of the men killed."

Lopukhin told them about the story Kherensky had told them to spread about the American—that he was an Englander, that he had killed a woman and child, and that he was dangerous. "It was very strange. He even told us to give a false description of the American. It was almost as if he didn't want him caught and yet . . . "

"From the look of things he had an accomplice—an accomplice who betrayed him." Max said.

"It is possible," Lopukhin said. "Two men say that they had the American under gunpoint and were going to deliver him to Kherensky for the reward when they were waylaid. Both have concussions to prove their story, but Kherensky simply had them thrown in solitary confinement and gave orders no one was to speak to them until he said so."

"But you did."

"This morning. They told me of two men who were trying to help the American. They are also missing, along with the older man's daughter. Their names are Isjet and Vilinia Yazhul and a friend known as Tazbir."

"It's safe to assume that all of them were at the embankment last night and at least one of them betrayed Alex to someone," Logan said.

"Whoever it was also betrayed the commandant," Max said.

"That would be Tazbir, I think," Lopukhin put in.

"Why do you say that?"

"I saw the commandant speaking with him." He shrugged. "It is as you say . . . an educated guess, but it is known to us that he wanted to replace Yazhul in the high councils of the Tartar people. He was also in much need of money. It is the kind of person Kherensky would use."

"I suppose you did a search for this Tazbir and the others at the spot where Kherensky was found collected in the fisherman's nets," Logan said.

Lopukhin nodded. "We found no sign of any others."

Max spoke. "Sergei Davidov and Kherensky had worked together for a long time, along with Andrei. For some reason Sergei decided to cut Kherensky out this time."

"The commandant was very excited after returning from a meeting with Davidov. Such excitement came only when money was his motive. It was very much money this time, I think," Lopukhin said. "He was very agitated and got upset over very small matters. He threw a fit when I questioned the two men who had seen the American with Yazhul and Tazbir. He cursed my family, then told me he would be glad when this was all over and he would never have to look on my face again."

"Enough money he was going to walk away?"

"Kherensky had made a lot of enemies. His days as commandant were coming to an end, and he knew it. He may have seen this as his chance to get out with his head still attached to his shoulders." Lopukhin said it with feeling, leaving Logan with no doubt about his dislike for Kherensky.

Lopukhin shifted down, approaching the gate cautiously. The broken wrought iron had been pulled back so vehicles could come and go, but no one was in sight. Lopukhin pulled over at the broken wall. All three got out and approached the edge, peering down into the ravine. The trees were blackened by fire all around the car, now nothing more than a burned-out hulk. There was no sign of a body.

"You say this man looked Chinese?" Lopukhin asked.

Max nodded. "Why do you ask?"

"No reason." Max sensed there was but left it alone. Janos was smart, but he was also dirt poor. Max knew he had a wife and four kids and that he shared a two-bedroom apartment with six other people of his extended family. It was natural for him to look upon this as a way to alleviate that pressure; it had been a way of life in the former Soviet Union. But he would make sure of his ground before he made his pitch. Max might even make the offer before Lopukhin had to give up his integrity and ask. From his sources, Max knew it would be a first for Janos Lopukhin. He was an honest man, but this situation might be too much of a temptation even for him.

They got back in the car and drove through the gate and up the cobblestone driveway to the front of the house. The place was deserted.

Logan was the first to reach the door, and all three men drew their weapons as he turned the knob and pushed the large door aside. The entryway was dark, the house quiet. Logan went to the living room door and pointed out the bullet holes in the wall where he and Max had been fired on. In the living room, furniture was neatly back in place, the broken table and chair removed.

They searched the rest of the living areas and found them in similar condition. Going into the library, Max searched through the desk while Lopukhin and Logan moved into the area where Max had shot the guard. The window still held the bullets and the cobweb effect they had created—not enough time to replace it or fix the holes in the wall. Some things just couldn't be done in a hurry—especially in Crimea.

The rooms were all unlocked, cleaned, spotless, with no indication anyone had been living in them. Logan could see they had gone to extra pains to clear away every sign of who had been there. He wondered if they had polished away fingerprints as well but decided they hadn't when he saw several obvious ones on the glass of the door.

They moved into one of the bedrooms. "Thorough," Logan said. Lopukhin shrugged. "There are many fingerprints, but it would take a good deal of time to discover who they belong to." He stooped and looked under a bed, then checked the wardrobes. "Time we don't have."

Logan went into the small den and started a search of his own. Max joined him a few minutes later.

"Except for shattered windows and a broken garage door, along with the skeleton of that car in the ravine, you'd think we'd just had a bad dream. Someone wanted this place clean enough that it would take some time to find a trail to follow," Logan said. "Have Lopukhin see if Davidov left anything lying around in the bedroom we came through last night."

Max nodded and went into the next room to send Lopukhin on his way. Logan removed a pocketknife and wedged it between the locked drawers. He jerked the knife handle up and pulled on the drawer. It popped open. Empty. He jimmied the others and found them empty as well.

Max walked through the door and planted himself on the couch. "You know Lopukhin hasn't been completely up front with us."

Logan nodded. "What do you think we should do about it?"

"Torture. It's the only way."

Logan laughed. "Sorry, I left my tools for such things at home."

"I think Barrett Bank should float him a no-interest loan. According to Ilya, he needs a house."

"Wait long enough and he'll make a deal—probably for a lot less than what's needed to build a house," Logan said.

"The man's never taken a bribe, Logan. He's one of the few honest ones left in his rather mean profession. I'd like to keep it that way."

Logan looked at Max. "By offering him money?"

"A loan, with easy payments."

"It will look bad. They'll think he's dishonest anyway."

"They already do. It comes with the position. It's what he thinks, what his family thinks, that's important."

"You're turning into an old softy," Logan said. "Claire will make the arrangements, you can count on it. But he'd better come through with something substantial. The trail is already cold, and Alex is out of time. Davidov knows the envelope isn't coming, and he'll lean on Alex. I'd say we have a day, maybe two if Alex is as tough as his father." He paused. "If they use the woman or her father as leverage, we have less. Alex won't keep any secrets if someone else's life is in danger."

Max moved to the chair behind the desk, the couch already giving him an ache in his lower back. "If Davidov had Kherensky killed and captured Alex and the others, why didn't he bring them up here?"

"Maybe he thought some other place provided better security."

"You can say that after what we went through last night?"

"Umm. Silly isn't it. What are you thinking?"

"The third party."

"The Giant?"

"Maybe. One thing is sure—we're behind in this one, my friend," Max said. "Way behind."

And they had been so close. If they had just been able to collar Davidov . . .

Logan stared out the window at the hills he had spent his night in. They looked less evil with a bright morning sun shining on them.

Lopukhin appeared at the door, a small notebook in hand. "I have some information for you."

Max stood, and Logan turned from the window, each glancing at the other.

Lopukhin looked at his notes. "I have been waiting for some details, but I think what I have may help. The Giant arrived with Davidov and came here, staying until after Kherensky met with Davidov. When the commandant left, the Giant followed."

"Then he is probably the one who killed Kherensky."

"He didn't seem that smart," Max added.

"My sources tell me he is mentally slow, but once he knows what is wanted, he does it extremely well."

"Your sources?"

"Two men who were here last night. One of them is in the hospital, the other mending at his home in Alupka. It took me a little time to convince them they should answer my questions."

"They wanted proof Kherensky was dead," Max said.

Lopukhin nodded. "They have seen what is left of the body. They know I can have them imprisoned. Now they cooperate. I'm sorry it took so much time."

"Under the circumstances, you did a very quick job," Max said.

"Do they know what the Giant did with Alex and the others?" Logan asked.

Lopukhin shook his head. "No, they were here until after your escape, but other information may give us some direction."

"You must understand, Kherensky was the man protecting Davidov and his family, but he used us as his manpower. Some, willing to sell themselves for a little money, were used more than others, but the rest of us knew a lot about what was going on."

"Family? You mean Andrei, his brother."

"And the Giant, also a brother. Over the past few years he has come and gone, but these men tell me the Davidovs and the Giant have the same father. The father was very secretive, coming in the middle of the night, seeing only his sons and keeping himself inside, out of sight. But as two of Kherensky's most trusted men, my sources tell me they knew of the relationship because they were inside the house and lived with the family. I believe they tell the truth."

Logan and Max looked at each other. Max spoke to Lopukhin. "If there's a punch line, Janos, give it to us."

"The father is in Crimea as well."

"You're sure?" Max asked.

"I wasn't until a few minutes ago when I completed my calls.

It is another reason I delayed speaking frankly with you. I wished to be sure."

"Where is he?" Logan asked.

"It is not certain, possibly at sea. My sources tell me he comes to Crimea only by private ship and that Kherensky made arrangements for it to be docked in Sevastopol. I called the port authority there, then the office of naval operations. They are looking and will respond to this number as soon as they have information for us."

"Alex is aboard that ship," Logan said.

Lopukhin nodded. "It is most probable, but finding it will take some time, and there are other possibilities."

"Let's hear them," Max said evenly. He could see he was wrong about Lopukhin. Money was not an issue, he hadn't been thinking about a bribe, and Max owed him an apology when the time was right. All Lopukhin was doing was being a good officer, an honest man.

"One of the men who was fighting you last night, the one you put in the hospital, said the father has been here often in recent months. He came secretly and stayed with Andrei and the Giant in a ten-room house near the Tsar's palace."

"Lividia Palace, outside the city," Max said.

Lopukhin nodded. "It seems he, not Davidov, was the first to pay Kherensky for his services, for protection and privacy. He seemed to be very wealthy even though he was of Russian descent. I have men going there now."

Logan started for the door. "I think we should join them."

"It is not necessary, Mr. Logan. I do not believe they are there; it is only a precaution. We should wait for the call from the port authority."

Logan collapsed on the couch.

———————————

Time clicked off on the clock. Logan alternated between sitting and pacing, often going to the window and staring at the hills, waiting. He hated waiting.

The phone rang. Lopukhin, who was closest to it, picked it

up and spoke in Russian. Logan didn't understand any of it but tried to read what was happening in the young Russian's face. Nothing. He looked to Max.

"What's he saying?" he said in a frustrated tone.

Max just raised a hand, concentrating. "It's Ukrainian. Hard to catch some—"

Lopukhin hung up.

"The yacht is of Chinese registration—a sixty-foot boat called the *Geisha.* The address of the owner is in China."

"Owner?"

"A Peter Dang. British passport. It's a phony name. The description is the same as the one given to me of the Russian father of Sergei Davidov."

"Where is it now?" Logan asked.

"It docked in Sevastopol harbor less than an hour ago, but only for a matter of minutes. Then it went to sea again."

"Do we know where it's going?" Max asked.

"No."

"Did anyone get off the yacht?"

Lopukhin shrugged. "Sevastopol is a big harbor. That the port authority gave them permission to dock and that they left shortly after is all I know."

Max frowned, thinking. "What if they dropped someone off in Sevastopol?"

"Did they refuel?" Logan asked.

"No," Lopukhin said.

"Then someone got off. Picked up a car, maybe a plane."

"Alex is taking them somewhere," Max said. "Check the airport to Sevastopol, private jets first. I want to know if any have left in the last hour."

"Double-check anything to Switzerland or even in that direction," Logan added.

Lopukhin dialed.

"You're playing a hunch," Max said. "The letter from the bank in Geneva to Charles Barrett. The fact that he was there in 1944, had a safety deposit box."

"If Claire's father took something out of Germany for safe-keeping, that's a likely spot. It isn't much, but it's all I've got."

Lopukhin hung up. "Three flights—one went to Kiev, another to Moscow, a third to Istanbul. None west."

"Check public airlines," Max said.

Lopukhin picked up the phone again. This time he talked to the passenger desk at the airport for what seemed like an eternity, then hung up again. "All flights were full, but no one with a passport under Alex Barrett's name attempted boarding. No one answering his description went through customs. And there is no passport under the name of this Britisher, Peter Dang, either." Lopukhin seemed hesitant.

"What is it?" Max asked.

"It doesn't mean they didn't hire a charter. These days such things can be done without identity papers. And private jets often come and go quietly—government officials and businessmen who don't wish to broadcast their whereabouts."

"Money under the table," Max mumbled under his breath. "That's how I got in!"

Logan stood. "You said Davidov used a private charter to get to Yalta from Kiev."

Max brightened. "Government planes don't have to register." He turned to Llopukhin. "Check. See if Davidov's plane was in Sevastopol, if it is still there."

Lopukhin got on the phone again. He hung up for the last time a few minutes later.

"It was in Sevastopol just twenty minutes ago but is now gone. Radar tracked the plane in the direction of Simferopol. Simferopol tower tracked it further north out of their jurisdiction. The tracking station at Kharkov never picked them up, and there is some concern that the plane has gone down."

"Fat chance; they're flying under radar."

"Did anyone see who boarded at Sevastopol?"

"No one in the tower. Someone at the main gate may have seen them come, or grounds crew may have seen them board the plane, but it will take some time to find out. I will have to question many people."

Logan took a deep breath. "I think that plane is taking some-one to whatever it is Davidov is after—either that, or Alex has sent them on another wild goose chase."

"I don't think they would let themselves be taken in twice. Alex has given them information they think they can trust, but they're holding some kind of leverage—possibly a hostage aboard the yacht. Possibly all of them are hostages, and Davidov and his father have sent someone else to check out what Alex has given them."

"Whatever he told them, it had to be convincing, good infor-mation."

"But we don't know where this plane goes," Lopukhin said.

"We might be able to find out." Max picked up the phone and dialed a number. By the time he had finished, Lopukhin was vis-ibly impressed. Max had been speaking with the head of intelli-gence for the state of Israel.

"My intelligence organization will cooperate." He jotted something on paper. "Logan, when you board your plane, call this number and they will feed you the information they gather."

"Gather? How? What can . . . " Logan stopped himself. They were stupid questions Max wasn't about to answer.

Max smiled. "The method is not important at this moment, is it. Just trust that if anyone can find and track that plane, they can." They headed down the hall for the garage and the closest exit to Lopukhin's car. "Lopukhin and I will try to find that yacht. Once we board her, we'll contact you."

He turned to Lopukhin. "I owe you an apology. You're a good cop, but we've just begun taxing the limit of your abilities. I need transportation—a helicopter."

Lopukhin smiled. "That, my friend, will cost you." He grinned. Max would get what he needed.

27

LOGAN GAZED OUT THE WINDOW at the mountains below, feeling more tired than he could ever remember. Claire, sitting next to him, had her eyes glued to the latest photo fax from Israeli intelligence.

Logan rubbed his eyes and yawned. The first report had come with his first call to the number Max had given him. The plane had been spotted flying through Romania, going west, then had crossed Hungary into Austria and had asked permission to refuel in Vienna. That had been nearly an hour ago, and they still hadn't taken flight again. Logan was getting nervous.

When Logan had seen they were definitely headed west toward Switzerland, he had told the pilot to fly a direct route to Geneva. They had made up the ground on Davidov's plane and were now nearly parallel with, but further south of, Vienna. Logan was sure both planes would end up in Switzerland, but the length of time Davidov was spending on the ground in Vienna was giving him second thoughts. They were going to have to make a decision in the next ten minutes to continue their course or turn for Vienna.

Logan was also worried about what they'd do even if they caught Davidov or whoever was aboard that plane. He and Claire were like fish out of water. They knew no one, official or unofficial, who could help them if they chased Davidov into some major airport! The police force would be unfriendly, possibly even antagonistic, surely bureaucratic, and certainly negative toward foreign police arresting or shooting anyone on their soil! It was the way every police force acted toward foreign cops! That alone might prove fatal or at least cause delays they couldn't afford. And that could mean life or death to Alex!

"What are you thinking?" Claire asked.

"Whether or not to turn north."

"Umm. It has taken a long time if they only intended to refuel."

"During World War II, Vienna was in the war zone. Whatever they're after could be there. It might have been as far as Charles got with it."

Claire sat back, her hand rubbing her forehead. "If only Alex hadn't removed the envelope from the safety deposit box!" she said with frustration. "My brother has always been such a neat freak, so careful about everything, about detail! This time . . . how I wish he had been sloppy for a change!"

Logan took her hand and held it tight. They had called Hal Frost. Nothing yet, but there were still dozens of box-holders to contact. "He knew he had enemies, Claire. He took precautions by putting that envelope in a safe place he could get to. All evidence says it has to be another safety deposit box; that's the only answer."

"But there are no others. Alex hasn't been in that bank since Mother's death, and he's never had a box of his own. He doesn't even have an account there."

"Your mother's death? Why would he go there then?"

"Mom had an interest in the bank. She kept her accounts there even after the divorce. As executor of her estate, he closed them."

"Then she had a safety deposit box at one time." Logan's voice was becoming animated.

"No, I don't think so. She and Dad kept everything together. You saw their boxes."

"She had nothing of her own after the divorce?"

"Everything was liquid assets—cash mostly. There was some jewelry, but she kept those things at home, and they were given to me after her death." Claire sat up, her eyes wide. "Wait! There was something!"

"What?"

"A diamond-studded watch that belonged to my father's mother, then my mother. Dad gave it to her when they were married, and it was to be handed down to the eldest son's wife. It wasn't for everyday wearing. It was more of an heirloom, and when Mom and Dad divorced, she stopped wearing it. She might have—"

"Put it in a safety deposit box? Has Alex mentioned it? Have you seen it in his possession since your mother's death?"

Claire put her head in her hand, thinking. "No, I can't remember . . . "

"Then there is a chance it was in a safety deposit box. Claire, don't you see it might be the answer? He had to leave that envelope in that vault. It has to be the answer."

"But we looked at the list, Logan. There wasn't any . . . Windham!" Claire picked up the phone. Logan was wondering what she meant. Moments later she was connected through to Natalie at the bank. "My mother's maiden name!" She ran her hand through her hair, her face in anguish. "Why didn't I think of it earlier?"

"Natalie, this is Claire Barrett. I want you to check your list of deposit box holders for a Fontana Windham or F. Windham." Claire could hear the keys of Natalie's computer.

"Yes, number 751," Natalie said.

Claire's breath caught in her chest. "Get it opened, Natalie! It's my mother's box! Alex put that envelope in there!"

"Keys. I have only the bank's," Natalie said in a despondent tone. "It will take hours to get a locksmith here."

Claire took a deep breath, rubbing her head, pleading for help. What would Alex have done? What would she have done? Alex wouldn't have gone to all that trouble to hide the envelope, then keep the key to their mother's box in his possession. He had gone straight to the airport. Was it with the other deposit keys? No, Frost would have noticed when Logan gave them to him. Alex would want them in a safe place—in the bank.

"He left the key there, Natalie. Probably in or on your desk. Think! What did he do? Did he act strange? Did he give you anything?"

"No, no! Nothing!" Natalie said.

"Did he look in your desk drawers? Ask you for anything?

Think!" Her voice was strained and full of impatient frustration. She could hear the desk drawers opening and closing with a bang, the frantic searching of papers, the clatter of items lifted and then dropped.

Claire took a deep breath, calming her voice. "You told us he was at your desk before you, when you were returning from the back room . . . do you remember?"

"Yes. He was standing with his back to me, in front of the desk."

"He was probably putting your keys back. You said he needed them to open a box, right?"

"Yes, he would have had to take them to get in any box."

"If he dropped them without your seeing what he was doing, he might also have put his key somewhere. He—" It hit her. She knew where it was. "Natalie! How many keys are in your set?"

There was a pause. Claire could hear the jingle of keys, then a scream.

"It's here! He put his key on the ring! Number 751!"

Claire grinned and squeezed Logan's hand so tight he thought he'd lose a finger.

"Good! Now, get the envelope! Hurry! It's time we took a look at my father's papers."

Alex watched through the window as the plane drifted toward the airport runway. Geneva. Time was closing in. He adjusted his position. With his hands tied behind him, there didn't seem to be a comfortable one.

There had been one delay, another hour of life registered. Grachev had switched planes in Vienna, leaving Davidov's easily identifiable Ukrainian jet for a smaller one owned by a private firm flying out of Liechtenstein, Austria. A diversion, Grachev told them, something that would throw anyone following off their trail, at least make them pause and consider, giving them more time in Geneva. Alex knew it was smart and would make them harder to follow, if anyone was even trying.

He glanced over at Vilinia. Without a miracle their lives, and

Isjet's, would be over soon. He knew Grachev would never leave
any of them alive. They knew too much, could prove the butcher's
guilt, and, in the end, take Grachev's dream away from him.
Grachev wouldn't allow that.

Alex still had a few doubts about Grachev's legacy. But even
if it did exist, he had no idea exactly where to find it. To bluff was
inviting immediate retaliation against Vilinia, but all he had was
the map, the name of a town, and the words on the key: *Beau
Rivage.* He could only hope for a miracle.

"What do we do?" Vilinia whispered as the plane's engines
cut back even further.

"I'm going to press him for your freedom. Then you bring
help. Find a Beau Rivage in Voltaire, a village outside Geneva.
There is one in Geneva, but it was not built in 1944 and doesn't
fit what I know. Voltaire. It is in Voltaire."

She nodded. "And if he won't allow my freedom?"

He glanced at Grachev, half dozing in a chair at the front of
the chartered jet.

"We look for our first chance—"

The gun butt came out of nowhere and left a knot on the back
of Alex's neck. The pain from the blow throbbed clear to his toes
and made his eyes water and his head spin. Then the gun came
under his chin and pushed upward.

"No talking, Barrett," Davidov said, "or I will wait no longer
to avenge my brothers."

Alex stared into the cold, heavily lidded eyes without really
seeing them, trying to shake loose the cobwebs. Davidov pulled
the gun away and went forward while looking over his shoulder.
He finally positioned himself next to the man he considered his
father and shook him lightly to wake him up.

Such hatred—Grachev's work over years of brainwashing.
Alex wondered what history the man had fed Davidov when he
was young, wondered if telling him the truth now could make a
difference. He didn't think so. The bond of hatred, the loyalty of
years of brainwashing had been complete with Sergei Davidov.
The history he understood was the only history he'd ever accept.
For Alex, it was a sad revelation. The real history was so much

better, more honorable. Sergei Davidov's father had given his life for his son, for his country, even for his good name. Arkadi Lutria was a man Sergei could be proud of, but Sergei would never accept that Arkadi was anything more than a traitor because of Grachev's poison.

Alex watched as Grachev shook the sleep off. From this vantage he looked like any other normal human being just coming out of a nap, but when you looked into those eyes—so empty, lifeless. Haunted. Alex wondered how many lies one had to tell to get eyes like those, how many deaths and how much guilt lay behind them. One thing was certain: Grachev was so devoid of the Spirit that the devil ruled the house.

"Alex. Are you all right?" Vilinia was visibly angry and concerned.

He put his head against the chair. "Just exhausted."

He looked out the window as the plane touched down and braked, then turned across the runway and moved in the direction of the terminal. It turned left and went toward some private hangars a short distance away. As they passed the far end of the main building, he looked over each person he could see, each plane. No one looked familiar. No one looked like police. Everything looked normal, and he felt the sinking in his heart. If only he hadn't hidden the envelope!

Claire had looked at everything at least ten times. She was sure now they were headed in the right direction.

Natalie had faxed copies of everything to the plane's machine. It had been frustrating when some of it hadn't come through and had to be re-sent, but they had finally received it, finally had everything Alex had seen the day he disappeared.

They spread everything out. Logan had gone through the poor copies of photographs, frustrated. A woman and two boys. Grachev, Lutria, Hainey, and Michael Poltoron. Photographs that told them nothing and yet a great deal. They had learned her father's former identity.

She caught herself shaking her head at everything she saw. It was so unreal, a dream. Her father, Michael Poltoron. Russian. Jewish. A stranger. A past she so much wanted to know and understand and was afraid she never would. She shook her head for the tenth time, brushing off the desire to let her mind wander into the past, forcing herself to concentrate on the moment—on saving Alex.

Claire had studied the map. It had been copied on a copy machine at the bank in sections, then fed through the fax. She had taped them together. It was dark and hardly readable, but Natalie had told them about the red line leading from Breslau to near Geneva—to a place called Voltaire. Other names were unreadable, and Natalie had given them over the phone while Claire wrote them again. That was how Claire knew Geneva was where they needed to be. Alex was going there.

"Anything from the Israeli intelligence service?" She asked.

Logan shook his head in frustration. "Why are they delaying in Vienna?" He looked at Claire. "Your father could have moved everything there. Alex might have taken something out of the box and—"

Claire shook her head adamantly. "No, Logan. They'll go to Geneva."

Logan ran his hand through his hair. He knew she was right. "The last fax wasn't readable. Possibly they've left by now. I asked the pilot to call the number Max gave us and have it sent again. Should come any minute."

"I checked a Swiss map from the plane's tour cupboard." Claire said. "Voltaire is about ten miles outside of town, a village with one hotel and an old castle from medieval times."

"Natalie said the line wasn't that exact. It might be just short of the village," Logan said.

Claire picked up the picture of the key. The words *Beau Rivage* were stamped on it. They had found a hotel in Geneva by that name but nothing in Voltaire. It wasn't in Geneva. She knew it, but there simply was nothing in Voltaire. "We'll have to check out the hotel in Geneva." she said with a disappointed tone.

"It's the only possibility."

Claire walked to the chair next to the window and sat down, staring at the clouds below. "They have to go to Geneva."

"Security is watching for them. That plane has *Ukraina* written all over it. It isn't going anywhere if it lands in Geneva."

There was a prolonged silence.

Claire was hoping. She knew there were other small airports in the surrounding towns. But she knew Alex—knew he was smart enough to realize his only chance was to be as visible as possible. He had to take them through Geneva.

"I wish Max would call," Logan said. He glanced at his watch. It had been nearly six hours since splitting up at Yalta airport. He hated being in the dark!

He shook it off. Claire was right. Alex knew what they knew. If he wasn't aboard that boat, he was on his way to Geneva. He would do it because he would be praying they had been smart enough to find the envelope and figure this whole mess out.

Smart wasn't the word for it; *dumb luck* fit better.

"I'm going to call the airport—have a car ready." Claire picked up the phone and called the operator. Logan stared out the window as the plane started a downward tilt. Geneva.

Outside the window were the Alps. It seemed like ages since they had flown over them, yet it had been only—two days? He wasn't even sure.

The door opened, and the co-pilot came in. "We're third in line, after an Air France liner and a private plane out of Liechtenstein."

"Any fax yet?" Logan asked.

The co-pilot shook his head. "Dumb thing is on the fritz. The captain is fiddling with it." He shrugged, then disappeared into the cockpit.

Logan followed. He had nothing else to do. He might as well see if he could help fix the idiot fax.

Alex watched through the window as the two pilots disembarked and walked toward one of the hangars a good hundred feet away. A car was coming toward them, and Alex knew they'd never see the inside of the terminal where he might get some help, make a ruckus, have a chance. Along the main street, just outside the fence and behind the hangars, he saw an airport security car parked against the curb, but nobody was in it. They must be inside one of the hangars or checking vehicles in the parking lot beyond the road. No help there.

He hoped Claire and Logan had figured it out, found the envelope. But even if they had, they didn't know what he knew, hadn't talked to Arthur Hainey and Pavel Grachev. He couldn't expect miracles.

He drew a deep breath. As near as he could tell, he and Vilinia were on their own. He had to convince Grachev to let her go.

Grachev came toward him, and Alex took a deep breath and said a silent prayer. Grachev stood in front of Alex, a gun at his forehead as Davidov shoved him forward a little and untied his hand. "Now you will take us to our legacy," Grachev said.

"Not yet." Alex felt his stomach start to churn.

"There will be no more hesitation, Mr. Barrett. You know I will hurt the woman."

"I know you intend to kill us anyway. Two or three hours of drawing breath will make no difference. She's innocent, Grachev, and has nothing to do with any of this. It's my father and I on whom you want your revenge. You have it. In full measure. My life. His life. The treasure you covet. You'll have them all. Another murder will only complicate things."

Grachev's face was like stone. "If I let her go, she will go to the police while you lead us on a merry chase. I am no fool, Alex Barrett."

"You have her father. She knows if she tries to help me, he will die. Promise her his life and she'll not speak of this to anyone. Her silence for his freedom."

The evil in Grachev's face glowed from his dark eyes. He motioned to Sergei, who grabbed Vilinia by the hair and pulled her to her feet. She screamed with the sudden pain, and her eyes filled with hatred. She scratched Davidov's face with her nails and ripped at his arm. He hit her, and she went limp. He held her away from himself by her neck, unconscious, nearly lifeless.

Alex started to react, but Grachev pushed the gun against his chest.

"Sergei is not pleased with how things have gone. He loved Andrei and Maxim. He blames you, and this woman, Mr. Barrett. At my word he will end the woman's life. I suggest you cooperate." Davidov accentuated Grachev's words by taking Vilinia's neck in a death grip.

Alex brushed Grachev's weapon aside and picked up Vilinia. "All right, Grachev," he said as calmly as he could. "You win. But if you touch this woman again, I swear, I'll die with my hands around your throat, and you'll never get what you're after."

Grachev took a step backward, the unexpected strength of Alex's statement hitting him like cold water. Alex went past him and started for the exit. "We need a car."

"What is our destination?" Grachev said, recovering.

"A small village. Voltaire."

28

Isjet kept rubbing the ropes against the edge of the metal housing. He was exhausted, his head pounding from an injection of drugs. How long had he been out? Where was he? The last he remembered was the guard punching him in the face, then on the back of the neck, knocking him unconscious.

Vilinia! Alex! Where were they? Why was he still here? What had happened?

The ropes loosened. He tugged at them, the last threads splitting and his hands coming free. His fingers fumbled in the darkness for the knot that secured the rope around his ankles, and seconds later he threw it aside and stood up.

The dizziness hit him like a wave. He staggered, then nearly fell, his head pounding. What kind of drug had they used? He grabbed a pipe with one hand and put his other to his head. He felt nauseous, then sick. Retching, he deposited what was in his stomach on the floor, then went to his knees, too weak to stand. After a few minutes, he wiped his mouth with the back of his jacketed arm. He felt better, yet his head still throbbed. He stood again, more slowly this time, then began searching for a light switch, finally finding one near the door. He flicked it on, then squinted, his eyes hurting. After they adjusted, he removed his jacket. The room was stifling.

He had to get out of there. He looked around the room for some kind of weapon and came up with a wrench in a toolbox. Careless of the guards—overconfidence or lack of wits, it didn't matter. Isjet was grateful to Allah.

The wrench was heavy, about the length of his forearm. He stepped to the door and placed an ear against it, concentrating on

340

the exterior sounds—all he could hear was the diesel motor's high-pitched tones in the next compartment.

He tried the knob. It turned. He opened it carefully, just enough to see into the outer hall. No one. He opened it more widely, then slipped out of his small prison. His head was throbbing so badly his eyes hurt, but he forced himself to look over his surroundings. Doors along each side, probably bedrooms. A stairway at the far end leading upward. He turned the knob on the closest door, revealing a small room with a bed. He closed it, then checked each successive door in the hall with the same results.

At the last door he thought he heard muffled noises, but he wasn't sure. He listened more carefully. Yes. Moans. He turned the knob and shoved the door open, the wrench ready to deal a blow if necessary. A man, tied, was lying on the bed with his face to the wall. Isjet stepped in and closed the door, then stepped close enough to roll his old friend over.

Tazbir moaned through puffy lips, his face so swollen his features had disappeared. His eyelids tried to open but delivered only thin slits.

"Your betrayal has cost you dearly, Tazbir," Isjet said in a sad voice.

The thin slits opened a bit wider. "Isjet . . . I . . . "

Isjet wanted to hate Tazbir but couldn't. He touched his friend's face, then began untying the ropes. "We have to leave this boat."

"We are at sea," Tazbir croaked. "There is no way to leave it."

Isjet had finished untying his friend's hands. "Then we will steal it." He tried a smile and got a small one in return. "We have to get help. Vilinia and the American . . . "

Tazbir looked down at his arms. Both were broken. Isjet felt sick to his stomach, then angry at the men who would do such things. Surely Allah would reserve a place for them in hell.

He took the blood-stained case from the pillow and made quick slings, placing Tazbir's arms gently in each.

"You can walk?"

Tazbir nodded.

Isjet helped Tazbir get to his feet, and they left the room

cautiously. With one arm around Tazbir's waist, Isjet moved to the stairs, praying to Allah for deliverance.

And wondering if his daughter and new friend were still alive.

"There!" Max said. He pointed, his binoculars still at his eyes. Lopukhin put his in place and focused. Right size, right description. He centered on the name printed on the back of the boat. *Geisha.*

" Yes, that is it!" Lopukhin tapped on the pilot's shoulder. The headset didn't work, and it was the only way of communication. He pointed at the vessel and signaled with a downward motion of his hand.

The Black Sea was a busy place. The satellite photos coming through Israeli intelligence had shown a number of vessels of the size and basic description of the *Geisha,* and it had taken some time to finally find the right one. Now they were in business.

The pilot began hailing the call numbers of the vessel on the proper frequency but received no answer. It was no surprise. He had been calling for them since leaving Yalta, and they hadn't responded. Why should they now? He shook his head, and Lopukhin returned to his position next to Max. Picking up his automatic weapon, he injected a shell into the chamber. Max pulled a large crate close enough that he could flip the lid and pull out the weapon inside. He attached the thirty-millimeter cannon to the side of the chopper door, opened the feeder, and placed a string of ammunition inside. Cocking the weapon, he planted his feet firmly apart and prepared himself for the cannon's powerful recoil.

Lopukhin removed a handkerchief from his pocket and attached it to the rifle barrel, then wiped the sweat from his forehead. He was hoping the yacht would let them board peacefully. He thought of his wife. Max had given him the promise of a new home, a promise written on a single piece of white paper they had picked up at the airport. He had it tucked safely away in his pocket. Not that it mattered. If something happened to the paper, or to him, he knew that Max was a man of his word. The house would be built, his family provided for. It was the first time in his life he had felt good about taking something for his services, and the only time he had done so. Even now he wondered if it was the honorable thing to do, if he had given up his honor. But it was a question for later, a decision to make if he survived what was to come. If he didn't, his family would not be lost. If he did . . .

He would decide then what to do with the note. He crossed himself after the orthodox way, then checked the sights on his weapon.

The chopper swooped down near the capping waves and came up to the yacht from behind. Max could see the bridge and two men looking them over through binoculars. He signaled Lopukhin to show the white flag. Lopukhin stuck the rifle out the window and waved it back and forth. Max watched the one he thought was the captain turn and give orders to the other. The second disappeared through a door on the inside of the bridge. Max suspected it led to the front outside deck. Two other men stood on the back of the lower deck and were quickly assembling a cannon of their own.

So much for white flags.

As Isjet and Tazbir worked their way slowly to the top of the stairs, they heard the thick whacking of a chopper overhead. The boat lurched forward and started a left-to-right swing as the sound of shouted orders came down the hall from where Isjet thought the bridge must be. He ducked aside as a man appeared at the other end, ran toward them, then past and out a door that led to the front deck. Isjet looked around the corner to see if others might follow. Nothing. A quick glance through the door's glass pane revealed the man lifting something from a long box. He placed the long tube, sleek and silver, on his own shoulder.

Isjet knew what it was, knew that the chopper overhead had no chance of surviving its nasty bite. That meant they had no chance to survive either. And Vilinia . . .

Quickly he lowered Tazbir to the floor and launched himself toward the door. He had only seconds.

As the chopper made its first pass, then swung left in a tight circle, Max saw the sailor coming through the front door onto the deck. He pulled a large crate into the open and removed the lid, then extracted its contents. Max caught the tube's glint in the sunlight and knew they were in trouble. He had seen the Russian-made missile in action during the excursions into Lebanon, had seen them bring down Israeli planes.

"Missile!" Max yelled.

The old chopper had no evasion devices and no missiles of its own. Their only chance was the cannon, and from their present position it was a long shot. Max widened his stance and was preparing to fire when he saw someone jumping through the door that led into the ship and catapulting into the sailor's back, knocking him down. The tube flew over the side into the sea, and both Max and Lopukhin let themselves breathe again.

As the chopper flattened out for a frontal pass, Lopukhin focused on the man wrestling with the enemy on the deck. The frame was vaguely familiar, the bald head . . .

"Yazhul!" he yelled. "It is Yazhul!"

Max recognized the hope in Lopukhin's voice, hope that the others might be aboard as well. But Max saw no one, and he knew that if they were aboard, they were in bad shape and would be of no help.

Those on board disappeared from his view as they passed over the ship and the rear deck came into view. The two men there had completed their assembly of the cannon and swung it toward the chopper as it passed over. Lopukhin recognized the danger at the last second, pulled his legs in, and covered his head as the heavy bullets tore into the old chopper's underbelly and ripped upward. Max felt a bullet graze his shoe but was busy aiming his own cannon. He fired, cutting up the back of the sleek vessel and forcing the two gunmen to jump for cover. The bullets ripped through the soft fiberglass and ended up in the engine room. As the chopper swung right in a hard turn, a puff of thick black smoke ejected itself from the back of the boat, and the vessel began slowing in the water. Then it came to a standstill.

The chopper flew toward the rear of the boat as the two gun-men were about to take up firing positions again. Max honed in with the cannon and shredded more of the deck, throwing chips of fiberglass and shrapnel into their feet and legs. They went down like rocks and begin rolling on the deck in pain.

The chopper passed over the radio tower. Lopukhin looked down at the front deck and saw only one man, unconscious. Yazhul was gone.

Isjet entered the hallway, the gun he had just captured at the ready, his heart pounding. His chin stung from the single blow his enemy had managed to inflict, and he was breathing heavily from the tussle with the now-unconscious sailor.

He moved past Tazbir toward the back of the yacht as the chopper cannon erupted, threw bullets toward the rear deck, then passed overhead. He hustled even more as he heard someone from the bridge curse and give another order. A man appeared in the doorway at the same time Isjet reached it. The surprised look on the sailor's face registered in hesitation, giving Isjet the chance to drive the rifle butt into the sailor's solar plexus, sending him reeling back into the room. Isjet followed, aiming the rifle first at the sailor gasping for air on the floor, then at the captain near the window.

"Hands up," Isjet said, motioning with the gun. The captain let the binoculars drop around his neck and slowly put his hands in the air. Isjet caught him glancing at a switch on the control panel, but before he understood the meaning of it, the captain reached out and flipped it upward. Isjet bolted at the captain and pummeled him with the weapon, knocking him to the floor. As the sailor took a step toward him, Isjet pointed the gun.

"You will die for nothing," he said. The sailor straightened, his hands raised above his head. Isjet looked down at the switch. A small display at its side registered numbers flashing in red and making a clicking sound.

"What is it?" he screamed at the captain. He got no response.

The sailor answered the question. "It is a detonator!"

"What? Why blow up the ship?" He looked at the captain with an unbelieving eye. "Are you that anxious to die?"

"They were his orders!" the sailor said. "If the ship is in danger, we are to destroy it!"

Isjet looked at the timer. It was still clicking down. 1:45, 1:44 . . . "Any way to disarm it?"

"No!"

Isjet looked again: 1:40. "Are we going to fight or try to get off this ship?"

"Get off," the sailor said.

"You have a mate on the front deck. Get him!"

The sailor ran for the hall. Isjet scowled at the captain, stooped and removed his weapon, then went back for Tazbir. As they came back to the bridge and headed for the exit, the captain was sitting in his chair near the wheel. Isjet dragged Tazbir through the exit and onto the deck. He screamed a warning to the two wounded men on the rear deck, who struggled toward the side, then went over.

Isjet was about to pick up Tazbir for the jump over the side when he felt his friend freeze.

"You go nowhere."

Isjet glanced over his shoulder. The captain had found a gun.

———————————

The chopper had been hovering at the rear of the vessel as Isjet came out of the bridge, dragging someone. Lopukhin leveled his rifle, preparing to shoot, but was unsure of his target. He watched as two sailors struggled out the other side and lunged over the edge, while the two men on the lower deck bounded over as well.

Lopukhin wondered about the reason for the sudden plunge into frigid water, and the answer in his mind gave him the chills. He kept his eye on the decks, waiting, apprehensive. He didn't like this; something was deadly wrong.

Then he saw the captain, gun in hand, standing in the doorway of the bridge, his weapon leveled at Yazhul. Lopukhin scoped the captain but couldn't get a clear shot with the door partially covering his target. The seconds were clicking by, but the shot didn't change. Isjet was being held hostage, the man he'd been helping standing helpless by his side.

"Shoot!" Max said over his shoulder. "You are their only chance."

Lopukhin fired.

The captain fell, a red splotch gathering on his white coat. Isjet hesitated with the shock of it, then realized that someone in the chopper had fired a rifle, the sound inaudible above the loud whump of the large bird's blades. He grabbed Tazbir, heaving him over the side into the water, then stepped up on the rail and . . .

The yacht exploded under him, catapulting his body high into the air, driving the wind out of him and replacing it with darkness. He was not aware of hitting the water.

Lopukhin let himself breathe again when he saw the captain fall. He watched with a smile as Yazhul threw his wounded companion over the edge into the water. But his relief was short lived.

The impact of the explosion drove the chopper back and up, sending it nearly out of control. Lopukhin was blown inside, across the deck of the chopper and nearly out the other door. Max grabbed his shirt and hung on as the chopper wavered, sunk, twisted, then got under control. Lopukhin struggled to his feet, his ears ringing. He grasped the side of the door, and he and Max stared into the sea below. They saw the last of the ship sinking below the water, debris landing all around it. A fireball had blown past them, dissipating into the air and leaving a thick cloud hanging over the scene.

Max and Lopukhin searched for survivors. Two were swimming toward a large chunk of the ship, something they could hang on to. Two others were face down, unconscious. One of them was Yazhul. Max signaled the pilot, whose face was pale and drawn from the emergency conditions he had just encountered. He maneuvered the chopper downward. When within range, Max propelled himself from the door and into the water some forty feet below. He kicked to the surface and came up near Isjet's floating body. Then he turned him over and began treading water as the chopper hovered above them.

Pulling a lifeboat to the door, Lopukhin pulled the automatic inflation device and shoved it out. It landed nearly on top of Max and his charge, fully inflated. Pulling Yazhul close, Max hoisted him over the edge and into the raft. Swimming to the second man, he checked for signs of life. There were none.

He turned him over and looked at the face. It was badly beaten, but Max knew it wasn't Alex. Both relieved and angry, he pulled the body toward the raft, lifted himself inside, and then pulled the dead man in after him.

Lopukhin launched another raft near the surviving sailors. They dragged themselves aboard, the unhurt sailor helping the others.

Max looked around for other survivors. They had all there were. Yazhul moaned, coughed up seawater, choked, then spit, his skull lolling back and forth. Max lifted his head.

"Voltaire." He blinked water from his eyes. "You must get to Voltaire."

29

CLAIRE STARED AT THE FLASHING LIGHTS of an ambulance, its European siren unnerving. It flashed past the window of the Lear jet as the plane pulled to a stop. She watched out the glass pane and could see the ambulance headed for a plane just a hundred yards ahead of them. *Liechtenstein Air* was written on the fuselage; the plane had landed only minutes before their own.

She felt her insides turn over and her heart begin to race. Liechtenstein was in Austria. Davidov's plane landed in Austria.

The pilot opened the outer door, and she and Logan quickly descended the stairs. The paramedics had reached the jet.

A number of security personnel had gathered. There seemed to be something, someone, lying on the tarmac near the plane's door, and as the paramedics reached the spot, they put down their equipment and began working. The fear climbed into Claire's throat.

A stranger moved through the crowd toward them, but Claire hardly noticed, mesmerized, her heart thumping. She could see the body now, could see that the height was right for Alex, and so was the weight. She picked up speed.

The stranger stepped to a position in front of them, holding out a set of keys. She hit him, knocking him aside and bolting past. They came to the edge of the crowd, and she started shoving her way through.

"What happened?" Logan stopped long enough to ask the man with the keys.

"A shooting—maybe fifteen minutes ago." He pointed toward the gate. "I was just headed there when I saw him lying at the foot of the stairs. I called an ambulance, and they got hold of another security guard."

"Do they have any idea—"

"No. The guard is unconscious and cannot tell. It is apparent he approached the plane and was shot." He gave Logan the keys.

"What are these?"

"The Mercedes Miss Barrett ordered. I was delivering it."

"Wait here," Logan ordered. He followed after Claire, catching up as she shoved her way back out of the crowd.

"It's not him," she said with a stern face. Logan told her what the attendant had said.

The pilot of their plane came running up, a sheet of paper in his hand. "This just came! It says Davidov's plane is still in Vienna. They chartered one out of Liechtenstein—" He cut himself off as he spied the name of the plane painted on its side. "Max called. They found the boat. Isjet Yazhul was aboard. He said Alex is headed for Voltaire!"

"It's them," Claire said. She turned and ran for the gate. Logan grabbed an arm and slowed her down. "We need to contact the police."

"No police," Claire said flatly as they passed through the gate. "They'll slow us down, ask hundreds of questions. Alex could get killed in the time it takes to fill out the forms." Her jaw was set in concrete. "Look back there, Logan. Look at that guard. They shot him before he even had his gun out of his holster. Does that look like the kind of men who are going to wait for us to work through the police? If Alex lives out the hour, I'll be surprised."

"We can't find them alone, Claire," Logan said. The car attendant caught up with them, a bit perplexed. Logan could see he was worried about his tip.

"We have to try." She turned to the attendant. "The words *Beau Rivage*. What do they mean?"

The attendant looked surprised by the question but encouraged by the fifty-dollar bill Logan had removed from his wallet. "Beautiful river, or beautiful shore." He took the fifty and walked away, smiling.

They were at the car. "This is crazy, Claire," Logan said.

"The police—" Logan opened the passenger's side door as Claire darted to the driver's side.

"Are visible and therefore dangerous." Claire cut him off. "If you were the enemy and saw a dozen police cars descending on the village of Voltaire, what would you do?" She didn't wait for an answer. "Use Alex and the woman as hostages? Try to run? Kill them and yourself?" Her voice was angry, frustrated at having to explain all this to him. "They'll kill Alex! And the woman! We both know it! Now are you with me?" Her voice was pleading now.

Logan turned, detected the person he was looking for, and walked to him. He pulled his badge and showed it clearly in the security guard's face as he removed the pistol from the man's hip holster.

"I'll return it."

He got into the car before the security guard had a chance of stopping him. Claire put the Mercedes in gear and sped away from the curb, the security guard dashing into the street after them, screaming in shock.

Logan couldn't help smiling. "He'll get the license plate and send the cavalry looking for us. They might come in handy."

———

Alex didn't know where to turn. They sat in the center of the village near a marble fountain, flowers cascading from its circular interior instead of water. The main road ran on through the village, the river at its side. A church tower stood behind them, showing off a clock that read nine. Obviously the showpiece wasn't working.

It had been close at the airport. The guard had recognized him and gotten shot for his effort. Grachev had nearly killed Alex as well, the hot flame of hatred boiling over in an instant as he realized Alex had friends closing in on him. He had nearly plummeted off the deep end, pulling all of them with him.

Luckily the car was waiting and they had made a successful escape without much notice. The plane was away from the regular part of the airport, and the noise had covered the shot. At least Alex considered it lucky. For now.

That had been half an hour ago, and he was beginning to

wonder if he had been wrong, if the Beau Rivage of the key was
the hotel there.

They had driven every street in the village of Voltaire and
found nothing named Beau Rivage. There was only one hotel, the
Martinet, two restaurants, and dozens of large houses on both
sides of the river. Dead ahead, on a hill overlooking the village,
stood an old castle, the town's one claim to fame, a tourist site off
the beaten path. He could see why it had been built where it was.
The river turned sharply just outside the town and ran directly
under the castle's walls, then flowed south into an expansive flat
plain. From the ramparts, its former inhabitants could have seen
for miles, a great advantage in keeping their enemies at bay.

It had to be here! In his gut he knew this was right! It was just
finding it . . . finding his father's secret.

"I am running out of patience, and you are running out of
time, Mr. Barrett. No more stalling!"

"I'm not stalling, Grachev. My father didn't leave a set of
instructions, just a map and a key with a name on it. The map
brings us here; the name is still a mystery." He started getting out
of the vehicle. Sergei stopped him.

"I'm going in that restaurant over there and ask some questions. You can tag along if you like, but we won't have time for
lunch."

"Questions?" Davidov asked.

"The place I'm looking for either no longer exists or has had
its name changed, that's obvious. Old-timers who eat in quaint
restaurants will know that sort of thing, don't you think?"
Davidov let go of his arm.

"I will accompany him, Sergei, but if we don't return . . . "

"Lay off the threats, Grachev. You made your point back at
the airport." Alex glanced at Vilinia, who sat quiet, saying nothing
since returning to consciousness just before reaching Voltaire.

"Are you all right?" Alex asked.

She nodded. Tears had stained her cheeks, but the determination was still there. Alex knew what she would do if given the
chance, and that gave him hope. They'd need all the strength they
could muster when it came down to life or death.

Getting out of the car, he and Grachev walked across the paved street and entered the sidewalk area of the restaurant. Taking a seat near two old-timers sipping black coffee and eating pastries, they ordered a couple of small cakes. Alex asked for milk, balancing out Grachev's request for coffee.

"Bonjour." Alex addressed the closest of the two men. "Do you speak English?"

They glanced at each other with a smile. "A little," one said. "May I help you?"

Alex spoke slowly. "Have you heard of the Beau Rivage?"

"The beautiful river? Of course."

Alex felt relieved.

"It is there; it runs through the country many miles."

Alex smiled at his own mistake. "I'm sorry. I meant a hotel, a place of some kind."

The man who spoke a little English turned to his friend and translated. They both shrugged.

"No such hotel or place of residence." His friend spoke to him in their native tongue, and they discussed something rather heatedly.

"My friend reminds me—a hospital for soldiers during the war."

Alex felt Grachev stiffen. "Where is this place?" Alex asked.

The man leaned forward and pointed toward the main road. "Turn right at corner. Follow the highway until you come to a bridge. Cross and go five kilometers. It is along the river—a deserted building, run down. You cannot miss it."

Alex stood, Grachev with him. His captor removed a wad of bills from his pocket and tossed an American twenty on the table even though the food hadn't arrived. Alex couldn't remember the last time he had had money in his hands and thought it a strange point to think about now, a sign of how worn out he really was.

They crossed the street and got back in the car. Excited, Grachev screamed the instructions. With tires screeching on the pavement, Davidov turned the car around and sped back to the main road.

Grachev had to repeat the instructions several times for

Sergei, and Alex realized Maxim wasn't the only slow one in the family.

Fifteen minutes later, they passed the lane but spied the run-down building in the woods. Grachev ordered Sergei to back up, and they quickly turned down the road, accelerating toward the old hospital. Above a pair of solid-oak doors were the words *Beau Rivage* carved in a stone arch. The doors must have measured at least eight feet wide between them.

The place was overgrown with crawling vines and had two towers, one at each end. The towers were round and constructed of the same stone as the rest of the building. They had conical, pointed roofs made of wood, now full of holes. A dozen windows lined the high walls on two levels right and left, but many of the panes were broken out, the frames unpainted and in disrepair. Beau Rivage was deserted and had been for years.

In wonder, Alex stepped from the car and opened the door for Vilinia. Grachev, laughing giddily, was already at the front doors but was disappointed when confronted with a large lock and chain that ran through the two rusting steel handles. Alex found himself wishing for the key in the deposit box, but from the look of the lock, it wasn't the right one anyway. This one appeared to be fairly modern.

Grachev started around the right end of the building. Davidov pushed Vilinia and Alex after him, anxious to keep up. Traversing the overgrown weeds and wild grass, they came to the back, where a patio of well-set stones and a large area of grass sloped toward the shore of a river. Even though the grass was weedy, tall, and burned in spots from lack of moisture, the sight was pleasantly shaded by numerous trees. Alex got a picture in his mind of the area filled with lounging soldiers bathing in the sun, searching for a little peace from shell shock and mayhem. Right then he could have used a little of that himself.

"This must have been quite a place in its time," Alex said to Vilinia.

She nodded, pointing to the view across the river where the castle stood atop the hill. Through the branches of the trees Alex could see a number of tourists atop the castle walls admiring the view of the river and valley. He wondered if they could see their little group at this distance and through the trees. It would be nice if one, just one, would get suspicious and call a cop before this place became their tomb.

Alex didn't like the idea of dying in a foreign corner of the world. He disliked even more the idea of Vilinia dying while he watched.

Sergei shook the locked door that led from the patio, but it didn't give. He placed his shoulder against it and shoved, then slammed his weight into it, and it sprang open. Grachev pulled his gun from under his shirt and waved it at Vilinia and Alex with a stupid grin on his face that said "I told you so."

They entered a large room featuring a stone fireplace in the center of a long interior wall. The enormous opening on the fireplace could have accommodated them all side by side. The chimney extended clear to the roof. On this side of the building there was no second story.

"A ballroom," Vilinia said. "This must have been someone's palace before it was a hospital."

Alex nodded but was busy watching their two captors, hoping they would lose their concentration and allow a chance to escape. No such luck—not yet.

The empty room and the marble floor were covered with dirt and fallen pieces of stucco from the ceiling high above. Alex could see where water had leaked in, causing much of the ceiling plaster to fall, leaving ugly bare lathe to greet the eye. Remnants of molded cornice atop columns indicated to Alex that the ceilings had once been decorated with murals.

"It's been some time since anyone lived in this place," Alex said, "and yet it is such a piece of work one wonders why."

Stepping through the archway at their right, they found themselves in an oversized kitchen. The sink was stained and filled with dirt, and the countertops, covered in mosaic tile, were cluttered and dirty as well. Vilinia brushed aside some of it, making the bright mosaic colors visible.

"It is beautiful!" She said. "I do not understand such a place being left alone without use. Many of my people could live in this house and be happy." She seemed animated with disgust, making Alex smile.

"The foundation may be crumbling, Vilinia. Possibly the place isn't safe."

Then again, Alex thought to himself, if Charles were hiding a treasure here for the past fifty years, he wouldn't want the neighborhood coming for tea and pastries.

They moved into a large dining room next but were on the front side of the house now, and the ceiling was only nine feet overhead. The room was empty, dirty, the walls covered with spots where plaster had eroded and fallen away, making the inside of the heavy stone outer wall visible. The large salon was the same, and they passed through the entry quickly. Davidov stepped toward the hallway that led to the left while Grachev motioned them upstairs.

The stairway was of wood and was still in fair shape, though each stair had a creak unique to itself. At the top, halls extended right and left with doors leading to rooms throughout the front and back. They searched each room—all were empty—then moved to the towers, where they found nothing but warped floors and a view of the sky through holes in the roof.

"Nothing." The disappointment was thick in Grachev's voice.

Alex pointed to the nails sticking out of the wall all along the hall. "Something was here at one time—dozens of pieces of artwork. Charles may have removed . . . "

"They were never hanging on these walls, Mr. Barrett. They are hidden, and we have but to find them."

"Excuse me for bursting your bubble, Grachev, but my father was no fool when it came to artwork. He would never leave expensive works in a place like this. You've seen the water damage. The humidity and mold alone would destroy works of art, discolor precious metals. Sorry, your treasure isn't here. Only my father knows where it is—if it exists at all."

Taking the steps two at a time, Sergei bounded before them. "Father! I have found them." It was all he said before disappearing the way he had come.

Alex looked at Vilinia, his heart dropping into his shoes. There must be a basement.

Claire pulled the Mercedes next to the flower-filled fountain. They had driven through the village and along the river, but there had been no sign of Alex, and they were losing hope.

Flashes of finding Alex dead, his eyes open in a face full of questions, haunted her now.

"Give me a second," Logan said. He got out of the car and walked to a young man standing by a team of horses. He tried communicating but wasn't having much luck when an old gentleman crossed the street from the cafe and entered the conversation. Logan seemed animated, heading toward the car quickly while thanking the gentleman profusely. As he got in and explained that Alex had been seen, the man approached his window. Logan rolled it down.

"The ones who went before you—they are in trouble, no?"

Logan glanced at Claire then nodded. "Yes. The one you described is being held captive, along with a woman."

"I saw the woman in a car, like this one. There were two other men. The one who came asking questions has very cold eyes. The other I only saw from a distance, also in the auto."

Claire started the engine, thanking the old man. He put his hand on the window frame and spoke.

"They went by road. There is a faster way."

"How?" Logan asked.

The man smiled. "I have a boat."

Alex peered into the black hole, the rotting steps and railing visible only a few feet beyond where he stood. Grachev, by his side, turned to his son with a questioning look.

"What do you mean you found them, Sergei? Where are they?"

Sergei grinned the same silly grin he had worn upstairs, reached overhead, and felt in the darkness until he found something and pulled it. A light flickered in the basement, illuminating the treacherous steps clear to the bottom.

Alex glanced at the light and wondered why such a place would be lit but never used. He shoved the thought aside for a more pressing problem—the stairs.

"Did you go down there?" Alex asked, staring at Sergei. The steps looked as if they'd collapse at the slightest touch.

"Yes. You have to be careful, but—"

"What did you find, Sergei?" Grachev asked impatiently, his excitement nearly uncontrollable.

"Crates. Lots of them."

Grachev pushed Alex aside and tried the first step. It started to give a little, and he stepped back—the floor was twenty feet down, filled with nothing but jagged rocks that had fallen away from the thick stone foundation. It didn't look very inviting. Alex smiled until Grachev grabbed his arm and pushed him ahead. Alex peered at Grachev as though he must be joking but received only a jab with the gun for his trouble. He took the first step, then the second. They held, and he worked his way down. Once he was there, Grachev told him to stop, using his gun as a point maker. Alex waited while peering into the confines of the musty cavern. Some crates were back there but much deeper in the basement and shrouded by the dim light of a small bulb. There were lots of them, but, as Sergei said, the number was relative. Alex could see only a dozen at the most.

Grachev was soon next to him, sweating. He turned and spoke to Sergei. "Watch the woman, Sergei, but don't hurt her, not yet. Do you understand?"

Sergei nodded, the disappointment evident. Staying behind while Grachev found the treasure was certainly not his choice.

Turning into the basement, Alex and Grachev worked their way back to the crates. Excited, Grachev approached the first crate and looked carefully at the markings in the dim light.

"The writing is German!" He said excitedly. "See! The swastika, and the German words for *weapons* and *caution.*"

The crates were old, even rotting in spots. Water marks stained them halfway up, as if they had been partially submerged at one time, possibly when the basement had flooded. Alex watched Grachev try to open one of them hurriedly while still trying to keep the gun on him. He prepared himself, ready to spring if the chance should come.

As Grachev broke off pieces, Alex sat down on one of the crates, getting closer to a large hunk of wood Grachev had just discarded. He was tired of bending over as well, the roof lower in this section of the basement than near the stairway.

The floor was of stone laid in mortar, thick with dust. The walls, of similar material, were several feet thick, but a number of the stones had fallen away and lay on the floor.

Grachev had made a good-sized hole in the box and stuck his hand in. He felt something that gave him a renewed desire to tear the box into small pieces with his bare hands but kept himself under control, the gun trained on Alex's midsection.

Grachev finally worked the side off the wide crate, and they could see inside. A frame, with a picture still encased. Alex felt his blood pressure go up as Grachev freed the item and pulled the picture out. It was a landscape of the French countryside, a nice print, its paper surface warped by water.

The disappointment on Grachev's face was refreshing for Alex and brought a smile momentarily to his lips. The smile disappeared when Grachev looked up with those empty eyes and pointed the gun at the bridge of his nose, defying Alex to say anything.

Alex watched as his enemy opened two more boxes and found similar items inside. They were damaged and watermarked worse than the first, but Alex knew that none of them was worth as much as the frames anyway. He figured those might bring about a hundred American dollars in an antique store. The pictures themselves were good for nothing but kindling for the huge fireplace in the ballroom.

"Probably the items that used to hang on the walls upstairs," Alex said. "They must have stored them down here for some reason when they closed the place up." He shrugged. "Has it occurred to you that Michael may have stayed here for a while—that the key is nothing more than another souvenir of his days in the military? The map I saw must have been exactly what I thought it was in the beginning, what Arthur Hainey thought it was—nothing more than a map designating a trip here for some rest and recuperation. Face it, you've lost. Michael fed you a story, knowing you were greedy, knowing only something like the Orlov legacy would tempt you enough to set Nadia and the children free."

"No! It exists! He didn't lie." His face was flushed. "Your father's treasure is here! And I shall have it!" He threw the piece of wood in his hand across the room, slamming it into a stone wall. "It has to be here! These are the crates. Look at them! They have the Nazi swastika on them! There is no other explanation for their being here!"

He picked up one of the smaller crates and threw it across the room. It shattered against the stone, and a picture fell to the floor. Another print. Grachev turned to stare at it. Alex saw his chance.

He grabbed the piece of wood and drove it into Grachev's head, hoping to knock him out without so much as a moan, but the rotting pine broke, doing hardly any damage. Grachev looked surprised, then angry, then sinister. Alex saw death in that look and jammed the jagged end of his broken stick into Grachev's arm. The explosion was deafening.

Vilinia had listened to the distant tearing of wood, the murmur of voices too far away to understand. She had watched Sergei's face for some sort of concern but saw none, sure his father was in complete control.

Then came the explosion of a fired gun.

Sergei stiffened, his eyes riveted to the opening at the bottom of the rotting stairway.

"Father?" he said in a loud voice. No answer. "Pavel?" He said it louder. Still no answer.

Vilinia could see the confusion, the debate going on behind his eyes. He glanced down at the rotting steps, then back at the opening. Vilinia could still feel the tension of indecision and fear, see it in the sudden droplets of sweat forming on his forehead.

She looked down to where Alex and Grachev had disappeared. She listened. There was something, but she couldn't tell . . .

Sergei took the first step; the stairway swayed dangerously. He stepped back to the solid first floor and grabbed Vilinia by the arm.

"Go!" he said, shoving her forward. "If they fall, you will be the first to die."

Vilinia pulled her arm away, the heat of anger thick in her chest. She glared at the coward before her, then took the first step.

Claire might have enjoyed the trip down the river if it hadn't been for the anxiety filling the pit of her stomach. The scenery was idyllic, and the sounds and smells of a warm summer afternoon surrounded them. The castle on the hill looked down on them in massive majesty, and the river water was clean and cool.

But Claire hardly noticed, her mind occupied with anxiety.

The Frenchman had delivered them to the shore behind the old house he had said was Beau Rivage and then turned his boat upriver for the return trip. They hadn't waited for him to disappear, hadn't even waved. Instead they had moved quickly to a hiding place just a short distance from the house.

"Now we do it my way," Logan said firmly, removing the guard's pistol from under his shirt and behind his belt. "These guys are dangerous, armed, and have nothing to lose if one of us gets in the way. *You* stay here!"

Claire started to protest, but he clamped a hand over her mouth. "Not this time, Claire. I mean it! You stay! You have Melissa and the baby to think about!"

She pulled his hand away but nodded reluctant agreement.

"You placed the call back there?" Logan asked.

Claire nodded. "You have maybe ten more minutes before this place is crawling with police. By the way, the security guard is ticked off about his gun."

Logan laughed, then grew serious. He was visibly pumped

with adrenaline, trying to decide if he should wait or make a move, at least try to get closer in case Alex was in trouble.

There was a sudden sound, a gunshot. Muffled, but a shot! He glanced at Claire; her face was turning pale.

"Get around front and bring the cops as soon as they get here!" He ran for the back door, throwing caution to the wind until he reached the opening, where he slammed himself against the outer wall. He took a deep breath, listening. Nothing.

He disappeared inside.

Vilinia took the second and third steps. They swayed dangerously. She paused, her anger at the man behind her turning first to caution, then to fear.

"Go! I will kill you if you don't!" He pointed his weapon at her chest from the safety of the doorway. She didn't move, glaring at him defiantly. He lifted the gun. She could tell he wanted to kill her. It was in his cold, lifeless eyes, but the glance toward the basement, the fear of reprisal from the man he feared more than death itself, kept his finger from squeezing the trigger.

She let a slight smile crease her lips, mocking his fear. It was a mistake.

Crimson flushed his face, and he cursed her as he lurched forward.

"No!" she yelled as his extra weight hit the decayed stairway. "You will—" She wished she could take back her defiance as the steps swayed and began to crumble.

Vilinia lunged toward the top of the stairs, was nearly past Davidov, when the stairs fell away. In desperation she grabbed for the handle of the open door just above her head. Sergei grabbed for her, for anything as he began the fall downward, his grasping fingers just missing the railing connected to the stone wall. He plummeted after the broken stairway, landing twenty feet below.

Vilinia hung from the rusting handle of the old, creaking door, a cloud of dust encircling her as it mushroomed from the pileup. Sergei was spread-eagled in the rubble, his eyes staring blankly up at her. Blood poured from the wound where a piece of wood protruded through his chest. She pulled her eyes away and tried to focus on her own safety, fearful of joining him in the mass of jumbled timber and foundation stone that surrounded his body.

She looked up at the small, rusty handle she was painfully gripping. She could already feel it beginning to loosen from the thin door. Carefully she tried swinging herself toward the doorway, hoping to reach it with her feet and pull herself over. It was no use; the door leaned at too drastic an angle.

Her fingers felt weak, the doorknob slippery. She braced herself for the fall she knew would come.

Logan heard the crash from the kitchen, where he had begun his search. He ran across the ballroom and into the hall, then cautiously checked each doorway for an enemy before coming to the opening that was belching dust. He placed himself against the wall and peered around the corner. A woman was dangling from the doorknob and staring downward.

Logan shoved his gun into his belt at the small of his back and repositioned himself to grab the door and swing it inward. The woman's head jerked up toward him, her eyes afraid until she saw he was trying to help her. He gave her his most confident and friendly smile.

"Hold on just a minute longer," he said. Her eyes registered understanding.

Logan pulled until the door handle was within reach. He grasped her arm and pulled as the rotting wood gave way and the handle ripped free. She let go, trusting herself to his grasp.

But the sudden weight brought him to his knees, then to his belly. She was still dangling but now below the floorline and the end of his arms. It wasn't going to be a problem until he saw the movement near the wreckage below them.

Alex stared up at Vilinia, who was dangling from Logan's arms. He felt a bit dizzy from the blow on the back of his neck that had been dealt by Grachev in the struggle for the gun. When he had jabbed Grachev's arm with the jagged stick and shoved, the gun had gone off. The bullet had whizzed past Alex's ear at the same time he had lunged for Grachev, but the old gentleman had been stronger than he looked, and, using the gun as an equalizer, he had pummeled Alex into submission.

Grachev pushed harder on the gun, making Alex flinch and forcing him further into the room.

Grachev caught sight of Vilinia dangling from the stranger's arms, then Sergei lying in the debris. His heart felt cold and his mind numb at the bloody end of his last son.

"Sergei, get up!" he said, refusing to believe his own eyes, what his mind was telling him. The body didn't respond. "Sergei!"

"He's dead, Grachev. All of them are dead. Another sacrifice to your gods." Out of the corner of his eye, Alex could see the blank, disbelieving look on Grachev's face.

"No. We are too close," he said in a cold, lifeless voice.

"Hello, Logan," Alex said.

Logan felt helpless. Both hands were occupied in keeping Vilinia from falling into the scattered and dangerous wreckage below, and his gun was in his belt at the small of his back. His head throbbed, and his arms were already aching with the strain. He tried to keep his voice even.

"Alex. You're a hard man to catch up with. Who's your friend?"

"Pavel Grachev. You may have heard of him."

"Umm, from your father's war years. I read the letters."

"Then you found the envelope." Alex said it with pleased relief.

"Claire did. Smart, putting it in your mother's box like that. But next time tell Claire what you're doing." He forced a smile. " A quick question: what are we after? I take it you haven't found anything yet." Logan worked his grip further down Vilinia's arms, forcing himself to forget the strain.

"I'm still trying to figure it out myself, but it's nothing worth dying for," Alex responded.

Logan looked at Davidov's body, then at Grachev. "Some people seem to disagree. Is this all of them?"

"All that's left." Alex looked at Davidov. "He's the last of three brothers. I understand you ran into one of them at Davidov's place—an Oriental."

"The gorilla. Yeah, I ran into him." Logan considered giving them the details of Davidov's cowardice in letting the Giant fall to his grave inside the Chaika, but he decided Grachev wouldn't handle it well at this point.

"I suppose you brought help," Alex said.

"Did Patton go anywhere without an army? There will be a ten-minute delay, however. Coffee break, croissants. You know the Swiss." He looked down at Vilinia. "You're a slim one, and I am grateful. Hang on. We'll see if we can all survive this business." He looked at Alex. "Claire came along; she's outside, waiting to show the cops the way in."

"Isjet Yazhul. Vilinia's father. He was aboard a ship in the Black Sea." Alex glanced at her, hopeful the news was good.

"Safe. A friend of mine took the boat about an hour ago." Logan paused, looking down at the woman. "He's fine." He could feel new strength in her arms.

"Listen, Alex, can't you convince your friend to give this up so we can all go home?" Logan was getting tired, but he had noticed that Vilinia was almost within reach of the rail. If he could get her a little closer . . . He nudged that direction, careful not to draw Grachev's attention to his intent.

"You've lost, Grachev," Alex said. "There's nothing here. If my father ever had what you say belongs to you, he either destroyed it, sold it, or hid it away where none of us will ever find it."

Alex felt Grachev's body stiffen. It scared him. Grachev had nothing to live for except vengeance. And vengeance could now be nothing more nor less than taking the life of Michael Poltoron's son. Alex looked up at Logan with pleading eyes, then saw what he was trying to do with Vilinia. He prayed there would be enough time. Maybe he could buy a little.

"Why kill Nadia, Grachev? If you loved her so much, why—"

"I did not kill her. She took poison. It was . . . suicide."

"She wouldn't have left the boys behind to suffer in Karaganda, or with you," Alex said evenly. "It wasn't suicide."

"It is your father's fault, you know. He ruined everything with his matchmaking. He had no right to give her parents the money he did. He knew I couldn't match his offer. He knew Nadia's father would have to reject me. For that I have hated him, hunted him!"

Alex decided to press for more, to buy time. Logan had Vilinia almost close enough.

"You were an Orlov. Surely Nadia's father would have taken that into consideration."

Grachev laughed. "You never believed that; we both know it. No, I am not the Orlov; your father was."

"Then it was his property he took from Germany."

"Yes. And Arkadi's. I didn't know it at the time but discovered it later. The Orlov family line was a large one. Count Orlov had many children, and Arkadi was descended from the sister of your father's great-grandmother."

"When did they find out—"

"They knew it all along, even before the war. When they found out your father was being sent to Moscow during the war, Arkadi asked to be transferred to represent the military. They used the chance to search for what had been lost when your father tried to have the legacy shipped out of Crimea."

"And found it in southern Germany."

There was no answer.

"Father helped Arkadi marry Nadia because he was family."

"And I lost Nadia. It is your father's fault. The children were mine. I took them."

"You tried to take Nadia as well, but she refused."

No answer.

"You got angry and killed her."

Still no answer.

"You made the children yours, but you blamed my father for destroying your happiness. You wanted revenge."

"To your father, his family, his heritage, was everything. I must take all these from him."

"So you stole the boys and turned Arkadi and Nadia's children against Michael by making them yours. Then you tried to take his family's wealth. It must have been quite a blow to you when your henchmen reported he'd been killed in their attempt at kidnapping him. Without him to torture, you had no way of finding the wealth he took out of Germany at the end of the war—the wealth that belonged to the Orlovs. Your intent to take it all away was thwarted."

"When I discovered he was still alive, my life took on new meaning," Grachev said. "When I discovered he had a son, an heir—you, Alexander Barrett, you who carried the name of your grandfather and great-grandfather—I knew my years of patience would pay me well."

"You're a sick man, Grachev. You've lost far more than you will ever gain."

"Your father is dead; you will die as well. It will have to be enough."

Vilinia was almost there. "But your real dream, your dream of *becoming* my father, of returning to a new Russia as head of the Orlov family, with the Orlov wealth, that will never happen now. The boys you raised to step into the shoes of my father once you eliminated him, the boys you needed to authenticate your efforts, are dead. It has all been for nothing."

Alex felt Grachev stiffen, prepare himself to end it all. He tried to keep calm, watched Logan move Vilinia closer to the rail. There was something wet on his arms, and he looked down at it. Grachev's sliver-infested arm was bleeding, dripping onto his.

"You told me you found my father by accident in 1985. Why didn't you go after him then?"

Grachev laughed. "Our research of who your father had become revealed two things to us. He loved his church, and he loved his wife and family. It takes time to take such things away from a man. And it takes planning."

Alex felt weak in the knees. "What do you mean?"

"He suffered as I suffered!" Grachev's voice hardened. "I

drove his wife away from him as he drove Nadia from me!" He moved his mouth right up to Alex's ear. "I hired the woman to lie about him, Alexander! Your father never committed adultery except in my mind!"

"That's impossible." Alex was shaking his head. "The Church would know! They would see . . . feel . . . "

"They could not deny the unmistakable evidence any more than you could. I learned everything I could about your church, discovered how it works. I used its justice system to my advantage. I made the evidence overpowering and very convincing! Even you believed it, Alexander!" He laughed. "And your mother! Even though her heart told her otherwise, she could not deny the evidence. In her mind, it outweighed everything!"

The anger burned inside Alex like a hot iron, his mind filling first with anguish, then with the desire to kill Grachev! He wanted to cry out, to scream! How could this be? The years of pain! The feelings between his parents, between him and his father—all because of this man's desire for revenge, a desire that was unjust in the first place! His fist clenched tightly, and his nails dug into his palms.

"Your soul will burn in hell for this, Grachev!" Alex said through his teeth, the muscles in his jaw so tight they ached.

Grachev pushed on the gun. "Even hell is acceptable if I know I have given your father great pain!"

Logan could see it coming. He had no more time. He flexed his arms, lifted, and threw Vilinia toward the rail. She grabbed it and hung on. It held. He reached for the gun at the small of his back . . .

The explosion echoed through the chamber.

Logan watched the shock wash over Alex's face as the blast knocked him sideways, saw the pain in his eyes as he fell.

Grachev raised the gun toward Vilinia, his eyes as empty as a dark night. Logan screamed and fired at the face peering down the barrel. Grachev's gun flew upward as it went off. The bullet went high and planted itself only a few inches to the right of Logan's face. Logan fired again. The bullet caught Grachev in the backbone and threw him against the wall, where he melted to the floor. He would never rise again.

Logan felt weak, his gun falling limp in his hand as he stared down at Alex lying unconscious on the floor, his blood draining into the dust. Vilinia's scream pulled him out of his stupor, and he grabbed her arm. She swung toward him. He put all his remaining strength into pulling her upward and through the doorway to safety, his heart full of pain. Vilinia was crying "No, no!" over and over as she rocked back and forth on her knees, staring into the pit. Claire came running down the hall, two policemen behind her, as Logan pulled Vilinia to her feet.

"Take her. Alex has been shot," Logan said.

Claire turned ashen but wrapped her arms around the young woman's shoulders while staring in disbelief at the body of her brother. Tears erupted from the corners of her eyes and ran down her cheeks as she held on tighter to Vilinia, trying to make the anguish go away and keep hope alive.

Logan looked for a way down and saw the railing.

He reached out, testing it, then letting it take his weight, his body dangling. He worked his way quickly down, hand over hand, then jumped the last six feet, twisting an ankle when he hit in the rubble near Davidov's body.

He moved to Alex and saw immediately it was bad.

"We need an ambulance! Now!" he yelled. One of the policemen rushed away. Logan ripped the lower part of his shirt away and applied pressure to the two wounds even though they didn't seem to be bleeding badly. The bullet had entered his lower right side and exited on the left. It had passed clear through his vital organs, and Logan knew the worst damage was inside. "We're going to need some rope, a ladder, anything to get him out of here fast! If the hospital doesn't have Flight for Life, call the airport, but get us a chopper!" Logan said to Claire, trying to keep his voice even, without panic. "You have to hurry, Claire. Every second counts!"

Wiping her tears away, Claire moved herself and Vilinia away from the opening, the remaining policeman by her side as she started giving instructions. Until then he hadn't known she could speak French.

Logan was left alone with Alex.

He placed his hand on the dying man's head. He didn't have oil, but this was no time to worry about it.

"Alex Barrett, in the name of Jesus Christ . . . "

30

Claire sat next to Logan in the waiting room of LDS Hospital in Salt Lake City, Melissa in her lap.

The Israeli Hospital jet had flown Alex and the rest of them nonstop into Salt Lake Airport. They had been home for nearly four hours.

Max had flown to Geneva with Vilinia's father, who had been lucky enough to sustain only a mild concussion, temporary loss of hearing, and some broken ribs from his experience aboard the *Geisha*. He had come when his daughter needed him most.

Alex had been flown from Beau Rivage to a Geneva hospital by helicopter. He was near death then but managed to hang on. Logan hadn't said as much, but Claire knew he had given him a blessing.

Then there had been long hours of surgery in which it was discovered that the bullet had destroyed both his kidneys. If he was to survive, he needed new ones.

Max had made arrangements for the Flying Hospital even before the doctors had made their diagnosis. The plane had arrived from a military air base in northern Israel by the time Alex came out of surgery. It was equipped with everything needed to sustain his life during the flight, and half a dozen nurses and two qualified doctors had made the trip with Claire, Logan, Vilinia, and Max. Isjet had returned to his home for a much-needed rest.

Now Claire was watching the door across the hall—her father's room. She knew that inside machines clicked, tubes fed, and monitors supervised the lifeless form that was once Michael Poltoron, then Charles Barrett.

She wanted more than ever to have him sitting by her, laughing, telling them about those mysterious years about which they had so little knowledge. She wanted Alex there, listening, questioning, discovering the past, able to put their father at ease about his love for him.

But Charles would never sit with them, and they would never have their talk—not in this life. Pavel Grachev had seen to that and nearly defeated Michael Poltoron. Except that he hadn't, and he wouldn't. Michael would still win.

Her eyes found the clock on the far wall. The doctors would be through with their preparations any time.

She got to her feet. "Give me five minutes alone, then come in, will you?" She said it to Logan, giving him the best smile she could muster.

Logan nodded as Melissa settled next to him, sensing her mother's need to say her good-byes alone.

Claire passed through the door, letting it swing shut behind her. Charles looked better than he had just a few days earlier. His face had a look of peace.

There were still no signs of life in his brain, and his organs functioned only because science willed it so, but Claire couldn't shake off the thought that he knew, somehow, what had transpired in their lives and was ready to do what was necessary.

She walked to him and touched the waxen flesh of his arm. The doctors had declared him capable of his role. In fact, they had been quite surprised to find that his kidneys were those of a man in his thirties. Claire had merely been thankful—and frightened.

The decision was right, she knew that—knew in the depth of her heart by the peace she had there. It was what her father would want, but, oh, how she would miss him! There were so many things she wanted to say to him, things both she and Alex wanted, needed, to know! His family, his past, his friends! They had been deprived of so much because of war and hatred and Pavel Grachev!

Logan had told her what Grachev had revealed about her father's excommunication. It hadn't shocked her. She had always known her father was innocent, even though she had been frustrated and angry, bitter toward the Church for not seeing what she could see. On one particular day when she had been railing against the stake leaders for what they were doing, her father had given her some counsel. She had rejected it then, understood it now.

"Claire," he had said, "the evidence was overpowering. If I admitted guilt, I would have given them a choice—they could have tempered their judgment of me. Because I refused to do so, they had a responsibility to put me outside the Church, an apparent adulterer who has broken the most sacred covenants. I cannot, will not, blame them for doing their duty."

"But what about inspiration, Dad?" she had asked him, frustrated. "God knows you're not guilty. If the leaders are really inspired . . ."

Her father had only smiled. "The Church is set up to give us the chance to make that connection, Claire—to get inspiration from him. He wants to guide us. But, although the Church may be divine, the average members are not. And because they are not, they are not infallible. What they see with their eyes in the natural world may cloud what they feel from the spiritual one, but that doesn't mean they are wicked or that the Church isn't true. When they make mistakes, God will right them. Soon or late, he will right them."

And he had never blamed them. He went to Church, suffered the losses, never grew bitter, even though it cost so much. It was then she realized just how strong her father's testimony was, and it was then she began having second thoughts about her own conduct, started looking at the Church again through different eyes— at its beliefs instead of its people. And it had made a difference, even though she hadn't come back. By then she had believed her own soul was too far gone for a move like that.

The tears rolled freely down her face as she lifted her father's hand and kissed it. She wanted his once-strong fingers to come to life again, to press against her fingers as they had so many times in her life. She wanted to tell him she understood it all now, that she loved him for what he had given her, for who he had been. She wanted a smile from his lips and eyes, the dimples in his cheeks, the sound of his voice, his laughter and his wisdom.

The tears turned to sobs.

She knelt by the bed and grasped her father's hand between hers, bowing her head. She prayed silently, her sobs filling the room as she poured out her soul to a Father in Heaven she needed more than she had needed anything or anyone in her entire life, the weight of her decision pressing down on her with crushing force.

Finally, standing, she leaned over her father and kissed his gray brow, then his eyelids. As she did, Logan opened the door, and he and Melissa came to her side. Claire took Logan's arm, and Melissa grasped her around the waist.

Moments later, a number of doctors, orderlies, and nurses came through the door and wheeled Charles Barrett into surgery. It would be hours before the vital organs were transferred from one Barrett to the other. As part of father became part of son. As Michael Poltoron welded his life to that of his heir.

Epilogue: One Year Later

ALEX AND CLAIRE STOOD IN FRONT of the old hospital, admiring the work that had been done. The windows had been replaced, the roof repaired, old removed and replaced with new. The workers, off for the day, would return to make the final embellishments inside before the place was opened.

Claire still had nightmares once in a while, but then, so did Logan and Alex. And Vilinia. None of them would ever be the same. Evil might not be able to overpower a strong man or a good woman, but it could change them. Things important once weren't so important anymore. Things that hadn't meant as much as they should have suddenly loomed as everything that mattered.

Alex walked to the door and opened it for Claire. They stepped inside, and Claire found herself immediately pleased with what the workers had done under her brother's direction. The elegant stairs had been repaired and polished. The walls were smooth and without blemish, the color of eggshell. The lights had been replaced, and a sparkling chandelier hung in the main entrance in front of the stairs, another in the living room. Other lights, ordered by Alex, were in place and shone against freshly painted white walls.

"The entire house is the same way," Alex said. "I hope you're pleased."

"Very," Claire said, impressed. "I didn't know you were an interior designer."

"Just a wayward son with a purpose."

They walked into the room Vilinia had called a ballroom so long ago. The fireplace had been cleaned, the rock renewed, the walls and ceiling repaired. Two more chandeliers hung equidistant from the ends of the room. Claire hadn't remembered that the room was so big, but then, other things had been on her mind the last time she was there. The large picture of their mother that had hung in their father's den was hanging over the mantel.

"It is a beautiful spot for that, Alex."

"Umm. I think she'd like it."

"Do you think they've worked this all out?"

"Not a question in my mind."

"Mother owed him a very big apology."

"She probably knew that even before he got there."

Claire smiled. "Do you think she was finally willing to admit it?"

Alex chuckled. "With reservations. She could be stubborn, couldn't she."

"Like her son. How are you feeling about things?"

"Better—a lesson learned. I won't jump to judge someone else very soon again. I think Father had forgiven me before he died. It's a little tougher forgiving oneself for such stupidity, but I'm getting there."

Alex had healed well. The surgery had gone as planned, but then one of Charles's kidneys had failed. It was nip and tuck for a while, but now Alex was getting along exceptionally well with just one.

Claire and Logan had arranged the funeral for Charles while Alex was still struggling for survival. It had been well attended, the stake center packed to overflowing with the famous and the ordinary neighbors alike. She had been proud to display his medals and pictures of the war years. Most people coming through the line didn't know what it all meant, but for her it had been an important passage. After the funeral, the coffin had been closed, then stored until Alex was well enough to be at the burial and dedicate the grave, a ceremony only for close friends and family. The tombstone sat next to that of their mother. On it were the names of Michael Poltoron and Charles Barrett. The inscription read, "He lived and died for his people, his family, his friends. No greater love hath any man." In the top center was the Star of David.

Most important of all, the president of the Church had given instructions for reinstatement, and Charles had been buried in his temple clothes. Logan had said it was an honor to explain everything, but the meeting had scared him to death.

Walking to the window, Claire looked across the lawn to the river. The weeds had been replaced with new green sod, flower beds, and stone paths. The trees had been trimmed, and a swimming dock floated in the river.

"The man in the village, the one who helped us find this place that day, talked to some of the veterans. They told me how it looked in the old days. I tried to restore it as closely as I could."

"It's beautiful," Claire said.

They moved to the kitchen. The mosaics were clean, glistening, the new cupboards white and shining. She stepped to the sink and tried the chrome hardware. Water, clear and cool, flowed freely. She smiled. It had been so dirty.

"Vilinia took care of this room. She fell in love with it from the beginning." Claire felt the affection in his voice and smiled at her brother. Maybe someone was finally going to get to wear their mother's diamond-studded watch.

They walked back through the dining area and living room, then down the hall. The bathroom was larger now, with new European fixtures. The room to the left and across the hall would serve as the property manager's office, at least for now.

"The upstairs, everything is finished?" Claire asked.

"Yes. Each room has a theme, and all the display cases are ready." Alex smiled. "We have our museum."

Claire returned the smile. "Just nothing to put in it."

He took her hand and guided her down the hall. Opening the door to the basement, he switched on the overhead light. He shuddered a little at the thought of how his life had almost ended there but shoved it aside. He had been working on this little project for three months now and had learned to deal with it.

New steps greeted them, the basement below cleaned out and the old stone floors and walls washed. The picture of Alex lying in the middle of the floor bleeding to death flashed across Claire's mind, then left, but she took his hand just the same.

"You've been after me for the past year to tell you what I

think happened to us, and why—how all the pieces of the puzzle fit together. I explained it the best I could, but I have a few more things you might be interested in." Alex smiled.

"It's about time you filled in the blanks."

"Don't get belligerent, or I'll let you stew for another year."

They took the steps and turned left at the bottom, working their way back into the depths of the cavernous basement. The crates Grachev had tried to rip apart with his bare hands stood in rows to their right, the pieces neatly stacked next to them. Claire had never seen them before, and Alex explained what they were.

"How many do you count?" Alex asked.

Claire looked them over. "Eleven."

"Nearly eighty were shipped out of Breslau."

"What happened to the others?"

Alex looked up. "Low ceilings, and yet we came down a good twenty feet from the first floor."

Claire looked up at the wood framing. Alex took the key from the deposit box out of his pocket, then reached up and let his hand wander over the dusty wood, tapping it with his knuckles.

"I was sweeping up down here the first day after the workers put the stairs in, and I bumped my head on this about half a dozen times." He gave a sheepish smile while he continued tapping with his knuckle. "It finally dawned on me that this might be an attic."

Claire laughed, then saw he was serious.

Alex tapped again. It struck Claire how hollow the sound was. Alex walked toward the far wall. There was a slight crack between the lowered ceiling and the stone foundation.

He showed her the key. "*Beau Rivage.* I knew it had to fit some kind of lock in this place." He reached up and felt along the edge until his fingers caught hold of something. He used the key. Claire heard a click, and part of the ceiling gave way an inch. She stuck her fingers into the crack and pulled. The section was hinged on one end, and the other end lowered to the floor.

"Steps!" Claire said, astonished.

"I went ahead without you but decided not to do much until you could get here." He smiled. "It's been hard waiting, but I thought we should do most of this together." He stepped back and waved a hand. "Ladies first."

Claire tested the old wood. It held, and she started up, her heart racing. They could stand upright; the attic roof, the bottom of the first floor, was a good six inches above Alex's head.

The wooden walls were lined with paneling, and a row of lights ran the length of the space. A switch hung near Claire's left shoulder. Alex turned it on. The lighting shined on crates and boxes that nearly filled the place.

Claire gasped. "There are so many!"

"Sergei turned on the cellar light that day. I couldn't figure out who might be paying the light bill to keep this ramshackle place lit. When I was well enough again, I made inquiries and found an account in a local bank out of which the taxes are paid and the electricity kept on. Money is deposited once a year by mail."

"So Father kept the place going. It seems a little breezy for such a confined space."

Alex pointed at the small furnace/air conditioner humming in the corner. There were two other pieces of equipment as well. "He had those installed. Art has to be kept at certain temperatures, and humidity has to be kept under control. The paneling is fairly new and conducive to cleanliness and keeping down dust and moisture."

Claire stepped to the first crate. The lid had been pried off but was lying in place without the nails. She lifted it and looked inside. She could see a framed painting but couldn't see what it was without lifting it from the box.

"A Tintoretto," Alex said. "According to an inventory we'll look at some time, most of the masters are represented here, along with a number of Russian artists and iconographers.

"City records show that our grandfather, Alexander Poltoronov, built Beau Rivage in 1921. He moved several doctors here, let them hire nurses and run a hospital."

"1921?"

Alex smiled. "Grandfather's journals are in a trunk here. This room was used for a special purpose, as was the hospital. When they smuggled Jews out of Russia, they brought them here. The necessary papers were printed and forged in this room. Lessons in various languages and cultures were given upstairs, and they had time to recuperate before being sent either to Israel or the United States."

"So Father, the family, has always owned Beau Rivage."

"And used it until 1948 when Israel was established as a nation. This place was no longer needed for immigration after that because everyone went to Israel with the full knowledge of the new authorities."

"Father brought all these things here earlier than 1948. It must have caused some curiosity among the Jews still being processed here."

"Father left a chest full of papers here that I've had a chance to look through. Among them I found a receipt for payment to a warehouse in Geneva. It's dated at approximately the time his military records show he left Breslau for some time off. Maybe he stored the shipment there, then moved it here later, when the place was no longer being used. According to the date of production stamped on the furnace, he put that in after 1950. The records he left for us show that Father spent a lot of time here in the early years, even had an office in Geneva. After his change to Charles Barrett, he came much less but often enough to keep tabs on things."

"The deposit box opened in 1944—have you ever found out what it contained?"

"The clue that gave you an idea Father had taken something from Germany and eventually led you back here?" Alex smiled. "Father kept his passports and identity papers in it when he was Poltoron. He used it for personal papers when he spent a lot of time here."

"That's it?"

He laughed. "That's it. He finally got around to closing it in 1985—probably decided he wouldn't need it any longer."

"Lucky for you."

"Knowing your determined spirit, you would have found me anyway."

"Grachev's rendition about the legacy was correct, wasn't it."

"Yes. Father really did try to use it to free Nadia and the children. To him, all of this wasn't worth the lives of good people. In papers that have been left for us, you'll find the story. The Orlov heirs suspected the revolution to come and protected their possessions by moving them out of Russia to Crimea. They kept them in vaults in the basement of a house specially built for them. When it looked like all of Ukraine and the western half of the Soviet Union might fall to the Germans, Michael made arrangements to get the items here, but they were captured. During the war, he used the intelligence apparatus to keep track of their approximate whereabouts. He heard reports that Himmler had them in Fribourg, but he couldn't be sure. When the opportunity to get close came through the plan to save the Russian pilots, he jumped at it."

"And involved Arkadi."

"Grachev told me they were cousins. When Father went into Russia as part of the underground, he found Arkadi, and they started working together to free Jews. During the war they got together again and expanded what they were doing."

"Then Arkadi's children—"

"Really were heirs to the legacy. At least they had some rights. Arkadi and Michael were not only friends but also family. That was why Michael went to such great lengths to procure Arkadi's bride for him. It was his duty as the heir of the Orlovs. Nadia was of royal lineage as well, and it made for a good match between the two families."

"But Grachev wanted Nadia."

"Michael's journal says that when he tried to buy Nadia and the children their freedom with the legacy, he told Grachev who he was, how he and Arkadi were related. Grachev saw it as a chance to take over the Orlov family line by marrying Nadia and killing Michael."

"Nadia knew what he was up to and took her own life."

"There was Siberia as well, but yes. She also poisoned the children."

"But I thought . . . "

"Grachev's way of continuing the dream. I don't know who Sergei and Andrei were, but they weren't Nadia's children. I had the boys in Father's pictures of Arkadi, Nadia, and the children compared to pictures of Sergei and Andrei. They don't match."

"Poisoning the children . . . " Claire said.

"I know—it makes me shudder. But they lived under different rules, Claire. To Nadia it was the necessary, the honorable thing to do—the only way of stopping Grachev."

"So Grachev selected two orphans and began their preparation to become the Orlov heirs—"

"While making arrangements to have Michael kidnapped and brought back to the Soviet Union so he could be forced to tell where the legacy was. When the attempt failed and Michael disappeared, it was a stunning blow. But Grachev didn't have time to think about it; he was busy trying to save his own skin during the Khrushchev purges."

"That's when he fled to China."

"From there he began the hunt for Michael, but he wasn't successful until Sergei was placed inside the archives, where he could do his research. You know the rest."

"Why didn't Arkadi get his family out of Russia at the end of the war? Father had the connections. They could have had a wonderful life."

"According to Father's journal, there were two reasons. Arkadi didn't feel he could leave his aging father, and he knew the old gentleman would never leave. He had to wait at least until his father passed away. And Arkadi loved his country as much as Michael did. He felt it important that one of them be on the inside in their work to free it again. Michael couldn't do it, and Arkadi wanted to.

"One of the most touching entries in Michael's journal is the one just after he found out that Arkadi had taken his life to save the rest of their friends."

There was a long but comfortable silence. Their father had experienced more than his share of hard things. Yet he had stayed true. It was something to be proud of.

"How could he just leave all of this in a place so vulnerable?

Vandals, children snooping around. He must have worried about it all the time."

"You have to remember, the items themselves were not that important to Charles—only what they stood for. Family. But he did take care of them. He hired a watchman, to begin with. A copy of the contract shows one Jean Louis Moudon and his family hired for the sum of one thousand American dollars a year to mow the hay in the lower acreage, keep down the weeds, and make sure vandals stayed clear of the property. They also kept the hay." He grinned. "Jean Louis lives across the main highway and down a quarter mile. I had an interesting talk with him about Father's visits and concern for the property. It sounds like he wanted it to be a bit of an eyesore, probably as a point of discouragement for curiosity."

Alex sat down, placing his back against one of the crates. "The crates in the basement, the ones that Grachev and I found, housed paintings Michael planned to return to their proper owners privately—things that Himmler had but that didn't belong to the Orlov family."

Claire stared at the room. "The Orlov family treasure—"

She had a question but couldn't bring herself to ask it.

"Why did he hide this stuff for so long?" Alex asked.

"You can read my mind."

"Always could. I even knew you were in love with Logan before you did." He laughed.

"Father kept the treasure hidden for several reasons. As long as the Soviet Union existed, he feared they would claim it if they knew what still existed."

"But they didn't have any real claim, did they?"

"The Communists had strange ways of thinking about things. Anything Russian, anything even remotely attached to Russia, they thought belonged to the Soviet people—especially something that might, at one time, have belonged to one of its leaders. And a lot of this belonged to Catherine the Great before she gave it to Orlov. The Communists were never shy about making such claims and even falsified some documents to make their case. It was a valid concern.

"Father didn't like the Communists, and he certainly didn't trust them. He didn't think they deserved his family legacy, nor did he think they'd give it the respect and honor it was due."

He stood again. Since the surgery, his back ached a lot, and he could never seem to find a comfortable position for more than a few minutes. He was certain time would heal it.

"The Russians will have considerable interest in what's in this room. Even now they may try to claim it, but the Orlov family papers Father left us leave no doubt that everything belongs to us. But I would like to work with them."

"How?" Claire asked. "You have intended from the beginning to keep it housed here. All these repairs, the creation of the museum, were done with that in mind."

"For a while. Eventually I would like them taken to the town where Father's ancestors came from in Russia. I'd like to build a permanent museum there, but things are so unsettled right now I don't think they'd be safe. Plus, there are arrangements to be made."

"Such as?"

"The purchase of property and the building of a museum."

"You have something in mind?"

"A house once belonging to Count Orlov himself. We're negotiating." He smiled. "In the meantime, I think the pieces should go on several tours. To Israel, Ukraine, and several places in Russia if we can get guarantees for the safety of the legacy."

"What will you do with this place?"

"We'll decide that later. It seems like a nice place to spend vacations, or we can leave it a museum of some kind. Then again, Voltaire needs a hospital." He shrugged. "It's an open field."

Alex walked to a crate that had the lid removed. It was one of the smaller ones. He lifted the lid and pulled out a beautifully lacquered box. The black background set off the wonderful colors of cossacks on the steppe, painted in bright oranges, yellows, reds, and browns. Alex opened the lid and revealed the gem-studded and enameled gold cover of a large and very old Bible.

"The Orlov family Bible." He turned to the first few pages. "A genealogy. Eventually we'll do the work for these people in the temple." He pointed to one of the names. "Grigorii, the man given much of this by Catherine the Great." He pointed at another line. "This is where Judaism came into the family tree—our great-great-grandmother. From there it became the family's religion. For good and evil."

He placed the book back in the lacquered box, rewrapped it in the faded silk cloth, and placed it back in the crate.

"The worth of that goes beyond gold and silver. I wonder what Grachev would have done with all this?"

"The Bible would have survived as authentication that his false sons were the rightful heirs. Of course, he would have had to make some changes."

"He set up the computer deal through you to get at both of you—to kill the true heirs and take over the legacy," Claire said.

"His destruction of Mom and Dad's marriage was only the first step. He took his time, relishing his revenge, doing everything in a way that would bring father the most suffering."

They came to a spot between two large crates where a chest made of polished wood sat. It was dusty but had Alex's prints on it from being opened.

"It was the first thing I looked for. I knew he left records, diaries, papers, and property deeds belonging to the Orlovs," Alex said. He lifted the lid, and Claire could see the neatly stacked and rolled papers. On top were two very fat envelopes, one addressed to each of them. Alex picked Claire's up and handed it to her. The seal on his had already been broken.

"Inside you'll find a letter from Michael Poltoron, dated about four years ago. It gives you a history, quite detailed, some recollections and a copy of his journal up to the time of his becoming Charles Barrett. If yours is the same as mine, there is also a small ledger giving the dates of Father's return here and short entries of pertinent information dealing with the treasure."

"And all of this was kept secret because he still feared Grachev."

"I think he knew Grachev was still alive; he just didn't know where. And he knew Grachev well enough to know he'd come after all this. And after us.

"Come on, it's getting late." They started back toward the stairs.

"At the time of his last writing in the ledger, Father's biggest concern was that Grachev might outlive him. As it turned out, he didn't. I don't think there is any further reason to leave all of this tucked out of sight. It's time to share Michael Poltoron's legacy with the world."

They wandered down through the crates, the boxes, but didn't open any more of them. Plenty of time for that. When they got to the stairs, they took one last look at the treasures spread out before them. Both knew that the ones of most importance they held in their hands.

Claire descended, then Alex, after turning off the lights.

"We'll be a few weeks seeing that these things are properly removed and taken care of," Claire said.

"I always liked Switzerland."

"When are you going to ask Vilinia to marry you?"

"Yesterday." Alex smiled.

Claire laughed lightly. "And what did she say?"

"That she'd always been kind to dumb animals and now was no time to change." He grinned. "What do you mean, what did she say?"

He pushed the stairs up and locked them in place. Then they ascended to the first floor, kidding each other as they had since they were knocking about on their father's two knees. As Alex reached the top of the stairs and prepared to close the cellar door, he looked back down at the pit where Pavel Grachev had died.

The Orlov legacy was finally safe.

He turned off the lights.